To

Hope you enjoy!

Fallen Prince

Jon Dietz

11. 29. 22

MW01128358

JON DIETZ

Copyright © 2021 Jon Dietz
All rights reserved
First Edition

PAGE PUBLISHING, INC.
Conneaut Lake, PA

First originally published by Page Publishing 2021

ISBN 978-1-6624-5563-6 (pbk)
ISBN 978-1-6624-5565-0 (digital)

Printed in the United States of America

Dedication

This book would not have been possible without the support of these incredible people:

Loving wife Debbie Dietz, who has been my rock for three decades.

My parents, Paul and Hannalene Dietz, who spent their lives in the pursuit of knowledge and who never sat on a couch without a book or a magazine.

My sisters, Patricia Startzman and Peggy Thalgott. Bringing laughter into one's life is the greatest gift of all.

The author owes a debt of gratitude to three individuals whose help proved to be of enormous value.

Dr. Harvey Schonwald is this book's contributing editor. His profession is urology, but his passion is history. He went over this manuscript with the eyes of an eagle and his suggestions were almost universally adopted.

Marty Glass designed the cover of this novel. He and the author have spent three decades discussing human foibles and the attendant political travesties. Marty is also a well-respected cartoonist.

Dr. Michael Jazzar is the author's biggest cheerleader. He extolled my first novel, "The Jerusalem Train," from mountaintops and low-lying valleys. He pushed me to write another novel, and he did not stop until I started typing.

Characters

Fictional
    Tito Bendado
    Tommy Borsino
    Arthur Jackson Burnell
    Vincent Carsini
    Frank Caruso
    Nick Cosentino
    Scott Dennis
    Pete Donatelli
    Francis O'Hara Dunleavy
    Kristin Dunleavy
    Matthew F. Dunleavy
    Michael Thomas Dunleavy
    Mike Dunleavy
    Patricia Cornell Dunleavy
    Peter Dunleavy
    Stuart Dunleavy
    Tom Greenwood
    Ivan Gorkin
    Thomas Higgins
    Curt Holmes
    Helen Holmes
    Mark Holmes
    Thomas Holmes
    Henry Jackson
    Amanda Johnson
    Arlene Montgomery
    Robert Xavier O'Halloran

Jackson Pickering
Woodrow Spencer
John Tunsten

Historical
John Adams
Ray Albert
Ignacio Antinori
Jacobo Arbenz
Vasily Arkhipov
Chester A. Arthur
Inga Arvad
W.L. Astor
Hugh Dudley Auchincloss
Bobby Baker
Antonio Imbert Barrera
Bill Barry
Dave Beck
Melvin Belli
Lavrentiy Beria
Romulo Betancourt
Richard Bissell
George Blake
Anthony Blunt
Hale Boggs
John Wilkes Booth
Jacqueline Bouvier
Janet Bouvier
Carolyn Lee Bouvier
John Bouvier
Lester Bowen
Calvin Brewer
Joe Brown
Pat Brown
Guy Burgess
Horace Busby

Charles Cabell
Judith Campbell
Alphonse Capone
Marshall Carter
Pedro Livio Cedeno
Vincent J. Celeste
Gene Cernan
Neville Chamberlain
John Cheasty
Winston Churchill
Joseph Colombo
John Connally
Nellie Connally
Calvin Coolidge Jr.
Calvin Coolidge Sr.
Sherman Cooper
Walter Cronkite
James M. Curley
Édouard Daladier
Richard Daley
Charles S. Dawes
Rufino De La Cruz
Antonio De La Maza
Frank DeSimone
Juan Thomas Diaz
Ngo Dinh Diem
Everett Dirksen
Herbert Von Dirksen
Anatoly Dobrynin
Allen Dulles
Fred Dutton
John Ehrlichman
Dwight D. Eisenhower
Paul Fejos
Jose Ramon Fernandez
John F. Fitzgerald

Gerald Ford
Laurence Hugh Frost
Yuri Gagarin
Carlo Gambino
James Garfield
John Nance Garner
Vito Genovese
Ella German
Sam Giancana
John Glenn
Joe Goldstrich
Barry Goldwater
Rosie Grier
Andrei Gromyko
Herschel Grynszpan
Amada Garcia Guerrero
H.R. Haldeman
Nathan Hale
Kohei Hanami
Warren G. Harding
William Henry Harrison
William R. Hearst
Adolph Hitler
James Hoffa
Abby Hoffman
Herbert Hoover
Sarah T. Hughes
Hubert Humphrey
John Husted
Andrew Jackson
Thomas Jefferson
Andrew Johnson
Bill Johnson
Lady Bird Johnson
Lyndon Johnson
Rafer Johnson

Ronald Jones
Joe Kane
Nicholas Katzenbach
Kenneth Keating
Estes Kefauver
Ethel Kennedy
Eunice Kennedy
Jean Ann Kennedy
Joe Kennedy Jr.
John Fitzgerald Kennedy
Joseph Patrick Kennedy Sr.
Joseph Patrick Kennedy Jr.
Kathleen Kennedy
Mary Augusta Kennedy
Patricia Kennedy
Martin Luther King
Patrick Joseph "PJ" Kennedy
Robert Kennedy
Rose Marie Kennedy
Ted Kennedy
Nikita Khrushchev
Andy Kirksey
Lawrence Klein
Robert LaFollette
Alf Landon
Mark Lane
Meyer Lansky
Robert E. Lee
Curtis LeMay
Nick Licata
Evelyn Lincoln
Henry Cabot Lodge Jr.
Henry Cabot Lodge Sr.
Peter Loeb
Charles Luciano
Bela Lugosi

Douglas MacArthur
Donald MacLean
Joseph Magliocco
Carlos Marcello
Harold Marney
John Martin
Edgar Maurer
Eugene McCarthy
Joe McCarthy
Robert McClelland
John J. McCloy
John McCone
Nick McDonald
George McGovern
John McGuire
Phyllis McGuire
William McKinley
Giuseppe Minacore
Luigia Minacore
Ho Chi Minh
Maria Mirabal
Minerva Mirabal
Patricia (Patria) Mirabal
Silvio Mollo
Bugs Moran
J. P. Morgan
Robert Morgenthau
Wayne Morse
Mohammad Mossadegh
Audie Murphy
Carrie Nation
Michael J. Neville
Richard Nixon
Dion O'Banion
W. Lee O'Daniel
Kenny O'Donnell

Lee Harvey Oswald
Marguerite Oswald
Robert E.L. Oswald
Alexander Pantages
George Parr
Oleg Penkovsky
Jack Pershing
Kim Philby
George Plimpton
Dave Powers
Eunice Pringle
Joe Profaci
Marina Prusakova
Ernest Rath
Sam Rayburn
Scotty Reston
George Henry Robertson
Erwin Rommel
Franklin D. Roosevelt
Theodore Roosevelt
Johnny Roselli
George Ross
Eileen Rubenstein
Jerry Rubin
Jack Ruby
Richard B. Russell
Kenneth Salyer
Valentin Savitsky
Donald Seldin
Alan Shepard
Sirhan Sirhan
Marilyn Sitzman
Al Smith
Ted Sorenson
Thomas Stafford
Joseph Stalin

Ray Starkey
Adlai Stevenson
Coke Stevenson
Henry L. Stimson
Gloria Swanson
Stuart Symington
Robert A. Taft
Zachary Taylor
Leonard Thom
Llewellyn Thompson
Luis Amiama Tio
J. D. Tippit
Jacqueline Todaro
Clyde Tolson
Johnny Torrio
Santo Trafficante Sr.
Santo Trafficante Jr.
Rafael Trujillo
Harry Truman
Mao Tse Tung
Alan Turing
John Tyler
Karl Uecker
Walter Ulbricht
Martin Van Buren
Horacio Vasquez
Henry Wade
Charlie Wall
George Wallace
Henry Wallace
Earl Warren
George Washington
Hymie Weiss
William Westmoreland
Byron White
Kaiser Wilhelm

Wilford J. Willy
Woodrow Wilson
Howard Yardley
Don Yarborough
Ralph Yarborough
Howard Yardley
John Young
Abraham Zapruder
Efrem Zimbalist
Arthur Zimmerman
Jerry Zinser

Foreword

Written By: Marty Glass

Is there anyone among us who was alive on that sad Friday in November of 1963 that can't recall where they were when they first heard the news of the death of John F. Kennedy? I remember the day like it was yesterday when Sister Roseanne interrupted my second grade class, announcing an immediate assembly in the school cafeteria to give us the tragic news.

And who hasn't imagined or given deeper speculation as to what the real story was of the assassination? "Who killed JFK?" has probably fostered more debate than any event in American history. The story itself has resulted in so many books and films that it serves to confirm how obsessed a nation became about this political tragedy.

In *Fallen Prince*, Jon Dietz lays out a thoughtfully improved account of the events surrounding the death of John F. Kennedy. His story, while fictionalized, leans heavily on the actual truth but with the added elements of conversations never heard and plausible actions that fill the gaps in a fascinating retelling of the story.

What Jon manages to achieve goes far beyond the more myopic literary offerings about JFK's assassination. There have been many excellent books that focus largely on November 22, 1963, but what some of these books miss is the broader history that made John F. Kennedy so undeniably vulnerable and so intentionally targeted. And what often is lost in narrow analysis is what a phenomenal story lies within. A classical story that beckons Shakespeare or other great tragedies in literature.

As an ardent follower of political science and a passionate student of history, Jon has a unique talent for historical staging of the telling of a great story. Jon's previous work, *The Jerusalem Train*, was also a historical drama that takes the reader back to a crucial period in history to serve as the backdrop of his novel. In that case the Russo-Japanese war, an often neglected chapter in history, played a pivotal role in our world's geopolitical landscape.

The historical focus for *Fallen Prince* spans multiple generations that cover the rich history of the Kennedy clan with particular focus on the patriarch, Joe Kennedy. Concurrently to the Kennedy story is the dark history of the world of organized crime and our nation's response to the criminal underworld. To understand what made Kennedy vulnerable, one must look at generations of family histories, government policies, and the machinations of the criminal underworld. All of this and more culminating in the assassination of John Fitzgerald Kennedy.

Chapter 1

Mike Dunleavy long ago stopped thinking of himself as a criminal.

The thirty-nine-year-old small boat mechanic had his last twinge of conscience four years ago. That was 1922. It was the year he decided to shed his scruples for the benefit of his family.

The tipping point came in 1921 when his wife, Patricia, announced she was pregnant with their third child.

Five mouths to feed. One salary. A lowly boat mechanic. A hundred dollars a week was considered a good week. Quite often it was less.

A lot less.

Dunleavy moved to Miami from Illinois in 1914. He was always good at fixing things. He loved the ocean.

He was single. Miami presented itself as an exotic paradise of warm weather and women who were unencumbered by heavy clothing.

He was not disappointed. In less than a week, he was hired as a mechanic. Miami was bloated with small craft and magnificent yachts. Most of them had internal combustion engines. An engine cannot repair itself. It needs a human being. It needs a Mike Dunleavy.

For three years, Mike was quite contented. His meager salary was more than enough to support a bachelor who owned a two-room apartment.

Dunleavy was employed at the Johnson Dockyard near South Miami Beach. There were plenty of bars near the dockyard, but Dunleavy preferred a pub called Ferguson's Reef about two miles inland.

An Irish bar for a proud Irishman.

Dunleavy's family hailed from Dublin, Ireland.

Mike Dunleavy saw his first sunrise in 1887.

In 1905, Dunleavy's father, Peter, moved the clan to the United States. Dunleavy's beloved uncle, Francis O'Hara Dunleavy, stayed behind.

Mike Dunleavy missed the Irish rebellion by eleven years.

On Easter Sunday, April 24, 1916 Irish patriots decided they had had enough of English rule. Numbering 1,500, they declared their independence. They thought their timing was propitious. England was locked in a death struggle with Imperial Germany. The war was two years old. Already tens of thousands of Englishmen were dead on the fields of France.

England, of course, would negotiate. The Brits certainly wouldn't want a two-front war. England's initial reaction to the seizure of public buildings in Dublin was anything but conciliatory.

British troops reacted with gunfire and the destruction of homes owned by Irish Republicans.

England's policy toward taking prisoners was flexible. British commanders greenlighted summary executions.

One of the men to surrender his life to the cause of Irish Independence was Francis O'Hara Dunleavy. He and four others were positioned in front of a stone wall. High-powered bullets raced through their flesh.

The rebellion, at least temporarily, was a failure.

Mike Dunleavy received news of his uncle's death a month after he was buried.

The telephone industry had progressed to the point it was possible for Mike to instantly contact his father in Illinois.

Mike wanted to board an ocean liner and head back to Ireland for some payback.

Peter Dunleavy convinced his son to stay put, at least for a while.

A seething Mike Dunleavy agreed. He would sit at the bar at Ferguson's Reef and denounce the bloody English. Virtually all of Mike Dunleavy's audience was sympathetic. This was an Irish hangout.

Dunleavy spent a year negotiating with himself over the pros and cons of going back to Ireland.

He decided he would go back. He was unmarried. No children. And the cause was just.

But events in Europe and America intersected in a manner that completely upended Dunleavy's plans.

Exactly one year after the Irish Rebellion began, President Woodrow Wilson asked Congress to declare war on Germany.

The proximate cause was not the sinking of the *Lusitania*, which was sent to the bottom of the Atlantic by a German submarine two years earlier.

Nope. The reason the United States decided to go to war was a decision by the Germans to incorporate Mexico into the struggle.

English spies had intercepted the famous Zimmerman telegraph.

Arthur Zimmerman was Germany's foreign minister. He knew Woodrow Wilson was an Anglophile and a hater of all things German. Zimmerman wanted to make certain that if the United States did enter the war on the side of the British, there would be consequences.

Zimmerman asked the president of Mexico to form an alliance. If war came, would Mexico agree to attack the US southern border?

England's secret service was ecstatic. The English government desperately wanted the United States to join this war effort.

Almost at the speed of light, England transmitted the Zimmerman telegraph to the White House.

It worked. Wilson regarded the provocation as if it were a live hand grenade. It was always suspected Wilson wanted to join the fight. But he had campaigned in 1916 on a slogan, "He Kept Us out of War." This promise was instrumental in getting him reelected.

Now, how does a politician break a promise? Simple, you keep poking your adversary. This all must be done clandestinely. Over time, the hated adversary will make a blunder, and there is the excuse to go back on a promise.

In 1917, Mike Dunleavy joined the US Army. He had dual motives. One was patriotism. The other motive was revenge.

The US government would be training Dunleavy in the military arts. And the US government would be paying all of Mike's travel expenses to Europe.

Mike Dunleavy would be stationed in England, while General Jack Pershing negotiated with his new allies about troop dispositions.

He would be in England, armed with a rifle. There were lots of Irishmen in England. Maybe Dunleavy and his countrymen could hook up.

But Dunleavy's stay in England was too short. He was shipped to France after only three weeks.

Dunleavy survived the war unharmed physically. But the carnage changed him from a romantic warrior poet into a pacifist.

War kills. War dismembers. War makes one long for peace.

Upon returning to the United States, Dunleavy had lost all his infatuation with armed combat. He decided he would support Ireland with money. But not blood.

Dunleavy was still wearing his uniform at Ferguson's Reef when he spied a new waitress named Patricia Cornell.

She was twenty. She was full-figured and moved like a gazelle across the wood flooring.

Dunleavy thought she was too good-looking and the competition for her affections had to be fierce. On that score he was right.

The first thing Patricia Cornell noticed was Dunleavy's uniform. It is an old cliché, but young Ms. Cornell loved men in uniforms.

It was she who approached him. As a waitress, it was expected she would saunter over to his table.

She did not just take his order. She engaged him in conversation. It took all of five minutes for Mike Dunleavy to decide he wanted to marry this woman.

He asked her out. She did not hesitate. He went home that night as light-footed as he had ever been in his life.

It took four dinners, but Mike Dunleavy finally bedded the woman of his dreams.

One night, as Patricia lay sound asleep beside him, Dunleavy was suddenly filled with terror. He was seeing a woman who could command the attention of millionaires.

Mike Dunleavy was no millionaire.

They were sexually compatible, and that was a big deal. But the art of fornication will not carry a man and a woman more than a few years. At some point, a woman will ask, "What kind of a provider is he? Can I do better?"

Dunleavy did not have a college education, a knowledge of finance, or any other recognizable skill that can generate lots of money.

He was devoid of social panache. He was basically a grease monkey.

Two months into the relationship, he decided to confront his demons. He asked Patricia to join him on the couch.

"Sweetheart, I love you more than anything. I want to marry you. Here is my problem. I fix things for a living. It is honorable work, but it doesn't pay."

Patricia put her arms around his neck. "I won't lie to you. I have been thinking about that very same thing. But I have faith in you. I want to be your spark plug. I want to be the person who helps you rise. But you have to promise me you are going to make the effort."

Dunleavy felt as if a heavy rock had just fallen off his back. "As God is my witness, I will."

Mike Dunleavy and Patricia Cornell were married in June of 1919.

A son, Matthew Francis Dunleavy, arrived nine months later.

In 1920, a daughter, Kristin Patricia Dunleavy, followed her brother into the loving arms of her parents.

Mike Dunleavy did not slack in his responsibilities. He worked sixteen hours a day and made enough money to cover life's necessities.

But he did not make enough money to clothe his wife in furs and jewels. And this bothered him. While Mike Dunleavy lay in bed in 1920 pondering how to improve his life, 1,500 miles away, another Irishman was playing with his three-year-old son.

Joseph Patrick Kennedy Sr. did not have to worry about money. He had plenty. He and his wife, Rose, lived in a palatial house in Brookline, Massachusetts.

On May 29, 1917, only thirty-six months earlier, Rose and Joe welcomed their second son into the family. He was christened John Fitzgerald Kennedy. This was the child Joe was watching romp around and who, like all toddlers, did not have a care in the world.

Chapter 2

The year 1919 does not resonate with average Americans.

Mention 1860 and most Americans can tell you that was the year Abraham Lincoln became president, setting the stage for the War Between the States. Or December 7, 1941, when the Japanese attacked Pearl Harbor.

That date draws about 100 percent recognition.

Mention 1919 to an average citizen and the year's significance will generally generate a blank stare.

But three events occurred that year that would enormously affect the lives of millions.

World War I ended in 1918, but it was a year later that the Treaty of Versailles was signed by the combatants.

Woodrow Wilson and his idealistic Fourteen Points for peace were each body-slammed by the leaders of Europe. The treaty blamed Germany, and only Germany, for the debacle. The treaty also hand-cuffed Germany to a highly punitive reparations mandate that was guaranteed to cause an eventual revolt.

The treaty spawned Adolph Hitler, a second world war, and fifty million dead.

There was another more benign development that reached fruition in 1919. Congress finally gave women the right to vote. The law was sent to the states for ratification, and it sailed through.

In August of 1920, a woman's right to vote became the Nineteenth Amendment to the Constitution. In Miami, Florida, Patricia Cornell Dunleavy celebrated her new right by making passionate love to her husband. Mike Dunleavy did not complain.

Mike Dunleavy did complain about the next momentous development that saw the light of day in 1919.

Congress passed the Volstead Act, also known as the National Prohibition Act. The law was ratified by thirty-six states.

It became part of the Constitution under the banner of the Eighteenth Amendment. In January of 1920, it became illegal to "produce, sell, and transport" alcohol in the Continental United States.

The Volstead Act did not outlaw the consumption of alcohol. If one had enough foresight, one could have stashed a great deal of alcohol in basements and attics. Family and friends could imbibe for years without violating the law—unless one sold a portion of one's stash. That could lead to a knock on the door by the authorities.

Mike Dunleavy was outraged that his favorite watering hole was shut down.

But Dunleavy was a law-abiding citizen. He fumed, but he never considered breaking the law.

Others did not hesitate for one second to notice an opportunity.

In the time it took a beam of light to traverse the core of an atom America's criminal class was gearing up.

The irrationality of the Volstead Act should have been apparent to a five-year-old. Alcohol has been a part of human civilization for as long as grain and barley has been cultivated.

Some experts believe beer was being made in China ten thousand years ago. And there are seven-thousand-year-old Mesopotamian clay tablets outlining the methodology for making beer.

Simply stated, alcohol is engrained in all human societies.

There is a case against alcohol.

The number of children and women killed by men who happened to be drunk is too high to calculate. Though there can be no accurate accounting, the number is unquestionably in the millions.

The number of children and women who have been beaten by men deranged by alcohol is probably a hundred times the homicide rate.

Not all women faced this curse with passivity.

In the nineteenth century, Carrie Amelia Nation would enter American saloons. But not to pontificate. This temperance movement leader would brandish a hatchet and go to work on the furniture and the mountains of alcohol behind the bars.

"I want all hellions to quit puffing that hell's fume into God's clean air!" she once stated. Ambiguity was not Carrie Nation's strong suit.

She was often arrested, but she had such cachet she became a cult figure.

Women loved Carrie Nation and her acolytes because women bore the brunt of alcohol's insidious side effects.

Throughout history, reaching deep into the twentieth century, women could not find protection from brutish men. The State often looked the other way.

A man was supposed to beat his wife. How else could he control his household? The ancient rule of thumb stated that it was okay for a man to beat his wife so long as the stick was no thicker than his thumb. It would take a dead body before the State would intercede.

For one hundred years, prior to 1920, the impetus for Prohibition came mainly from women.

And in 1920, women won the right to vote. Now politicians had no option but to listen.

During WWI, Woodrow Wilson temporarily forbade the manufacture of alcohol to conserve grain supplies.

When the male population failed to rebel against the edict, Temperance Movement leaders saw their chance. They became busy little bees. They lobbied their friends in Congress. And they got the deed done. What was just a presidential order became a constitutional amendment.

The Mike Dunleavy's of the country were stunned. He and two million other men were overseas fighting for democracy. It never occurred to them that a temporary wartime exigency could morph into a lifetime ban.

But that is exactly what happened.

Supporters of Prohibition called it a noble experiment. Detractors labeled it a fool's errand.

These two philosophies intersected in Mike Dunleavy's life in May of 1921.

It was near closing time at the Johnson Dockyard. A large man strolled down the pier to Mike's workstation. Dunleavy gave the man an intense visual examination. The man generated a tiny cautionary neuron alert in Mike's brain. Dunleavy grabbed a rag and started cleaning his hands.

The man wore a raincoat and a fedora, which Dunleavy thought was odd. It was Miami, and the temperature was in the mid-eighties.

The man was white, but he was dark complexioned. Dunleavy thought he looked swarthy.

Swarthy Man extended his right hand. "Hello, Mike, how ya doing?"

Dunleavy was slow to shake hands. "Do I know you?"

"No, you don't. But I have been asking around. People tell me there isn't anything about boats and engines that you can't fix."

"Well, give me the tools and the parts, and I can fix anything that's run by gasoline." Dunleavy did not regard the remark as bragging. It was a fact.

"That's what I have been told," Swarthy Man said. "Listen, can I get five minutes of your time?"

"Sure, what's on your mind?"

Swarthy Man locked his arms behind his back. He smiled and adopted a most solicitous demeanor. "I represent certain out-of-state business interests. These businessmen need small craft in order to facilitate their operations. Yachts, cabin cruisers, that sort of thing."

"Are we talking about fishing or tourism? What are we talking about?" Dunleavy did not detect anything up to this point that was improper.

Swarthy Man looked down at his shoes. "No, we are talking about regular excursions to Cuba. No tourists. Just you."

"And what do I do when I reach Cuba?"

"You pick up a product and return it to these docks."

Now the curtain was being drawn back. Dunleavy instantly suspected skullduggery was afoot.

"This product wouldn't happen to be rum, scotch, or bourbon, would it?"

"It would indeed," Swarthy Man responded.

Dunleavy stared hard at his counterpart. "What's your name, friend?"

"You can call me Nick."

"Okay, Nick. Listen, I know why you are here. The government just outlawed booze nationwide. I do not like the law. I think it is stupid. But if I bring booze into Miami and I get caught, are you going to go to jail with me?"

"I'm not going to jail, and I don't believe you will either."

"How can you say that? The law is the law!"

"There are laws that people take seriously, like bank robbery or murder. We are not asking you to do anything like that. Then there are laws against prostitution and gambling, which people don't take seriously, and neither do the cops. Listen, Mike, this prohibition against alcohol is a joke. People are not going to stop drinking. It ain't gonna happen."

Dunleavy had a retort. "I read in the newspaper about two guys who were busted for running booze out of Cuba. You want to explain that?"

Swarthy Man unlocked his arms from behind his back. He put his left leg on a folding chair and leaned into Mike's face.

"They got busted because they didn't do their homework. They failed to get permission from the right people. They jumped the gun."

Dunleavy was beginning to lose interest.

"Listen, pal, I have a wife, two children, and one on the way—"

"We know," Swarthy Man said. It was a statement that sent a small chill through Dunleavy.

"If I'm in jail, how are they going to survive?"

"Your wife and kids, all they are doing now is just surviving. Do you ever take your wife out for steak and lobster? Besides her wedding ring and engagement ring, does she have any jewelry? Imagine if you had two cars in your garage instead of one."

"Yeah, she could use her new car to visit me in the slammer."

"I told you we are working on that."

Dunleavy pressed on. "In order for your plan to work, you must buy off cops, judges, politicians, even the Coast Guard. Where do you find enough money to do all that?"

Swarthy Man smiled. "We have it."

Dunleavy was impressed that his potential recruiter did not hesitate for even a second to state, "We have it."

"What do you need me for? Anyone with a compass and a cabin cruiser can find Cuba."

"True, but none of my people can do what you can do, Mike. If an engine cuts out on the way there or, worse, on the way back, they can't fix it. You can."

Now Dunleavy realized why Swarthy Man was pushing so hard. A cabin cruiser with a dead engine in the Florida straits was subject to rolling over, taking along thousands of dollars in profits.

Dunleavy was positive that he could fix any engine regardless of what company manufactured it. Knowledge is power. Dunleavy now knew he was powerful. And valuable.

Dunleavy rubbed his chin and looked away from his guest. His next words exited his mouth at a glacial pace.

"I...just...don't...know."

Swarthy Man felt he was making headway, so he pressed his ace in the hole card.

"Mike, how would you like to make two thousand dollars a month?"

Dunleavy froze. The math was simple. Two thousand dollars a month was twenty-four thousand dollars a year. In cash.

Now this was something to ponder.

An absolute fortune. He currently made four thousand dollars a year. No, that was his best year ever. He usually made a lot less.

Dunleavy decided it was too good to be true.

"How could you possibly pay that much? How much would you and your associates pocket?"

Swarthy Man was never at a loss for answers.

"Mike, we won't be selling bathtub gin to the public. We are only interested in the good stuff. Alcohol made overseas by reputable firms. We won't be poisoning people. We will be recruiting customers, not killing them. Human nature being what it is, people will pay double for something that is forbidden. Especially if that product has status and quality."

Dunleavy was beginning to believe Swarthy Man could sell ice to an Eskimo.

It was all happening too fast. Dunleavy needed time to process this out of the blue bonanza.

"Look, pal, I have only known you for..." He looked at his watch. "Twenty minutes. If you expect an answer right now, the answer is no."

Swarthy Man straightened his back and spread his arms until his shoulders locked like a preacher concluding a sermon.

"Take your time, Mike. Take all the time you need. I live here now. You'll be seeing me around."

He reached into the left pocket of his raincoat. He produced a wad of money at least three inches thick.

Swarthy Man carefully fanned the money so Dunleavy could see that each bill had the number one hundred printed on it. He extracted one of the bills and shoved it into Mike's shirt pocket.

"This is a gift, not a loan, Mike. Take your wife out to dinner."

Swarthy Man moved away too quickly for Dunleavy to reach into his pocket and return the obvious bribe. In any event, Dunleavy was not inclined to hand the money back to his new friend Nick.

Swarthy Man walked back down the pier with the air of an aristocrat. Dunleavy watched as he approached a 1921 Dorris 6-80 Touring Car. He saw a man open the door for his new benefactor.

Swarthy Man got in the back seat. The other man got behind the wheel.

In 1921, you could buy a Ford Model T for seven hundred and fifty dollars.

A 1921 Dorris 6-80 Touring Car cost seven thousand dollars.

Dunleavy pulled the bill out of his shirt pocket. He stared at it. Yes, he would take his wife to dinner. Any place she wanted to go. And he would tell her to order anything she wanted.

What he would not do was tell his wife the provenance of this one-hundred-dollar bill.

How do honest men become corrupted?

It takes time. There are psychological barriers that must be traversed.

A retail clerk might start by stealing a dollar from a cash register. The dollar will be replaced later.

Except no one notices the dollar is missing.

Another dollar disappears. Then two dollars.

No one notices.

The clerk begins to depend on the small stipends that suddenly disappear.

The clerk rationalizes the theft as inconsequential. The company is large; the salary is small.

The larceny could go on for years except for one small human defect.

It is never enough.

Suddenly ten dollars disappears. The store manager pulls the clerk into a small room. Since there is only one logical explanation for the missing money, the clerk caves.

Then comes the confession. Then the dismissal. Maybe even a court date.

It always comes down to a question of money versus reputation. Which is more important?

This conundrum has been in play since the dawn of time.

Mike Dunleavy was battling these two conflicting forces.

He had trouble sleeping. His family had needs. His reputation was a fragile flower. Once gone, it might never again bloom.

Dunleavy was determined not to be pushed into a transcendent decision.

But now domestic forces were in play. His wife, Patricia, was emotionally slowly moving away.

It began when Dunleavy took Patricia out on the town with Swarthy Man's money.

It was a great night. Nothing on the menu was out of reach. They ate like royalty.

Then came the dancing and Dunleavy telling his wife it was okay if she cut loose and drank all she desired. The booze came out of her purse.

Dunleavy used his own private stock. His wife felt a very guilty pleasure smuggling it in.

Little did they know that the nightclub they were visiting was renovating to become a speakeasy.

At the end of the night, the one hundred dollars was gone, but Dunleavy's wife was radiant. Sex was the capstone of the evening.

But Patricia wanted more, not fewer, of those evenings.

Her pregnancy was starting to show. She again would watch her figure disappear into a bloated lump.

Soon there would be a third child. More money out the door.

Less time for dining and dancing.

Patricia loved her children, but raising human beings is never easy. And it never ends. Children require a 100 percent of a mother's time.

And Mike Dunleavy had to work two shifts in order to keep his family afloat.

When Dunleavy got home, neither he nor his wife had any energy for sex.

It had been two months since Swarthy Man made his appearance at the dockyard. Mike Dunleavy did not know that Swarthy Man was back in Chicago.

He had been summoned there by a man named Johnny Torrio. Johnny Torrio was Chicago's leading mobster. But he did not control the entire city.

Torrio had to coexist with another hoodlum named Dion O'Banion. There was an uneasy peace between the two gangs. It would all come crashing down in 1924 when Torrio ordered a hit on O'Banion. The assassination was successful.

A year later O'Banion's lieutenants retaliated. Bugs Moran and Hymie Weiss ambushed and shot Torrio four times. He survived, but psychologically he was finished. He retired and named Al Capone as the new leader.

Al Capone's reign was only six years in duration, but he became the most famous gangster in world history.

But that was all in the future. From 1920 to 1921, Torrio and O'Banion were racing to organize the incipient bootlegging industry.

Prohibition was an absolute godsend to the country's criminal class. Millions of dollars were at stake. But it was critical to be the first one out of the gate.

Money builds armies. And armies can destroy competitors.

O'Banion and Torrio were determined to scour the country looking for opportunities. Neither man was interested in selling rotgut liquor. To obtain quality product, it had to be brought in from overseas. With one exception.

Chicago's proximity to Canada made that country the Golden Goose.

But ninety miles off the coast of Florida was another haven of sin and corruption.

Cuba.

Swarthy Man's real name was Nick Cosentino.

Johnny Torrio ordered Cosentino to Miami to organize bootlegging operations. This market was too rich to leave to others.

Cosentino was told to recruit men who could navigate the high seas.

Priority number one was not to lose forty thousand dollars in high-grade alcohol to a storm at sea.

That is why Cosentino approached Mike Dunleavy just one week after arriving in Miami.

By no means was Dunleavy Cosentino's only contact. The goal was to create a flotilla of thirty yachts, speed boats, and cabin cruisers.

That meant thirty high-paying jobs for those men whose special talents kept those platforms from sinking.

The moral dam for Mike Dunleavy broke when his third child was born. Another son. They named him Stuart.

Stuart was a joy to behold. But he did not come free.

More money. Always there was a need for more money.

Patricia was completely swamped. Three children under the age of five. All of them howling monsters.

One night they were debating what they could afford at the grocery store that week. Patricia was not happy with the answer.

She stood up. She picked up an ash tray and flung it against a wall. "It was you and your goddamn penis that created this mess!"

She stormed out of the house. She did not come back for hours.

Mike used this incident to come to a decision.

He was going to hunt down Swarthy Man. He was going to take the job.

The very next morning Dunleavy's determination collapsed.

On the front page of the newspaper was a story about five men arrested for rum-running. They even ran their photographs. Dunleavy knew two of the five.

Dunleavy sat down with his head in his hands. There was a money tree right within his grasp. But he was too afraid to grab it.

"I'll give it a year," he said to himself. "Maybe something will come up."

Dunleavy had no way of knowing that his decision to wait would prove to be highly propitious.

The early years of Prohibition were the law's golden days.

The public was still willing to give this experiment a chance. Most Americans believed that alcohol consumption was far too high. Maybe abstinence was the proper road to travel.

This was the general consensus in the years 1920 and 1921.

But by 1922, there was a sea change in public opinion.

Those who believed alcohol was a God-given right were boldly flaunting the law. Enough Americans were determined to keep on drinking that the Volstead Act was essentially neutered.

By 1922, the cancer was becoming visible.

It took organized crime twenty-four months to get the bribe money flowing to everyone nationwide who needed to be compromised.

Police. Judges. Deputies. Coastguardsmen. Anyone who could interrupt the flow of alcohol from the Mob to its customer base had to be bought off.

By 1922, the machinery was oiled.

In 1920 and 1921, there was a good chance anyone engaging in rum-running could end up in handcuffs.

By 1922, that possibility had greatly diminished. Still possible but highly unlikely.

In February of 1922, Dunleavy finally located Swarthy Man. "Can we talk?"

Cosentino smiled. "Sure. I have a thirty-five-foot cabin cruiser with your name on it."

Dunleavy asked, "How did you know I had changed my mind?"

"Why else would you be inquiring around the docks about my whereabouts."

"Do the original terms still apply?"

Swarthy Man was all sunshine and roses. "You betcha, Mike. You are just the kind of man we need. You can treat this boat as if you had title to it. And, Mike, I would not worry too much about the law. That's all been taken care of."

"When do I start?"

"You can quit your job right now. In three days, you will be on your way to Cuba."

They shook hands.

It was by design that Dunleavy knew his new employer only by the name Nick.

None of the rumrunners knew Nick's last name. They just knew him as the man who handed them envelopes filled with cash.

And how the money did flow.

Mike Dunleavy loved his new cabin cruiser, even if he did not own it.

Had he bothered to check at the courthouse, he would have discovered that the listed owner was Frank Caruso from Baltimore, Maryland. Mike Dunleavy would never know the cabin cruiser's actual owner.

That person did not live anywhere near the danger zone.

The real owner was Joseph Patrick Kennedy of Brookline, Massachusetts.

Chapter 3

The Kennedy clan might have come to America on their own, but it was a cruel twist of nature that propelled them across the ocean.

In the 1840s, Ireland's potato crop suffered a crippling blight. Men and women became walking skeletons. Children died in the arms of helpless parents.

They gathered on ships by the hundreds of thousands. The Earth is a large planet with plenty of nation-states but the Irish were only interested in one—the United States of America.

Joseph Patrick Kennedy's grandparents on both sides sailed into New York harbor. They were not greeted by Lady Liberty. That great iconic landmark was still forty years in the future.

They were greeted instead by a hostile population of Protestants who regarded the Catholic Irish as an army of potential job-stealing interlopers.

Storefronts posted signs that read, "We Don't Hire Irish."

The police reveled in arresting young Irishmen in such numbers that the conveyances used to haul them away became known as paddy wagons.

Joseph Patrick Kennedy was born into this social milieu on September 6, 1888. He was the son of Mary Augusta Hickey Kennedy and Patrick Joseph "PJ" Kennedy. PJ Kennedy was a successful investor, saloon owner, and a local political bigwig. His family lived comfortably inside the environs of Boston.

Joseph Patrick Kennedy was accepted at Harvard. He graduated in 1912 with a degree in economics.

While at Harvard, Kennedy experienced the hurt of social rejection.

The highly regarded Porcellian Club blackballed his membership application.

This club was started in 1791 by a student who hid a pig in his room and used the animal's screeching to torment the school proctor who resided one floor below.

Hearing that the offended proctor was going to tear apart the building in order to find the pig, the student and his friends butchered the beast and ate every bit of it.

This became a yearly ritual, and eventually the students started a club to honor their victory over an authority figure.

From this ridiculous beginning, one of Harvard's most prestigious clubs was instituted.

Young Mr. Kennedy had no doubt his Irish background was the fuel that generated his rejection.

That was exactly the reason.

Kennedy was elected class president, but he could not enter a building housing a club named after a butchered pig.

Kennedy's determination to succeed and elevate his family in society no doubt partly sprang from this incident.

Kennedy wasted no time in his determination to begin the long climb to the very apex of American society.

It is impossible to pinpoint the exact moment Kennedy decided he wanted to become president of the United States.

But anything short of that towering plateau would be unworthy of a Kennedy—the first Irish Catholic president.

Not snow, nor rain, nor the insufferable sniggering of Protestant elitists was going to stand in the way of his quest.

Only two years out of college, Kennedy decided to marry.

Rose Elizabeth Fitzgerald was the daughter of Boston Mayor John F. "Honeyfitz" Fitzgerald.

This was considered a union among equals.

But Joe Kennedy had chosen a partner whose moral compass was 180 degrees away from his own.

Rose Kennedy was fanatical about her Catholic faith. Throughout her life, Rose would hold many exulted positions inside the Catholic bureaucracy.

She would need all the steady pillars of Catholicism in order to sustain her marriage to Joe.

Joe regarded marriage as a necessity for social advancement. And Joe wanted to spawn lots of children to carry on the family name.

From day one, Joe had no intentions of allowing the Catholic marital injunction against infidelity from interfering with his sexual machinations.

Fun for Joe Kennedy meant pursuing other women. Lots of other women.

Joe Kennedy would inculcate infidelity into the very genes of his male offspring.

His marriage to Rose Fitzgerald was inspired.

So strong was her Catholic faith that there is no historical record of Rose having an affair with another man. Or woman.

Rose stoically put up with Joe's philandering. She had no choice. Joe was not about to stop chasing women. This option was an impossibility.

Rose, on the other hand, believed she would burn in hell if she violated the marital vows.

One can imagine Rose gritting her teeth each time Joe demanded sex so he could enlarge his brood.

She had to wonder if she was the second, or even third, woman Joe had bedded that day.

She was in a prison. Divorce was not an option. In Rose's eyes, divorce was also a conveyor belt to hell.

Rose did not disappoint Joe's yearning for immortality.

The children came in rapid succession.

Eventually there would be nine. The sons—Joe Jr., John, Robert, Theodore. The girls—Rose Marie, Kathleen, Eunice, Patricia, and Jean Ann.

Not one of these children would ever experience a moment of material deprivation.

The price they paid for this security was high. They had to obey the royal edicts emanating from the mouth of Joseph P. Kennedy.

Rose was permitted to express her opinions. But there was only one decision maker in this family.

Joe Kennedy would explode at the slightest insubordination. He treated his business associates with the same Napoleonic disdain.

If Joe Kennedy ever suffered a business reversal, history has not recorded it.

Right out of college, Kennedy landed a job as a state bank examiner. One would assume someone so young would need years of training for this challenge, but Kennedy's family contacts negated that requirement.

In 1913, Kennedy became president of the Columbia Trust Bank. He was all of twenty-five-years old. He bragged he was the youngest bank president in the country.

The fact that his father was a major shareholder in the bank played no role in his ascension. No one believed that fairy tale.

In 1917, just as Woodrow Wilson was dragging America into war, Kennedy became assistant general manager of the Bethlehem Steel Shipyard.

It was during this time frame he met Franklin Delano Roosevelt, who was then assistant secretary of the Navy.

Bethlehem built ships under Kennedy's direction. Roosevelt needed Kennedy's managerial skills to make certain the ships were properly constructed.

The brevity of America's participation in WWI was stunning. War was declared in April of 1917. Peace was declared in November of 1918.

The careers of both Kennedy and Roosevelt benefited from the war. The men would remain political allies until Roosevelt's death in April of 1945.

Roosevelt always respected Kennedy's business acumen. But truth be told, FDR watched Kennedy as if he expected the household silverware to disappear.

In 1919, Kennedy became a prominent member of the stock brokerage firm of Hayden and Company.

A year later, the story almost ended.

In 1920, the Grim Reaper passed right next to Kennedy.

American anarchists wanted to make a statement. And they wanted to make it in a big way. They loaded dynamite into a horse-drawn cart and parked the conveyance at the intersection of Wall and Broad Streets in New York. They chose this location with a purpose. The J. P. Morgan building was the target. Morgan was the living embodiment of American capitalism.

Joe Kennedy was maybe fifty yards away.

The explosion sounded like Judgment Day.

Kennedy was knocked to the ground. But the bomb's deadly shrapnel missed him.

Not so lucky were the forty victims who died from the blast. Another three hundred were seriously injured.

The suspected anarchist fled the country. He was never caught.

If Joe Kennedy ever once got on his knees and thanked his Creator, this was probably the day.

Year 1920 was also the year Warren G. Harding was elected president. The progressive Wilson was gone. A true capitalist was now in the White House.

This is the year the Kennedy legend really took off.

Wall Street was completely unregulated. It was Tombstone before Wyatt Earp moved in with his brothers.

From 1919 until 1929, America boomed. There were financial slowdowns, but they were quickly subsumed by the march of prosperity.

Everybody wanted in. A stock might sell for one hundred dollars. If Joe Blow could not afford it, no problem. Joe Blow could buy the stock for ten dollars.

Joe Blow was told he could pay the difference from future earnings.

No one seemed to see the danger in this formula.

For ten years the country went on a binge.

Ninety-nine percent of the investors in the stock market had no pertinent information about the companies they were investing in.

They couldn't know. There were no rules mandating a company to report on its collateral, its earnings, or its liabilities.

People got their stock information from neighbors and relatives.

Or maybe the shoeshine boy.

Joe Kennedy was not part of the 99 percent. He was part of the 1 percent of investors who made it their business to know exactly what was going on.

Kennedy knew which companies were solid and which companies were empty shells.

Insider trading was not illegal. Joe Kennedy made it his mission to know a company from top to bottom.

Kennedy and his allies also had newspapermen in their pockets. These ink-stained collaborators hyped stocks at Kennedy's command, and they maligned stocks at Kennedy's whim.

It is called winning coming and going.

Kennedy's golden touch made him a millionaire by 1923. He started his own investment firm, and in no time at all, he was a multimillionaire.

In 1926, Kennedy became enamored with Hollywood.

America during the Roaring Twenties was gaga over movies and movie stars.

At this stage of his life just being rich was not good enough for Joseph Patrick Kennedy.

No. There was a garden of Eden in California.

Kennedy got his feet wet by purchasing Film Booking Offices of America. It is a testament to Kennedy's genius that he recognized the film industry was on the cusp of a titanic change.

Talking movies were just a few months away.

Some of the old bulls in Hollywood thought that talking movies would prove to be just a fad.

Kennedy thought these old bulls were idiots. He was right.

He wanted to get the jump on them. He bought the technology that made talking movies possible. Now major studios would have to come to him for technical support.

Kennedy's Hollywood period also highlighted the cracks in his character.

He rotated his time between Massachusetts and California. Kennedy was a slightly constrained playboy when Rose was close. When she was three thousand miles away, he was unencumbered.

He began in the late 1920s a very public relationship with mega movie star Gloria Swanson.

It lasted three years. She broke it off when she discovered he bought her an expensive gift and then charged the item to her account. Swanson also found out she was not the only horse in the barn.

More troubling was the role Kennedy played in the destruction of a business rival.

In 1928, Alexander Pantages owned sixty-three profitable movie theaters nationwide.

Kennedy wanted to buy him out. He offered him eight million. This was the equivalent of one hundred million in today's money.

Kennedy was shocked when Pantages said no. Instead of moving on, Kennedy schemed.

Kennedy plotted to destroy Pantages's reputation thus forcing him to sell.

Out of the blue, Pantages was arrested for rape. Once Pantages got over his initial shock, he immediately accused Kennedy of setting him up.

It took two trials, but Pantages was finally acquitted.

The alleged victim in this drama was a woman named Eunice Pringle.

On her deathbed many years later, Pringle said she committed perjury on the orders of one Joseph Patrick Kennedy.

Pantages's only victory was on the legal front. His reputation in society was ruined.

Pantages eventually sold his interests to Kennedy for three and a half million dollars. He felt he had no choice.

Kennedy spent three years reorganizing and refinancing Hollywood studios.

He made money with every maneuver.

In 1928 and 1929, alarm bells sounded inside Kennedy's sagacious brain. Kennedy knew the stock market was way overdue for a correction.

Most of the fortunes the market generated were hollow. When one buys stocks for a dime on the dollar, one is looking at a Potemkin Village of wealth.

The market was a balloon filled with hot air. The boundaries of the balloon were stretched to their limits.

Kennedy started selling. And selling. By October of 1929, Kennedy had transferred about 92 percent of his money out of the market.

His timing was perfect.

By the end of October, the market had crashed in an epic manner. Tens of thousands of Americans saw their fictitious wealth disappear. The federal government then compounded the problem by tightening the money supply.

More jobs were lost than in any other time in American history.

Soup kitchens and shantytowns sprang up everywhere.

America was on the rocks.

But not Joe Kennedy. His wealth increased.

In 1929, Prohibition was nine years old. It had another four years to go.

Historians are quite split on the theory that Joe Kennedy was involved in bootlegging.

Those who wish to exonerate Joe Kennedy point to the absence of a written record. After all, Joe's other business ventures were well documented.

Wow. No written record. Therefore, Joe Kennedy could not possibly be involved in bootlegging.

The exoneration of Joe Kennedy is counterintuitive. Does one really believe that Harvard graduate and self-made millionaire Joe Kennedy would leave a paper trail attesting to his criminal behavior?

Is it possible to conduct business face-to-face? Is it possible to buy boats and cabin cruisers using cash?

Is it possible for a millionaire to hire cutouts and front men?

The answer of course is yes to all these questions.

Forty and fifty years later, the most prominent of Prohibition's gangster class would all state Joe Kennedy was up to his eyeballs in bootlegging. Frank Costello. Sam Giancana. Johnny Roselli. Carlos Marcello. Santo Trafficante Sr. and Santo Trafficante Jr.

Teamster Boss Jimmy Hoffa told anyone who would listen that the Kennedy fortune was tainted.

Joe Kennedy's upfront business dealings were considered questionable. It is not too difficult to believe that a money-making machine such as Joe Kennedy would never pass up the opportunities Prohibition provided.

Joe Kennedy had no way of knowing that his association with gangsters in the 1920s would lead to the death of a US president forty years later.

And that the president who would die in a barrage of bullets would be his second son.

Chapter 4

Mike Dunleavy was a nervous wreck.

He was two miles from the docks that service Havana, Cuba.

The ninety-mile trip itself had been uneventful—calm seas, fair weather, and beautiful blue water.

His new cabin cruiser performed flawlessly. Mike fell in love with the engine and the way it purred. The rooms had been hollowed out to make space for the cargo.

This boat was not renovated to carry tourists.

This was Mike's first excursion to Cuba. He did not know the language. He had no friends anywhere in the country.

And for the first time in his life, he was engaged in criminal activity.

Dunleavy vowed that if he spotted uniformed men on the dock at Havana he would turn around.

Nick had told him he would be met by an American. Nick did not tell Dunleavy that his contact was an Irishman. He wanted it to be a surprise.

Now just one hundred yards from the dock, Dunleavy's eyes were as wide as soup bowls.

It all looked normal. There were dozens of boats and hundreds of people loading and unloading all manner of goods.

Dunleavy was told to look for a man with a bright red shirt and black pants.

And there he was. Standing. Smiling. Hands on his hips.

Dunleavy eased the cabin cruiser into a slip. He shut down the engine.

The man in the red shirt sauntered over and extended his hand to help Dunleavy out of the bobbing craft. "Hello, Mike! How ya doing?"

Dunleavy grabbed the man's forearm and pulled himself onto the dock. "Fine, I guess. Nick described you, but he didn't tell me your name."

"I am Robert Xavier O'Halloran, a true son of Ireland."

Dunleavy's anxiety melted away. "No, you don't say! And where do you hail from?"

"Dublin."

Now Dunleavy was over the moon.

Without intending to, Dunleavy transitioned over to Gaelic.

O'Halloran did not miss a beat. He spoke the melodic Gaelic language as well as he spoke English.

After five minutes, Dunleavy was relaxed, even giddy. The two men talked about Ireland, the rebellion, and the bloody English.

They were interrupted by a young Cuban dockworker whose shirt had seven different colors.

"Senor, we are ready."

O'Halloran put his hand on Dunleavy's shoulder. "Mike, it's time you found out what you'll be hauling back to the states."

"I am more than a little interested."

O'Halloran ripped the tarp off a small hill of cases. "Dewar's White Label Blended Whiskey." O'Halloran spoke each word slowly, almost reverently.

Dunleavy was thoroughly impressed. Whenever he had a little extra cash, he would tell the bartender at Ferguson's Reef to serve him a Dewar's, no water, no ice. How he missed those days.

Dewar's White Label was first created in 1899. It evolved into the choice of drink among aristocrats and the moneyed classes.

Simply stated, Dewar's had panache.

Dunleavy pulled a bottle out and caressed it. "How many cases?"

"One hundred and sixty," O'Halloran barked back.

"Damn, are you trying to capsize me?"

O'Halloran laughed. "You have thirty-five feet of boat under you. You'll be just fine."

"Do you mind if I call you Bob?"

"Absolutely not."

"Bob, how long have you been in Havana?"

"Eighteen months."

"Any trouble?"

O'Halloran laughed. "You know what, this is a beautiful city. Let's go have a drink. I'll bet there's a whole bunch of questions you want to ask."

"You got that right. What about the cargo? Shouldn't we keep an eye on it?"

"No problem. That's my man Jose over there in that God-awful flowery shirt. He won't let anything happen."

Reynaldo's restaurant was less than a hundred yards from the docks.

"Dos cervezas, Pronto!" O'Halloran motioned Dunleavy to have a seat. "Mike, you know we picked you because you have skills that are absolutely invaluable to us."

"I have been told. But I have spent my whole life standing on the right side of the law. I'm not yet convinced I am doing the right thing."

"Mike, weren't you ready to go back to Ireland and shoot Englishmen dead?"

Dunleavy was stunned. "How did you know that?"

"We hear things, Mike. We do our research."

Dunleavy felt a little defensive. "I believed it was for a righteous cause."

"As do I! But an Englishman would say you were committing a crime. Not just any crime. Murder."

"Was it murder when they blasted my uncle off the face of the earth?"

"You and I say yes, they say no. It never ends."

"All right, I get the point. But have you had any trouble with the authorities?"

O'Halloran leaned into Dunleavy, so close their eyes almost melded together. "Mike, it is perfectly legal in Cuba to produce, sell, and transport alcohol. No one cares. Sure, the authorities know where our stuff is headed. And we have to grease them to make certain they don't manufacture an excuse to come after us. But everything down here is peaceful. Cubans regard Prohibition as pure stupidity. They can't believe we actually outlawed alcohol."

"It seems like your organization—"

O'Halloran interrupted. "Our organization."

"Okay. Our organization. It seems like we are constantly handing over money to lots of people just to keep them off our backs."

"It's the nature of the game. There is no other way to do it."

"Okay, I get it. If you know, how much do we have invested in this little enterprise?"

O'Halloran rubbed his chin. He rolled his eyes toward the ceiling while he did the math in his head. "Oh, in the two years since Prohibition began, we probably have half a million invested." He uttered the amount with complete insouciance.

Dunleavy's back straightened. "Half a million! Who has that kind of money?"

"We do, Mike. You, me, Nick, and a whole bunch of other guys that hopefully you will never meet."

"Can we recapture that amount?"

"Mike, each one of those cases you bring back will get us double and sometimes triple what we could have made before Prohibition. Now times are good. Lots of people have lots of money. And they all want to have a drink. But the people we are aiming for want the good stuff, Mike. They won't settle for rotgut."

"I wouldn't move rotgut, Bob. If I am going to break the law, it has to be done in style."

"You are my kind of guy, Mike. Want another beer?"

"I better not. I must keep my wits about me. Nick said you were going to tell me where to unload the product."

O'Halloran reached into his pant pocket and produced a map of Florida. His right index finger picked a spot that Dunleavy knew well. The Johnson Dockyard.

"Here's where you used to work. Five miles northwest, there's an inlet. It is called Blue Flamingo. Have you heard of it?"

"I know exactly where it is."

Blue Flamingo was a small insignificant inlet with no commercial activity except for the occasional lazy fisherman.

"At three a.m. tomorrow, one of our men will be there with a crew of five. He will signal you with a flashlight."

Dunleavy was concerned. "Hang on. That inlet close to shore is about three feet deep. Am I supposed to throw the stuff overboard?"

"Nope. Our guys will unload it on the dock."

"There is no dock there."

O'Halloran smiled. "There is now. Eighty feet of dock."

"When did this happen?"

"We completed it three months ago. The dock has already paid for itself. We also own the land near the inlet."

Dunleavy was mightily impressed, but he had another concern. "There is a road right next to that inlet. What if a cop comes by?"

"Between three a.m. and five a.m. tomorrow, there will not be a police vehicle anywhere near that inlet."

Dunleavy stared at O'Halloran as if he were a magician who just pulled a building out of a top hat.

"One more thing, Mike. There will be a paymaster there with an envelope. Inside will be five hundred dollars. A week later, you'll get another five hundred. A week after that, same thing. Now what do you think?"

"I just hope the government doesn't repeal Prohibition." Dunleavy laughed.

"Don't even joke about that. And Mike…"

"Yes?"

"When you get home, take your wife to dinner."

Chapter 5

The year 1929 saw America blissfully sailing along on a sea of prosperity.

Everyone was doing well. The Republican Party was crushing the Democrat party in local, state, and national elections.

The years 1920 to 1929 were the golden age of capitalists, rugged individualism, and entrepreneurs.

Warren G. Harding died in office in 1923. He was succeeded by Vice President Calvin Coolidge.

Coolidge had the reputation as the most laconic politician in the United States, but his lack of verbosity did not hurt him.

Coolidge's sad demeanor during the campaign of 1924 had its roots in a true tragedy.

His sixteen-year-old son Cal Jr. died that year.

He was playing lawn tennis at the White House. He developed a blister.

The blister got infected by deadly bacteria called *Staphylococcus aureus*. The bacteria morphed into sepsis—blood poisoning.

This was quite common in the early twentieth century.

Coolidge could barely bring himself to campaign that year. The death of Cal Jr. generated sympathy amongst the voters.

People showed up at the polls in big numbers.

So popular were Republicans during this period that even a third party candidate could not sway the election.

Senator Robert M. LaFollette of Wisconsin broke with the Republicans that year. He formed a new party, the Progressive Party.

Democrats hoped the split would redound to their favor. After all, when Teddy Roosevelt ran under the banner of the Bull Moose Party in 1912, the split cost the Republicans the White House.

Woodrow Wilson probably would not have been elected save for this development.

But in 1924, even a man as popular as Robert LaFollette could not change the election results.

Coolidge and his vice presidential nominee Charles S. Dawes beat LaFollette and Davis by a combined vote of two and half million.

They carried every state outside of the Old South, save for LaFollette's home state of Wisconsin.

Coolidge could have run again in 1928, but he never got over the death of his son. He announced his retirement.

Coolidge had no way of knowing it, but his retirement timing was perfect.

In 1928, Republicans nominated Herbert Hoover for President. The Democrats chose Al Smith. He was the first Catholic ever to run for the presidency.

Eight years of prosperity was enough for Hoover to crush Smith.

Republican rule looked to continue for a generation.

One American regarded himself as truly blessed.

Mike Dunleavy of Miami was climbing the ladder of success.

Dunleavy had now been running alcohol from Cuba for seven years.

His employers loved him. In that seven-year period, Dunleavy had saved eleven shipments of contraband from a watery grave.

Engine trouble which would have confounded most people was no problem for Mike Dunleavy. He truly could fix anything that is powered by gasoline.

In 1926, Nick Cosentino asked Dunleavy if he could make eight trips a month to Cuba instead of four.

It took Dunleavy just a split second to do the math. Eight trips a month meant the Mob would pay him forty-eight thousand dollars a year.

Forty-eight...thousand...dollars...a...year.

Maybe 2 percent of all Americans made that kind of money. Maybe it was 1 percent.

It was Nick Cosentino who probably saved Dunleavy from making the one mistake which could be his undoing.

"Watch yourself, Mike. Do not flash your money around. A lot of people know you. Big houses and new cars draw attention. And envy."

Cosentino told Dunleavy to find a city where he was completely unknown.

He told Dunleavy that whenever he entered a financial institution, he should wear the most expensive finery money could buy.

Cosentino said, "You need to adopt an air of aristocratic disdain, as if having money was no big deal. Once people assume you have always been wealthy, no one will question where it came from."

Dunleavy knew just the city. West Palm Beach.

He decided he would build his wife a house that had four bedrooms and four bathrooms. And two acres for a backyard.

Patricia Dunleavy would love West Palm Beach. The best people lived there.

Back in 1922, it took Patricia all of one hour to come on board with her husband's new occupation.

Mike stalled until he had a large wad of cash. Then he waited for his wife to come back from the store. He spread the money out on the kitchen table.

Patricia came home with her meager purchases. She opened the door and saw a sea of green. "What's this?"

"Our future, honey. But only if you are on board with it."

Patricia had not known her husband had quit his job. She assumed his long absences were because he was working a double shift.

Mike did not pull any punches. He told her everything. He told her this was the only way they could rise above their station.

Mike also told Patricia they had to be patient. There could be no ostentatious displays of wealth. "Our day will come, honey. I promise you."

Patricia stared at him for a full minute.

"You have to give me something right now," Patricia said. "I want help raising these kids. I want a nanny."

Dunleavy pored the idea over in his head. A woman coming and going from a modest house would not attract too much attention.

"Okay, done. Hey, let's hire someone who is fluent in Spanish. I wouldn't mind having three bilingual kids."

"Mike, one more thing. Can we take trips out of town and really cut loose?"

Mike smiled. "You bet we can, baby. You just wait."

That night Patricia rewarded her husband with some very artistic sex. It had been a long time.

It took seven years, but by 1929 Dunleavy was sitting pretty.

Dunleavy made two decisions that proved to be lifesaving. He put his money in out-of-town real estate.

And he did not go near the stock market.

Dunleavy's decisions proved to be brilliant. Because in October of 1929, the entire house of cards came crashing down.

Historians would call it the Great Crash of 1929. Billions of dollars of wealth would be wiped out.

The disease started in the United States, but it spread like an epidemic overseas.

Proud men now found themselves walking the streets not on the way to work but looking for work.

Herbert Hoover proved to be the unluckiest president since Abraham Lincoln. Hoover did everything wrong. Instead of loosening the money supply, he tightened it.

In 1930, 133 businesses a day failed.

Soon the economy reached such a nadir it was labeled the Great Depression. Twenty-five percent of the workforce was unemployed.

There were at least two Irishmen who did not feel the sting of deprivation.

Mike Dunleavy of Miami, Florida, and Joseph Patrick Kennedy Sr. of Brookline, Massachusetts, did not have trouble putting food on the table.

The two men had never met, nor would they ever meet.

Dunleavy never knew that the thirty-five-foot cabin cruiser that he maintained was owned by Kennedy.

Nick Cosentino knew. But he was sworn to secrecy. On pain of death.

Chapter 6

Mike Dunleavy and Nick Cosentino met for the last time in a little roadside café in the very heart of Miami.

It was August 1932.

The two men had been working together for ten years. They had both used the government's attempt to force virtue on America as a vehicle to prosperity.

Dunleavy showed up at the café driving a 1932 Packard Light Eight Model 900 four-door sedan. Cosentino drove a 1932 Ford Model B Hemmings. Each man had paid cash for his conveyance.

It was no sweat.

"Hello, Mike." Cosentino grasped Dunleavy's hand with a firm and friendly grip.

"It's been a while, Nick. What's the emergency?"

"Business can wait, Mike. How's the family?"

"I have three kids about to become teenagers. I'm considering suicide."

Cosentino chuckled. "I navigated four kids through their teen years," he said. "You are going to need a bracer. How's Patricia?"

Dunleavy leaned forward. "Thanks to you we are still together."

"Glad I could help, Mike." Cosentino looked outside at Dunleavy's new car.

"I see you didn't lose your money in the Crash."

"No, I didn't. And that's one more thing I can thank you for."

"How are things in West Palm Beach?"

"Great city. Good schools. The kids love it. And thank God so does my wife."

A waitress brought over two cups of coffee. Cosentino waited for her to walk away. He adjusted himself in his chair. "Mike, it looks like our days of doing business are coming to an end."

"Anything wrong on the legal front?" Dunleavy was momentarily concerned.

"No, nothing like that. It's politics. It looks like Roosevelt is absolutely going to trounce Hoover. If that happens, our people in Washington tell us Prohibition is on its way out."

"Repeal?"

"Yes, Mike, outright repeal."

Franklin Delano Roosevelt was exactly three months away from beating Herbert Hoover like a drum. It was in the air.

Roosevelt campaigned on reversing the Volstead Act as a well-intentioned failure.

The country was behind him. Even supporters of Prohibition had undergone a psychological adjustment.

Bribery. Corruption. Crime organizations becoming so powerful they acted as if they were independent nations. Murder in the streets. Politicians selling their souls.

The tipping point came when ordinary Americans who had never broken the law decided to flaunt their contempt for Prohibition.

"How long?" Dunleavy asked.

"I give it a year," Cosentino did not sound dejected. "Mike, in many ways, you had the perfect job. You were low enough on the totem pole that you did not attract the attention of the authorities. But you were important enough to compel us to pay you handsomely. When this thing comes to an end, do you have enough to carry on?"

Dunleavy smiled. "I and the family will be just fine."

Cosentino did not know that Dunleavy owned a waterfront restaurant and an office building in West Palm Beach. He had also held on to his first house in Miami. The rent money came each month.

In one more year, Mike Dunleavy would be making money legitimately, and all concerns about a midnight knock on the door by the police would be put to rest.

"Mike, I never told you who you were actually working for. But I guess it doesn't matter now."

"Why doesn't it matter?"

"When you first came on board, you were working for a man named Johnny Torrio. When he retired, your new boss was a man named Alphonse Capone. I'm sure that name rings a bell."

Dunleavy's eyes widened in disbelief. Scarface Al Capone was his benefactor?

From the beginning, Cosentino had told Dunleavy not to ask about his superiors in the organization.

Dunleavy was left to speculate.

He thought maybe the head guy was Charlie Wall. He was a major gangster who ran Ybor City.

Or it could be Ignacio Antinori the crime boss of Tampa.

Or it could be Santo Trafficante Sr.

Wall and Antinori would eventually fight a ten-year war for dominance. When it ended, the last man standing was Santo Trafficante Sr.

It never occurred to Dunleavy that Johnny Torrio's and Al Capone's tentacles could reach all the way from Chicago to Miami.

Dunleavy had followed Al Capone's trial in the newspapers. The entire country was engrossed by the legal proceedings.

In October of 1931, the government put Capone on trial for income tax evasion.

It was a brilliant maneuver. Capone assumed the government would come after him for murder or bribery. Charges he could easily defeat.

Capone kept his hands away from the actual crimes. He just issued orders and others did the gritty street work.

The government did a head fake. Prosecutors researched his finances for two years, and then they leaped like a lion on a wildebeest.

Capone had no way of explaining his lavish lifestyle. He had flaunted his wealth in public. Where did it come from?

Capone's lawyers could not explain the wealth, and the jury convicted him on five counts. Capone expected he would be given two years and ordered to pay back taxes.

But the judge hit Capone with an eleven-year sentence. No doubt the judge was feeling the heat from the White House.

In February of 1929, Capone's soldiers lured members of Bugs Moran's gang to a Chicago garage.

Two men disguised as police officers sprayed bullets at them with Thompson submachine guns.

Seven men lay dead. Bugs Moran was not one of those men. He had missed the meeting by a few minutes.

It was known as the St. Valentine's Day Massacre.

To this day it is the most famous Mob hit in history.

Capone was in Florida. He wanted an ironclad alibi. But no one was fooled.

Brand-new President Herbert Hoover read about the massacre. He was enraged.

He ordered his subordinates to "Get Capone!"

It took two years, but they got him. Federal agents spent twenty-four months pretending to look for witnesses who could put Capone at a murder scene with a smoking gun in his hand.

Capone laughed at the government's incompetence.

He was not laughing when he was handcuffed and led out of the courthouse in 1931.

Cosentino knew there was no reason now to keep Dunleavy in the dark about the leadership of the organization he worked for so diligently.

"Mike, the organization would like to give you something for all those trips you made to Cuba. You can keep the cabin cruiser."

Dunleavy was pleasantly surprised. He had fixed, painted, and reconditioned the boat for ten years. He had grown attached to it. "Are you sure, Nick?"

"What are we going to do with it? Alcohol is going to be legal in a year, maybe less. My people are not big into fishing."

Dunleavy laughed. "Well, Nick, what are you going to do?"

"I'm going back to Chicago. The government hopefully will not go crazy and legalize gambling and prostitution. If that happens, I'll be bugging you for a job."

Dunleavy stood and watched his friend walk out of the café.

Neither man had ever been questioned by law enforcement let alone arrested. They were lucky.

Thousands of their contemporaries were either dead or living in eight-by-eleven prison cells.

Dunleavy walked outside and let the sun caress his face.

Now his only worry was how to put three children through college.

Mike Dunleavy was now fully committed to getting on the right side of God.

Chapter 7

Joseph Patrick Kennedy Sr. gently massaged the glass holding the smooth liquid scotch he had poured after hanging up the telephone.

The date was November 9, 1932.

Kennedy was in his palatial house in Massachusetts. He had just gotten off the telephone with Franklin Delano Roosevelt of Hyde Park, New York.

Kennedy would not allow any family members into the room where he had just communicated with the president-elect.

Twenty-four hours earlier, Roosevelt had beaten incumbent President Herbert Hoover in the largest electoral landslide in American history.

Kennedy had placed a congratulatory call to Roosevelt. Kennedy never doubted for a second that Roosevelt's staff members would put him right through.

They did.

It was "Hello, Joe" and "Hello, Franklin." These two powerful Americans had been friends for eighteen years.

Only after Roosevelt was sworn in would Kennedy refer to him as "Mr. President."

Kennedy did not in any way regard himself to be inferior to the man holding the title president-elect of the United States of America.

Truth be told, Kennedy regarded himself as smarter, tougher, and more adept than the wheelchair-bound Roosevelt.

"A cripple in the White House," Kennedy mused to an empty room. "Who would have thought that could happen?"

Kennedy admired how Roosevelt had conned the press into covering up his paralysis. Roosevelt had contracted polio at age thirty-nine. His legs did not work.

Roosevelt knew his infirmity would kill his political ambitions. Americans expected their politicians to be sturdy as an oak. Much like his now dead cousin, Theodore Roosevelt.

Franklin Roosevelt used several tricks to make it appear he was ambulatory.

He had rigid unbending leg braces. And whenever he walked, he had a death grip on the man next to him. The supporting partner was usually a family member.

Roosevelt also polished his rhetorical skills so voters would concentrate on his voice instead of his frame.

It worked. Roosevelt was elected governor of New York and then president of the United States.

Beginning in 1931, Kennedy had grown envious of Roosevelt.

Twelve months prior to the election, Roosevelt had emerged as the leading candidate for the Democrat Party nomination.

Roosevelt. Roosevelt. The ubiquity of his name began to irritate Kennedy. He was slightly irked that Roosevelt now occupied the highest political office in the land.

Kennedy believed he was better suited to represent the nation.

Kennedy was forty-four years old. Plenty of time to get there.

First things first. Kennedy needed to acquire a federal job in order to build a resume.

This is where his friendship with Roosevelt could pay dividends.

Beginning in March of 1933, Roosevelt would start to staff his administration.

Democrats intended to vastly expand the federal workforce. A myriad of new agencies was imagined.

But priority number one for Kennedy was severing his relationship with the Mob.

Kennedy had used surrogates to shield his relationship with Mob bosses, but even this firewall could not be relied upon to save him from some enterprising journalist with a nose for corruption.

This was the main reason Kennedy just gave away his armada of smuggling boats. He wanted out quickly and quietly.

Kennedy had five months to get his private affairs in order before he could join the Roosevelt Administration.

Alcohol legalization was just over the horizon. No need to abandon that sea of profitability.

Kennedy had a brilliant plan for making money off America's pent-up demand for booze. If he could become the exclusive agent for a major distillery, the money would flow like Niagara Falls.

He pulled it off.

In 1933 Kennedy became the exclusive agent for the United States market involving Haig&Haig Scotch, Gordon's Dry Gin, and Dewar's.

The distillery was in Scotland, but the money flowed to America.

Kennedy was convinced there would never be a depression in alcohol consumption.

In this analysis he was dead-on accurate.

Convinced he was financially set for life, Kennedy decided to enter public service.

Roosevelt had the perfect assignment for America's most famous financial robber baron.

To no one's surprise, Americans had lost faith in the stock market. For a decade, thousands of investors thought they had found El Dorado.

It proved to be a chimera. They were rich one day and poor the next.

Roosevelt had to convince the public that they could safely reenter the stock market.

His brain trust created the Securities and Exchange Commission. Marching orders for members of the SEC were to bring order and transparency to Wall Street.

Roosevelt believed Kennedy was the perfect person to head the SEC.

His logic was impeccable. If you want to secure a bank, hire a successful bank robber.

Kennedy knew all the tricks of the market. And he had no problem reining in his former friends.

Kennedy's stay at the SEC was exceedingly short. He was interested in establishing a resume, not a record.

He had an equally short stay as chairman of the US Maritime Commission. There was no way such a piddling office was going to tie down the time of the likes of Joseph P. Kennedy Sr.

The year 1936 saw America in a better mood. The Depression still roared like a lion, but Americans believed Roosevelt was at least trying to solve the problem, unlike that dunderhead Hoover.

Kennedy requested a face-to-face with Roosevelt who in November of that year crushed Republican Alf Landon for the presidency. People were still mad at Republicans (and would be until 1952).

Kennedy wanted a position that projected stature and importance. If he did not get it, he would move back to the private sector.

Roosevelt had a perfect solution. Would Mr. Kennedy be interested in becoming US ambassador to England?

Kennedy did not hesitate even for a second.

The ambassadorship to the Court of St. James was the most prestigious diplomatic posting on the planet.

Now here finally was an assignment worthy of the talents of Joseph P. Kennedy Sr. Kennedy intended to dazzle the world for three years and then come back to the United States a hero. Using his vast personal wealth, he would run for the presidency.

In the year 1937, Kennedy had no way of knowing that his behavior in England would doom his political fortunes forever.

When the Kennedy family arrived in England, it was all sunshine and roses. Kennedy was formally installed in office on March 8, 1938.

The English press treated the photogenic family as if American royalty had arrived.

Invitations to the Kennedy clan poured forth like a raging river.

Everyone wanted to be seen with the patriarch and his cohort of beautiful children.

Joe Kennedy's ego, already gigantic, became galactic.

Kennedy's reputation was at its apex. The fall began almost immediately.

Private citizen Joe Kennedy could express his opinions without paying a price either politically or socially. But when one is America's chief representative at the Court of St. James, one must curb one's tongue or face the consequences.

Kennedy was not used to having newspapermen follow his every movement and record his every utterance.

Soon after arriving in England, Kennedy became friends with a vicious anti-Semite. Her name was Viscountess Nancy Witcher Langhorne Astor. She was immensely rich. She was also immensely cruel.

She was the leader of what became known as the Cliveden set. These were Europeans who despised the Jewish race and who admired Adolph Hitler. They would congregate at Astor's huge estate.

Astor was also anti-Catholic. She asked Joe Kennedy to overlook this presumed failing.

He did. Kennedy's own Catholicism was a veneer.

Kennedy was also an anti-Semite. And he was also an admirer of that WWI corporal who had become chancellor of Germany five years earlier.

Hitler, Kennedy said out loud, was a man of action. He came to power on January 30, 1933. Germany was flat on its back.

Hitler had taken a broken country and reconstituted its economy with lightning speed.

By 1938, Germany, under Hitler, was roaring ahead while America under Roosevelt was still stagnating. Kennedy unexpectedly expressed that opinion knowing newspapermen were present.

Joe Kennedy despised weakness. Everywhere Kennedy looked, he saw frightened little men.

Hitler was just the opposite.

Kennedy was still in America when Hitler in 1936 marched into the Rhineland in defiance of the Versailles Treaty.

And what did the Europeans do? Nothing.

And what did the United States do? Congress passed a series of Neutrality Acts signaling to the entire world that America would not help anyone overseas who was threatened by fascism.

The carnage of WWI was still very much a burning memory for civilized Europeans. No sane person wanted a repeat of that calamity.

In the mid-1930s, the whole world endorsed appeasement. The thinking was thus: if we toss meat at the wolf, perhaps the beast will stay in the woods.

Hitler was a wolf with far greater ambitions.

Kennedy had seen how Hitler treated communists. He killed them. Or he put them in concentration camps and worked them to death.

That solution was just fine to the mind of Joe Kennedy. He hated communists as much as he hated Jews.

Kennedy mused in public that the Roosevelt Administration was too soft on communism.

All of Joe Kennedy's mutterings reached the ears of the man sitting in the Oval Office. Roosevelt was furious.

But recalling Joe Kennedy so soon after his appointment would be an admission of a mistake in judgment. Roosevelt gritted his teeth and held back.

In 1938, Kennedy was convinced his political acumen was infallible.

In that year, Adolph Hitler managed to expand the German Empire twofold without firing a shot. Hitler told the entire world that he would go to war to complete the task of rounding up all German-speaking people and placing them under his jurisdiction. The world listened. And it recoiled in fear.

Hitler seized the Sudetenland from Czechoslovakia.

He marched into Austria and swallowed up the entire country in two days.

Kennedy watched the supine leaders of France and England as they acquiesced to this territorial rampage.

He publicly saluted Hitler. He predicted the Germans would subdue the entire continent.

Kennedy told the German ambassador to England, Herbert Von Dirksen, that the future belonged to the Third Reich.

Dirksen wired back to Berlin, "Kennedy is Germany's best friend in London."

Kennedy faced a conundrum when in November of 1938 a Jewish teenager in Paris murdered a German diplomat.

Herschel Grynszpan shot Ernest Vom Rath five times. It was rumored the seventeen-year-old had a homosexual relationship with Von Rath. But the public excuse for the killing was the treatment of Jews inside Germany.

The Nazis, with Hitler's blessing, went crazy. Beginning on November 9, 1938, and continuing until the next day, everything Jewish was under attack.

The SA and the SS rounded up thousands of Jews. The number of summary executions cannot be determined. But they were not rare.

Jewish businesses and synagogues were firebombed and looted.

The savagery became known as Kristallnacht, the Night of Broken Glass.

The situation was ready-made for an American ambassador to speak out and condemn the violence.

Kennedy was upset not because the rapacious behavior of the Nazis offended his conscience but because the incident was a setback in his campaign to elevate Germany.

The year 1939 saw the release of *Gone with the Wind*. It would become the most-watched movie of all time.

It was also the year Roosevelt announced he was seeking a third term.

Kennedy was furious. But this was one incident he kept quiet about.

As a loyal Democrat, he had no choice but to stand and salute.

But Kennedy knew that the power-mad Roosevelt could easily seek a fourth or even a fifth term. There was no law against it.

A long dynastic run. A disaster. Kennedy knew that when Roosevelt did leave office, the American people would probably elect a Republican for eight years. That was the normal rotation of politics in America.

By then Kennedy would be too old to seek the office.

Seeing his dream slip away, Kennedy became even more bombastic in his rhetoric.

In August of 1939, Hitler and Russia's Joseph Stalin signed a nonaggression pact. The two dictators agreed not to go to war. They also secretly agreed to carve Poland in two.

For the democracies, the nonaggression pact was tantamount to being bitten by an electric eel.

The leader of England, Neville Chamberlain, and the leader of France, Edouard Daladier, issued simultaneous statements that an attack on Poland would lead to a world war.

Hitler scoffed at the threat. Kennedy laughed.

On September 1, 1939, Hitler invaded Poland.

On September 3, 1939, England and France declared war on Germany.

The two most surprised men on the planet were Adolph Hitler and Joe Kennedy.

It is one thing to declare a war. It is another to fight one.

Hitler and Stalin crushed Poland in one month. With his eastern front stable, Hitler moved his troops west.

This began a period known as the Phony War. With the exception of the battle of the North Atlantic, there was very little action.

This inactivity convinced Kennedy that the democracies were hollow and had no intention to fight.

In the spring of 1940, Kennedy's predictions appeared to be correct.

Hitler roared through the Ardennes forest and marched on Paris. The French Army had no stomach for a fight. The English found their expeditionary army trapped in the coastal town of Dunkirk.

Using every small craft England had, the average citizen managed to sail across the English Channel and rescue three hundred thousand men.

It was called a miracle.

But in military terms, it was a massive defeat.

After the debacle at Dunkirk, Kennedy told anyone within earshot that England was finished.

The quote that finished Kennedy's political future came during this period. "Democracy is dead in England," he said. "And it probably is in America too."

Joe Kennedy suffered from the smartest kid in the class syndrome. He could not conceive his insights could ever possibly be wrong.

Kennedy, like Hitler, believed too much democracy bred rot in the national fiber.

But the opposite is the truth. Those who have tasted freedom will fight viciously to protect it.

On May 10, 1940, the weak Neville Chamberlain resigned his office.

Winston Spencer Churchill became prime minister of England. And Mr. Churchill had had enough of Joe Kennedy.

Churchill began corresponding with the one man who could shut Joe Kennedy up—Franklin Delano Roosevelt.

The final nail in Kennedy's coffin occurred in the summer of 1940.

America was officially neutral, but Roosevelt was shipping arms to England. England alone stood against the Nazi menace.

Kennedy bitterly opposed helping England with lethal weapons.

Wheelchair or not, Roosevelt was no weakling. He decided it was time for Joe Kennedy to come home.

Kennedy resigned on October 22, 1940. He had no choice.

England had just beaten the Luftwaffe in the Battle of Britain.

It should have been a heroic period for whoever held the title US ambassador. Instead, Joe Kennedy came home in disgrace. He was excoriated by radio announcers and newspapermen.

No doubt Kennedy believed that the passage of time would enable him to recover his footing and maybe salvage his ambitions.

But thirteen months after returning to the United States, Japan bombed Pearl Harbor.

Four days later, Adolph Hitler declared war on America.,

This was the same dictator Kennedy praised for three years.

Now, without a doubt, Joe Kennedy's ambitions were dead. But he had an ace up his sleeve.

He had a son. A son named Joseph Patrick Kennedy Jr.

A son who would take orders. Even if the son held the title "President of the United States."

Chapter 8

It is not like either of the Kennedy brothers had a choice.

Joe Kennedy Jr. (born 1915) and John F. Kennedy (born 1917) were both going to fight for their country.

Most Americans had four branches of the military to choose from for service to flag and country.

Not the Kennedy boys. They were going to join the Navy.

Their father decreed it. And their father's desires are always obeyed.

Joe Kennedy Sr. was in the shipbuilding business in WWI. This is how he met Franklin Delano Roosevelt, who was assistant secretary of the Navy.

Kennedy's ties to the Navy and its bureaucracy guaranteed he could get his sons those choice commissions denied average Americans. And he did.

Joe Kennedy Jr.'s credentials were stunning. He attended Choate and the London School of Economics before moving on to Harvard. He graduated in 1938 cum laude.

He was attending Harvard Law School when the Japanese bombed Pearl Harbor.

His father decreed that he would become a pilot.

He became a pilot. He mastered the B-24 Liberator better than any other man in the US Navy.

John F. Kennedy's acceptance into military service was anything but smooth.

Most Americans do not have a clue how sickly John Kennedy was as a lad. Three times between 1930 and 1940, John Kennedy was given last rites.

Growing up, Kennedy was a twig. His clothes hung awkwardly off a frame devoid of meat or muscularity.

Doctors misdiagnosed Kennedy's ailments until 1946 when the medical profession finally got it right.

Young Mr. Kennedy had Addison's disease.

This disease causes adrenal insufficiency. The adrenal glands are located just above the kidneys. When they fail the body does not receive enough cortisol and aldosterone.

Kennedy contracted the disease at an early age. In the 1920s and 1930s, the medical profession did not know how to look for causation.

Doctors inflicted constant enemas on John Kennedy and other medieval practices.

What saved John Kennedy from an early death was the discovery of cortisone. Beginning in 1947, Kennedy would receive this treatment, and his body finally responded.

Kennedy had been skeletal all his life. He could finally start putting on weight.

But all that lay in the future.

In 1941, Kennedy was suffering from Addison's disease as well as a spinal malfunction that pretty much crippled him for life.

The discs in Kennedy's spine did not fuse properly.

Kennedy's true medical history would have kept him out of every branch of the US Military.

Joe Kennedy Sr. knew how to pull enough strings to get his son in the Navy. Damn the pain. No Kennedy was going to sit out the war.

Robert Kennedy (born 1925) and Ted Kennedy (born 1932) were too young to put on a uniform in 1941. Bobby had to wait two years.

Had they been over the age of seventeen, all four brothers would have been frog-marched into military service by their father.

The elder Kennedy's machinations were masterful. He now had two sons in the Navy, and both held the title lieutenant commander.

Joe Kennedy Jr. was sturdy as an oak tree. The rough and tumble of flying B-24s was not something that would affect him dramatically in terms of physical wear and tear.

John Kennedy was another matter. His delicate back required a platform that was huge and stable. Something like an aircraft carrier.

Except John Kennedy aboard an aircraft carrier would be an ant amongst thousands of other ants.

It takes twenty years of service before the Navy even considers a man for the title of captain aboard a carrier.

But there is one section of the Navy where a man can get his own platform almost immediately—a PT boat.

The letters PT stand for patrol, torpedo.

These eighty-foot manmade killing machines were just what John Kennedy wanted for an assignment.

At age twenty-five, he would be calling the shots. He would be in command.

Kennedy's decision would seem to be counterintuitive.

A PT boat bounces along the water in the same manner an unbroken horse seeks to expel its rider.

It is precisely the wrong platform for a man with a soda cracker spine.

History does not record if Joe Kennedy Sr. pushed his son into the decision to join a PT squadron. The elder Kennedy would certainly want his flesh and blood to be calling the shots.

John Kennedy might have just assumed his father would endorse the decision.

Whoever supplied the initiative, John Kennedy became a PT commander in 1942. He would be heading for the South Pacific and a shot at immortality.

Joe Kennedy would end up in England.

The gods of war had a sadder ending in mind for Joe Jr.

Chapter 9

"Mr. Kennedy! Hang onto your hat! We have a volunteer."

John F. Kennedy looked up from his tiny desk at his executive officer, Leonard J. Thom. Standing to Thom's right was a young handsome ensign in navy whites so pristine they could only belong to a man who had been in the South Pacific for all of ten minutes.

Kennedy leaned back in his chair and examined the newcomer.

"Well, Len, what you have brought me?"

"We have a fresh face who, I have been told, was yanked out of the halls of Harvard and sent here to single-handedly win the war."

Kennedy's eyes lit up. A Harvard man.

"Well, Ensign, who are you, and what are you doing in my hut?"

The young sailor approached Kennedy. "Dunleavy, Stuart, sir. Thank you for seeing me."

A Harvard man. And an Irishman. Kennedy grinned. And he held out his right hand.

The two men shook hands like warriors do, with a hard grip and a purpose.

"Mr. Dunleavy, this is a PT squadron. We are very informal here. May I call you Stuart?"

"You may. Thank you, sir!"

"And you can call me Jack. Unless we are being shot at. Then I expect you to say, 'What can I do to save your ass, Commander?'"

All three men laughed. It was a sincere laugh as the statement was pretty funny.

"Well, Stuart, have you been assigned to the 109?"

"Actually no. I was assigned to PT 152."

Kennedy was puzzled. "Then why are you here, and what are you volunteering for?"

"My orders and classification don't become operational until the commander of PT 152 signs off on them. That won't happen until tomorrow."

"Well, what good am I to you for a grand total of twenty-four hours?"

"I understand you are going out on patrol tonight. I would like to come along."

Kennedy leaned forward. "Stuart, you are going to have plenty of time to see action in this war. Don't rush it!"

Dunleavy had a retort. "The mosquitoes and bugs on this island are more dangerous and crueler than the Japanese could ever hope to be."

Kennedy and Thom chuckled. It was true.

The Americans had set up a base on Rendova Island, a spit of land immediately north of Guadalcanal. The battle for Guadalcanal was the second great Allied victory over Japan. The first was the June 1942 Battle of Midway.

Midway stopped the Japanese rampage through the Pacific theater of war.

Japan was determined not to suffer another defeat. The Japanese fought ferociously to hang onto Guadalcanal, but by early 1943, they had lost.

General Douglas MacArthur now began his famous island-hopping strategy.

American sailors would patrol the waters off Rendova looking for Japanese ships that became known as the Tokyo Express.

It was dangerous work. PT boats were fast, but a Japanese destroyer was a hundred times more powerful.

Kennedy was worried about protocol. "Is your commander going to chew my ass if I take you along?"

"No, sir. I cleared it with him not twenty minutes ago."

Kennedy looked at Len Thom. "Well, Len, what do you think?"

Thom took a step forward. "We are two men short. I know I can find something for him to do."

Kennedy grinned at Dunleavy. "Stuart, as a Harvard man, I thought you would have more sense than to volunteer."

"Commander, everyone knows Harvard men have intelligence but no common sense."

Kennedy laughed. "Where do you call home, Stuart?"

"Born in Miami. Raised in West Palm Beach."

"Your old man got you into Harvard. That is no easy trick. What does he do for a living?"

Dunleavy hesitated for just a microsecond. He long ago learned that his father got rich breaking the law.

He decided he would tell a little white lie to Lieutenant Junior Grade John Kennedy.

"My dad made his money in the small craft industry. No one builds better boats than Mike Dunleavy."

Kennedy locked his hands together. "Your dad and I have a lot in common. No one loves sailing more than I."

With that, John Kennedy stood up and stretched out his right hand. Dunleavy shot to his feet and reciprocated.

"Glad to have you aboard, Stuart. Be back here in four hours. Were I you, I would find a bug-free section of this island and get some sleep. There won't be any naps aboard PT 109 tonight."

For the second time in just minutes, the two men shook hands vigorously.

Each man liked the other. Kennedy wished Stuart Dunleavy had been assigned to his squadron.

Dunleavy had no idea that his impulsive desire to see action would alter his life forever.

The date was August 1, 1943. In twelve hours, Stuart Dunleavy, John Kennedy, Len Thom, and the rest of PT 109 would be facing either capture by the enemy or death by drowning.

Chapter 10

The men of PT 109 were finishing their patrol logistics when Len Thom told them to take five.

"All right, you swamp rats, listen up. We have some fresh meat coming with us tonight. He is only going to be with us on one patrol, so try not to make his life too miserable."

Thom wiggled his index finger, and Stuart Dunleavy went from the dock to the deck of PT 109.

"Gentlemen, I give you Ensign Stuart Dunleavy, who gave up all the comforts of West Palm Beach, Florida, just so he could get killed for Uncle Sam."

Ensign George Henry Robertson Ross stepped forward and grabbed Dunleavy's right hand.

"Glad to have you, Mr. Dunleavy. Let me introduce you around."

"That mopey character over there is Edgar Maurer, our quartermaster. Next to him is our radioman, John McGuire. Another friggin' Irishman. Those three guys next to the 37-mm Jap busters are not Moe, Curley, and Larry. They're our gunners, Ray Albert, Harold Marney, and Bill Johnson. The Cro-Magnon covered in grease is our motor mechanic, Jerry Zinser. The grease monkey next to him is Pat McMahon. Our two torpedomen are Ray Starkey and Andy Kirksey. Ever notice torpedoes resemble phallic symbols?"

The entire crew found that jibe hilarious.

Dunleavy made certain he shook each man's hand.

Len Thom waited for the niceties to be completed, and then he approached Dunleavy. "I think we will assign you to Mr. Ross. When he's not shooting at Japs, he is looking for them. How is your eyesight, Ensign?"

"Twenty-twenty," Dunleavy said.

"Good. It is going to be dark as hell tonight. Any speck of light you see, you come and get me. Do not yell. Just walk over. Got it?"

"Right as rain. Where's the commander?"

"Jack? Oh, he is always the last on board. As a matter of fact, here he comes now."

John Kennedy walked down the dock with an air of patrician indifference that somehow did not rankle his working-class comrades.

Kennedy had a gift, a style that conveyed, "Yes, I am a rich man's son" but also "no, I'm not an insufferable jackass."

Self-deprecating humor has been the salvation of many aristocrats. But it cannot be phony. Kennedy was no phony.

John Kennedy was comfortable in his skin. He did not have a Napoleonic complex, and he distrusted those who did.

Kennedy swung his skinny frame onto PT 109 and headed straight for Stuart Dunleavy. He put his hand lightly on Dunleavy's left shoulder. "I hope you are not prone to seasickness because we are going to be out there all night."

Dunleavy smiled. "If I puke, we'll use it for chum and do some fishing."

Kennedy laughed. He really liked this kid. And the feeling was reciprocated.

The mission this night was the same as all the others.

Intercept the Tokyo Express. Launch torpedoes. Pray for an explosion. And then get the hell out of Dodge.

To date, not a single Japanese destroyer, battleship, cruiser, or aircraft carrier had been sunk by a PT boat.

The concept seemed sound. Build a fast platform that could close on the enemy, shoot, and run.

But to be effective, a PT torpedo had to close within a mile of a target.

A destroyer's sixteen-inch guns could launch a deadly projectile twenty-five miles. A battleship's eighteen-inch guns could hurl one even longer.

It was a question of speed versus power. So far power was winning.

PT boats were effective as a mechanical cavalry. With the exception of scout planes, nothing was better at gathering intelligence than a crew of PT men.

But every man in the PT universe was hungry for a big score.

Perhaps John Kennedy could make it happen. Perhaps the night of August 1 and the morning of August 2 would be the time frame that saw a real victory at sea.

PT 109 had a radio, but it did not have radar.

And the eight PT boats on patrol that night were ordered to maintain radio silence.

No radar. No communication.

John Kennedy was back in the nineteenth century. He knew only what his eyes and ears told him.

The Japanese had one hundred thousand men stationed at the island of Rabaul. The main function of the Tokyo Express was to keep this linchpin supplied with men and material.

Joe Kennedy Sr. never wanted his second son to be in this position.

The elder Kennedy had wrangled John Kennedy an assignment patrolling the Panama Canal. His only danger at that location would be tropical diseases and ennui fostered by boredom.

Young Kennedy defied his father. He wanted action. He requested and was granted a South Pacific posting.

On February 23, 1943, John Kennedy was sent to Tulagi Island in the Solomons. Exactly one month later Kennedy took command of PT 109.

On May 30, 1943, Kennedy was ordered to the Russell Islands to help the US Navy prepare for an invasion of New Georgia. In the straits around the Russell Islands was the Island of Rendova, where the PT Squadrons set up a base.

Hundreds of PT men would patrol the Ferguson and Blackett straits looking for the Tokyo Express.

It was here that the legend of John Fitzgerald Kennedy was born.

Without radar or running lights, PT 109 was forced to keep its speed at four to five knots.

On the night of August 1, 1943, eight PT boats engaged the Tokyo Express. Thirty torpedoes had been launched. Not one scored a hit.

Stuart Dunleavy was whipsawed with emotions. This was his first combat experience.

And it was all taking place in the dark.

Dunleavy and Ross tried their best to penetrate the ubiquitous darkness, but it was to no avail.

They had no way of knowing that a sea beast was bearing down on them.

The Japanese destroyer *Amagiri* was built in 1930. It was a child of the Japanese victory over the Russians in 1904–05.

The Japanese Navy so thoroughly routed the Russian Navy that a belief in the efficacy of sea power was embedded in the brains of every militarist and civilian in that island nation.

In the 1920s, Japan decided to build a navy second to none.

The *Amagiri* was the fifteenth of twenty-four Fubuki-class destroyers ordered built by the Japanese Navy.

The ship was 387 feet long. It displaced 1,750 tons. Top speed of the *Amagiri* was thirty-eight knots.

In other words, the massive *Amagiri* was just as fast as John Kennedy's small greyhound, PT 109.

The man in charge of *Amagiri* in 1943 was Lt. Commander Kohei Hanami. His paramount mission was to keep Japanese forces on Rabaul supplied no matter what.

Avoiding the US Navy or, if that was not possible, sinking the US Navy became his only goal in life.

At 2:25 a.m. on August 2, 1943, Hanami spotted the outlines of an American torpedo boat. He did not hesitate.

He bore down on the American menace with a deadly resolve.

At 2:27 a.m., the *Amagiri* hit PT 109 at midsection and neatly bisected the boat. Ross and Dunleavy spotted the danger with only ten seconds of reaction time available to them.

Dunleavy cried out "Mr. Kennedy! Mr. Kennedy!"

There was absolutely nothing that could be done.

Like a scalpel going through soft flesh, PT 109 became two pieces, neither of which was seaworthy.

A fireball one hundred feet high lit up the darkened waters off the islands of Kolombangara and Ghizo.

Crewmen Kirksey and Marney were killed instantly. The rest of the men were badly injured or facing the prospect of drowning.

The *Amagiri* did not stop. Hanami's orders were to get to Rabaul unmolested.

He assumed the collision was cataclysmic. For certain, no one could survive.

The sea beast sailed into the opacity of a black night.

The surviving crew of PT 109 did have two things in their favor.

The watertight compartments at the front of the boat did what they were designed to do.

They kept half the boat afloat. A crippled life support system.

The other advantage the crew had was in the person of their commander, John Kennedy.

Up until this very moment, John Kennedy had been a playboy and a raconteur, someone who would dominate a fraternity party with his charisma.

But until August 2, 1943, no one knew John Kennedy had what it takes to survive a devastating tragedy.

Over the next five days, Stuart Dunleavy watched John Kennedy assume command.

For twelve hours, the men hung on to the broken hull of PT 109.

When it became apparent that a rescue operation was not coming, Kennedy ordered his men into the water.

Dunleavy was uninjured. He could swim. He watched as Kennedy pulled wounded comrade Patrick McMahon through the water by putting his life jacket strap in his mouth.

The entire crew made it to a spit of land called Plum Pudding Island.

Some were healthy. Some were in bad shape.

John Kennedy decided he was going to be the only one taking chances in order to survive this disaster.

Dunleavy did not know Kennedy had a deadly disease. He did not know Kennedy's spine was a rubber band.

But what Dunleavy saw over the next five days was a man who took on one dangerous assignment after another in order to help his men.

Kennedy took a lantern and a life jacket and swam out into Japanese-held waters hoping to intercept a PT boat on patrol. Then he made another swim in the dark. And then a third. Each episode was deadly dangerous.

He could easily have drowned. Or been pulled down by sharks.

Kennedy told his men to stay out of sight. He alone exposed himself to the elements and the Japanese.

Dunleavy grew to admire—no, he grew to love John Kennedy.

And when, after five days, two friendly natives stumbled across this misbegotten crew, it was John Kennedy who exposed himself and convinced the interlopers to help.

Kennedy cut a coconut in half. He wrote a message inside the husk. He had no idea if the natives would deliver it.

But deliver it they did. And they told the US Navy where they could find the crew.

Naval personnel had assumed PT 109 was sunk and all hands had gone down. That the Navy failed to launch a comprehensive search was a disgrace.

Kennedy never held it against his superiors.

Two men were dead. But the rest were alive. And grateful they had John F. Kennedy as their leader.

Back in the United States, Joe Kennedy Sr. went from the very pit of hell to a resurrection. The government told the ambassador his son was lost at sea and was presumed dead.

Joe Kennedy Sr. was a ruthless tyrant with individuals outside of his family. But he dearly loved his children.

He was certain his son was dead. Rose Kennedy retreated to the confines of the Catholic Church to find solace. Her despondency was crippling.

After seventy-two hours of grief came news that John Kennedy was alive and unharmed.

Not only was he alive, he was hailed as a hero.

A very prestigious Navy medal was going to be placed on the emaciated frame of John Kennedy—the Navy and Marine Corps Medal for heroism and actions that resulted in the saving of lives.

Joe Kennedy Sr. was ecstatic.

Rose Kennedy spent hours thanking Almighty God for this miracle.

Joe Kennedy Jr. was glad his brother was alive, but he was in possession of a darker and more selfish impulse.

Joe Kennedy Jr. had been upstaged by his younger brother. This had never happened before.

John Kennedy's role in life had been mapped out by Joe Kennedy Sr.

"Support your older brother at all times. Help him become president of the United States. And never put yourself in a position where your achievements dwarfed those of Joe Kennedy Jr."

In a family as hierarchical as the Kennedys, some things are never done.

Joe Kennedy Jr. knew he had to do something to reverse this family dynamic. He needed a medal.

And his medal could not be less prestigious than his brother's. It had to surpass it.

That meant the Navy Cross or the Congressional Medal of Honor.

These honors were tall orders. The military did not hand them out unless the proposed recipient had done something spectacular.

Joe Kennedy Jr. was stymied. And he did not like it.

It has been reported that when the two brothers finally got together after the sinking of PT 109, Joe Kennedy Jr. hit John Kennedy in the face with a haymaker. It knocked the younger man across a room.

John Kennedy instantly forgave his brother. He knew the motive behind the punch.

But the die was cast.

The newspapers were lauding John Fitzgerald Kennedy. His brother was being ignored.

Joe Kennedy Jr. must, without fail, do something to restore the family chain of command.

The war would not last forever. The deed must be done quickly.

Chapter 11

Lt. Commander Joseph P. Kennedy Jr. was morose.

It was August 1, 1944. He had completed twenty-five combat missions, and under Navy directives, he was eligible to go home.

Absolutely no one would have faulted him for going back to the United States. He had done everything military command had asked him to do.

But sticking in his craw were those medals the Navy had given his younger brother.

Joe Jr. had a distinguished service record. Not a black mark anywhere in his personnel file.

He still could not stand it. He just could not stand it.

He would be facing a lifetime of Thanksgiving dinners where John Kennedy would be toasted as the superior warrior.

Time was running out.

The invasion of France on June 6, 1944, heralded the end of Adolph Hitler's thousand-year Reich.

Joe Kennedy Jr. knew the end of the war was coming and coming very quickly.

He had to do something!

Salvation came that very day.

Kennedy's superiors told him about a new technology that would revolutionize warfare—drones.

"What the hell is a drone?" Kennedy asked.

Radio technology had advanced to a point where the Navy believed it could control a bomber after the pilots had parachuted out.

A following aircraft, known as Mother, would direct the plane to a target and crash-dive the plane into an enemy installation.

Pack the plane with enough explosives and even the most hardened enemy facility would be reduced to a smoldering cinder.

It was all very new. And dangerous.

But the idea, if successful, held great promise.

It held the promise of a Navy Cross for the two men who could pull it off. The plan called for one pilot and one expert radioman.

Navy brass wanted Joe Kennedy Jr. to be the first man in history to test a drone aircraft.

The Germans had a version of the drone called the V-1 and the V-2.

The V stood for Vengeance.

But these were rockets. Not airplanes.

Drone technology in August of 1944 had not advanced to the point where controllers on the ground could get a bomber into the air without a pilot.

That is why the Navy needed Joe Kennedy Jr.

The Navy regarded Kennedy as their best pilot.

It was an honor but also a curse.

All advances in aircraft design come at a risk of death or injury.

Navy scientists told Kennedy he would be flying an airplane loaded with 21,700 pounds of high explosives.

This, too, was new. No one had ever packed an airplane with that amount of explosive power. No one had ever wired so much explosive in such a contained environment.

Just one mistake and...

Joe Kennedy did not hesitate. He accepted the assignment.

The other man selected was radio expert Wilford J. Willy.

On August 2, 1944, the two men were spirited away from Fersfield AFB in England to a highly classified country location.

They would spend the next ten days training. Neither was allowed to communicate with the outside world.

On August 10, 1944, the Navy gave Joe Jr. permission to write his brother a letter. The training was almost over. On August 11, 1944, the two volunteers would be taken back to Fersfield. And one day later they would be airborne.

The letter was the last communication Joe Jr. would ever have with John or any other member of his family.

He had just forty-eight hours to live.

> Dear Jack,
>
> Your letters are always a great source of enjoyment. My tardiness in writing is not attributable in any way to an attempt at discouragement of such a fine pen relationship. For the last ten days, I have been stuck in the country far beyond striking distance of any town. Every day I think will be my last one here, and still we go on. I am really fed up, but the work is quite interesting. The nature of it is secret, and you know how secret things are in the Navy."

On August 12, 1944, Kennedy and Willy climbed aboard a B-24 Liberator at Fersfield. The men who loaded the explosives on board were doing something they had never done before. No one had.

With the exception of the cabin, every inch of the plane was loaded with the Navy's most advanced chemical explosive compound.

The target was a V-2 launch site in western France. The V-2 was the one German weapon that scared the pants off Allied leaders.

It was the world's first intercontinental rocket. It traveled at twice the speed of a bullet.

It could not be intercepted. It could not be seen or heard until it hit the ground.

The V-1 was a clumsy slow-moving rocket that could be shot down by a Hurricane or a Spitfire. Even by ground fire.

Not so the V-2.

Hitler told his people this would be the weapon that changed the course of the war. From pending defeat would emerge absolute victory.

Joe Kennedy was never told the real reason his mission, code-named Operation Aphrodite, was pushed ahead with such alacrity.

The reason the V-2 rocket frightened strong men was its future potential.

It was the perfect conveyance for an atomic warhead.

Kennedy did not know because only a few men on the planet knew of the Manhattan Project. This was America's multibillion-dollar plan to build a uranium bomb.

Both Churchill and Roosevelt greatly feared that the Germans had a corresponding program in the works.

How far had the Germans progressed? No one knew.

But the Germans did have something the Allies were not even close to having—an unstoppable intercontinental rocket.

That is why the V-2 launch sites had to be destroyed.

It is why Adolph Hitler had to be run to ground and exterminated.

The nation that possessed atomic bombs and intercontinental rockets was the nation that controlled the world.

Joe Kennedy and Wilford Willy coaxed their B-24 Liberator off the ground at 6:00 p.m. August 12, 1944. A second bomber immediately lifted off behind them.

For twenty minutes, everything appeared to be functioning properly.

The two bombers would soon leave English air space and head for occupied France.

Kennedy and Willy were minutes away from parachuting to safety on English soil.

But the god of war plays no favorites.

That Kennedy and Willy were honorable men fighting for a noble cause meant nothing to this cruel entity.

Maybe the plane's vibration generated a spark. One tiny spark.

That is all it took.

Twenty-one thousand seven hundred and fifty pounds of explosive ignited instantaneously. The explosion was so massive it could be heard one hundred miles in every direction.

Debris from the B-24 Liberator fell like snow on the ground.

But no trace of either Kennedy or Willy were found.

The two men had been reduced to their atomic level.

Operation Aphrodite was a resounding failure.

Getting rid of Adolph Hitler and the V-2 was now the sole responsibility of Dwight Eisenhower and his ground forces.

Radio-controlled airplanes lay in the future.

Joseph Patrick Kennedy Sr. was inconsolable. He cried for days. Rose Kennedy again entrenched herself in the confines of the church.

The entire Kennedy clan was cast down in a communal depression.

Joe Kennedy Sr. could not even bury his son. There was nothing to bury.

This event probably shattered whatever faint belief Joe Kennedy Sr. had in the existence of a benign God.

In 1943, God tortured the elder Kennedy with the news of his second son's death in the South Pacific.

Then came the joyous news that the story was false. John Fitzgerald Kennedy was alive and well.

But there would be no happy ending this time. No miracle telegram announcing a mistake had been made.

Joe Kennedy Jr. was gone. There would be no earthly resurrection.

And Joe Kennedy Sr. did not believe in a heavenly resurrection either.

His most treasured child, his namesake, was dust in the wind.

It took six months for Joe Kennedy Sr. to recover from his son's passing.

Gritting his teeth, he pounded his desk. "I have another son! He and I will carry on! And damn the God who did not protect my firstborn child!"

Chapter 12

The greatest war in human history ended in September of 1945.

John Kennedy survived four years of combat. But not without a toll on his less-than-robust body.

Psychologically he needed a break.

His father had other ideas.

The clock was ticking. His son was eighteen months away from turning thirty.

Joe Kennedy Sr. had plans for his son's future. Whether or not his son was on the same wavelength was irrelevant.

Joe Kennedy's word was law.

And Joe wanted his son to run for Congress.

To keep John Kennedy occupied, Joe called up his old friend William Randolph Hearst.

Hearst was probably the only man in America who could hold his own with Joe Kennedy in a wrestling match over who was the most ruthless.

Hearst ran the largest newspaper chain in America. In the blink of an eye, John F. Kennedy became a correspondent for the *New York Journal-American.*

Kennedy always wanted to be a writer. He did not know his father was merely keeping him occupied with something he liked until the real occupation he was destined for rolled up in his lap.

Joe Kennedy Sr. knew the ins and outs of Massachusetts better than any man alive.

Kennedy wanted his son to run for the US House of Representatives in the Eleventh Congressional District.

There was only one problem. That seat was held by a Democrat named James Michael Curley.

And Mr. Curley was a popular politician who could beat back any competitors who exhibited the temerity to run.

There was no way Joe Kennedy was going to put his son up and watch him go down in defeat.

Something had to be done about Mr. Curley.

Joe Kennedy had the financial means to convince Mr. Curley that retirement from the House was the smart thing to do.

If Mr. Curley wanted to run for mayor of Boston, or even governor, that was just fine. Joe Kennedy would provide money no matter what office Curley selected.

To the surprise of newspapermen everywhere, James Michael Curley announced he would not seek reelection in 1946.

He also bought himself a new Cadillac.

He nicknamed it the JPK (Joseph Patrick Kennedy) Roadster.

When Joe Kennedy was certain Curley was out of the way, he told his son he would be the next congressman from the Eleventh District.

John Kennedy just nodded his head. It never occurred to him to object.

The Eleventh Congressional District included the towns of Cambridge, Somerville, East Boston, the North End, Brighton, and Charlestown.

Rose Kennedy had been born in the Eleventh District.

John Kennedy's maternal grandfather John F. Fitzgerald (Honeyfitz) once occupied the seat.

Joe Kennedy Sr. picked the Eleventh District precisely for these reasons.

In October of 1945, John Kennedy began giving speeches around the state. He was a decorated war veteran. He was articulate. He had a smile that devastated female voters.

Stuart Dunleavy was back in West Palm Beach Florida. His mother and father were grateful that he was home with all his arms and legs intact.

One day Stuart read a small article in the local paper about the hero of PT 109 running for Congress.

Stuart nursed a cup of coffee and pondered what to do with this information.

He had no plans for his life. He was the manager of his father's restaurant, but this provided him no real joy at all.

It took only twenty minutes of contemplation before Dunleavy made a decision.

He would take a train all the way to Boston. He would not tell Jack Kennedy he was coming. His plan was to knock on his door and just look at the expression on his friend's face.

Stuart Dunleavy would offer to help Jack Kennedy become a United States congressman. He would do whatever Jack wanted. For free if it came to that.

Two weeks later, Jack Kennedy was shaking hands at a factory in Charlestown.

Stuart Dunleavy had his hat pulled down low so the contours of his face could not be discerned. He grabbed the young politician's right hand.

"Hi, I'm Jack Kennedy, and I'm running—"

"You are nothing but a drunken Irishman who couldn't score in a women's prison with a handful of pardons."

Dunleavy pushed back his hat and grinned. Jack Kennedy was overwhelmed.

For five days in the South Pacific, Dunleavy and Kennedy had forged a bond that could not be broken.

Dunleavy had done everything he could to make Kennedy's command easier.

When Kennedy returned from his nightly swims off Plum Pudding Island, Stuart would sit next to him while he slept, spending hours fending off the bugs that sought to make a meal out of the young lieutenant.

After the rescue, the two warriors sat down for an hour alone, and each man promised that when the war was finished, they would not become strangers.

Kennedy grabbed Dunleavy and nearly crushed his rib cage.

"Goddammit, Stuart, what are you doing here?"

"I read in the newspapers you were engaged in some futile endeavor at improving your station in life. I'm here to watch you fall on your face."

Kennedy laughed loud and hard. He was oblivious to the line of factory workers seeking to shake his hand.

Realizing he was slighting potential voters, Kennedy decided to act.

"Dammit, Stuart! I can't believe it! I'm a little busy right now. But you must come by the house tonight. Don't even think of saying no. Dave, come here!"

Kennedy's friend and confidant Dave Powers rushed over to see why his candidate was so animated.

"Dave, this is Stuart Dunleavy. You have one job today. Make sure he is at my house at eight p.m. Are we clear?

"Clear as mud, Jack. I'll get him there."

Normally Joseph Kennedy Sr. is cold as stone to young people he does not know.

Kennedy long ago decided he would spend whatever time he had on this earth communicating with people who were his equals or who could help his family.

But when the elder Kennedy learned that the young man standing in front of him was an Irishman who helped keep his son alive, he grinned like a chimpanzee.

Joe Kennedy was even more impressed when Stuart Dunleavy offered to work for the campaign for free.

"Mr. Dunleavy, I guarantee I will find you a spot in this campaign. Would you care to join us for dinner?"

Dinner was held in abeyance until Jack Kennedy got home at 9:00 p.m. He had been shaking hands for fourteen hours.

The elder Kennedy was immediately impressed by Dunleavy's intelligence and articulation. He was a most convivial dinner guest.

Over dessert, Joe leaned and whispered in Jack's ear. "Son, tomorrow you tell Dave Powers to find a responsible position for this young man."

"Dad, I've already taken care of that."

The elder Kennedy had the power to send Dunleavy back to Florida in the blink of an eye. But he decided to give his son this tiny triumph.

In no time at all, there was a quartet of men attending John Kennedy at all times.

Dave Powers. Advisor Kenny O'Donnell. Kennedy's first cousin Joe Kane. And Stuart Dunleavy.

Dunleavy became part of Kennedy's Praetorian Guard. He, O'Donnell, and Kane were in charge of managing crowds and scheduling.

Dunleavy was also given an assignment that was a bit more esoteric.

He had to get the phone numbers of those women Kennedy found attractive on the campaign trail.

In no time at all, Dunleavy had collected more than a hundred numbers.

Naturally as a confidant of Massachusetts' most eligible bachelor, Dunleavy was able to consort with Kennedy's leftovers.

He did not protest one bit. Nor did he object to the envelopes of cash that arrived on his desk each Friday afternoon. Dunleavy did not have to work for free.

Dunleavy was stunned by the amount of money John Kennedy managed to scrape together.

His campaign never lacked for anything. Billboards. Pamphlets. Balloons. Ballrooms. Endless buffets. Transportation.

Ten men were running in the Democratic primary.

Joe Kennedy outspent them all by a factor of a hundred.

But the best ammunition Joe Kennedy had was his son.

John Kennedy did not slouch through the race. He ran hard.

He gave hundreds of interviews to newspapermen. He used radio.

He buttonholed ordinary people on the street.

He never put in less than a twelve-hour day.

And it paid off. On primary election day, John Kennedy garnered 22,183 votes. His closest competitor, Michael J. Neville, received 11,341.

The general election was a slaughter.

Kennedy in November 1946 got 69,093 votes to the Republican challenger's meager 26,007.

The man he beat, Lester Bowen, congratulated the young Democrat for running a great campaign.

Bowen told his friends that going up against Joe Kennedy's money was a suicide mission.

In January of 1947, John Kennedy took the oath of office. Standing ten feet away were Kane, O'Donnell, Powers, and Dunleavy.

And of course, Joe Kennedy. The emperor of the Kennedy clan was already musing to himself about the United States Senate and how nice it would be to knock off Republican incumbent Henry Cabot Lodge in 1952.

The Senate was prestigious, but it was not going to be the apex of John Kennedy's career.

Joe Kennedy was determined to spend whatever amount of money it took to ensconce his son inside a famous structure located at 1600 Pennsylvania Avenue.

Chapter 13

Congressman John Fitzgerald Kennedy romped through the 1948 and 1950 election cycles.

He was not a policy wonk. John Kennedy used his money and status to enhance his sybaritic impulses.

He spent as much time sailing and courting females as he did in the marble halls of Congress.

He was gregarious and charismatic. But the high lord of the House, Speaker Sam Rayburn of Texas, regarded him as a dilettante.

Rayburn assumed Kennedy would spend ten years in the House and then join his daddy in some business enterprise where he could pretend to be calling the shots.

When Rayburn heard that John Kennedy was going to challenge incumbent Republican Henry Cabot Lodge for a United States Senate seat in Massachusetts, he laughed.

"That little punk is going to get his ass kicked," Rayburn told Senator Lyndon Johnson of Texas.

Johnson heartily concurred. "The boy is a lightweight, Sam. He'll never amount to anything."

Rayburn regarded Lyndon Johnson as the son he never had. The all-powerful Speaker nurtured Johnson through his years in the House.

When Johnson announced he was running for the Senate, Rayburn promised him his unqualified support. The year was 1948.

Johnson was going up against popular former Governor Coke Stevenson. Stevenson was a beloved figure in Texas, and beating him would necessitate some creative voting.

Johnson won just enough votes to force Stevenson into a runoff.

When the vote totals in the runoff were counted, Stevenson was ahead. Johnson's men went to work.

They knew the number they had to beat. And they knew the man they had to recruit to pull it off—Democrat power broker George Parr.

Parr was the law in several counties in Texas. One of them was Jim Wells County.

In tiny little Alice, Texas, 202 previously unknown ballots were found. When the counting was over, Johnson was ahead of Stevenson by eighty-seven votes.

Johnson would forever be tagged with the appellation Landslide Lyndon.

The election was as crooked as a dog's left leg. Stevenson fought the issue in the courts, but when the US Supreme Court refused to intervene, Johnson was certified as the winner.

After only one year in the Senate, Johnson was given an astounding promotion.

The all-mighty Senator Richard B. Russell of Georgia maneuvered to have Johnson declared the leader of all Democrats in the Senate.

Russell wanted his own man in that position to make certain that no civil rights legislation ever saw the light of day.

In 1951, Lyndon Johnson was ascendant. He assumed the skinny kid from Massachusetts was on his way out.

Johnson rated Kennedy's chances of beating Henry Cabot Lodge in 1952 as less than zero.

The Lodge family was royalty in Massachusetts.

They were the bluest of the blue bloods. A Protestant dynasty.

The Kennedys were Roman Catholic. And the patriarch may or may not have been a rumrunner.

Then there was Joe Kennedy's lamentable tenure as US ambassador to England. This was only twelve years ago. People had not forgotten.

John Kennedy also rated his chances of winning as slim.

He argued with his father about the wisdom of going up against the Lodge family.

Joe Kennedy could not be swayed from his mission.

In order to take the White House someday, young John Kennedy would have to obtain gravitas, something he could not do in the House of Representatives.

He needed to be part of that one-hundred-member fraternity known as the Greatest Deliberative Body on the planet.

Joe Kennedy knew that this race would cost a fortune. He did not care.

He had a dream.

His son one day would be addressed as Mr. President.

But the man behind the curtain, the real wizard, would be Joseph Patrick Kennedy Sr.

Everything his son did would have to go through the clearinghouse that was Joe Kennedy's brain.

His son could host the state dinners, make speeches, and enjoy all the pomp and circumstance of the presidency.

But the important part of the job involved policy. It would remain firmly in the hands of the patriarch.

Taxes, spending, troop deployments. All that had to remain under his purview.

It was not a perfect solution. Joe Kennedy would have preferred to be the actual president.

But he could live with being the power behind the throne.

Now Joe Kennedy faced a Mount Everest of politics—the Lodge family.

Lodge's grandfather, Henry Cabot Lodge Sr., had been a United States senator. He was a close friend and confidant of President Theodore Roosevelt. To make things even more personal, the man Henry Cabot Lodge Sr. beat in 1916 was Rose Kennedy's father, John F. Fitzgerald.

This was intolerable.

Henry Cabot Lodge Jr. ran for the Senate for the first time in 1936.

This was the year that Franklin Delano Roosevelt and the entire Democratic Party absolutely crushed Republicans nationwide.

Lodge was the only Republican to beat a Democrat for the US Senate in that pivotal year.

Lodge was reelected in 1942. Then he took three years off to serve his country in the military.

He reclaimed his Senate seat in 1946.

All the political wise men of that era believed Lodge could hold on to power in Massachusetts for decades.

Joe Kennedy knew the task was Herculean. But it had to be done.

The elder Kennedy marshaled his entire clan into the effort.

The ever-photogenic Kennedy women held tea parties, where they charmed the common people with unusual intimacy.

Joe Kennedy had a perfectly legal liquor monopoly that fed waterfalls of money into his coffers.

He spent money like no man in America had ever done before.

When the *Boston Post* newspaper announced it would endorse Lodge, John Kennedy believed his cause was sunk. These were the days when a newspaper endorsement had actual political weight.

Joe Kennedy knew what had to be done. He purchased the paper for five hundred thousand dollars. In today's dollars, that was twenty million.

Joe Kennedy did not bat an eye.

Not surprisingly the *Boston Post* rethought its position and endorsed war hero John F. Kennedy.

The turning point of the race occurred when Henry Cabot Lodge made a decision powerful men often make when they believe their political sinecures are impregnable—he took his victory for granted.

Lodge took time off from campaigning to help Dwight David Eisenhower win the Republican nomination for president.

Lodge wanted Eisenhower to defeat Ohio Republican Robert A. Taft, the popular Senator and leader of the conservative movement in the party.

Taft was a strong ally of Wisconsin Republican Senator Joseph McCarthy, a man who believed communists were infesting the US government. McCarthy was a wrecking machine, attacking people without solid evidence of communist sympathies. This does not mean McCarthy was completely off base. There were communists in the government. But McCarthy used a shotgun when he should have used a revolver. He tarnished too many innocent people.

Eventually, the US Senate would censure McCarthy. A few years later he died of alcoholism.

While Lodge was off helping Eisenhower, John Kennedy was blanketing the state.

Billboards supporting Kennedy were ubiquitous. Kennedy never slighted a newspaperman looking for an interview. Nor did he say no to a radio broadcaster looking to fill in some time.

Kennedy's innate ability to massage the press would pay huge dividends over the next ten years. But it was Joe Kennedy's ability to provide low-level pols with "walking around money" that provided the fuel for the election effort.

There was no inch of Massachusetts land that Joe Kennedy could not seed with campaign money.

No village was too small. No town too insignificant.

Lodge's wall of Jericho began to crack.

On November 4, 1952, the people of Massachusetts made the final call. The election was brutally close.

Kennedy received 1,211,984 votes. Lodge garnered 1,141,247 votes.

John F. Kennedy was now the senator-elect from the great State of Massachusetts.

In exactly eight years, Kennedy would face Lodge for a second time.

Richard Nixon chose Lodge to be his running mate in the 1960 election.

For the second time in a decade, Lodge would feel the sting of defeat at the hands of America's newest dynasty.

Among those celebrating on November 4, 1952, was campaign aide Stuart Dunleavy. He had just turned thirty. He telephoned his parents in West Palm Beach on election night.

Mike and Patricia Dunleavy wanted their son to be with them on his thirtieth birthday, but that was impossible.

He told his parents that the man he was working for had a future. "Don't be surprised if John Kennedy runs for president," Stuart said.

His folks chuckled.

Chapter 14

Now that his son was ensconced in the majestic halls of the US Senate, the ever-calculating Joe Kennedy made his next move.

Young John Kennedy's days as a roaming playboy were about to come to an end. At least in public.

Joe Kennedy knew that a bachelor with a reputation for partying would never be elected president of the United States.

The public demanded a man who had stability. He had to be a family man. He had to be a man who at least pretended to adhere to the strictures of whatever religion he espoused.

The voters wanted a man who had a wife, children, and a dog. It had to be a dog. A cat simply did not have enough warmth to be known as the White House pet.

Joe Kennedy asked his son to join him one afternoon in the library of his family's spacious home. It was the day after his son beat Lodge.

Joe Kennedy did not suggest his son start looking for a wife. He ordered it.

John Kennedy, of course, knew he would one day have to look for a wife. He just did not want to do it right now. He was thirty-five. He still enjoyed the chase. He wanted variety. The cortisone treatments he started receiving in 1947 had stabilized his Addison's disease. For the past six years, his energy level had increased substantially.

Energy meant sex. And how those Kennedy men loved sex.

Just not monogamous sex.

Kennedy men were notorious for fooling around. All of them.

Joe Kennedy's four sons had seen their father flaunt social convention a hundred times. Joe Kennedy told his sons that all powerful and successful men chased women. And there were damn few exceptions.

Maybe George Washington was faithful. Maybe Abe Lincoln.

But they were the outliers. Their contemporaries in business and politics were not about to go through life having sex with just one woman.

John Kennedy knew without being told that he would have to be faithful, at least until the honeymoon was completed.

After that, as long as he was discreet, he was free to enjoy the charms of the countless beautiful women who populated his universe.

Now the actual selection of a wife was a tricky issue.

It was okay to chase waitresses and secretaries, but under no circumstances could a Kennedy man entertain marrying one.

Any female under consideration had to have an aristocratic pedigree. And the target had to be beautiful.

That narrowed the search considerably.

Joe Kennedy believed he had found a perfect solution.

Her name was Jacqueline Bouvier. She was the daughter of John Vernon and Janet Lee Bouvier.

She was twelve years younger than John Kennedy. Joe Kennedy knew his son would like possessing a much younger wife.

Joe Kennedy knew her father. He was known as John "Black Jack" Bouvier.

Both men had been stockbrokers on Wall Street. Both had been successful. And each man enjoyed all the pleasures of life. Especially pleasures of the flesh.

But only one of them, Joe Kennedy, had seen the coming storm.

In 1929, the year Jacqueline Bouvier was born, Joe Kennedy had taken his money out of the market.

Bouvier had not seen the danger. He stayed in.

He was cleaned out. And he did not handle it well.

To dull the pain of poverty, Black Jack began drinking heavily. And he became more arrogant in his pursuit of women other than his wife.

His one saving grace was his love for Jacqueline. And she reciprocated.

When Jacqueline was seven, her parents separated. They divorced four years later.

Salvation came when Janet met and then married Hugh Dudley Auchincloss. He was an heir to the Standard Oil company.

The Auchincloss family was rich and connected to the best Protestant families on the East Coast.

Hugh Auchincloss did not ask Janet or Jacqueline to switch their religion.

This was Auchincloss's third marriage. He wasn't about to cause problems by insisting his wife and stepdaughter submit to a forced conversion.

He told his sniggering friends to just deal with it.

The Auchincloss family had two palatial homes. One was Merrywood Estate in McLean, Virginia. The other was Hammersmith Farm in Newport, Rhode Island.

Jacqueline and her younger sister, Caroline Lee Bouvier (b. 1933), did not want for anything material.

They also got along with their stepfather, a development that was not the norm in such a high-profile family blending.

Jacqueline was a very intelligent child. She eventually mastered four languages. She spoke English, Spanish, and Italian, but her favorite was French.

Auchincloss money got Jacqueline admitted to Vassar.

A *Hearst* newspaper columnist labeled her Debutante of the Year.

She spent her junior year (1949–1950) at the Sorbonne in France.

Returning home, she told her parents she did not like Poughkeepsie, New York, the city that housed Vassar. She said the city was too boring.

She transferred to George Washington University and graduated with a degree in French literature.

Jacqueline went to work at *Vogue* magazine, but she quit after only one day. One of the editors told her she was now twenty-two, and it was time she got out of the writing business and find a husband.

There was no way Jacqueline Bouvier was going to work for such a troglodyte.

She found a job as a photographer at the *Washington Times Herald*.

In 1952, she got engaged to stockbroker John Husted. She broke it off after three months. She found him "too boring and immature."

Then in May of 1952, she met John Fitzgerald Kennedy at a dinner party. She found him extremely handsome. And he liked her immediately.

But John Kennedy at that time was in a life-and-death struggle for the United States Senate seat held by Henry Cabot Lodge.

He did not have time to court Jacqueline Bouvier. But he did not forget her.

In early November, the people of Massachusetts put Kennedy in the United States Senate.

And Joe Kennedy told his son that the institution of marriage could no longer be put on hold.

With plenty of time on his hands, Kennedy pursued the pretty brunette.

She fell in love quickly. And he proposed.

Several of Jacqueline's closest friends told her not to do it. "Those Kennedy men are all philanderers," they intoned.

Jacqueline Bouvier was not a woman who stuck her head in the sand.

She well remembered the pain her father had caused her mother. He, too, thought the world was his oyster and damn the consequences.

But maybe, just maybe, she could convince John Kennedy to behave, and if he did, she would make his life a heaven on earth.

The couple got married on September 13, 1953, at St. Mary's Church in Newport, Rhode Island. There were seven hundred guests. There were twelve hundred at the reception.

Stuart Dunleavy was at both events. He felt honored.

He liked Jacqueline Kennedy. He felt she was a classy woman and a real asset to his friend.

The couple honeymooned in Acapulco, Mexico. When they returned, Jack Kennedy was back at work with a suntan and smiling good humor.

Stuart Dunleavy brought Jack Kennedy a cup of coffee. "Well, Jack, how does it feel to be handcuffed and hog-tied?"

Jack Kennedy took a small sip and then slowly placed the cup on his desk. With a small but wry smile, Kennedy responded, "You're kidding me, right, Stuart?"

Chapter 15

Joe Kennedy admired Lyndon Baines Johnson.

In 1954, Johnson became Senate majority leader. Prior to Johnson, the title of Senate majority leader had status but no power.

Each senator regarded all other senators as absolute equals. Individual senators jealously guarded their power and sovereignty.

A senator could ask for a favor. But a senator could not demand a favor. Such a demand would elicit umbrage in an extreme form.

It is one reason why senators did not seek out the title majority leader of the US Senate. The hassles were pronounced, and the rewards were little.

This formulation held true until Landslide Lyndon entered the US Senate in January of 1949.

The Senate's most respected member was Richard Russell of Georgia. He asked Johnson if he would consider taking the job.

The freshman senator did not hesitate for even a second.

Lyndon Johnson had a knack. Even going back to high school, Johnson could take a ceremonial assignment and turn it into a source of power.

This attribute appeared when Johnson was a mere legislative aide in the 1930s. He became the most powerful legislative aide in Washington. He maneuvered into positions of power when he became a member of the US House of Representatives in that same decade. He did it by groveling at the feet of House Speaker Sam Rayburn.

The life-long bachelor eventually regarded Johnson as the son he never had. Johnson milked this sentiment into real power.

Upon entering the US Senate, Johnson became a fawning protégé of Richard Russell. Russell's motives were always the same.

He wanted Southerners in positions of power so that no liberal civil rights bills would see the light of day.

Voters who lived in the Old South had a foolproof method of obtaining and maintaining power.

They elected white men who were in their twenties or early thirties. And they kept reelecting them every two and six years.

The seniority system in both houses of Congress meant that the longest-serving members got the important committee chairmanships. And whoever held the title Mr. Chairman had God-like authority over legislation.

Lyndon Johnson had no intentions of being a ceremonial leader. By sheer force of personality, and the secret backing of Russell, he transformed the title into power.

It only took twelve months. Powerful senators started referring to Johnson as Leader. Johnson simply took control of the levers of power in the Senate and dared anyone to object.

None did.

By 1955, newspapermen were writing stories about the transformation of the Senate under Lyndon Johnson's guidance.

The lazy and sedate institution had become a railroad yard of efficiency and movement.

Johnson's passion for work came with a price. In 1955, he suffered a serious heart attack.

Lyndon Johnson always feared his time on earth would be truncated. Johnson men were known for their weak constitutions. And early deaths.

But modern medicine kept Johnson alive, and after several months he was back in action.

And he did not slow up. He was on a mission. It was a trek he began while still in his early twenties.

Johnson wanted to become president of the United States. It was all he ever thought about. Every action he took in life was designed to reach that summit.

But now Johnson could hear the tick-tock, tick-tock of his biological clock.

The presidential year of 1956 was not going to be his moment. Johnson was savvy enough to know that Dwight David Eisenhower was a shoo-in for reelection.

No, Johnson's target was 1960, when Eisenhower, by law, would have to step down.

Johnson would be fifty-two years old in 1960. And Johnson men had a habit of dying in their sixties.

He knew that by 1960, he would have a strong record of Senate leadership in his resume. Johnson believed he could channel his personal relationships into political power by relying on smoke-filled rooms occupied by Brahmins and old Senate bulls.

In short, Johnson believed he could win the Democratic nomination by bypassing the primary process.

It was one of the few miscalculations Johnson would ever make concerning political strategy.

Johnson did not see that the sands of time had passed him by. The actual phrase "smoke-filled room" had become a pejorative.

Joe Kennedy was not that blind. He knew that the art of public speaking and one's attractiveness on television would prove to be a game changer.

Joe Kennedy would not ask the old bulls to hand over the levers of power. He and his son would instead hand them a fait accompli.

Joe Kennedy decided to use Lyndon Johnson as a conduit to power.

In 1955 and 1956, no one was seriously talking about John Fitzgerald Kennedy running for president in 1960.

There were rumors and mutterings. But then again there always are.

Lyndon Johnson did not regard John Kennedy as serious competition. He called him "the boy" or "that kid."

Johnson assumed that Kennedy would have to marinate in the Senate for at least twelve years to acquire the experience necessary to run for president.

Johnson believed Kennedy would be ripe for a run in 1968. That would be the moment Lyndon Johnson would be leaving the White House after eight successful years.

Johnson did not see the trap that Joe Kennedy was setting.

In 1956, Joe Kennedy picked up the phone and called Lyndon Johnson. "Would it be possible, Senator, if my son could have a seat on the Senate Foreign Relations Committee?"

This was a coveted assignment. Any politician with presidential aspirations would kill to get on this committee.

Johnson knew what Joe Kennedy was doing. But Johnson assumed he was grooming his son for 1968.

Johnson also wanted to have access to Joe Kennedy's wallet. Joe Kennedy was the fifth or maybe the fourth richest man in America. By putting John Kennedy on the Senate Foreign Relations Committee, Johnson would be in a position to ask for a boatload of money to run against the 1960 Republican nominee.

"Why, yes, Mr. Ambassador. I believe I can find a spot for the senator from the great state of Massachusetts."

And that is how John Kennedy jumped over the heads of senators with much more time in office.

But Joe Kennedy was not done. He had another favor to ask of Lyndon Johnson.

"Would the Senate majority leader also consider putting John Kennedy on the newly formed Senate Rackets Committee?"

Lyndon Johnson, again failing to see the danger, agreed.

John Kennedy was now positioned to buttress his foreign policy record, and he was also in a position to appear to be tough on organized crime.

A one-two punch.

Still, Joe Kennedy was not done playing Johnson like a violin. He got Johnson to agree to put his third son, Robert, on the rackets committee as its chief counsel.

Joe Kennedy had thrown a right hand to Johnson's temple, a left to his jaw, and another right to his solar plexus.

Johnson was on the mat. And he did not even know it. Johnson's desire to get his hands on Joe Kennedy's money blinded him to the ambassador's machinations.

Sun Tzu, the man who wrote *The Art of War* in fifth century BC China, would have seen the trap immediately.

Unfortunately, for Lyndon Johnson, he never read *The Art of War*.

Chapter 16

In the late 1950s, organized crime was a huge cancerous tumor on America's soul. Prohibition had caused the cancer to grow exponentially.

When the fuel that fired the growth of the Mafia, the Volstead Act, was rescinded in 1933, organized crime had the financial heft to move onto other areas, mainly drugs.

But organized labor was another source of profit.

Unions had grown mightily under the New Deal. Millions of men and women held union cards in their wallets and purses.

Union membership meant union dues. Someone had to manage all that money.

The men (they were almost always men) who were entrusted with union dues were not always paragons of virtue. Quite the opposite.

The temptation to dip into union bank accounts proved irresistible. Why not? The federal government was not watching them. And the membership did not have access to the records.

The leadership of many AFL-CIO-related unions regarded pension funds as their personal piggy bank.

Organized crime figures quickly ascertained they could bully, threaten, and even kill union leaders who refused to lend them money.

No union was richer, or more corrupt, than the mighty Teamsters.

America was a nation on wheels. Trucks were the nation's lifeblood.

The Teamster pension fund housed millions and millions of dollars. The leader, Dave Beck, became Teamster president in 1952.

Beck had helped to create the Teamsters in 1917. He battled his way through the snake pit of union politics to become its leader thirty-five years later.

By the 1950s, the federal government became concerned about graft and corruption in the union movement.

In 1957, Congress established the United States Senate Select Committee on Improper Activities in Labor and Management.

This ponderous title was a nightmare for newspapers, so it was universally referred to as the McClellan Committee. It was named after its chairman, Senator John McClellan of Arkansas.

The committee had four Republicans and four Democrats. One of those four Democrats was thirty-nine-year-old John Kennedy. And the committee's chief counsel was thirty-two-year-old Robert Kennedy.

Joe Kennedy had instructed both of his sons not to be wallflowers when the committee was in session. The ambassador wanted headlines featuring his sons. He did not care about the other members.

John Kennedy managed to maintain decorum. But his little brother was a different story.

Robert Kennedy went after Dave Beck like a wolverine on the hunt. He insulted Beck. He demeaned him. He badgered him until Beck decided to exercise his constitutional rights.

Beck invoked his Fifth Amendment rights 117 times. Only then did Robert Kennedy let him go. But not before he got his scalp.

Beck resigned as Teamster president when he refused to explain what happened to three hundred and twenty-two thousand dollars in union money.

In 1959, Beck was indicted for racketeering, embezzlement, and income tax evasion. He went to prison in 1962. He got out in 1965. He was pardoned by Gerald Ford in 1975.

Beck lived to be ninety-nine years old. He died a multimillionaire, having invested in parking lots. He also died earning fifty thousand dollars a year in Teamster pension money.

The man who succeeded Beck was the Teamsters second-in-command, James Riddle Hoffa.

Robert Kennedy was even more vicious toward Hoffa than he was toward Beck. The conflict between Hoffa and Robert Kennedy would become legend.

Robert Kennedy was not above using skullduggery against his enemies. He decided to get Hoffa by using a sting operation.

Kennedy knew Hoffa was corrupt. He was certain Hoffa would fall into his trap.

Hoffa wanted a spy in his employ on the committee staff. He believed he found such a man. It was a New York lawyer named John Cye Cheasty.

But Cheasty was a Kennedy man. He agreed to bait Hoffa with the promise of staff documents.

On March 11, 1957, Hoffa and Cheasty met face-to-face. Hoffa gave Cheasty two thousand dollars for a bundle of records that purportedly belonged to the McClellan Committee.

Hoffa was immediately arrested. The new Teamster boss was enraged by the trap and was furious at the man who orchestrated it.

Robert Kennedy gloated over the arrest. He boasted he would "jump off a building" if Hoffa beat the case in court.

Hoffa did beat the case. A jury decided Hoffa was entrapped by an overzealous young man named Robert Kennedy.

Robert Kennedy did not jump off any structures. But after that stinging defeat in court, Robert Kennedy made it his life's mission to "get Hoffa."

Hoffa made it his life's mission to destroy the Kennedy family.

Robert Kennedy's acerbic personality would over the next eight years create two mortal enemies, both of whom vowed to get revenge.

One was James Riddle Hoffa. The other was Lyndon Baines Johnson.

Chapter 17

Poor Vincent J. Celeste.

This was the sacrificial lamb the Republican Party put up to try and unhorse John F. Kennedy from the US Senate seat from Massachusetts in the year 1958.

Celeste had hardly any money to combat the millions Joe Kennedy was prepared to spend.

But even if Celeste had a billion dollars, it would not have mattered.

John Kennedy had six years to work his charm on the people of Massachusetts.

And work it he did.

It began with his spectacular wedding in 1953 to the unbelievably beautiful Jacqueline Bouvier. Mrs. Kennedy proved more valuable to her husband than all the wealth King Solomon purportedly owned.

Then there was the candidate who, thanks to cortisone and more weight on his skinny frame, presented himself to the world as a handsome prince. The kind of man little girls dream about.

And not just little girls—John Kennedy owned the women of Massachusetts.

Not only was John Kennedy a politician, he was an author.

His 1956 book *Profiles in Courage* garnered praise from critics, most of whom wanted to be his friend and receive invitations to Hickory Hill.

The book was researched and written by his top speechwriter, Ted Sorenson. But this embarrassing fact was kept away from the public for decades.

Kennedy slapped his name on the cover. And he won a Pulitzer.

That should have been enough literary praise for most people, but his father, Joe Kennedy, wanted more.

The patriarch reached all the way back to his son's senior year at Harvard.

John Kennedy's thesis *While England Slept* was turned into another book. It was released to the public as proof of his sagacity involving world events.

While England Slept chronicled the mistakes the democracies made in dealing with the rise of fascism in Europe.

It is not known if this work was ghostwritten. But it would not have been out of character.

Joe Kennedy wanted his own mistakes about fascism smothered and doctored. He used his son as a conduit for redemption.

John Kennedy graduated cum laude with a BA in government. A more prestigious matriculation could not be imagined.

This is what Vincent J. Celeste was up against in 1958.

John F. Kennedy was young. Handsome. Educated. Athletic. Rich. Articulate. Suave. And he was a war hero.

All his life John Kennedy was part of the in crowd. In fact, he was the leader of the in crowd.

The bitter sting of social rejection never visited this anointed young man.

Vincent J. Celeste lost to John Kennedy by 874,680 votes.

It was the largest senatorial election massacre in Massachusetts history. In Washington, there was one man who took note of events in Massachusetts and knew what was coming next.

Lyndon Baines Johnson realized he had made a huge mistake.

John Kennedy was not grooming for a presidential run in 1968. Or in 1964. He was going to make a move in 1960.

And guess who had helped propel this young dynamo into prominence? None other than Lyndon Johnson.

Kennedy's position on the Senate Foreign Relations Committee and his position on the McClellan Committee were all the result of an intervention by the Senate majority leader.

Johnson realized he had been blinded by his lust for Joe Kennedy's unlimited bank account. That possibility was now gone forever. Every penny Joe Kennedy had was now going to be used for his own blood.

Johnson poured himself a stiff drink and contemplated his options.

On the plus side was Johnson's reputation as the master of the Senate, the man who had transformed the institution.

Johnson was a decade older than Kennedy. The public would view him as more seasoned.

Johnson could count on the backing of Congressional heavyweights in both houses of Congress. More importantly, Johnson had the support of Sam Rayburn.

And Johnson knew there were other northern liberals who wanted the top job. Men who had been in power longer than John Kennedy. Men who believed they, not he, were the best choice to run the country.

Adlai Stevenson, who had twice run against Dwight Eisenhower, was the sentimental favorite of Democrats. But he was a two-time loser.

Minnesota Senator Hubert Humphrey had a huge following among liberals. It was certain he would run.

Governor Pat Brown of California was making presidential noises. And so was Oregon Senator Wayne Morse.

Stuart Symington, the senator from the Show Me State of Missouri, was interested and he was expected to run.

Johnson was confident these men would all enter the same primaries. And each man would cancel out the next. No one would run the table.

It would all come down to a simple number. If no man had a grip on the delegate count on the first ballot, the Democratic Convention would be deadlocked.

To win the nomination, a candidate must have 761 votes.

Johnson was positive that if all these men made a run for it, no one could reach this number.

The convention was scheduled to be held in Los Angeles in July of 1960. There was plenty of time for Johnson to get his ducks in order.

The year 1959 arrived, and Johnson formally mapped out his strategy to his allies. He would run for president—by not running for president.

Johnson was positive his friends in the House and the Senate, if faced with a deadlocked convention, would simply hand him the nomination.

He would not enter a single primary. He would not even allow a nationwide "Johnson for President" campaign to get off the ground.

His long-time aide, Horace Busby, thought this strategy was insane. But Johnson could not be moved.

His excuse for not running would be that his duties as Senate majority leader could not be subsumed by any outside interests. The job was too important. The work of the American people must come first.

And the American people, he believed, would be appreciative of his selfless behavior.

Johnson was blind to the forces of modernity. He was a nineteenth-century politician running in the twentieth century.

Johnson's greatest mistake was underestimating the importance of television.

Television had certain requirements.

One must be articulate. Johnson was not.

One must be attractive. Johnson most certainly was not.

John Kennedy was perfectly crafted for the age of television.

Lyndon Johnson was built by God to exist in dark rooms, where a small group of powerful men decided the fate of millions.

By 1960, this type of governance was destined for the dustbin of history.

Johnson was confident he could massage the old ways of doing business into a successful foray. He believed Kennedy's Roman Catholic background would slay his ambitions.

America was a Protestant country. America had rejected Al Smith in 1928 primarily because the electorate believed he would be beholden to the Pope in Rome.

Johnson did not believe that thirty years later the country had changed.

John Kennedy's quest would die in the state of West Virginia. It was the most Protestant of any state in the Union.

Kennedy could not bypass the West Virginia primary. He had to prove to the party that he could win over Protestant voters.

The linchpin of Johnson's strategy was that Kennedy could not bridge this river. Lyndon Johnson sent out orders nationwide that all "Johnson for President" movements must be quelled. He would wait for the prize to fall into his lap.

Chapter 18

Stuart Dunleavy was summoned into Joseph Kennedy's office on a cold January day in 1960.

Present were Kennedy Sr., John Kennedy, Robert Kennedy, Ted Sorenson, and Kenny O'Donnell.

Joe Kennedy asked Dunleavy if he would like to participate in an adventure.

The end goal of this adventure, he was told, would be acquisition of the presidency of the United States.

Dunleavy said he would be honored to participate in any capacity. In the seventeen years he and John Kennedy had been friends, Dunleavy had developed a man crush on the young senator.

Dunleavy told Joe Kennedy that he was planning on getting married the first week in February.

"Do you plan on a honeymoon?" Joe Kennedy asked.

"Yes, sir."

"Can you postpone the honeymoon? If you do, I will pick up all your expenses."

Dunleavy tossed the idea around in his head.

He met his fiancée at a 1958 tea party hosted by John Kennedy's sisters. It was one of those innumerable social gatherings designed to help the senator get reelected.

Arlene Montgomery worked at a Boston bank. She was an avid Kennedy fan.

She was twenty-five. She was smashingly good-looking. She had suitors chasing her from one end of the state to the other.

John Kennedy saw how Stuart was looking at Arlene. Kennedy deduced his friend might be intimidated by such a creature.

Kennedy had considered making a play for this Massachusetts Aphrodite. He knew it would be successful. Maybe 1 percent of all the women Kennedy met ever said no to his advances.

Kennedy was so fond of Stuart Dunleavy that he decided to stand down and help his friend.

"Hey, Stu, would you like to meet her?"

"You are damn right I would."

With studied nonchalance, Kennedy walked over to the brunette bombshell.

She, of course, was over the moon at the attention she was getting from the senator.

But Kennedy introduced his friend to Ms. Montgomery, and he extolled the virtues the former sailor possessed.

When Kennedy made his apologies and left, Arlene gave him a long look goodbye. Then she looked Stuart over from head to foot. She liked what she saw.

He was not John Fitzgerald Kennedy. But he was lean, handsome, mature, and he did not have a ring on his finger.

They talked for half an hour. Her body language was favorable, so he worked up the courage to ask her out.

She said yes.

Stuart Dunleavy was thirty-six years old in 1958. He had never been married. His association with John Kennedy meant he had access to the most beautiful women in America.

Stuart Dunleavy did not let any grass grow.

But maybe it was time to find the one.

He proposed Christmas Eve 1959. The answer was an immediate yes.

His parents in Florida were ecstatic. Having a thirty-six-year-old unmarried son was causing talk.

Their other two sons and their daughter had been married for years.

Dunleavy did not like the idea of having a woman as attractive as his soon-to-be wife left alone for weeks, maybe months.

Human beings are, well, human.

"Mr. Ambassador, in lieu of a honeymoon, would it be all right if my wife accompanied me on this adventure?"

Joe Kennedy laughed. "Man does not live by bread alone, Stuart. Sure, she can accompany you. Do you think she would like to be part of the campaign?"

"She would like that more than anything else on this earth, Mr. Ambassador."

"Consider it done."

Joe Kennedy rose from his chair and walked over to where his second son was sitting. John Kennedy had not said a word. He knew better than to interrupt his father.

The elder man put his hand on John Kennedy's left shoulder.

"This young man is going to be the next president of the United States. I will not rest until it happens. I will spare no expense, nor will I tolerate any summertime soldiers. Do you get my message?"

"Mr. Ambassador, you have my unqualified support."

"Good. Good." Joe Kennedy took his hand off his son's shoulder. He folded both hands over his chest and addressed Dunleavy as if he were Zeus and the younger man was a mere mortal.

"Stuart, you have been with us for fourteen years. You have been there for every election in the House and again in the Senate. I know you are a capable man. And you know I don't suffer fools."

Dunleavy knew that fact very well indeed. Joe Kennedy fired aides with lightning speed if they did not measure up. And he did not let people go in a soothing, compassionate manner. Some men ran out the door in absolute terror.

"Stuart, we Kennedys are Roman Catholics. Do you know what that means?"

"It means we have a problem," Dunleavy said. "It means millions of Americans are going to be worried that the Pope is going to tell your son what he can and cannot do as president."

"Precisely. We are going to change that narrative. I understand you are a Methodist."

"Technically, yes, but I am not a practicing one. I spend my Sundays watching sports."

The men in the room chuckled. None of them was what you would call a religionist.

"I want you to use your Protestant credentials, slim though they may be, to help convince other Protestants they have nothing to fear. My son does not answer to the Pope!"

"Whatever limited value I have in that endeavor, consider it done."

"Good. Now, my son tells me you are a whiz in mathematics. He also tells me you have become enamored with a new invention, something called, ah, ah, what is it, John?"

"A computer, Dad."

"Yes, a computer. Is this something we can utilize in our campaign?"

Dunleavy was impressed. He could see that Joe Kennedy was leaving no stone unturned in his quest.

"Mr. Ambassador, in 1943, an English mathematician named Alan Turing invented a computation machine that cracked the German naval code. His invention probably shortened the war by twelve months."

Dunleavy shifted in his chair as he continued. "Now, in twenty years, every facet of your life will be controlled or influenced by computers. But has the science progressed to the point where a computer is necessary to win a political campaign today? I don't think so, but in 1964 when your son seeks reelection…"

"I like the way you think, Stuart," the ambassador said.

Dunleavy pushed forward. "When your son seeks reelection in four years, we will need a battery of computers."

Joe Kennedy marched forward, put his hands on both knees, and leaned into Dunleavy's face.

"If you change your mind, if you feel we need one, then buy a damn computer! I do not care what it costs. Is that clear?"

"Yes, sir, Mr. Ambassador."

Joe Kennedy again found his favorite chair and sat down.

"Now, as for your assignment, you will be working with Kenny O'Donnell. We are going to be entering ten primaries. Ted, give him the itinerary."

Sorenson stood up. "You might want to write this down, Stuart."

In an instant, Dunleavy had a yellow legal pad and a pen in his possession.

"The New Hampshire Primary is March 8. The Wisconsin race is April 5. On April 12, we have Illinois. Then it is our home state on April 26. That same day we are on the ballot in Pennsylvania. On May 3 we will be in Indiana. A week later, Nebraska."

"Now, we want you to pay extra attention to what I am about to say. On May 10, we will be competing not only in Nebraska but in West Virginia. This is the big enchilada, Stuart. Do you know why?"

"I am guessing that West Virginia has a dearth of Catholics and a whole bunch of Protestants?"

"Give the man a cigar," Sorenson quipped. "You are exactly right. If we can carry West Virginia, the religion thing goes away."

Sorenson continued. "The last two contests are Maryland on May 17 and Oregon on May 20. From then on, we spend our time rounding up delegates not connected to any primary races. It is going to be a long, tough slog. Are you ready, Stuart?"

"Just tell me where to be and I will be there," Dunleavy said with conviction.

Joe Kennedy got back on his feet.

"Gentlemen, let me be as clear as glass. I—I mean we are going to win every one of those ten primaries. Is that crystal clear?"

The response was universal. "Yes, sir!"

"Gentlemen, thank you for your time."

Joe Kennedy had just issued a dismissal order, and all save his son left the room.

"Well, Dad, I think we have put together one hell of a team."

"Sure, sure, we'll be fine. But I want you to sit back down."

"What's up, Dad?"

Joe Kennedy looked into his son's eyes and spoke very slowly. "We need to discuss this Lyndon Johnson situation."

Chapter 19

Senate Majority Leader Lyndon Baines Johnson cradled a glass of scotch in both hands. He was sitting down on a thick leather chair in his ornate office in the US Senate building. He was staring at the floor.

He had ordered his secretary not to allow anyone in and not to put through any telephone calls. He was miserable.

The date was Wednesday, May 11, 1959.

Twenty-four hours earlier, John Kennedy had prevailed in the West Virginia primary. And it was not even close.

Kennedy had just won his eighth straight primary. There were two contests left. Maryland and Oregon had yet to make their intentions known, but Johnson had no reason to believe these two states would behave differently from the others.

Johnson thought for certain that his old friend Hubert Humphrey would prevail in West Virginia.

The war machine Joe Kennedy had constructed bulldozed the amiable Minnesotan right out of the race.

Kennedy had neutralized the issue of religion.

He had blanketed the state with rallies. He appealed to the innate sense of fairness Democrats had for their fellow countrymen.

"I refuse to believe I was denied the right to be president the day I was baptized," Kennedy intoned repeatedly.

Over and over Kennedy told the coal miners and factory workers of West Virginia that he would not under any circumstances take orders from Rome.

The message resonated. And it did not hurt that Jacqueline Kennedy and all the other women inside the Kennedy clan were hobnobbing with the common people of West Virginia.

Nor was anyone offended by the amount of money Joe Kennedy was spending.

An aristocrat's son he may be, but John Kennedy had easy manner and a self-deprecating sense of humor. And he had one more thing—those medals he received for serving his country in the South Pacific.

West Virginians were enormously patriotic. West Virginia had split from Old Virginia in 1861 when the South went to war with the North.

Hubert Humphrey was well-liked. But he did not have any medals.

Johnson was now forced to admit to himself what he would never admit to anyone else—he had made a mistake.

His decision to run for president by not actually running for president had been a boneheaded strategy.

Six years of running the US Senate in the same manner as Napoleon had run France had convinced Johnson he was respected everywhere.

Everyone in Washington knew who Johnson was, and they all treated him with extreme deference.

But to the rest of the nation, it was "Lyndon who?"

It is an absolute truism that 99 percent of all the people living in America can identify the name of the man holding the title president of the United States.

Go below that office, and name recognition drops off a cliff.

It is the reason why perceptive candidates spend hundreds of hours campaigning in villages, hamlets, and small towns.

Name recognition is everything in politics. But one must work for it.

Lyndon Johnson wanted the highest office in the land. But he did not want to work for it. He wanted Washington elites to hand it to him.

Johnson could hear the clock ticking. In fact, he heard two clocks. The political clock of 1960 was ticking away. And his biological clock was also forging ahead.

He could not wait. In a flash, Johnson made a decision. He bolted out of his chair, spilling scotch on a two-thousand-dollar rug.

"Goddammit, this race is not over yet," he said to an empty room.

In that instant, Johnson decided he was going to fight. There would be no surrender.

Johnson's passivity had allowed John Kennedy to gain a huge amount of momentum. Johnson cursed himself for not listening to his staff and allies about the stupidity of his strategy for achieving the presidency.

Well, that strategy was now dead.

Johnson was no stranger to hard work.

He nearly killed himself in his very first run for the US House of Representatives. He was up at daylight, and he did not fall asleep until every possible small farm had been visited. He was determined to shake hands with each voter in his district.

And it worked. He won a race no one thought he had a chance of taking.

That first race was the springboard to the very pinnacle of power he now held in 1959. For it could be truthfully asserted that Lyndon Johnson was the second most powerful man in America.

He did not want to be the second most powerful man. He wanted Dwight Eisenhower's job.

Johnson flung open the door and shouted at his secretary. "Get me Sam Rayburn! Now!"

Chapter 20

Marine private Lee Harvey Oswald fiddled with his watch as he sat alone in a twenty-by-twenty-two-foot room in a building at Naval Air Facility Atsugi near Tokyo. It was the summer of 1959.

The facility housed Marine Air Control Squadron 1. This was Oswald's second stay at Atsugi. He had been stationed there before being shipped to the Philippines.

In the Philippines, Oswald had screwed up again. While on guard duty, he was sipping vodka. For no reason at all, he decided to fire his rifle into the green morass of jungle surrounding his base.

The unlawful discharge of a firearm is a big deal in the military. This was Oswald's third and probably final offense.

He had been court-martialed and demoted for shooting himself accidentally with a .22 caliber handgun. He was not authorized to have this weapon.

He was court-martialed a second time for striking a sergeant. Oswald believed the man was responsible for turning him in on the weapons violation.

Now this latest event. The Marines were certainly going to have him dishonorably discharged. They had given him two chances. They were not going to give him a third.

Lee Harvey Oswald was born on October 18, 1939, in New Orleans. He never knew his father. Robert Edward Lee Oswald died of a heart attack two months prior to his son's birth.

His mother, Marguerite, was distant and unaffectionate.

At age seven, Oswald was diagnosed as disturbed.

His mother's peripatetic behavior did not help. Oswald lived in twenty-two locations and attended twelve schools by the time he was seventeen.

He did not stick around to get a high school diploma. He joined the Marine Corps before his eighteenth birthday. He told his siblings he just had to get away from his mother.

Oswald was five feet, eight inches tall, and he weighed 135 pounds.

He was a small man in a branch of the military that prized muscularity, height, and physical presence.

Oswald comforted himself in the knowledge that America's most decorated war hero was about the same height and weight as he. That man was Audie Murphy.

Another barrier between Oswald and his compatriots was politics.

At age fifteen, Oswald declared himself a socialist. He had done just enough rudimentary reading to fall for the siren song of Marxism.

His fellow Marines were collectively about 99 percent opposed to leftwing ideology. They gave Oswald two nicknames: Ozzie Rabbit and Oswaldkovich.

Oswald believed his philosophy gave him moral imprimatur and a sense of intellectual superiority.

Marines he shared a barracks with predominantly thought he was a jackass.

Now he was alone in a room waiting for Lt. Col. Jackson Pickering to give him the inevitable news. He was out. And he was disgraced for life.

Suddenly the door flung open. Jackson Pickering, in full Marine regalia, entered without saying a word.

He was not alone. He was with a civilian. Why this man was here Oswald could not fathom.

Oswald shot to his feet and saluted.

"At ease, Private!" Pickering had a deep voice and a commanding demeanor. He took a chair immediately in front of Oswald. Mystery man sat in a chair that had its back against the wall.

"Private, you are in a hell of fix." Pickering did not mince words.

"I know I am, Colonel." Oswald lowered his head and stared at the tabletop.

"You have to have an awfully damn good reason to discharge a rifle while on guard duty, Private."

"I know, sir, I know."

"Three court-martials. I have never heard of such a thing. This time there is about a one hundred percent chance you will be dishonorably discharged."

"I am aware of what I am facing, Colonel."

Pickering broke his gaze away from Oswald and glanced at the civilian. The man said nothing.

Pickering returned his attention to Oswald.

"Private, I am going to break protocol here. We are going to move this interview in a different direction. Do I have your permission to address you as Lee?"

Oswald was stunned. Marine colonels did not address subordinates by their first name as if they were equals.

"I...I...suppose that's okay."

"Lee, do you believe in redemption?"

"Excuse me?"

"Redemption, Lee. A second chance. If you were raised a Christian, you know what I am talking about."

"I know exactly what the word means, Colonel. But how does that apply to me?"

"Lee, if you go through life with a dishonorable discharge on your record, you will be blacklisted. You will be consigned to menial labor jobs from now until eternity. It will be as if you have a bowling ball attached to your leg, and you can never shed the weight."

Oswald looked at the civilian. "Sir, can I ask you who this man is?"

A split second later, mystery man was standing and pulling his chair over to the table. He did not ask permission.

"Lee, this man is a United States intelligence officer. You do not need to know at this juncture either his name or the agency he works for. Is that clear?"

Mystery man folded his hands and leaned into Oswald. "Hello, Lee. Is it okay if I call you Lee?"

More informality. Oswald was beginning to detect that these men wanted something. Something important.

"What do I call you?"

"Well, for right now, just to facilitate matters, you can call me… Bob Jones."

"Like the golfer?"

"Yeah, like the golfer."

"Listen, Bob, I may be a screwup. But if you are here to accuse me of treason—"

Bob grabbed Oswald's forearm. "Oh, no, no, nothing like that. I am not here to accuse you of anything, Lee. I am here to offer you…redemption."

"There's that word again. Colonel, what's this all about?"

Bob answered the question. "Lee, I have been told you taught yourself to speak Russian in just one year."

"Not true. I had help from the Marine Corps."

"Yes, you did, but I spoke with your instructor. He said you picked it up quicker than anyone else in the class."

"I did not find it all that difficult." Oswald was losing all fear and resorting to his normal demeanor—arrogance.

"That's amazing, Lee, because I have been told Russian is one damn hard language to learn."

"Where are we going with this, Bob?"

"We, Colonel Pickering and I, and the entire United States government want to clear your record. Instead of going through life a disgraced Marine, you can travel a completely different path."

Now Oswald knew for certain what card was being played. "Espionage?"

"Yes, Lee, espionage. We want to recruit you as a bona fide American intelligence agent."

"Why me?"

"You are perfect, Lee. We do not even have to manufacture you a false record. Your actual record contains an enthusiasm for Marxism. Your civilian record contains a host of antisocial behavior. And best of all your military record is a wreck."

"You want me to defect?"

"Yes."

"Sounds dangerous."

"Oh, it's very dangerous. If you are caught, you could end up in Lubyanka Prison. Or you could be shot."

Oswald stood up from the table and turned away from his interlocutors. Spying in Russia. In a thousand years, Oswald never would have suspected today's interrogation could move in this direction.

He weighed his options. A no answer would indeed herald a lifetime of mediocrity. He would never amount to anything.

A yes answer would mean danger ending in possible torture.

If he got out of Russia alive, all kinds of doors would open up. He could get rich writing a spy novel. Other men have done it.

Oswald turned back and faced his interrogators. "This is a big decision. When do you have to have an answer?"

Bob stood up. "I'll give you seventy-two hours, Lee. Then I am back on a plane for the States."

Walking back out the door, Bob just could not resist one more inducement. "Lee, you could be the next Nathan Hale."

"They hanged Nathan Hale, Bob."

"True, but at least he is in the history books."

Chapter 21

Lyndon Johnson was working the phones. He was doing it ferociously. Time was not his friend.

Immediately after the West Virginia primary, Johnson's passivity had transformed into a nuclear reactor of energy.

His very first call was to Speaker of the House Sam Rayburn. The speaker could not help but chide his former protégé. "Nothing like waiting until the last minute, Lyndon!"

"I know, Sam, I know. I screwed up. Will you help me?"

"Of course, I will. But you let Kennedy get a big jump on you. It might be too late."

"I can't believe the leaders of our party would put up that boy to challenge a street fighter like Richard Nixon." Johnson never referred to Kennedy as Senator. It was always "the boy" or "the kid."

"That boy just won ten primaries in a row." Rayburn did not have to remind Johnson of this fact, but he did anyway.

"Sam, if you could just talk to people, I know it would make a difference. You are the most respected man in America."

Lyndon Johnson's lifetime modus operandi was to treat powerful men with complete obsequiousness. When dealing with people he considered inferior, he was a rude and raging tyrant.

Johnson used flattery because he found it highly effective. Even a man as towering a personality as Sam Rayburn was not immune.

"I am going to help you, Lyndon. I will use all my influence. But you might want to prepare yourself for the possibility this could end badly."

In the back of Johnson's mind, he knew this was true. He just could not accept it.

Beginning in mid-May, Johnson started telephoning Democratic leaders in the south and west. He had to sit through the same lecture, every time.

Senators, governors, mayors, even sheriffs told him the same thing.

A compilation of their complaints reads as follows: "We were ready to go six months ago. But every time we talked to your man Busby, we were told to shut everything down."

"For God's sake, Lyndon. My people were fired up and ready to go. We received no encouragement whatsoever."

"John Kennedy has been all over my state. He has this thing wrapped up."

"Listen, Lyndon. You said you could not run because the job of Senate majority leader was too important. Well, if it is so damn important, why don't you stay there?"

Lyndon Johnson wanted to say his current job as leader of the Senate was just an excuse to keep reporters off his back.

But he could not say that. He could not tell his supporters the real reason he did not throw his hat in the ring.

He did not run because he was afraid.

He was afraid he might run and then lose.

Lyndon Johnson was the emperor of the Senate. He was used to having powerful men simply surrender their pride and agree to do his bidding.

But a voter cannot be ordered around. A voter must be approached with humility.

Lyndon Johnson was a Southerner. He was terrified of entering a primary in a northern state and then getting slaughtered in the vote count.

He was right to be concerned. Northern newspapers knew why Richard Russell tapped him to be Senate majority leader. It was to keep liberals at bay.

Fear was the reason Johnson chose to run for president in the dark.

His entire strategy was the inevitability of attrition. Let all the announced candidates attack each other and divide the primary races between them.

If no man had enough delegates for a first ballot victory, then Johnson would humbly offer his services to save the party from defeat.

Joe Kennedy's money and John Kennedy's charisma had just blown that strategy right out of the water.

It was now the first week of July, 1960. Democrats would be convening in Los Angeles in less than two weeks.

Come hell or high water, on the fifteenth of July, someone was going to be giving a nomination speech.

Johnson was determined to be that man. He would use his Machiavellian talents to steal the prize away from the Kennedy clan.

Tick tock. Tick tock. The sands of time wait for no man.

Johnson had one more card up his sleeve. He was going to hold it until the very last moment.

A week earlier, Joe Kennedy had called him. Kennedy told Johnson he was in the mix for a vice presidential slot.

Johnson thanked the ambassador, but he could not, of course, admit he was throwing in the towel.

Johnson was ever so careful not to be disrespectful in his conversation with Joe Kennedy. One must never blow up a bridge when one is not certain how a battle will progress.

Johnson then gave his staff a research assignment. How many men holding the office of vice president succeeded in winning the top job, beginning with Washington and ending with Eisenhower?

The facts convinced Johnson there were two roads to the presidency. John Adams was elected president upon the retirement of George Washington. Tom Jefferson was John Adams's vice president. He beat Adams in the 1800 election.

Martin Van Buren succeeded Andrew Jackson. Van Buren only served one term. John Tyler became president when William Henry Harrison became ill and died after only thirty-one days in office.

Andrew Johnson became president when John Wilkes Booth shot his boss, the beloved Abraham Lincoln. It was also a bullet that made Chester Arthur president. James A. Garfield was felled by an assassin.

Theodore Roosevelt was also the beneficiary of a killer. William McKinley died in the same manner as Lincoln and Garfield. Calvin Coolidge became president when Warren G. Harding died in office from natural causes.

The same held true for Harry Truman. Franklin Roosevelt died from a stroke one month after his fourth inauguration.

The numbers were encouraging. Nine men out of thirty-four had succeeded from the vice presidency to the presidency.

Three of those nine had become president via criminal actions.

If Johnson accepted the job, there was one chance in four he would become president.

Thanks to the Civil War and its aftermath, no Southerner had held the job since Zachary Taylor.

Johnson knew that John Kennedy had health issues. He knew exactly how many times Kennedy had been given his last rites.

The vice presidency could be a humiliating job.

Franklin Roosevelt's first vice president was former Speaker of the House John Nance Garner. Garner once famously said the position "wasn't worth of pitcher of warm spit."

Garner's mistake was in not sticking it out. Garner was replaced by Henry Wallace in 1940. Harry Truman replaced Wallace in 1944.

Truman suffered the humiliations of the office for just one month.

Roosevelt died on April 12, 1945. Truman, who could never have been president via his own efforts, took the oath of office without so much as a fine how-do-you-do to the voters of America.

That road to power was perfectly acceptable in the eyes of Lyndon Baines Johnson.

Chapter 22

On July 11, 1960, Democrats sojourned to the City of Angeles to pick their nominee for the most important job on the planet.

The Biltmore Hotel was selected as ground zero for the staffs of the many men seeking the office. John Kennedy set up shop two floors above Lyndon Johnson.

There were twelve men seeking the nomination, but only three were considered serious contenders—Kennedy, Johnson, and Stuart Symington.

All the momentum appeared to be with Kennedy. But Lyndon Johnson refused to throw in the towel.

He and Sam Rayburn plotted and schemed, but Johnson's decision to run for president by not running for president proved fatal.

Johnson was relentless. He did not decide to run openly until mid-May. By mid-July, he managed to cobble together four hundred and nine delegates. They all came from states that did not hold primary contests.

Johnson knew he could have swept almost the entirety of the southern and western states had he campaigned in a traditional manner.

But he did not. And now he watched as John Kennedy received the votes of eight hundred and six delegates. "The boy" had beaten the emperor.

The only decision left to be made was the selection of a running mate.

None of the Kennedy supporters ever believed for a second that man would be Lyndon Johnson. John Kennedy's feelings toward Johnson were highly negative.

That was nothing compared to the feelings Robert Kennedy had for the Texas politician.

Robert Kennedy hated Lyndon Johnson. Passionately. Johnson was a Roosevelt man. And Franklin Roosevelt had humiliated Robert Kennedy's beloved father.

Johnson was a great storyteller. In the early 1950s, Johnson enjoyed telling friends and reporters about the day he was in the Oval Office with Franklin Roosevelt.

The telephone rang. It was Joe Kennedy, then US Ambassador to the Court of St. James. Roosevelt purportedly put his hand over the phone and whispered to Johnson, "Watch and learn, Lyndon."

According to Johnson, Roosevelt was playing Joe Kennedy like a fiddle.

"Hello, Joe! Great to hear from you! How are things in London?"

The conversation continued for ten more minutes. Roosevelt could not have been more complimentary about Kennedy's tenure in England. Joe Kennedy naturally offered his unqualified support for Roosevelt in the 1940 presidential race.

The two men engaged in as much bonhomie as any two men had ever done.

The call finally ended. Roosevelt put down the receiver and turned toward Johnson. "I am going to fire that son of a bitch as soon as it is politically expedient."

Fire Kennedy he did. Joe Kennedy came home with his reputation in tatters.

Whenever Lyndon Johnson told this story, he would slap his knee and howl with laughter.

Robert Kennedy was once in the same room with Johnson. The majority leader did not know he was there. He told the story, and Robert Kennedy heard the laughter of sycophants trying to please the emperor of the Senate.

Robert Kennedy was the runt of the family. Born in 1925, he was too young to enlist in 1941. By 1943 he was in the Naval Reserve, but he never saw action.

Both of his brothers had fought. One was dead. He was a celebrated hero. The other brother was alive. And he was a decorated hero.

What Robert Kennedy wanted more than anything in life was the approbation of his father. The only way to achieve that recognition was for Robert Kennedy to become John Kennedy's biggest cheerleader.

Robert Kennedy threw himself into this endeavor. He was John Kennedy's campaign manager in 1952, 1958, and 1960.

The greatest moment of Robert Kennedy's life was when Joe Kennedy put his arms around his third son and congratulated him on a job well done.

Robert Kennedy hated two things. Robert Kennedy hated anyone who opposed his family. And he hated congenital liars.

In the eyes of Robert Kennedy, no one was a more epic liar than Lyndon Baines Johnson.

There was truth in that belief.

Lyndon Johnson grew up poor near Johnson City, Texas. His senior class had six students. They chose him as class president. Johnson early on acquired the appellation "Bull" Johnson.

"Bull" was not an encomium. It was short for "Bullshit."

One classmate reportedly stated: "Lyndon lied all the time. He lied about everything. If he were wearing gray socks, you could see the socks, but he would lie about the color of his socks."

Johnson, of course, lied about the origins of his nickname. He would claim all his life that the name Bull Johnson was a salute to his physical prowess and athletic ability.

In reality, Johnson's reputation was one of a boy who was terrified of getting into a fistfight and who was so uncoordinated he excelled at nothing.

Johnson learned early that if one combined a powerful personality with clever mendacity one could rise above one's station.

It can be argued that Johnson was not proven wrong. He had risen to become the second most powerful man in America. And he had done it by stretching the truth or completely abandoning it all along the way.

This was the man Robert Kennedy had outmaneuvered in the 1960 race for president.

It was John Kennedy who would lead the ticket.

There was certainly no room on that ticket for the likes of "Bull" Johnson.

There was one Kennedy family member who held a different opinion. This was the family's most important member.

Joe Kennedy Sr. summoned his sons into his room at the Biltmore hotel. It was the day after Kennedy won the grand prize, Thursday, July 14.

The elder Kennedy told John to offer the vice presidential nomination to Lyndon Johnson. Robert Kennedy's eyebrows nearly leaped off his head. John was equally as incredulous.

"Dad, you can't be serious!" Robert adopted a pleading tone.

"Pop, I cannot for the life of me understand what you are thinking." John had every intention of fighting his father on this edict.

Normally Joe Kennedy would issue an order, and that would be the end of it. He felt no reason to explain himself to people who prospered under his watchful guidance.

He was going to make an exception in this case only because of the magnitude of the decision and the fact both of his sons had to be fully on board.

"Boys, let me explain. My money got us this far. But I cannot buy off the entire country. We are going to need to think strategically."

Kennedy leaned forward in his chair while both sons stared at him in rapt attention. "In order to win the White House, we have to carry two states above all else, Texas and Illinois."

He pressed on. "If we lose either of these two states, Richard Nixon becomes president. Now, Dick Daley assured me he can handle his state."

Dick Daley was the mayor of Chicago. Elected in 1955, Daley took a job that was designed to be subservient to the city council, and he reversed the polarity of the two competing entities.

Daley became the boss. The city council became his rubber stamp.

Dick Daley knew Joe Kennedy Sr. quite well. Kennedy in 1945 purchased the Chicago Merchandise Mart for thirteen million. This was one of the world's largest commercial buildings.

The rents from this massive enterprise funded the Kennedy family until 1998 when the grandchildren sold it for more than half a billion.

It could be said with great accuracy that two men ran Chicago—Daley and Kennedy.

But Chicago was not held up by a two-legged stool.

There were three legs on this stool. But Joe Kennedy did not want his sons to know the name of the third man.

That man was Sam Mooney Giancana, Mob boss of the Windy City.

Joe Kennedy did not tell his boys that in the near future he would be meeting with Giancana.

Joe Kennedy believed in insurance policies. He knew the Chicago Mob could find votes where none existed.

In a close election, Sam Giancana could make the dead walk and vote. He also had the muscle to get lethargic voters out of their slumber and get to the polls.

Giancana would of course ask, "What's in it for me?"

Joe Kennedy would tell Giancana, "You will have a friend in the White House."

Joe Kennedy knew Giancana from their bootlegging days.

The elder Kennedy in his zeal to get his son elected failed to consider the danger involved in breaking a promise to a Mob boss.

Sam Giancana's nickname was Momo. It was Italian for "crazy."

Joe Kennedy kept the name Giancana out of his conversation with his sons. The less they knew about this connection, the better.

"That brings us to Texas. I know you boys do not care for Lyndon. Truth be told, I don't either. But if Lyndon Johnson can get us over the goal line, then biting this bullet is worth it."

Robert Kennedy was having none of it. "Dad, we can double up our efforts in Texas. I will move there if I have to, but please, not Lyndon Johnson!"

Joe Kennedy knew something his third son did not. Lyndon Johnson owned George Parr. And Parr controlled five counties in southwest Texas.

These five counties had a history of shady elections. If George Parr wanted a politician elected, he found a way.

Assume Richard Nixon was ahead of John Kennedy by ten thousand votes. George Parr would find twelve thousand previously unknown Kennedy ballots. No problem.

Joe Kennedy was not about to allow the concept of fair play keep him from his dream.

Lots of American elections had been fraudulent. The republic still survived.

Lyndon Johnson knew how to play this game. He was first a victim of fraud. Then he became a beneficiary of foul play.

In 1941, a Senate seat opened up in Texas. The two strongest candidates were Johnson and Texas Governor W. Lee "Pass the Biscuits" O'Daniel.

Johnson, who had entered the US House of Representatives in 1937, looked to be the winner late on election night in November 1941.

O'Daniel and his minions were unfazed. They simply waited for the final count to be announced. Then they went to work.

Ballots suddenly started showing up in counting houses all across the state. In short order, O'Daniel took the lead. As a sitting governor, O'Daniel had the muscle to crush any complaints about election fraud.

O'Daniel won the election by 1,311 votes. No need to overdo a good thing. Just get the win and move on.

This incident seared Johnson to the core. He vowed it would never happen to him again.

Eight years later, Johnson, with a helping hand from George Parr, stole a Senate seat from another Texas governor, Coke Stevenson. Johnson used the exact same formula that was used against him in 1941.

This was the expertise Joe Kennedy was counting on when he decided Lyndon Johnson had to be on the ticket.

Texas could not be lost under any circumstances. John Kennedy finally resigned himself to offering Johnson a spot on the ticket.

Robert Kennedy was having none of it. "Dad, this is crazy. First, he will never accept the offer. Why would he give up all that power he has in the Senate!"

Joe Kennedy managed to keep his temper in check. "He might not take it, Bobby. But we are going to make the offer."

Joe Kennedy then ordered his sons into another room. He wanted to make certain no outsiders could hear what he was about to say.

Kennedy told them that Lyndon Johnson and FBI Director J. Edgar Hoover were "best of friends."

It was completely possible that Johnson, feeling snubbed, might work against John Kennedy in the general election. Surreptitiously, of course.

J. Edgar Hoover was no fan of Joe Kennedy or any of his progeny. But Hoover loved Johnson.

A world in which Johnson and Hoover were feeding newspapermen negative stories about the Kennedys would be a world called living hell.

Joe Kennedy knew that Hoover was a soulless bureaucrat who could break the career of anyone he deemed an enemy.

Placing Johnson on the ticket was just one more of Joe Kennedy's insurance policies.

Joe told John to pick up the phone and said, "Make that call."

John Kennedy made the call. "Lyndon, may I come see you in a couple of hours?"

"By all means, Senator, come on down!"

John told Bobby to relax. "It will be a pro forma offer, Bobby. He won't take it."

Bobby Kennedy was white with terror at the possibility Johnson might say yes. He was concerned that his brother's credibility with the liberal wing of the party was about to be shattered.

All throughout the winter and spring of 1960, the Kennedys told labor bosses and liberal heavyweights that under no circumstances would the vice presidency "be offered to Lyndon Johnson."

It was this pledge that kept liberals from deserting the Kennedys and moving back once again to the camps of Adlai Stevenson and Hubert Humphrey.

How does one explain away such duplicity? Bobby was concerned it could not be explained away.

John Kennedy's suite at the Biltmore was room 9333. Two floors below was the Johnson suite. The number was 7333.

Exactly midway between these two powerful men was the suite used by Bobby Kennedy. His suite number was 8315.

John Kennedy walked down the back stairs in order to avoid the press.

Lady Bird Johnson and Lyndon Johnson greeted the party's new standard-bearer with great deference.

There was the inevitable small talk before John Kennedy asked if Johnson might consider joining him on the ticket.

Kennedy was mumbling and was almost inaudible. He was clearly signaling the Texan that the offer was not serious. He was stunned when Johnson grabbed the offer. He grabbed it so definitively there was no room for a retraction.

Kennedy thanked Johnson and bade farewell. Five minutes later, John Kennedy was trying to keep his younger brother from jumping out a window.

"Go back down there and tell him you have changed your mind!" Robert was screaming and not caring who heard his rant.

John said that was not a course of action he could follow.

However, if Bobby talked to Lyndon, perhaps…

Bobby Kennedy did not need any inducement.

He ran down the one flight of stairs and banged on Lyndon Johnson's door. Johnson confronted what could only be described as a Tasmanian devil.

It did not matter that Bobby Kennedy was addressing the emperor of the Senate. He treated Johnson as if the majority leader were a country bumpkin who had stumbled into the clubhouse of the cool kids.

Over the next three hours, Bobby Kennedy made not one, not two, but three trips to Johnson's suite to get the Texan to agree to withdraw.

Johnson was both a proud and an insecure man. Each time Bobby invaded his suite, Johnson was forced to call John Kennedy and ask if the offer was still on the table.

These theatrics were not taking place in a vacuum. Johnson's people, men such as Sam Rayburn and future Texas Governor John Connally, witnessed the humiliation.

In the end, Joe Kennedy told Bobby to "cut it out!"

The damage had been done. Kennedy and Johnson prior to this point had never liked one another.

After July 14, 1960, Lyndon Johnson and Bobby Kennedy became mortal enemies.

Weeks later, Stuart Dunleavy was having a drink with Bobby at the family mansion in Hickory Hill.

Lyndon Johnson had been given his marching orders. He was to travel the Old South via railroad and campaign in the small towns of the former confederacy.

Dunleavy asked Bobby if he believed Johnson could hold Texas for the Democrats.

"Maybe he will and maybe he won't," Bobby said with a sneer. "But if we win, I am going to make him wish he was on another planet!"

Chapter 23

Stuart Dunleavy was thrilled that John Kennedy wanted him inside his cabal of close advisors.

It did not hurt that Joe Kennedy liked Dunleavy and endorsed his proximity to power. Joe Kennedy had the absolute authority to veto anyone seeking a close connection to his son.

The election of 1960 took place exactly one hundred years after Abraham Lincoln assumed the presidency, which catapulted the nation into a civil war.

The war ended the institution of slavery. But it spawned two ugly stepchildren: Jim Crow and segregation.

Southern Democrats latched onto these evil twins and promulgated them via law and force of arms.

For sixty-four years, after the Civil War, black Americans were fanatically Republican. In every presidential election from 1868 until 1932, nine out of ten black votes went to the Grand Old Party.

Franklin Delano Roosevelt managed to garner a larger portion of black votes even though he stopped a federal anti-lynching statute from making its way through Congress in the 1930s.

He did it by pushing antipoverty programs that tangentially benefited blacks nationwide.

More blacks began to migrate to the Democrat Party when Harry Truman ordered the armed forces integrated in 1948.

During Dwight Eisenhower's administration, about half of all blacks had moved to the Democrats.

Eisenhower managed to staunch the flow when in 1957 he ordered federal troops to Little Rock, Arkansas, to enforce integration laws mandated by the US Supreme Court in its Brown Versus Board of Education ruling.

John Kennedy was facing two headwinds when he won the nomination. The first was religion. The other was race.

Would Protestants vote for a Roman Catholic?

Would Southern Democrats bolt the party because of civil rights?

Each of these questions posed a mortal threat to his campaign.

Kennedy repeatedly addressed the religion issue. Only he could do this. This assignment could not be farmed out to other liberals.

Lyndon Johnson's job was to keep the South in line. He spoke the language of Southern bigotry. For thirty years, first in the House and then the Senate, he had been a bulwark against black advancement.

Now Johnson had to walk a tightrope. He could not be seen as a segregationist. Nor could he be seen as firebrand liberal.

This required verbal dexterity. Johnson was proving he could pull it off.

Johnson could read people better than any politician in America.

In a crowd heavily white and loaded with voters holding Confederate flags, Johnson was Robert E. Lee reborn. In a crowd heavily populated by blacks, Johnson pretended he was the man who wrote "The Battle Hymn of the Republic."

Joe Kennedy did not pick Johnson because he was a principled man. He picked him because he was a chameleon.

Two developments proved to be decisive in the election of 1960. One development was the advent of television. The other was the arrest of a single citizen.

For the first time in history, presidential aspirants were scheduled to debate the great issues of the day live on television.

The Republicans had nominated Richard M. Nixon because he had served for eight years as Dwight Eisenhower's vice president.

Eisenhower in 1960 had a 63 percent approval rating.

Nixon was a known quantity. Kennedy was not.

The decision to debate Kennedy appeared to be counterintuitive. Why give a lesser-known opponent all that publicity?

Nixon did it because he believed he could outdebate the Massachusetts senator.

That argument had merit if the debate were on radio instead of television.

On television, the countenance of each man would be a factor. The looks and bearing of each candidate would be just as important as the words coming through the airways.

This was the trap Nixon did not consider.

John Kennedy was a very handsome man. Nixon looked like a nerd who took his mother to his senior prom.

Stuart Dunleavy was backstage when Nixon and Kennedy met in Chicago in September 1960.

Dunleavy knew instantly Nixon had made a huge mistake.

Nixon had injured his leg weeks earlier during a campaign stop in North Carolina. It got infected.

The injury drained Nixon of his energy and his weight. He looked sickly.

Nixon eschewed putting on makeup. He did not understand the importance of hiding facial imperfections behind foundational coloring. It is the reason even the best-looking people in America do not go on television with pale white faces glowing in bright lights.

Nixon also suffered from darting-eye syndrome. His black orbs raced left and right like a soldier trying to locate a sniper.

Kennedy was articulate, cool, graceful, and lithe. Had Nixon and Kennedy attended the same high school, there was no doubt who would be the prom king and who would be president of the chess club.

Nixon's only chance of overcoming these deficiencies was to paint Kennedy as unprepared for the job.

He did not succeed.

On issue after issue, Kennedy matched Nixon's presumed knowledge. Nixon's strongest asset was his reputation as an anti-communist crusader.

John Kennedy was the son of Joe Kennedy. And Joe Kennedy was the most anti-communist human being on the planet.

He made certain that every one of his progeny despised Marxism as much as he did.

Kennedy in the fall of 1960 railed against the Eisenhower-Nixon administration for allegedly falling behind in the race for space, for allowing a so-called missile gap to exist, and for not standing up strongly enough for Taiwan in that country's cold war with mainland China.

In Nixon's worst nightmare, he never envisioned a politician getting to his right on anti-communism.

John Kennedy did just that.

At the end of the debate, the best political minds in the country said John Kennedy had won.

Sixty-six million people watched the debate. Half of them were women. And the majority of those women wanted John Kennedy, not Richard Nixon, to take them to the prom.

There would be three more debates. Neither man clobbered the other. Experts rated the last three debates a tie.

It did not matter. Nixon never recovered from his first encounter with John Kennedy on live television.

There was another development that redounded to Kennedy's benefit that fall.

Martin Luther King was thirty-one years old in October of 1960. His youth did not lessen his importance to black Americans.

Five years earlier, King had led the Montgomery bus boycott in Alabama. The standoff was a success, and it propelled him into the forefront of civil rights leadership. King was a preacher. He used the English language as a weapon. King's voice and his mastery of tone and timing made him a force of nature.

King was arrested with fifty-two students at a lunch counter in Atlanta, Georgia, on October 19. They were trying to get served.

The city fathers regarded the students as a nuisance. But they were determined to make an example out of Dr. King.

King was sentenced to six months of hard labor for having the temerity to sit at a lunch counter in defiance of Jim Crow.

Nixon asked Eisenhower to immediately pardon King. He refused.

Nixon took no further action. This would turn out to be a huge mistake.

John Kennedy picked up the telephone and called King's parents. Kennedy then pressured Atlanta authorities to release King. He succeeded.

All this was played out on the front pages of America's newspapers.

Prior to King's arrest, it was estimated that 50 percent of the black vote was heading in Richard Nixon's direction.

All that changed following Kennedy's efforts. Black America swarmed to Kennedy's campaign.

Three weeks later, this voter migration played a huge role in the making of a president.

But it was not the only role. Dwight Eisenhower inadvertently made Richard Nixon look like a fool.

At the very height of the campaign, a reporter asked Eisenhower to give him one example of a policy or program Nixon had excelled at while in office.

"Give me a week and I might think of something." Eisenhower smiled after he said it, thinking it would get a laugh.

Boom. In one second, Nixon's strongest argument for getting elected evaporated. Eisenhower tried to save the day by stating he had only been joking.

Joe Kennedy made certain every American heard about this remark. And the Kennedy boys declared, "Ike was not kidding."

American voters were left to wonder: *If Eisenhower does not believe Nixon is anything special, why should we?*

Joe Kennedy's machinations were also determinative. On election night, November 8, 1960, his insurance policies became operational.

After the polls closed the tally began.

It was neck and neck.

By midnight on election day, the race was still not determined. It was destined to be razor slim.

Now it was time for Dick Daley in Chicago and George Parr in Texas to step up.

The Democrat machines in both states knew what the final count was going to be. Or at least they had it narrowed down.

Dick Daley telephoned Sam Giancana. "Time to make the dead walk again," he said.

George Parr did not have to make his own army of walking corpses. He had his henchmen "help" the poor people of southwest Texas.

Parr's people would drive voters to the polls. Most of Parr's men had pistols strapped to their hips. In Texas, no one thought twice about it.

Parr's goons would walk into the voting booths with terrified citizens and make certain the right lever was pulled.

Parr also salted away thousands of ballots in case they were needed in an emergency.

Kennedy won Illinois by 9,000 votes. He won Texas by 46,000 votes.

Lyndon Johnson had insisted on a healthy cushion in order to impress his new boss.

On November 8, in Fannin County, Texas, there were 4,895 registered voters. Somehow 6,138 votes were cast.

In one precinct in Angelina County, there were 86 registered voters.

Yet John Kennedy received 187 votes, and Richard Nixon got 24 votes.

And on and on.

By 7:00 a.m. on November 9, the count was in the bank.

John Fitzgerald Kennedy: 34,220,984. Richard Milhous Nixon: 34,108,157.

Kennedy had won by 0.17 percent of the votes cast.

Illinois and Texas were in his pocket.

Joe Kennedy's dream had come true. He knew his son would wear the crown, but it was he who would call the shots.

Sam Giancana was also a happy man. He and Daley had gotten Kennedy elected.

And each man wanted something in return.

There was only one problem. Joe Kennedy did not inform his son that a deal had been made with a powerful gangster.

This would turn out to be a calamitous mistake. Joe Kennedy's decision to keep his son in the dark about Sam Giancana would prove lethal.

But that fact was not evident on the joyous two days of November 8–9.

The storm that would hit the Kennedy family was three years away.

Chapter 24

"The president will see you now, Mr. Dunleavy."

Evelyn Lincoln was John Kennedy's devoted secretary.

She joined his staff in 1953 shortly after his miracle victory over Henry Cabot Lodge. She was in his presence more hours of the day than any other human being, and that included Jacqueline Bouvier.

John Kennedy regarded her as a member of the family.

Mrs. Lincoln knew Stuart Dunleavy occupied a special place in the heart of John Kennedy. He had been president three days when Dunleavy asked to see him.

Entering the Oval Office for the first time can have a profound effect on most visitors. It is the epicenter of world power. Kings, queens, ambassadors, presidents, dictators—they all seek entrance into this one room because they all know here lies the heart and soul of the most important branch of the government.

Newly minted president of the United States John Fitzgerald Kennedy stood up out of his seat and walked five paces to embrace his old comrade.

"Stuart, you old horse thief! I have not seen you since the inauguration. What have you been doing?"

"I have been down in Florida, Mr. President. My old man's health is getting a little shaky."

"Is he okay? You know, I met both your parents at one of the balls. I'm sorry I couldn't spend more time with them, but you know, there was a lot of handshaking I had to do that night."

"Pop is seventy-three. They're running tests to see exactly what the problem might be."

"Is there anything I can do? I can have the best doctors in the world down there in twenty-four hours."

"No, Mr. President, he is in good hands. And you need to run a country, not worry about just one of its citizens."

"You have been calling me Jack since 1943. It seems weird to hear you say Mr. President."

"My days of addressing you by your first name are over. And I could not be happier about that fact."

Kennedy smiled. He knew their relationship had forever been transformed. "Come on over and sit down. I told Evelyn not to disturb us unless the Russians are invading New York."

Stuart Dunleavy sat to the right side of the Resolute Desk. Queen Victoria had given the desk to President Rutherford B. Hayes in 1880. The desk was made from the timbers salvaged from the exploration ship HMS *Resolute*. It was perhaps the single most famous piece of furniture on the planet.

"Well, Stuart, what are your plans? You know you can have any damn job in this administration you want." Kennedy leaned forward and stated with mock sincerity, "And that includes the vice presidency." He leaned back laughing heartily.

"Mr. President, as much as I love you, I don't want to be attending funerals all over the planet."

Both men laughed at that remark. It was the fate of most vice presidents that boring ceremonial functions were the heart of the job.

"Actually, Mr. President, I have given this a lot of thought. I would like to serve you and my country by working at the NSA."

Dunleavy's reference to the National Security Agency, located at Fort George C. Meade in Maryland, did not surprise John Kennedy.

The agency was formally founded in 1952, but its parentage went all the way back to April of 1917.

Woodrow Wilson and Congress had just declared war on Germany. The United States needed intelligence. Failure to garner accurate intelligence could lead to the deaths of thousands of men.

The government set up the Cipher Bureau. The job of this new agency was to crack German diplomatic and military code traffic.

The Cipher Bureau after the war developed into the ominous-sounding Black Chamber. But its functions remained the same until 1929.

In that year, Secretary of State Henry L. Stimson pompously stated, "Gentlemen do not read each other's mail."

Stimson convinced newly elected President Herbert Hoover to shut down the clandestine intelligence agency.

During the 1930s, when dictatorships were popping up all over the planet, the US had to rely on the British for intelligence.

Franklin Roosevelt corrected Stimson's high-minded mistake. After Pearl Harbor, Roosevelt created the Office of Strategic Services (OSS).

Following the war, Congress made intelligence gathering a permanent priority. It created the Central Intelligence Agency.

In 1952, outgoing President Harry Truman signed into law a companion intelligence bureaucracy called the National Security Agency.

The agency was tasked with global monitoring, collection, and processing of data for foreign and domestic intelligence purposes.

Information was to be shared with the CIA and the FBI. The agency was authorized to engage in wiretapping overseas. No building was considered out of bounds, including those housing heads of state.

John Kennedy chewed on the end of a pencil while contemplating Dunleavy's request. "Let me guess. You want to work at the NSA because they have the most advanced computers in the world."

"You nailed it, Mr. President."

"Well, Stuart, getting you a job there will require a background check by the FBI. Is there anything in your past you want to tell me about?"

"Yes, there is, Mr. President."

Kennedy was taken aback. "What did you do? Abscond with some church's charity fund?"

"It is nothing I did. It pertains to my father."

"What did he do?"

"Remember years ago, I told you my dad made his money manufacturing small boats? That was a lie. He was a bootlegger."

Kennedy chuckled. "A bootlegger! No kidding!"

"He ran booze from Cuba to Florida for ten years. He made a pile of money. And I am not certain how much he told the IRS."

"Stuart, let me ask you a couple of questions."

"Yes, sir."

"Was your dad ever arrested?"

"No, sir."

"Positive?"

"Yes, sir."

"Did he ever engage in any rough stuff?"

"No."

"Did he ever bribe anybody that might still be alive?"

"My dad worked for a man named Nick Cosentino. He was the person who handed out the bribe money."

"Was Nick Cosentino ever arrested?"

"I asked my dad about that when I was in Florida. He said no."

"So, your father was never arrested, and there is no evidence linking him to rum-running at a time when that activity was considered illegal?"

"That's true, but if I am asked about it, I will not lie."

"Then as your commander-in-chief, I am ordering you not to volunteer that information."

"Are you sure, Mr. President?"

"Stuart, how old were you when Prohibition ended?"

"I was ten."

"When you were ten years old, did you drive any boats to Cuba and bring back any contraband?"

Dunleavy laughed. "My dad wouldn't let me. He thought I might do a better job of it than he was doing."

"Stuart, there is an old saying about the sins of the father being visited upon the son. It isn't fair."

"I would never do anything to hurt you, Mr. President. I felt compelled to tell you."

"You know, Stuart, a lot of people believe my old man was in the bootlegging business."

"Was he?"

"My older brother asked him once at the dinner table. Dad ripped him a new one. After that tongue lashing, the subject never came up again."

Kennedy stood up and came around the Resolute Desk to shake his friend's hand. "I am going to call a man at the NSA named Curt Holmes. You go over there and see him tomorrow. We'll have you sitting in front of one of those fancy computers in less than a week."

"Mr. President, you have made me a very happy man."

"Does this mean I can count on your vote in '64?"

"I can't make any promises. Your brother Bobby might decide to make a run for it in three years."

Kennedy howled in laughter as he escorted Dunleavy out the door.

Chapter 25

It was only ten minutes after Stuart Dunleavy left the Oval Office that the phone once again rang on Evelyn Lincoln's desk.

"Mr. President, your father is on line two."

Kennedy grimaced. His father since the inauguration had adopted even more Napoleonic tendencies, if that was possible.

John Kennedy wanted to be president. So did his father. Unfortunately for the son, when it came to a test of wills, Joe Sr. never lost a battle.

"Hello, Dad. How's Mom?"

Kennedy the elder wanted to get right down to business. "Never mind about that. There is one cabinet appointment we must absolutely get right. It is a matter of maximum importance."

"Which cabinet position are we talking about?"

"Attorney general."

"Who did you have in mind?"

"Your brother."

John Kennedy laughed. He assumed his father was doing something he rarely did—make a joke.

"Dad, you cannot be serious. It is an impossibility."

"I disagree."

"Dad, please, Congress will never allow my brother to become my attorney general. We will get laughed out of the Senate."

"You underestimate Lyndon Johnson. He makes one phone call, and the deed is done."

Kennedy knew his father was not playing games. John Kennedy had intended to marginalize Lyndon Johnson now that the race was won. By requesting his number two to perform such a monumental favor, Kennedy would be acknowledging Johnson was a leading member of the administration. He did not want to do it.

"Listen, Dad, there are so many gifted lawyers who are leaps and bounds better qualified for that office than Bobby. How do we explain it?"

"You tell the press that Bobby is your closest advisor, and you must have him in your cabinet."

"Dad, this will be regarded as the rankest form of nepotism this city has ever seen."

"We don't have a choice, son. And I will explain why. We have a problem. And that problem has a name. J. Edgar Hoover."

John Kennedy suddenly realized his father was not completely off his rocker. The diminutive Hoover had been a force in Washington, DC, for forty years.

He had transformed the Federal Bureau of Investigation from absolutely nothing into the greatest law enforcement agency on the planet.

He regarded the FBI as his personal property. He had no family life or anything recognizable as a normal social life.

Hoover was supposed to be subordinate to the man running the US Justice Department. What a joke.

Hoover had found a scheme to neuter whatever pettifogging bureaucrat got in his way. That included the man holding the title attorney general of the United States.

Hoover had two sets of files. One set of files was available to the secretaries and FBI lawmen who shared the building they occupied in Washington. The other set of files was kept in a room in which he and his number two, Clyde Tolson, had the only keys. Tolson was also his lover.

These files were rich in derogatory material about presidents, politicians, celebrities, judges, businessmen—anyone who might pose a threat to the power of one J. Edgar Hoover.

He used these files as blackmail whenever a perceived threat appeared.

Joe Kennedy suspected there were files dedicated to his entire family. Files that probably reached from the floor to the ceiling.

Joe Kennedy knew that Hoover had one weakness. Hoover did not want to retire. Ever. He wanted to die sitting at his desk issuing orders.

Hoover had an implied contract with every US president going back to the great Franklin Roosevelt: "Leave me alone and I will protect you. Fire me and you might not like what you read in the newspapers."

Decade after decade the contract was honored.

Joe Kennedy did not trust Hoover. The two men were not close.

Joe feared Hoover might subvert his son's administration with selected leaks.

Hoover had always wanted Lyndon Johnson to become president. It was conceivable Hoover had information about the Kennedy clan that was so explosive it could wreck everything.

Hoover needed to be watched.

Joe Kennedy pushed this point home during his January phone call.

"Son, we have to put a dog collar around Hoover's neck. And I want a blood member of this family holding the chain. Now do you understand?"

"I had every intention of asking Hoover to retire. If he refused, I was going to show him the door."

"We cannot do that! Let me give you just one example. Do you remember what you were doing twenty years ago?"

"Serving my country in the United States Navy."

"That's not all you were doing. You were also banging that beauty queen from Denmark."

John Kennedy raced through his memory bank back to the days just after Pearl Harbor. He was still in Washington. And he met an incredible Aryan beauty named Inga Arvad.

The lady was married, but for the men spawned by Joe Kennedy, that was always described as a minor impediment.

Inga and her husband, Hungarian film director Paul Fejos, came to the United States in 1940. She got a job at the *Washington Times Herald*. John Kennedy's sister, Kathleen, also worked at the newspaper. It was she who introduced Inga to her brother.

Kennedy went after Inga with the speed of a bullet. They began a passionate affair.

It was Inga's past employment and the company she kept that proved to be problematic.

In 1935, the Copenhagen-born temptress was a freelance reporter.

Her looks caught the attention of one Adolph Hitler. He granted Inga three interviews. This was something Der Führer hardly ever did.

She wrote glowing stories about the dictator.

The exact nature of Arvad's and Hitler's relationship is clouded, but everyone knew the chancellor of Germany was smitten.

Inga Arvad believed Germany under Hitler was being "reborn."

When Inga and Fejos emigrated, the FBI took judicial notice of her presence in the United States. They followed her. And they wiretapped her. She was suspected of being a Nazi spy.

The allegation was never proven. But on December 11, 1941, Germany declared war on the US.

This development did not stop John Kennedy from seeing Inga. This love affair had three partners: Inga, John Kennedy, and the FBI.

Kennedy's ruminations with Inga during their nighttime assignations were being monitored by J. Edgar Hoover.

Joe Kennedy had to wonder what bombshells Hoover had in his files concerning his son's relationship with Inga.

It was the reason Hoover could not be fired. But he had to be controlled and watched.

There was one more reason Hoover had to be coddled.

Joe Kennedy could not know how much information Hoover had salted away concerning his relationship with mobsters during the 1920s.

Kennedy had always been careful. He used intermediaries when dealing with men such as Johnny Torrio, Sam Giancana, and Carlos Marcello, just to name a few.

The specter of scandal hung like an albatross around all the Kennedys. It was the price one paid for living on the edge.

The good humor Kennedy had felt during his meeting with Stuart Dunleavy was gone. John Kennedy was now morose and angry.

"Okay, Dad. I will grovel in front of the press and we will get Bobby on board."

"Good! I'll tell Lyndon to make the call."

Two hours later, Lyndon Johnson was meeting with Georgia Senator Richard B. Russell. Russell's eyebrows shot up when Johnson told him the president of the United States wanted his brother as the next attorney general.

Russell spent the next twenty minutes telling Johnson that this was a very bad idea.

The normally loquacious Johnson did not interrupt. When Russell had expended his monologue, Johnson played his ace card.

The vice president told Russell that he was the only man in the administration standing as a bulwark against the many liberals who wanted to cram through civil rights legislation.

Johnson needed this favor because failure meant disaster. Johnson could be dropped from the ticket in 1964 in favor of some Harvard Bolshevik.

Russell finally came around. Richard Russell was the only man in the United States Senate who had the power to get his fellow senators on board with such an outrageous request.

And it took every bit of Russell's prestige to pull it off.

His fellow senators agreed to ratify Bobby Kennedy's ascension to the Justice Department. But there was a caveat. The vote had to be by a show of hands. No one wanted a roll call vote that would be on the record.

The deed was done. Robert Francis Kennedy moved into the Justice Department building before the month of February rolled around.

He had not lobbied his father for the job. Joe Kennedy told him he was going to be US attorney general and that was the end of it.

Joe Kennedy had unknowingly set in motion forces that would later haunt the family. Robert Kennedy's ascension infuriated J. Edgar Hoover.

He regarded Robert Kennedy as a puppy, a whippersnapper, someone who had not paid his dues to achieve such a high office.

Hoover turned purple with rage the day a telephone man showed up in his office with a red phone.

"What's that?" Hoover glowered at the workman.

Hoover's secretary timidly entered his office. "It is a direct line to the attorney general." She got the words out of her mouth, and then she beat a hasty retreat.

Clyde Tolson had to physically restrain the director. Hoover wanted to storm down to Robert Kennedy's office and toss the phone in his face.

Robert Kennedy would later tell Hoover that when the phone jangled, he was to drop whatever else he was doing and he was to answer it.

Kennedy also told Hoover he was to be kept apprised of every investigation initiated by the FBI. No exceptions.

Hoover vowed at that moment he would find a way to destroy the Kennedys.

Robert Kennedy's rise to power also stunned those men who had helped get his brother elected.

From 1957 to 1959, Robert Kennedy was chief counsel for the Senate Labor Rackets Committee.

Powerful Mob leaders had to sit still while Robert Kennedy grilled them about their activities. These men had to sit through insults and sarcasm. They were not used to being talked to this way. An ordinary citizen engaging in this type of harangue would end up dead in an alley.

Joe Kennedy promised these men, "You will have a friend in the White House."

Bobby Kennedy was not their friend. He was their mortal enemy.

Sam Giancana picked up the phone and talked to mobsters all over the country. "Let's wait and see," he said. "This could be a brilliant head fake. We all know Joe runs the show. Maybe he's got the kid in there to look tough while we can go about our business."

"You better be right, Sam," Carlos Marcello said. "You are the one who told us we could trust Joe Kennedy. If he is playing us, I for one will not sit idly by."

Chapter 26

The outgoing Eisenhower Administration left behind some unfinished business.

In late December 1959, Fidel Castro routed the forces of Cuban Dictator Fulgencio Batista. When Castro rolled into Havana, he was sitting atop a tank and smoking a cigar. He cut quite a figure.

The bearded revolutionary had carefully hidden his political philosophy from his own troops as well as the world.

In January of 1959, Eisenhower was willing to give Castro a chance. The guerilla leader had made noises about restoring Democracy to Cuba.

Castro slowly revealed his true self. He started off by shooting his presumed enemies. The execution squads in Cuba were kept busy day and night.

One man waiting for the executioner's bullet was Santo Trafficante Jr. of Tampa, Florida.

He was sitting in a Cuban jail. Outside his window, men were being gunned down with frightening regularity.

Trafficante had gone to Cuba hoping that Castro was just another Latin American Caudillo who could be reasoned with. Especially if the price was right. Trafficante had huge financial interests in Havana's casino industry. The effort to reach an understanding with Castro was paramount.

Trafficante did not realize the true nature of the new government. Cuban security forces tossed Trafficante in jail as soon as he arrived.

In the end, Trafficante escaped death by a whisker.

A mafia bagman showed up in Havana with a suitcase full of money. Even communists, it would appear, are susceptible to bribes.

The man who ushered Trafficante out of jail and back to the United States was a Dallas nightclub owner named Jack Rubenstein. He was often referred to by an abbreviated moniker, Jack Ruby.

Carlos Marcello sent Ruby to save his friend. It is not known how much money was in that suitcase.

Cuban exiles started pouring into the United States. They brought with them stories about Cuban soldiers expropriating property and Cuban political leaders extolling Marxism-Leninism.

By July of 1959, panic permeated the corridors of power in Washington.

There was a very real possibility a communist state might be coming to fruition just ninety miles from Florida.

If true, it would be the first one. Allowing it to survive might encourage other revolutionaries to get busy.

Eisenhower ordered his security agencies to get involved. The CIA, the NSA, the FBI, and Naval Intelligence were ordered to come up with contingency plans for getting rid of Castro.

Lethal force was authorized. This decision was best kept quiet and away from the American people. But Castro's spies were ubiquitous. His security people told him the United States was serious about getting rid of him and his cause.

Relations between the two countries went into a death spiral.

In early 1960, oil from the Soviet Union began to arrive in Havana. Castro ordered three American firms (Esso, Standard Oil, and Shell) to refine it.

The companies refused. Castro ordered his troops to expropriate the companies. Cuba refused to pay for the takeover, and this turned out to be the straw that broke the camel's back.

Diplomatic relations between the two countries were severed. A virtual state of war now existed.

Castro's depredations had caused 250,000 men, women, and children to flee Cuba.

They wanted their country back.

Uncle Sam wanted to help them get it back.

Clandestine CIA operations were instituted. Training camps for potential liberation movements were created in Nicaragua, Guatemala, and Florida.

Exiles created the Democratic Revolutionary Front (DRF). Potential soldiers were formed and trained under the umbrella of Brigade 2506.

John Kennedy was kept in the dark about this activity until he beat Richard Nixon in November 1960.

Eisenhower decided the president-elect needed to be brought up to speed. He had two meetings with Kennedy specifically to discuss the Cuban issue. The first meeting was on December 6, 1960, and the second meeting was on January 19, 1961, the day before he became president.

Eisenhower told Kennedy thirteen million dollars had been set aside from a so-called Black Budget. This money was designated to getting rid of Castro.

Kennedy was just getting his feet wet as a new president when he learned of Operation Zapata. This was a CIA plan to invade Cuba with soldiers from Brigade 2506.

Kennedy ordered CIA Director Allen Dulles to give him a briefing on Operation Zapata.

Dulles said the plan would work. Kennedy was dubious. He asked the members of the joint chiefs of staff about the proposed invasion. Each member signed off on it.

The director of the National Security Agency was a rear admiral named Laurence Hugh Frost. Kennedy asked Frost for an opinion. Frost circulated Operation Zapata among five top members of his bureaucracy.

One of those men was Curt Holmes, a casual friend of JFK. Holmes studied and restudied the plan.

He told Frost the concept was littered with problems.

Frost did not agree. He was blinded by anti-communism. Frost also did not want to contradict members of the joint chiefs of staff.

Frost told Holmes he was going to recommend the plan be adopted. Holmes was greatly concerned. He decided to bring in another man without telling Frost.

That man was Stuart Dunleavy.

In early March 1961, Holmes asked Dunleavy to join him for lunch. He gave Dunleavy the forty-five-page logistical outline for Operation Zapata.

"Take it home, read it, bring it back tomorrow, and then you and I are going to lock ourselves in my office and discuss it," Holmes said.

Dunleavy knew that taking documents outside the building housing the NSA could be construed as espionage.

"Curt, why me?"

"Everyone at the NSA knows you and John Kennedy have a special bond," Holmes said. "If this plan is implemented, it could destroy his presidency."

The statement was enough to convince Dunleavy to take a chance.

Operation Zapata was going home to Dunleavy's three-bedroom house in Georgetown.

Dunleavy kissed his wife and said, "Honey, I am going to lock myself in our bedroom for a couple of hours. And I can't tell you why."

"Well, I know you don't have a girl in there, so go ahead." She gave him a peck on his cheek.

The next morning Dunleavy and Holmes spent two hours together in a secure room that could not be monitored by any known audio device.

When they walked out, each man had a fixed jaw and a look of determination.

One day later, Dunleavy called the White House. He asked Evelyn Lincoln if she would convey a message to the president.

Lincoln responded, "Of course I will."

"Please ask the president to give me a call. And tell him it is urgent."

So strong was Kennedy's affection for Dunleavy that the call came in less than two hours. "Stuart, what's up? Is it your father?"

"No, Mr. President. He seems to be recovering. But I won't beat around the bush."

Dunleavy gulped and pressed ahead. "Mr. President, I am going outside the chain of command. The director of NSA does not know about this intercession. If you feel this is improper, we can stop right now."

Kennedy could not fathom what this was about. But his curiosity had been piqued, and there was no way he was not going to press ahead.

"Stu, if you feel so strongly about this, maybe you should get it off your chest. What exactly are we talking about?"

"Operation Zapata."

Kennedy was taken aback. "Are you on a secure line, Stu?"

"I am."

"I was not aware you were authorized to see the planning for Operation Zapata."

"I was not. But Curt Holmes thought it was imperative."

"It sounds like Holmes is trading in on our relationship to gain access he would not otherwise be granted."

"That is exactly what he is doing, Mr. President. But I also believe he is acting out of a patriotic sense of duty. If you disagree, we can stop right now."

Kennedy paused for a full ten seconds.

He did not want to encourage this kind of behavior. If word got out that anyone in the bureaucracy could call the White House and ask to speak to the president, there would be a deluge.

"Stuart, exactly how many people know about this phone call?"

"Two, Mr. President."

"Do I have your word as a naval officer that no one else will be brought into this little conspiracy?"

"You do, sir."

"Okay, Stuart. What is this all about?"

"Mr. Holmes and I believe Operation Zapata cannot succeed. If we go into Cuba under the parameters outlined in Zapata, we will lose."

Kennedy was relieved. He believed the plan was pie-in-the-sky. But he had run into a wall of support for Zapata from people who held the top positions in his government.

Kennedy no longer believed Dunleavy's unusual intervention was a bad thing. "Why don't you tell me what objections you and Mr. Holmes have in your mutinous little brains."

Dunleavy let out a heavy sigh of relief. The president could have told him to back off. Most presidents would have done just that.

"Mr. President, Operation Zapata states we are going to land fourteen hundred exiles on a beach in southwest Cuba. These men have been given rudimentary military training. Holmes and I do not question their bravery. We question the wisdom of sending men armed with rifles and hand grenades against an army possessing heavy weapons."

Kennedy stated, "Go on."

"Not only will they be outnumbered twenty to one, the number of US Marines assigned to back them up is nowhere near sufficient."

Kennedy did not interrupt, so Dunleavy pressed ahead. "We believe the main premise behind Zapata is faulty. The success of this operation rests on the assumption that the people of Cuba will join the fight and the cascading effect of hundreds of thousands of aroused citizens rising up to toss off their oppressors is inevitable."

"You don't think they will?" Kennedy asked.

"Mr. President, it is just as likely the people of Cuba will rise up to support Castro."

"I thought the Cuban people hated communism."

"Mr. President, this revolution is brand-new. The people have not yet seen the malignancy of communism. Millions of people have been told they will have free health care and a free education. The rhetoric coming from the government is touching all the right nerves."

Kennedy could not help but agree with Dunleavy. Why didn't the brahmins he hired to run these agencies have the same insight?

"Stuart, I am not certain I can allow a communist government so close to the borders of the United States. I could be impeached."

Dunleavy did not hesitate. "If we go in, then go in Normandy style. Commit a hundred thousand well-trained American troops backed up by five thousand tanks and two thousand airplanes. Castro will be gone in a week."

Kennedy recoiled. "Stuart, if we went in that heavy, the whole world would denounce us as modern-day Nazis."

"True, they would attack us in public, but in private they'd thank us."

"So, I would have to take a public beating, but no one would know about the private approbations."

"No one said being president of the United States was going to be easy."

"Come on, Stuart, a hundred thousand men—"

Dunleavy did something he had never done before. He interrupted Jack Kennedy. "Mr. President, if you were in a boxing match, would you prefer to knock out your opponent with one punch in the first round or would you prefer to slug it out over fifteen rounds?"

"I hate it when you always make sense."

This was the first attempt at levity since the conversation began.

"Mr. President, Curt and I believe the landings have a one in a hundred chance of succeeding. Imagine what failure will look like on the world stage."

Kennedy decided to pay Dunleavy the ultimate compliment. "Do you have a recommendation?"

"Call the whole thing off. Go to Congress. Explain the stakes involved. Do not forget that your job is to manage a war. Only Congress can declare one."

Kennedy knew he was right. But he was in a trap. And he could not explain the trap to anyone—not even the loyal Stuart Dunleavy.

Kennedy was handcuffed by one man. His father.

Joe Kennedy knew all about Operation Zapata. Joe knew everything that happened in this administration.

Joe Kennedy hated communism and all communists.

He wanted Castro gone. Immediately. He saw Operation Zapata as the tool to get the job done.

It was Joe Kennedy who would greenlight Operation Zapata.

It was John Kennedy who would pay the cost of any failure.

Kennedy thanked Dunleavy for his phone call. He told his friend there would be no repercussions this time, but he said, "Don't do it again."

John Kennedy hung up the phone, stood up, and walked over to a large Oval Office window.

"I'm president of the United States. What a joke!"

Chapter 27

Lee Harvey Oswald was miserable.

Living under communism was turning out to be a lot different than imagining life under communism.

Oswald landed in Russia in October of 1959. To no one's surprise, he was considered an odd duck.

One can count the number of US Marines who defect to Russia on the amputated hand of a one-armed man.

Soviet authorities immediately suspected he was a CIA plant. Had Joe Stalin still been crawling around the Kremlin, Oswald would have been sent to Lubyanka Prison immediately.

The KGB did not want to discourage defections. Locking people up the instant they land in Russia would end this potential source of human capital.

The Russian government initially tried to send him back. Oswald panicked. A quick return would certainly negate his deal with US Intelligence.

Oswald produced a knife and cut his wrist. He was hospitalized, and a Soviet psychiatrist ran a battery of tests.

Oswald's fake suicide attempt had its desired effect. The Soviets began to believe he might be what he contended he was all along, an aggrieved American looking for a social paradise.

They allowed him to stay. But they never took their eyes off him. Oswald was sent to Minsk, the capital of Belarus. Minsk was annexed by the Russians from Poland in 1793.

The government found him a reasonably comfortable apartment in the heart of the city. They got him a job as a lathe operator at the Gorizont Electronics factory. The job was intellectually deadening. The company was not a high-value military-connected entity.

The Soviets never grew to trust Oswald. He was under twenty-four-hour surveillance, seven days a week.

The CIA had no way of bridging this security blanket. No drop zones could be established. Not that Oswald had anything of value to send to the West.

Night after night Oswald sat in his apartment waiting for someone to contact him.

No one ever did. A KGB operative was never more than fifty yards from his abode.

The CIA knew that sending Oswald to Russia was a long shot. US Intelligence gave it a year. Allen Dulles told his subordinates to pull the plug.

Now they had to find a way to tell Oswald he had fulfilled his end of the bargain and it was okay to come back home.

It took another three months for a CIA agent to accidentally bump into Oswald at a coffee shop and slide a piece of paper into his coat pocket.

The note described his meeting with Lieutenant Colonel Pickering. Oswald knew it was authentic. He needed no prodding to come home.

Oswald had been dating a fellow factory worker named Ella German, a Jewish girl who was moderately good-looking.

She eventually rejected him. Ella correctly deduced Oswald would not rise any higher than his current job at Gorizont.

In March of 1961, Oswald met a nineteen-year-old pharmacology student named Marina Prusakova. Six weeks later, they were married. The union never would have happened except that Oswald told her he was going back to the United States. He, of course, could take a wife with him on the journey back.

Marina was not enamored with life in Russia. Life in the United States sounded much better.

Now began the delicate dance to get Oswald out of the Soviet Union.

Oswald contacted the US Embassy in May of 1962. He and Marina had a three-month-old child.

Embassy officials contacted their Soviet counterparts.

It all went so smoothly. The Russians wanted him out. It was costing a fortune just to keep him under surveillance.

US Embassy officials could have told Oswald to stuff it. He was, after all, a traitor.

That did not happen. The CIA told the embassy to facilitate the return of Oswald, his wife, and his daughter. And do not ask any questions.

The US government even gave Oswald traveling money—pretty nice treatment for a defector.

Oswald moved back to Dallas-Fort Worth. He knew the area well.

It was June of 1962.

He would not be writing any spy novels. His sojourn to Russia produced absolutely nothing of value.

On the bright side, he faced absolutely no legal repercussions for his treason.

Now a man who did not have a high school diploma, who did not have marketable skills higher than a soda jerk, had to find gainful employment.

He did find work. All of it was just as mind-numbing as his job as a lathe worker in Minsk.

And the longer Marina was in the United States, the more confident she became. She began to wonder why she needed Lee Harvey Oswald anymore.

Oswald's homelife began its slow but inexorable slide toward divorce.

By January of 1963, Lee Oswald was an angry man. Very angry.

Chapter 28

Robert Kennedy gave his brother a bear hug as he left the Oval Office the first week of April 1961.

It had been a grand meeting. The younger Kennedy had great ambitions for the US Justice Department, but he needed his brother's unequivocal support.

He got it.

Minutes after Robert Kennedy left, the president asked Evelyn Lincoln to find NSA Director Laurence Frost.

The admiral was on the line in less than five minutes.

Kennedy told the NSA director to clear his calendar for tomorrow morning. "I'm sending my brother over to see you," Kennedy said. "I want only four people at this meeting. You, Bobby, Curt Holmes, and Stuart Dunleavy."

"Yes, Mr. President." Frost debated asking the president the topic of the proposed gathering, but he decided to just accept the order.

Frost was a bureaucrat with keen instincts. He noticed that Holmes and Dunleavy appeared to have formed a two-man cabal. Each man had a connection to the president, so any attempt to get them in line might be dangerous.

Frost spent the entire day wondering why the attorney general of the United States was coming to visit the NSA.

He found out twenty-four hours later.

Robert Kennedy showed up alone. Frost found the absence of an entourage strange.

Robert Kennedy did not waste time on small talk. He shook Frost's hand and then asked that they find the most secure room in the building.

Frost noticed that Kennedy was animated, even giddy. He was a fountain of energy. Frost's bureaucratic antenna told him now was the time to listen and not to try to dominate.

Kennedy sat at the north end of a long rectangular table. To his right was Dunleavy. To his left was Holmes. Frost sat at the south end of the table. His distancing established him as the least most important man in the room.

"Gentlemen, thank you for agreeing to see me on such short notice." Kennedy smiled. Everyone in the room knew his status as the president's brother meant he could command a meeting with only five minutes' notice.

"Gentlemen, this administration has reached a determination that there is a domestic threat that has been ignored for decades but now must be dealt with."

Frost immediately assumed Kennedy was talking about the worldwide communist threat. He could not have been more off base.

"I am talking about organized crime, also known as the Mafia, or La Cosa Nostra."

All three men just stared so Kennedy continued. "Thanks to Prohibition, organized crime had a gusher of money for thirteen years. When Prohibition ended, the Mob moved into the drug business. Money begat influence and power. Money buys judges, cops, prosecutors. Money allowed the Mob to infiltrate the labor movement."

Kennedy stood up and walked behind his chair. "When I was chief counsel for the Rackets Committee, I saw what corruption looked like. I learned firsthand how the Mob dipped its fingers into the Teamster's pension fund and made it their own. Millions of dollars siphoned away from honest men trying to feed their families by driving trucks."

Frost decided it was time to assert his status as the ranking NSA employee in the room. "Mr. Kennedy, this sounds like a subject for the Federal Bureau of Investigation. We here at the NSA have been assigned quite a different mission."

Kennedy resumed his seat. "You are absolutely right, Mr. Director. We are revamping the FBI and the US Justice Department.

We are putting both on a war footing. I am hiring twenty attorneys who will spend all their time prosecuting the human scum polluting this great nation."

"Mr. Kennedy, I salute and endorse your mission. However, Congress created this agency to combat threats from outside our borders. Congress made it clear the NSA was to keep its nose out of domestic affairs."

"Your analysis is correct Admiral. But I believe I have found a loophole we can all live with."

"Mr. Kennedy, I am dubious that this loophole exists. I presume you want this agency to wiretap suspected criminals. Congress has stated it manifestly does not want us doing that."

"Admiral, I concur with your assessment of what Congress intended to do with the NSA's mission. And you will not be wiretapping."

"Then, Mr. Kennedy, I am confused as to the nature and purpose of this meeting."

"Mr. Frost, inside this building are the world's most advanced computers and the best code breakers anywhere on God's green earth. Is that correct?"

"I humbly concur with your assessment, Mr. Kennedy."

"If criminal A is making a phone call from New York to Criminal B in San Francisco, the NSA can trace this connection, correct?"

"Yes, we can, Mr. Kennedy, but that scenario again butts up against the will of Congress."

Kennedy rose from his chair, put both hands on the table, and leaned forward if only to close the distance between him and Frost by few inches.

"It violates the will of Congress only if the NSA is listening in to the conversation between criminal A and criminal B. You will not be listening, Mr. Frost."

"Could you be more specific, Mr. Kennedy?"

"If the NSA can tell my people there have been multiple contacts between criminals, that is all the information we need to go to a judge and get a warrant. The people asking for the warrant will be attorneys for the US Justice Department. NSA personnel will not be involved in any court proceedings."

Frost was turning this statement over in his head, looking for any land mines. The idea was very clever. The NSA would be surveilling without actually surveilling in the traditional sense of the word. This might survive judicial scrutiny.

Frost still wanted to protect his agency and his reputation. "Mr. Kennedy, would you be willing to give me assurances in writing that this proposal meets constitutional standards?"

"I will. With the understanding that this is a national security matter and any such letter will be deemed classified at the highest level. Is that understood?"

Kennedy was telling Frost that if the details of this meeting ever leaked, there would be hell to pay.

"One more thing, Admiral. The president wants Mr. Dunleavy and Mr. Holmes to be placed in charge of this operation. They will, of course, answer to you."

"Mr. Kennedy, I am on board with one caveat. If I get a phone call or a memo from anyone at the Justice Department or the FBI asking me to wiretap a conversation, I will resign."

Kennedy smiled. "Don't worry, Admiral, all wiretap requests will be handled by a man named J. Edgar Hoover. I understand he just loves listening in on people."

Kennedy laughed, stood up, shook hands with Dunleavy and Holmes, and gave Frost a quick wave.

In an instant he was gone.

Chapter 29

"Evelyn, I'm going for a walk."

"Yes, Mr. President."

Evelyn Lincoln saw the strained look on John Kennedy's face. He had not slept much for the past seventy-two hours.

The president of the United States wanted to be alone to ruminate in his own mind about the events of the past week. The Rose Garden provided the perfect scene for a solitary walk.

Three days earlier, John Kennedy terminated Operation Zapata just hours before the Cuban exiles at the Bay of Pigs were about to be massacred.

From April 17 through April 20, a pitifully small band of Cuban patriots had battled Fidel Castro's army.

The United States Air Force had bombed Cuban airfields. Sitting offshore aboard the aircraft carrier USS *Essex* were thousands of Marines eager to jump in and help the exiles.

The gun was cocked. But the trigger was never pulled.

John Kennedy froze. He realized that even if the Marines aboard the *Essex* were thrown into the fight, he did not have the logistical support necessary to carry the battle all the way to Havana.

The reason he did not have the logistics in place was his intention to hide the fact the US was at war.

The entire premise of Operation Zapata was ludicrous.

On the first day of battle, the US government told the world that the fighting was strictly a local affair between pro and anti-communists on the island of Cuba.

Except no one on the planet believed the lie. How could they? The fingerprints of US personnel were all over the affair.

Did Cuban exiles have their own aircraft carriers? Did they own sophisticated jet planes? Did they have an armada of transport ships loaded with millions of dollars in military equipment?

One week before the invasion, Radio Moscow announced it was coming. Everyone at the United Nations knew it was coming.

United Nations Ambassador Adlai Stevenson was forced to tell a bald-faced lie. "We are not involved, and we will not intervene," he intoned.

On the day of the landings, John Kennedy told the world: "I have emphasized this before. This is a struggle of Cuban patriots against a Cuban dictator. While we could not be expected to hide our sympathies, we made it repeatedly clear that the armed forces of this country would not intervene in any way."

A more oleaginous statement never left the lips of a world leader in recent memory.

Kennedy had asked the world to make a choice: "Who are you going to believe? Me? Or your own lying eyes?"

Kennedy was forced to make a deal with the Cuban government. If they restrained themselves from slaughtering the surviving exiles, he would call off the Marines.

It was a deal Castro was happy to make.

Now he had hostages who could later be traded for American goods.

Castro had fought the all-mighty United States, and he had won. His international prestige soared.

John Kennedy's reputation plummeted.

Kennedy said the fiasco was entirely his fault. This statement was at least halfway Churchillian.

But now the entire world knew Kennedy was a punk, a ninety-eight-pound weakling who would not fight back if sand were kicked in his face.

Men such as Mao Tse-tung, Nikita Khrushchev, and Ho Chi Minh were watching.

These were men who were survivors of a world where politics was a blood sport and the losers ended up dead. They were cold-eyed serious men who would not think twice about kicking sand in the face of a weakling.

In six weeks hence, John Kennedy was going to meet Nikita Khrushchev in Vienna for a summit.

He could not call it off. Such a move would radiate weakness.

"Why the hell didn't I listen to Stuart!" He spoke the sentence out loud, but there was no one there to respond.

Kennedy had lost all faith in the elites who had counseled him to take down Castro with this half-assed invasion.

He was exceptionally mad at one individual. CIA Director Allen Dulles. He was the chief architect of Operation Zapata.

Dulles told Kennedy, "I have done this before, Mr. President. I know what I am doing."

In 1953, the CIA orchestrated the removal of Prime Minister Mohammad Mosaddegh from power in Iran.

A year later, the CIA got rid of President Jacobo Arbenz of Guatemala.

Each man was suspected of having communist sympathies. Each man was violently removed from power.

Dulles was full of himself. He did not think Castro's fate would be any different.

Dulles was telling his friends the failure of Operation Zapata lay at Kennedy's feet. He accused Kennedy of pusillanimous indecision at the exact moment when courage was needed.

Kennedy hated Dulles even more because he knew the criticism was partially correct.

Kennedy vowed to get rid of Dulles.

There was one man intimately involved in this disaster Kennedy could not get rid of under any circumstances—Joseph Patrick Kennedy Sr.

Chapter 30

While John Kennedy was patrolling the Rose Garden cursing his own indecisiveness, his brother was a mile away holding sway at a meeting of prosecutors and FBI men.

Robert Kennedy was holding court at the US Justice Department. Fifty men were listening to the young attorney general map out a plan of action.

Robert Kennedy's war plan did not suffer from indecision. Just the opposite. He was determined to fight and win this war.

Kennedy told the assemblage the US Government was going to take down the Mob—in all fifty states.

He intended to accomplish this feat in record time. He wanted the Mob on its knees by the time his brother ran for reelection in 1964.

Normally such a Herculean task would take ten years. The US justice system is not known for its alacrity.

Kennedy wanted immediate action. He hired two chief lieutenants to help run the operation—Byron White and Nicholas Katzenbach.

Under their guidance, twenty prosecutors were assigned just one function. They were to spend all their time on putting mobsters behind bars.

The US Justice Department had enough prosecutors to handle all the non-Mob-related cases that came under its jurisdiction.

These poor souls became Robert Kennedy's orphans. He assigned subordinates to handle management of cases not connected to the Mafia.

Robert Kennedy was only interested in crushing La Cosa Nostra.

The men in the Mob Squad became the golden boys of the Justice Department.

Robert Kennedy did not invite J. Edgar Hoover to this meeting. He did not want Hoover's scowling countenance putting a damper on the proceedings.

Hoover was both relieved and enraged he had been excluded. He was relieved because he could not stomach being in the same room with a pipsqueak authoritarian, which was how he viewed Robert Kennedy.

He was enraged because a meeting of this importance should have commanded his presence.

Hoover sent thirty FBI men to monitor the meeting. He wanted to know every detail. Some of these men carried hidden tape recorders.

Kennedy welcomed their presence. These were the men who would have to do the leg work and find evidence his prosecutors would need in a court of law.

Kennedy felt he could bond with these men. But not if Hoover's towering personality interjected itself in the bonding process.

Kennedy took immediate command of the room. "We have a cancer in our society, and until this day it has been allowed to fester," he said. "The Mob does its business with impunity. It kills with impunity. It corrupts law enforcement and the courts wherever its malignant roots are allowed to grow and flourish. We cannot rely on witnesses and informants as our chief law enforcement tool. The Mob knows how to intimidate, to bribe, and to silence anyone it perceives as a threat. We are going to wiretap these bastards day and night. We will convict them by using their own words against them. We are going to shadow them. And we will not be discreet. I want these bums to know we are watching them twenty-four-seven. For too long this nation has had a live-and-let-live attitude toward the Mob. I am announcing the end of this practice. If anyone in this room believes differently, now is the time to state your case. I only want true believers."

No one spoke up.

"You gentlemen who work for Mr. Hoover, you are the bone and sinew of this operation. Everything relies on you. This country has a constitution, and that document states you cannot deprive a man of his life and liberty without real evidence. We don't want to shred the Constitution. We want to put these men behind bars using evidence that will withstand judicial scrutiny. I need you men to get inside the homes, the nightclubs, the fraternal organizations that these criminals occupy and get that evidence. If you have to bend a few rules, know this: I will have your back!"

Kennedy had won the day. The men left the meeting with a real sense of purpose. They now had a mission in life, a campaign they could one day proudly tell their grandchildren about.

J. Edgar Hoover immediately listened to the concealed tapes his men had carried into the meeting.

What he heard disturbed him.

His men were clapping for Robert Kennedy. His men were swearing their loyalty to a personage not named J. Edgar Hoover.

Until this day Hoover was the only sun in the universe that was the FBI. He could not stomach two suns pouring rays down on the same planet.

He was trapped. And he hated that fact.

Hoover had to tread carefully. The Kennedy clan could destroy Hoover just as easily as he could destroy the clan.

Hoover was a homosexual at a time in America when that fact was considered a moral failing.

Hoover's relationship with Clyde Tolson was well known in official circles. Amazingly, the establishment kept quiet about the scandal. The American people had no idea.

For years Hoover had told reporters, "I am married to the FBI."

Reporters did not believe it, but Hoover's status as a bona fide American hero saved his skin.

Hoover had created a cult of personality around the glorious FBI and its reputation of incorruptibility.

Hoover's men did not take bribes. They did not succumb to the siren song of dubious women. They were the embodiment of red, white, and blue.

By the 1950s, Hoover's army of Boy Scouts was revered by millions of Americans. They even had their own television show, beginning in 1965, starring Efrem Zimbalist Jr.

No one wanted to rain on Hoover's parade.

Except polite society did not reckon on the Mob's ability to use Hoover's homosexuality against him.

For decades, Hoover denied organized crime existed. This was no accident.

Hoover made a devil's bargain with the Mob—"I will leave you alone if you leave me alone."

Organized crime figures had newspapermen on their payroll. They could have blown Hoover out of the water had they chosen to do so.

With Hoover at the helm, crime bosses only had to fear local police agencies. This threat was miniscule compared to the potential threat of the FBI.

The status quo lasted through the administrations of Roosevelt, Truman, and Eisenhower.

Now the Kennedys were in town.

The Mob regarded John Kennedy as an irritant. But Robert Kennedy was a mortal threat.

Previous attorneys general had been obsequious in Hoover's presence.

Robert Kennedy was exactly the opposite. He loved ordering Hoover around and telling the FBI director what to do morning, noon, and night.

Robert Kennedy told Hoover, "We are going after the Mob, and you better get on board."

Hoover would do anything not to lose his job. He acquiesced.

There was one more American personality Robert Kennedy wanted to bring down.

Technically he was not a Mob boss. He was a union boss.

His name was James Riddle Hoffa, president of the powerful Teamsters.

Kennedy had tangled with Hoffa between 1957 and 1959. He dragged Hoffa before the Rackets Committee and proceeded to humiliate him.

Kennedy knew that Hoffa was greenlighting money from the Teamster pension fund toward Mob interests.

There was no RICO (Racketeering Influenced and Corrupt Organizations) Act in the 1950s.

Proving Hoffa was guilty of embezzlement was difficult. The books had either been destroyed or manipulated to hide the malfeasance.

Robert Kennedy was so determined to win this fight he created a "Get Hoffa" squad inside the US Justice Department.

The Kennedy boys had in the space of three months acquired two monumentally powerful enemies—the Teamsters and the Mafia.

Neither man seemed to understand the lengths to which these entities would go in an effort at self-preservation.

Chapter 31

It was a chastised and weakened president who met with Nikita Khrushchev on June 4, 1961 in Vienna, Austria.

The Bay of Pigs disaster was only six weeks old. The event had ruined Kennedy's introduction to the world.

Nikita Khrushchev was a short man with unique survival skills. He had survived thirty years of Joseph Stalin's murderous term as dictator of the Union of Soviet Socialist Republics.

Nearly every man who served in close proximity to Stalin ended up dead or in prison.

Stalin may have allowed Khrushchev to live because of the role he played in the defense of Stalingrad in 1942 and 1943.

Adolph Hitler wanted the city because it was named after the leader of the USSR. Stalingrad in Russian meant, "Stalin City."

For this exact reason, Stalin was prepared to sacrifice any number of men to win the battle. He put Khrushchev in charge. It was the bloodiest and most consequential battle of WWII.

Khrushchev hurled men in front of German machineguns until the enemy ran out of bullets. Stalin did not care. The city must be saved at all costs.

The Germans surrendered in February of 1943.

The victory provided Khrushchev with just enough status to allow him to survive until March of 1953. That was the month and the year that the Grim Reaper took away Joe Stalin.

Khrushchev manipulated his way through Russian politics until he became general secretary in 1955.

A year later, he denounced Stalin. It was a bold step that allowed him to be seen as his own man.

Khrushchev had enormous respect for Dwight Eisenhower. No one could question his manhood. He liberated half of Europe.

Kennedy on the other hand was a spoiled child of a multimillionaire capitalist. What had he ever done besides getting his torpedo boat cut in half?

The entire world watched the Bay of Pigs unfold in real time thanks to television.

Khrushchev chuckled as John Kennedy lied and vacillated. Khrushchev, of course, had no problem with a world leader prevaricating. They all did it.

It was the vacillation that drew his ardent scrutiny.

It certainly appeared that John Kennedy was a pushover, a man with a banana for a spine.

Khrushchev was going to use the Vienna Summit as a lab experiment on leadership.

John Kennedy went to Vienna hoping he could reverse his image as a man out of his depth.

The US Ambassador to Moscow was a man named Llewellyn E. Thompson. Thompson warned Kennedy that Khrushchev "was a true apostle of communism."

He added that Khrushchev cared about one thing—the worldwide expansion of Marxism-Leninism.

Kennedy was desperate for a successful summit. If Khrushchev smelled the desperation, he would strike like a rattlesnake.

The two men discussed three subjects: West Berlin, Laos, and Cuba.

Khrushchev told Kennedy he was going to sign a separate treaty with the German Democratic Republic. This ridiculous euphemism was the moniker communists gave to the country known to the West as East Germany.

Beginning in 1945, four countries governed Germany: Russia, France, England, and the United States.

Nothing substantial was supposed to happen in Germany unless all four powers signed off on a solution.

Khrushchev was desperate to change this paradigm.

There existed in this arrangement a huge embarrassment that Russia could no longer abide.

The city of Berlin existed one hundred miles inside the Soviet sector. Half of the city was under totalitarian control. The other half was free.

East German citizens were fleeing their country by the tens of thousands. All they had to do was walk past the barriers and enter West Berlin. From there they could go anywhere they wanted.

They wanted freedom. No one went in the opposite direction.

East German leader Walter Ulbricht told the Russians his country would be empty in fifteen years.

This rejection of communism was excruciating to watch.

Khrushchev said it was time to unify the city. Kennedy told him that was not on the table.

Khrushchev knew if he could not convince Kennedy to pull out of West Berlin, then he was going to have to build a wall and fence in all those seeking a life in the West.

That day was fast approaching. Could he get away with it? He was not going to try until he had talked to Kennedy eyeball to eyeball.

The tiny country of Laos was also discussed. Communist Pathet Lao troops were in active combat against the pro-American government.

Khrushchev regarded the government as illegitimate because it was mainly a creation of the CIA.

Kennedy asked if Khrushchev was open to a ceasefire and perhaps a declaration of neutrality.

Khrushchev regarded the American offer of neutrality as a sellout, and it indicated Kennedy did not want to commit troops to an American ally.

Good to know.

When the subject of Cuba came up, Khrushchev really turned into a bully. He hammered the young president on this international violation of sovereignty.

He told Kennedy America's pronouncements about what had happened at the Bay of Pigs were taken seriously by absolutely no one at the United Nations.

Khrushchev wanted assurances this incipient communist state would not be attacked again.

A different president would have told Khrushchev that under the Monroe Doctrine, what happened in the Western Hemisphere was "not Russia's business."

Truman would have said that. So would have Eisenhower.

Kennedy waffled. He was ambiguous about what lay ahead for Cuba.

Khrushchev took notice. The summit concluded without solid agreements on any of the subjects discussed.

World leaders deemed the summit neither a failure nor a success.

John Kennedy would later tell *New York Times* reporter Scotty Reston, "He (Khrushchev) really beat me up."

The summit did have consequences. It convinced Khrushchev that John Kennedy could be pushed around. If Kennedy were faced with a fait accompli, he would back down and accept it.

Up until the summit, Nikita Khrushchev was undecided about placing nuclear weapons on Cuban soil.

After the summit, he knew he could get away with it.

Chapter 32

In April of 1961, Sam Giancana was getting an earful.

The biggest names in organized crime were burning up the telephone lines complaining about FBI surveillance in or near their homes and businesses.

New York had five families. These crime entities were the children of Charles "Lucky" Luciano. In 1931, after he masterminded the murders of two old-time Sicilian warlords, Luciano decided to modernize the syndicates.

Luciano wanted no more crime emperors lording over all the other members of La Cosa Nostra.

He created a commission, a board of directors. The leading members of the commission were the heads of the Bonanno, Colombo, Gambino, Genovese, and Lucchese crime families.

The goal of the commission was to prevent internecine warfare. No murders could be committed without the permission of the board of directors.

Territorial disputes were negotiated instead of gangsters going to war.

Sam Giancana might be seven hundred miles away, but he was still answerable to the commission.

Giancana was spending an inordinate amount of time talking on a phone at Stubby's coffee shop, which was three blocks from his house.

Giancana was not stupid enough to discuss Mob business using his home telephone.

Giancana was hearing from the top men—Joe Profaci, Joe Magliocco, Carlo Gambino, Vito Genovese, Joe Colombo, John

Roselli, Santo Trafficante Jr., Joe Bonanno, and of course, Carlos Marcello.

The complaints were all the same. Where was this deal you made with Joe Kennedy?

Instead of a lovefest, the Kennedys were going after the Mob likes wolves.

Men from the FBI were shadowing them everywhere they went. Subpoenas were showing up at their places of business. Underlings were being dragged downtown for interrogations.

Mob leaders were spending a fortune hiring electronic experts to track down bugs.

Giancana was stunned by the Kennedy family's attitude toward the mobs. He had looked Joe Kennedy in the eye when the quid pro quo was discussed.

There was no misunderstanding. Joe Kennedy's refusal to rein in his two sons appeared to be a deliberate in-your-face betrayal.

Giancana could not dismiss the howls and baying of his compatriots. His credibility and his life were on the line.

Robert Kennedy had been attorney general less than three months, and he was turning into a hurricane of destruction.

The apex of the government's crackdown occurred on April 4, 1961. Robert Kennedy could not have picked a more dangerous and vindictive victim.

Carlos Marcello was born Calogero Minacore on February 6, 1910, in Tunis, French Tunisia.

His parents were Giuseppe and Luigia Minacore. In 1911, the family moved to Jefferson Parrish, Louisiana. Guiseppe got a job at a sugar plantation.

The plantation's overseer was also named Minacore. To avoid confusion, Giuseppe changed his name to Marcello.

Giuseppe had eight children. All that breeding must have worn out the parents, because they did not supervise their eldest son.

Carlos became a gang leader in his midteens. He and his followers committed so many armed robberies the newspapers in New Orleans decided to give him a moniker. They called Marcello "Fagin," the deplorable character from the novel *Oliver Twist*.

In 1929, Marcello was convicted of robbery and sentenced to nine years in prison. He served five.

In 1936, he married girlfriend Jacqueline Todaro. They would eventually have four children.

In 1938, Marcello was caught smuggling and then selling twenty-three pounds of marijuana. He was looking at some serious prison time, but money placed in the right political hands ended that threat. He served four months.

Marcello decided a change of scenery was appropriate. He sojourned to New York where he befriended gangsters Frank Costello and Meyer Lansky.

Costello and Lansky decided to take advantage of Marcello's Louisiana roots. The trio started skimming money from casinos in the New Orleans area.

Costello made a living selling slot machines. He and Marcello convinced casino owners their product was superior to all others.

A casino owner who did not agree could count on a severe beating.

During WWII, the government lost interest in domestic gangsters and concentrated on killing gangsters overseas.

Marcello used this hiatus to consolidate his position in the hierarchy of crime in Louisiana.

In 1947, Marcello was in charge of all illegal gambling in the state.

The New York Commission named him a godfather, and this title protected him from the threat of up and coming gangsters.

With power comes publicity. State and federal authorities now had Marcello on their radar.

In 1951, Marcello was called before the Kefauver Committee looking into organized crime nationwide.

Marcello would give the committee members nothing of value. He pleaded the Fifth Amendment 152 times.

The committee labeled Marcello "one of the worst criminals in the country." Marcello regarded the insult as an encomium.

Eight years later, Marcello was again summoned in front of a high-powered political committee investigating organized crime.

This was the McClellan Committee. Marcello met Senator John Kennedy and his brother Robert Kennedy for the first time.

Marcello once again parroted the phrase, "I am exercising my Fifth Amendment rights, and I refuse to answer that question."

Robert Kennedy grew tired of hearing those words. He began to get snarky with Marcello, baiting him, trying to humiliate him.

It was all for naught. Marcello did not crack.

But Marcello did not forget, nor did he forgive, the treatment he received from the Kennedy boys.

A year later, John Kennedy was elected president of the United States. Three months after the election, Robert Kennedy became attorney general.

Sam Giancana told Marcello not to worry. "I put Joe Kennedy's kid in the White House," he told Marcello. "He owes me big time."

That is why the events of April 4, 1961, came as a shock to both Giancana and Marcello. Marcello was not born in the United States. He was subject to deportation.

He was periodically summoned to an immigration office to discuss his status. His 1938 conviction for marijuana hung over his head like a sword of Damocles.

The government kept trying to deport him. Just one problem. No other nation on the planet agreed to take him.

By law, the government could not deport a person unless a foreign power was officially on board with an acceptance letter.

Marcello's odious record acted as a wall of security. No one wanted him.

Robert Kennedy believed he had discovered a loophole.

Kennedy had heard Marcello was in possession of a phony birth certificate from Guatemala. Kennedy decided he would simply regard the document as authentic.

Marcello walked into a New Orleans immigration office for what he believed would be a routine interview. He could not have been more wrong.

Waiting for Marcello were four federal officers, all of whom had received their orders directly from Robert Kennedy. "Pick him up and then dump him."

Kennedy told the agents to place Marcello on a government plane. He would be the only civilian on the flight.

The CIA had a jungle airstrip in the heart of Guatemala. Kennedy did not ask the government of Guatemala for permission.

The plane landed. Marcello was grabbed by his coat and tossed off the aircraft.

"Robert Kennedy sends his regards," one agent told the fuming godfather of Louisiana.

Marcello was left in the jungle with no money, no supplies, and no support system of any kind.

One could deduce that Robert Kennedy did not care if Marcello lived or died.

No judge would have sanctioned Kennedy's methodology for the deportation of Marcello. That was why Kennedy did not ask.

Marcello had to navigate through a jungle thick with vines and occupied by venomous snakes and spiders the size of dinner plates.

It took two months for Marcello to get back into the United States.

He was a changed man.

He did not care that John and Robert Kennedy were the two most powerful men in America. He was going to make them pay.

In July of 1961, Sam Giancana was sitting in Stubby's listening on a telephone to an enraged man.

Carlos Marcello wanted payback. He wanted it now.

The Kennedy boys might be untouchable. The father was not.

Marcello knew that Joe Kennedy had business interests in Chicago. He visited the city quite frequently. "I want you to kidnap that son of a bitch, take him to a warehouse, and work him over. It will be okay with me if he never walks again!"

Giancana had no intentions of doing anything of the kind. But he had to placate Marcello. "Listen, Carlos. We cannot manhandle the father of the man who is president of the United States. The heat on us all would be unbelievable."

"Sam, if you don't have the balls to do something about this, I'll handle it!"

Giancana could not allow Marcello to engage in a vendetta against the most powerful political family in America. At the same time, he could not allow the insult to Marcello to go unanswered.

"Carlos, listen, let's try one more stab at negotiation. I know Joe Kennedy. It is entirely possible he never told his sons about our deal. Let me have one more go at it."

"You want to get Joe Kennedy's attention? Let me send the Battering Ram over to talk to him."

The Battering Ram was a nickname given to Marcello's chief enforcer, a man named Vincent Carsini.

Carsini was six feet, five inches tall. He could lift the front end of a car. Carsini had killed four men. Not with a gun, but by picking them up and snapping their necks.

Carsini was a legend in the Mafia. No one wanted to see him coming through a door.

It took Giancana a full hour to calm down Marcello. He extracted from Marcello a promise not to engage in unilateral action.

Marcello said he would wait. He also told Giancana the clock was running.

Giancana hung up the telephone. He mused about his problem. How does one deal with a man like Joe Kennedy?

Kennedy had power and money. Tons of money. The kind of finances that would allow him to fund a private army.

Giancana decided that sending a heavy to talk to Joe Kennedy would be futile. Even dangerous.

This was a job for a diplomat. A man who could navigate in the upper crust society that Joe Kennedy inhabited.

Giancana knew a Chicago lawyer whose blood was so blue it ran all the way back to the *Mayflower*.

Arthur Jackson Burnell had the social status that would allow him to pick up a telephone and get Joe Kennedy to pick up on the other end of the line.

Giancana decided he would put Jackson on retainer. That would shield him from revealing any information as lawyer/client conversations were protected.

This would allow Giancana to tell Burnell about the deal he had with Joe Kennedy.

Burnell might be shocked by the details, but with a fifty-thousand dollar retainer, Giancana was confident Burnell would accept the assignment.

Giancana prayed Burnell could convince Kennedy to call off the harassment.

If he failed, Marcello would take draconian action, and Giancana would have to go along for the ride.

Chapter 33

Two CIA men sat in their government-issued blue Pontiac right outside Sam Giancana's house in Oak Park, Illinois.

They were waiting for someone to open the door and leave. That person was American singer Phyllis McGuire.

Giancana's wife, Angeline, was out of town. Normally this was a green light for Giancana to see his girlfriends.

Sometimes the overnight guest was Judith Campbell.

This night it was McGuire.

The CIA men did not want to embarrass McGuire, so they remained unseen until she got inside her Cadillac and drove away.

The driver of the Pontiac looked at his partner. "Let's go."

The two men walked up to Giancana's front door on a Monday morning in August of 1961.

Giancana heard a knock. Thinking McGuire had forgotten something, he opened the door without first checking a window to see who was there.

Giancana opened the door and scowled. These had to be cops.

"Good morning, Mr. Giancana. My name is Woodrow Spencer. This is my partner, Tom Greenwood. May we come in?"

"Not until you tell me who the hell you work for."

"Certainly, Mr. Giancana."

Spencer pulled out a wallet. Greenwood was a second slower.

Giancana grabbed both wallets. He stared hard. There were big red letters that announced the holders worked for the Central Intelligence Agency.

"Spooks?" Giancana had not seen this coming.

"We prefer the word agents," Spencer said. "May we come in?"

Giancana stepped outside his door and looked north and south. He wanted to make certain there were no hidden figures waiting for a summons to storm the house.

"Come on inside, boys. Care for some coffee?"

"We would love some, thank you."

The three men made meaningless small talk until the coffee had been made and distributed. Giancana bade them to sit down at his kitchen table.

"You know, this is not the first time someone from your agency has contacted me," Giancana said.

"We know," Spencer replied.

Giancana took a large gulp and then put his cup down. "Back in the spring of 1960, you guys asked for my help. You said Castro was a commie and we had to get rid of him."

"I have been informed of that meeting," Spencer retorted.

"Yeah, you boys were all hot and bothered to get Castro, and then you stopped calling me. What happened?"

This time Greenwood answered. "We, I mean the government, developed an alternative plan that did not involve members of your profession."

"That alternative plan wouldn't happen to be the Bay of Pigs, would it?"

Spencer and Greenwood looked at each other. Neither man was eager to confirm Giancana's question. The Bay of Pigs fiasco was a huge embarrassment to the CIA.

"Let's just say that getting rid of Castro is an ongoing process and there will be ups and downs." Greenwood put the softest interpretation of the disaster on the table for Giancana.

Giancana chuckled. "Well, I would say that right now you boys are in the down mode."

Spencer then again took control of the conversation. "Be that as it may, we are here once again to see if we can reconstitute our previous relationship."

"Help me out here, boys. All you had to do was put twenty thousand Marines on the beach and Castro would be dead or in exile. What happened? Why the cold feet?"

Neither man wanted to touch that question with a ten-foot pole. A truthful answer would entail a scathing indictment of the president of the United States. These two bureaucrats were not about to go there.

"We are not here to dissect previous actions. We are here to see if you want to help your country." Spencer put his palms open on the table in a welcoming gesture.

"Then I will ask the same question I asked a year ago. What's in it for us?"

"I cannot tell you what actions the government intends to take to eliminate this threat. Just use your imagination. But if you and your friends get the job done before we do, the United States will be very grateful."

Giancana leaned into both men's faces. "Gratitude doesn't pay any bills. Again, what is in this for us?"

It was Spencer who answered. "Mr. Giancana, when Castro is gone, there will be considerable unrest in Cuba. The United Nations will insist on getting involved. America will be called upon to provide security while the political factions negotiate a peace. If we are in charge of security, it means we will be calling the shots. I have been authorized to tell you that under these circumstances you and your associates may reopen your stolen casinos and operate them unimpeded."

This was the answer Giancana was looking for when he posed the question.

The Mob lost millions of dollars in revenue when Castro seized power. The Havana casino business was a license to print money. Getting those casinos back and running was the Holy Grail of top gangsters everywhere in the United States.

Giancana wanted to find out if he could extract any other concessions. "What else?"

"You can have your brothels back."

This was no small deal. Selling sex was every bit as profitable as gambling.

"Is that it?"

Enough was enough. Greenwood stood up. "Mr. Giancana, we have offered you all we intend to give. If you use Cuba to bring drugs into the United States, we will come after you."

"You can't fault a man for asking, can you?"

Neither agent laughed. Giancana had one more question. "Who is footing the bill for this operation?"

Spencer supplied the answer. "For obvious reasons, there will be nothing in writing. You and your associates can ask for money, and if we believe the request is warranted, cash will be provided. We won't be stingy, but all requests have to be job-related."

"If we kill Castro, how do we know you will keep your word?"

"You won't know. You will have no guarantees. You take this offer on faith or you don't take it at all."

Giancana pondered if he should explain his question about possible double-dealing by the government. He had a deal with Joe Kennedy that greatly benefited his son. Yet the government was coming after the Mob harder now than it ever had before.

Representatives of the same political family were looking for another huge favor. Giancana knew he would have to bring Marcello and Trafficante into this conspiracy.

Marcello was certain to say, "Are you crazy? You want to trust these people again?"

Trafficante was sure to be equally dubious. But his participation was mandatory. It was he who had the contacts in Cuba to carry out an assassination.

Giancana's reputation could not survive another betrayal by the government. Death by Mob gunfire was a certainty if the Kennedy boys played him false for a second time.

Giancana decided against telling these two CIA bureaucrats about the deal he had with Joe Kennedy. They were certain to run this information back to their superiors, and then all hell would break out.

Now the proposed meeting between his lawyer Burnell and Joe Kennedy took on maximum importance.

Burnell would have to extract from Kennedy an absolute guarantee that the US government would stand down from Mob prosecutions. Robert Kennedy was the problem. And Joe Kennedy controlled his third son lock, stock, and barrel.

If all went according to plan, Castro would be dead, and the Mob would regain Shangri La.

Giancana shuddered to think what a different scenario would bring. "Okay, boys, I will see what we can do to help us all with our mutual problem."

All three men rose at the same time. They shook hands, and Giancana walked them toward his front door.

Spencer had one more piece of business. He handed Giancana a card.

"If you need anything, call this number. Below this number is a code word. Just utter the word one time and hang up. Do not say anything else. Someone will contact you in person."

Giancana opened his door. "Gentlemen, I feel compelled to say just one more thing."

"Of course, Mr. Giancana."

He stopped smiling, and his countenance looked hard and menacing. "If you knife us in the back, do not assume for one minute we will just roll over and take it."

The two agents smiled and walked back to their car.

Each man was thinking the same thing: *Who is this guy that he thinks he can threaten the government of the United States?*

Chapter 34

The spring and summer of 1961 were alive with clandestine activities.

Nikita Khrushchev told East German leader Walter Ulbricht, "Kennedy is a weakling. He is nothing like Eisenhower. We need to take advantage of this fact."

First and critical on Ulbricht's wish list was stopping the flow of East Germans to the West.

Four party access to all four military occupation zones in Germany had been in effect since 1945.

This reality was driving the Russians crazy. They wanted the world to believe that communism produced paradise. The world instead watched as people walked, ran, or crawled to get away from Marxism.

When Truman was in the White House, even Joe Stalin curbed his ambitions. Truman dropped an atomic bomb not once but twice. Stalin decided not to poke this bear. At least in the European theater.

Eisenhower was equally threatening to the Russians. His army knocked the pants off Hitler's best troops. Eisenhower certainly would not hesitate to go nuclear if provoked.

The current president of the United States was a Harvard playboy. He did have an honorable war record, but those medals were given because he survived a calamity of his own making.

Two events convinced Khrushchev he could roll Kennedy. The Bay of Pigs was one. Kennedy's behavior and demeanor at the Vienna Summit was another.

Khrushchev did not know that Kennedy spent the entire Vienna Summit wondering how his father would view his performance.

Joe Kennedy had ripped his son a new one over the Bay of Pigs. That verbal lashing hung heavily over Kennedy in Vienna.

Every decision John Kennedy made in 1961 had to pass muster with the patriarch. It was a crippling handicap.

Ulbricht told Khrushchev, "We need to build a wall. We need to do it now!"

Prior to the Vienna Summit, Khrushchev would have said no.

After Vienna, Khrushchev gave Ulbricht the green light.

On August 13, 1961, Ulbricht gave written orders authorizing the construction of what would become known as the Berlin Wall.

The very next day troops and barbed wire showed up at the crossing point between East and West Berlin.

The world media descended on Germany.

Desperate East Germans saw the writing on the wall. Procrastination meant a life behind bars.

Some ran for the border. Some of them were beaten and arrested. Some of them were shot.

American military commanders ordered tanks moved right up against the Berlin border crossing. These same commanders asked John Kennedy for permission to pull down the barbed wire.

The Russians moved tanks into the flash point.

There were days when American and Russian tanks were only fifty yards apart.

The construction of the wall continued.

Would Truman or Eisenhower have pulled down the wall? Such speculation was futile.

Each man was now retired. Kennedy consulted them both. They told him the decision was his alone.

Kennedy decided to let the construction continue.

Khrushchev viewed this decision as further confirmation he could push around the president of the United States. This belief led Khrushchev to make another decision—a decision ten times more significant.

Khrushchev summoned Fidel Castro to Moscow for a face-to-face.

Castro had previously asked Khrushchev to place nuclear weapons on Cuban soil to prevent another Bay of Pigs invasion. Khrushchev had always demurred. Too risky.

The Bay of Pigs, the Vienna Summit, and the Berlin Wall convinced Khrushchev he could now get away with it.

In September 1961, Khrushchev met with his top commanders and told them to start rounding up one hundred tactical nuclear weapons for possible transshipment.

Khrushchev told his underlings to move very slowly so the CIA would not detect anything suspicious.

In 1961, America did not have satellites in outer space. Human intelligence was the lodestar of espionage. This was the CIA's bailiwick.

Working hand in glove with the CIA were the whiz kids and codebreakers inside the NSA.

A prime target of NSA employees was Russian military radio traffic.

In October 1961, a report landed on the desk of Curt Holmes. He read it one time, and then he hurriedly walked out of his office over to Stuart Dunleavy's cubicle. "Stu, would you come over to my office?"

Dunleavy did not ask any questions. He followed Holmes without speaking.

"Close the door, Stu."

Holmes picked up a red folder and handed it to Dunleavy. "Tell me what you think."

The folder held an intelligence report gleaned from radio traffic from the Kremlin to the naval military commander in Sevastopol. The report commanded that Admiral Ivan Gorkin begin preparations for Operation Damascus.

The Kremlin ordered Gorkin to institute the highest security procedures. In two days, Gorkin would be receiving a visit from the number two man in the KGB.

It was the last sentence of the report that caused Dunleavy's eyebrows to march northward. "Make certain that radiation protocols are in place."

Dunleavy looked up from the document, and he saw Holmes nodding his head. "Did you find anything in that report that tickled your fancy, Stu?"

"You and I are in the intelligence business, not the stupid business. The word 'radiation' should be enough to stir the juices in all of us."

"I could not agree more. I am just spitballing here, but what if…"

"What if what?"

"Hear me out. Sevastopol is Russia's main deepwater port. It can handle the world's largest ships. Assuming I was going to send something of great value to a foreign country, I would have to send the cargo out via Sevastopol."

Dunleavy interjected his thoughts. "Something of great value, such as military equipment?"

"Exactly. Except what military equipment would require the instituting of a radiation protocol?"

Dunleavy did not hesitate. "A nuke."

Holmes nodded his head in agreement. "The Russians would not need a deepwater port to move nuclear weapons into Eastern Europe. They would need a deepwater port if—"

Dunleavy stopped Holmes in midsentence. "Cuba."

Holmes again nodded his head. "Right now, this is all speculation. I'll have to bring Frost up to speed. But I want you to jump on this like a chicken on a June bug. Drop whatever you are doing and get on it!"

Dunleavy did not need any prodding. He shot out of Holmes's office, like Jesse Owens at the Berlin Olympics.

He was already trying to concoct a cover story for why his wife would be dining alone tonight.

Chapter 35

Arthur Jackson Burnell stepped out of a taxi at a golf course in Palm Beach Florida.

The date was December 19, 1961.

His flight from Chicago to Florida that day had been pleasant. The weather was beautiful, and Burnell had plenty of time to rehearse his pending comments to the father of the president of the United States.

Sam Giancana had one month earlier strolled into Burnell's plush office, one that was ironically located at the Chicago Merchandise Mart. This was Joe Kennedy's signature real estate possession in the heart of the Windy City.

Burnell was not a criminal attorney. He did not understand why Sam Giancana wanted his services. He agreed to meet with the mobster out of curiosity.

Giancana made small talk with Burnell for the sole purpose of evaluating his demeanor. No question about it. Burnell was a blue blood who had a supercilious disdain for most of humanity.

Burnell did not have any disdain for money. He loved it. It provided him with expensive toys and beautiful mistresses. He needed lots of money to buy his wife's compliance.

Giancana pulled his cigar out of his mouth. "How strong is the law governing attorney/client privilege in this state?"

Burnell did not hesitate. "It is sacrosanct, Mr. Giancana. However, if you or I were to mutually plot to rob a bank, the privilege would disappear. Do you understand the difference?"

"If you and I were not part of a conspiracy, anything I told you would be protected forever. Is that right?"

"That is correct, Mr. Giancana."

Giancana put a briefcase on Burnell's desk. He opened it. Inside was fifty thousand dollars.

"That's only half of what I will pay you if you accept my assignment," Giancana said.

Burnell stared at the money for a full ten seconds. "How can I help you, Mr. Giancana?"

Giancana for the next hour spilled his secrets to a very astonished Arthur Jackson Burnell.

He told Burnell about the deal he struck with Joe Kennedy. He also told Burnell that the mayor of Chicago was fully involved in manufacturing votes for John Kennedy.

The three of them acting in concert made John Kennedy's ascension to the presidency a reality.

Giancana's voice took on a sharp edge when he told Burnell about how the Kennedy boys repaid their benefactors.

"They are treating us like dirt. We are being hounded from New York to San Francisco. It has never been this bad."

"Mr. Giancana. I am a real estate attorney. What do you want me to do?"

"You know Joe Kennedy, don't you?"

"We have met twice socially. We are not close friends. He might not even remember our meeting one another."

"Mr. Burnell, I represent an organization that normally takes care of its own problems. Our methods are not always pleasant."

Giancana let that remark settle in Burnell's brain. "Some of my friends want Joe Kennedy to understand that a deal is a deal, and any backtracking can have serious consequences."

"Mr. Giancana, it sounds like you just made a threat against the father of the president of the United States. If that is the case, I am afraid I am going to have to terminate this meeting."

Giancana stood up. "You don't understand! I am not threatening Joe Kennedy. I am trying to protect him. There are powerful men in this country who want Joe Kennedy roughed up or even killed. Right now, I have those men on a short leash. But I cannot restrain them indefinitely!"

Now Burnell stood up. "What exactly do you want me to do about all this?"

"You and Joe Kennedy come from the same social class. He'll take a phone call from you. He might even meet with you in person."

"Can't you pick up a telephone and call him?"

"Come on, Mr. Burnell. Think! He has his son in the White House! He does not need us anymore. He has tossed us aside like trash!"

"Yes, I understand. Now, you are willing to pay me one hundred thousand dollars to do exactly what? And please be specific."

"I want you to explain to Joe Kennedy that he made a deal, and we expect him to rein in his two sons. We know who runs this country, Mr. Burnell. And it's not John Kennedy."

Burnell turned and sat back down. "That's all you want me to do? Ask him to be nice?"

"Yes, Mr. Burnell. But do it in a way that doesn't leave any ambiguity about noncompliance."

Burnell rubbed his chin. He wanted that one hundred thousand. He had a new girlfriend. She was twenty-two. He wanted to take her to Hawaii, and Mr. Giancana's money could provide for a very pleasant trip.

"I will call Mr. Kennedy. There is no guarantee he will agree to meet."

"You better hope he does. Or I will be asking for that fifty grand back."

Burnell did make the call. And he did get Joe Kennedy on the phone.

Burnell asked the ambassador if he could have fifteen minutes of his time at a date and location of his choosing.

"I am a very busy man, Mr. Burnell. Let's see. Yes. On the nineteenth of December, I will be at my golf course. We can meet briefly between nines."

"I will be there, Mr. Ambassador. And thank you!"

It was close to noon on the nineteenth of December. Burnell was sitting on a veranda. He looked out at the course, and he saw Joe Kennedy reach the last green on his front nine.

He waited for Kennedy and his three friends to finishing putting.

He stood and waved. Joe Kennedy waved back. Burnell saw Kennedy address his friends, and he was probably telling them to take a short break.

Joe Kennedy walked like an aristocrat. Wherever he went he was the dominant personality.

"Mr. Burnell! Nice to see you again! I do recall we have met before."

"And that occasion was an extremely pleasant day for me, Mr. Ambassador."

"As you can see, I am pressed for time, Mr. Burnell. How can I help you?"

Burnell had hoped he could pour on his oily charm before getting down to specifics. No such luck. He was in a minefield, and he had to trod carefully.

"Mr. Ambassador, first, I want to tell you that I and my entire family are great supporters of you and your son. John Kennedy's election generated a celebratory party at my house."

"Yes, thank you."

"Mr. Ambassador, you are probably aware that I am an attorney. Recently a certain party entered my office. This individual is the head of a very powerful concern. This individual claims that you and he entered into a verbal agreement involving the presidential election in the state of Illinois."

Joe Kennedy stopped smiling. "This individual wouldn't happen to be Sam Giancana, would he?"

"I would never disclose that information, Mr. Ambassador. Let us just say that your guess is very perspicacious."

"That's a very fancy word. It means your client is Sam Giancana."

"Without confirming or denying, may I go ahead?"

"You may. Keep in mind I am teeing off in ten minutes."

"My client contends he has heard from several of his associates. These men are concerned that their efforts on your son's behalf have not been rewarded with…respect."

Joe Kennedy debated his next response. He could tell Burnell to go screw himself. He paused and got control of his temper.

Joe Kennedy had put his third son in the Justice Department for one reason—to keep an eye on J. Edgar Hoover.

The elder Kennedy was surprised when his son Robert went after organized crime like he was Wyatt Earp.

Joe Kennedy was fully vested in his son's performance as president. He did not pay attention to the direction the US Justice Department was taking.

First the Bay of Pigs, then Vienna, then the Berlin Wall. It was just one thing after another. He did not have time to spend on Robert.

It suddenly dawned on him that Sam Giancana had a legitimate beef. Joe Kennedy would never admit this in a thousand years, but he had told Giancana, "You'll have a friend in the White House."

Burnell had been kept waiting for a full minute while Joe Kennedy pored through all this in his mind. Burnell was about to explode with anxiety.

Suddenly a small smile crept up on Joe Kennedy's lips. "Tell your client he has nothing to worry about. In one week, the Justice Department will be moving in a different direction."

Burnell let out an audible sigh of relief. "Mr. Ambassador! I cannot thank you enough!"

Burnell stood up and shook Joe Kennedy's hand so hard it hurt. "Mr. Ambassador, I predict you are going to shoot thirty-six on the back nine. Goodbye and thank you again!"

Arthur Burnell was wrong. Joe Kennedy did not par the back nine. In fact, Joe Kennedy never again played a round of golf.

Five minutes after Burnell left the veranda, an aneurysm in Joe Kennedy's brain split in two pieces.

Blood poured into his brainpan.

Kennedy fell to the ground. His face hit the dirt because his hands could not break the fall.

An army of men and women surrounded the stricken aristocrat. An ambulance was summoned. Dozens of phone calls were racing across the country.

Joe Kennedy was dead.

Except he was not dead. He was alive. But just barely.

Five miles away, Rose Kennedy was also playing golf. She and her husband almost never played together.

Rose Kennedy watched as a young man ran at full speed in her direction. She and her friends froze.

Gasping for breath, the messenger said, "Mrs. Kennedy! Your husband has suffered a stroke! He is in the hospital!"

Rose Kennedy stared. "Thank you for the information, young man. You may go."

It was reliably reported that Rose Kennedy finished her round of golf.

It was retaliation for a lifetime of humiliation.

When Rose finally deigned to go to the hospital, a nurse swore she heard this comment from a very composed wife directed at her supine husband: "Why are you still alive?"

Chapter 36

John Kennedy immediately boarded Air Force One and flew to Florida. He consulted with a battery of physicians who were fighting to keep his father alive.

He entered his father's hospital room. For the first time in his life, John Kennedy saw his father in a position of weakness instead of strength.

Kennedy was told the stroke had been a serious cranial event. A normal life was now not possible, assuming he survived.

Publicly the president of the United States presented the expected picture of a man in distress. Privately John Kennedy was rejoicing.

Joe Kennedy had been his sun and moon for four decades. John Kennedy had never once made a decision that was not ratified or dismissed by his father.

John Kennedy did not enjoy his presidency. He knew it was his father's presidency. He was the cardboard man sent out in public to charm the masses while the real decision-making took place in his father's head.

All of that was going to change.

When the three Kennedy boys got together immediately after the news of the stroke had gone over the wires, there was a change of attitude in each of them.

It was unspoken, of course. But all three men felt as if a stone had been excised from each man's shoulders.

The emperor was not dead. He was in a hellish purgatory from which he could never emerge as he was before God's intervention.

John Kennedy was now the unquestioned leader of the entire Kennedy clan.

All of Joe Kennedy's children experienced a feeling of liberation.

No one felt this emotion more intensely than Rose Kennedy.

Her days of pretending she was inside a true Catholic marriage could now come to an end. Joe Kennedy would never again consort with a woman of low virtue.

Equally liberating was the knowledge that Joe Kennedy would receive the best medical care available. Rose would not have to lift one finger to help her husband through his rehabilitation. An army of strangers would handle that tedious task.

On December 20, 1961, Arthur Jackson Burnell was in Chicago. He was pacing his office cursing his luck. He reflected on the last twenty-four hours.

Just one hour after meeting with Joe Kennedy, Jackson was on the telephone with Sam Giancana.

Burnell could not hide his elation. "I believe we have reached an agreement, Mr. Giancana. I will fill you in when I land in Chicago."

The flight from Palm Beach to Illinois had been most enjoyable. Burnell told the stewardess, "Keep the scotch coming."

Burnell sat in Giancana's kitchen and gave him a verbatim report on the Palm Beach meeting. It was the night of the nineteenth of December.

Giancana was pleased.

Burnell could almost smell the sweet Hawaiian air. He envisioned his girlfriend naked under the moonlight on a sandy beach.

The two men were smoking cigars and laughing while the ice tinkled in their glasses.

Suddenly Sam Giancana noticed a news flash on his black and white television set. Programming was interrupted to announce that the father of the president of the United States had suffered a stroke.

No two men anywhere in the United States were more stunned than Sam Giancana and Arthur Jackson Burnell.

"What the hell did you say to him!" Giancana was shouting.

"He was fine when I left him!" Burnell could not process this development.

Giancana slammed his glass on a table. For the next five minutes, neither man spoke. Each listened intently as the newscaster gave what few facts he had.

Giancana arose from his chair. He rubbed his forehead. "Let's give this time to play out. Maybe it's not that bad. I will meet you in your office tomorrow at noon. Understood!"

It was a command not a suggestion.

"Okay, Sam, tomorrow."

An hour later Burnell was explaining to a dejected young female that their trip to Hawaii was on hold.

Burnell slept for maybe half an hour that night. The next morning he met with clients, but he was so distracted he appeared to be high on drugs.

Exactly at noon, Giancana arrived. Burnell closed the door. Giancana did not sit down.

"You are going back to Florida. I want you to camp out in that hospital and find out exactly what kind of condition Joe Kennedy is in. If he is a drooling incompetent, our deal is off!"

Burnell did not argue. Giancana was a Mob boss, and he was not in a happy mood.

Losing a hundred thousand dollars was better than losing a life.

Burnell told his secretary to book him another flight to Florida. She tried to explain he had a lot of clients scheduled for the next two days. She was stunned when her normally composed boss blew his stack.

"I don't give a damn! Do as you are told!"

Twenty-four hours later, Burnell was sitting on a chair outside the intensive care unit. He told Kennedy's attending physician he was a close friend of the family.

"I know you are constrained by medical privacy doctor, but can you tell me anything?"

The doctor was impressed by Burnell's expensive suit and polished bearing. "It is very serious, Mr. Burnell. He may never walk again. He might not ever speak again. He will need close attention for the rest of his life. That's all I can tell you within the bounds of my medical obligation."

Burnell's second flight back to Chicago was nothing like the first. He did, however, consume the same amount of scotch.

Burnell reported to Sam Giancana that Joe Kennedy was no longer relevant.

"So, the Kennedy boys are on their own." Giancana made the remark as much to the ceiling as he did to Burnell.

Burnell was waiting for the other shoe to drop. He was waiting for Giancana to demand the return of his briefcase and its contents.

Giancana knew exactly what Burnell was thinking. "You can keep half the money I gave you, Mr. Burnell. I may need your services in the future. Consider yourself retained!"

Once again it was a command and not a suggestion. Burnell was happy to comply.

Chapter 37

Lyndon Baines Johnson was not a happy man. He had been vice president of the United States for eleven months.

He thought back to that day when he was standing next to John F. Kennedy during the inaugural address. It was a cold January afternoon.

"Ask not what your country can do for you. Ask what you can do for your country."

It was a great line. Ted Sorenson was constantly coming up with sentences that made the speaker rather than the author look like a genius.

Johnson had worked like a dog during the campaign to get the Democratic ticket elected.

He had succeeded. He held Texas for Kennedy.

Joe Kennedy appreciated his efforts.

His two sons had a different opinion of his value.

The very instant the election was over, John and Robert Kennedy turned on poor Lyndon Johnson of Texas.

They did not, of course, do it in public. In front of reporters, Johnson was saluted as a valuable member of the New Frontier.

The knives came out in social settings. Lyndon Johnson was the consummate outsider, the country bumpkin moping around the halls of the coolest fraternity on campus.

The Kennedy crowd and the Johnson crowd were yin and yang.

Kennedy was a Harvard man, and he brought so many Harvard graduates to Washington it was as if the school had picked up its roots and moved to the federal capital.

Johnson had a degree from a college squirreled away in the hill country of Texas. The degree conveyed zero status even in the state of Texas.

Among "the Harvards," as Johnson called them, his schooling was the butt of endless jokes. There was nothing wrong with Johnson's native intelligence. He was just as smart as all those bright young men from Massachusetts.

Society prizes credentials, and it was here that Johnson had nothing to offer.

Johnson's main tormentor was, of course, Robert Kennedy. The attorney general went out of his way to humiliate Johnson.

Robert Kennedy liked to crash uninvited into meetings called by Johnson. He would then bombard Johnson with esoteric questions that few humans could answer. He loved to stand up and abruptly leave in the middle of a Johnson soliloquy.

In the federal government hierarchy, it was Johnson who held the superior office. It mattered not in Camelot.

Robert Kennedy made certain that Johnson was never invited to any event unless protocol mandated his appearance.

Everyone in Washington knew Johnson was an outsider. Johnson knew John Kennedy had to assent to this treatment, or else his brother would not have pursued it.

The Kennedy boys knew what they were doing. They both regarded the isolation of Johnson as smart and necessary.

For six years, John Kennedy had to kowtow to Lyndon Johnson. Kennedy came to the Senate just a few years after Johnson arrived.

Kennedy did not take his job seriously. He pursued women instead of legislative victories.

Johnson was also a world-class womanizer. But he took his job responsibilities very seriously.

Johnson, by force of personality, took two nothing jobs and turned them into real power centers. He did have the full cooperation of Senator Richard B. Russell, but it was his own determination that carried the day.

By 1957, the entire Senate was kowtowing to Lyndon Johnson. It was an extraordinary power grab, and it did not go unnoticed by the press.

The Senate had a reputation for fifty years as "the place where bills go to die."

Johnson changed all that. Under Johnson, the Senate became "Action City."

This reputation chilled the bones of even the strongest men. Give Lyndon an inch and he will take a mile.

The Kennedy boys were determined not to give him an inch. Immediately after the election, Johnson came up with a plan for holding onto his personal power in the Senate.

Johnson visited the Old Bulls and asked if he could have his office back. This was the large imposing office that had a nameplate on the door that read "Senate Majority Leader."

Johnson assumed they would consent. He was wrong.

The Senate regards the separation of powers as the most important constitutional principle in existence.

Johnson was now a member of the executive branch. For him to even think he could run the Senate was outrageous.

Johnson failed to see how ludicrous the idea was because of his lust for power.

The Constitution gave Johnson exactly one job. As vice president, he could cast a vote only if the Senate were stymied fifty votes to fifty votes. In all other matters, Johnson must be no more than a spectator.

John Kennedy had to tell his vice president to "back off" all attempts at returning to power in the Senate.

John Kennedy could muzzle Johnson, but he could not fire him. Under the Constitution, Johnson was duly elected along with the president. To get rid of Johnson, Kennedy would have to call for his impeachment. There was zero chance of that occurring.

John Kennedy knew that Johnson could take an acorn and in no time at all grow it into a mighty oak.

The man had to be watched and controlled.

Johnson knew the power of symbolism. Immediately after the election, he asked John Kennedy to provide him with an office.

In the White House.

Right next to the Oval Office.

He also asked Kennedy if he could move fifty staffers into the White House so they could work hand in glove with the president's staff.

Kennedy, of course, told him no. No president would ever agree to such a request. That Johnson made the argument for side-by-side offices with a straight face demonstrated his obsession with power.

The Kennedy boys decided to marginalize Johnson. His most prominent responsibility involved working with NASA to advance the space program.

They had to give him something to do.

Johnson had no choice but to suck it up. His self-control was tested again and again. He was powerless in a town that recognized power as the only currency worth having.

One insignificant incident encapsulated the distance Johnson had fallen since he became vice president.

It was a rare occasion where he had finagled an invitation to a Washington cocktail party. He went without his wife. She had not been invited.

Johnson snaked around the room looking for someone, anyone, who would turn and recognize him.

Two Kennedy staffers were sipping drinks and leaning against a wall.

Johnson walked up and stood close to them for about thirty seconds. He fully expected they would at least say hello.

They did not.

Johnson turned and walked away.

One of the staffers said to his friend, "Did we just insult the vice president of the United States?"

The other staffer replied, "Fuck him."

Johnson heard the comment. He turned and glared. Then he just lumbered away.

From Mount Olympus to the Valley of the Damned—that was how far Lyndon Johnson had fallen in just eleven months.

Now he had just learned that his one and only ally in the Kennedy clan was neutered. Joe Kennedy could no longer save his skin. He was flat on his back and spitting up on himself.

If John Kennedy decided to drop him from the ticket in 1964, there was nothing and no one to prevent it from happening.

Johnson had no choice but to bide his time.

Life is a crap shoot. Something always comes up.

Chapter 38

Everyone noticed there was a change in John Kennedy's demeanor.

Christmas at the White House was constrained in deference to the calamity that had struck Joe Kennedy.

Two weeks after the stroke, doctors declared that the patriarch would survive the wreckage inside his brain.

The key word was "survive." His quality of life was gone forever.

Following the Christmas holidays, John Kennedy made certain that every medical resource was made available to his father.

Once the medical infrastructure was in place, John Kennedy allowed his new freedom to blossom.

He had a lighter step. His morning greetings were warmer and more personal.

John Kennedy presided over meetings with a new confidence.

His sunnier disposition had one origin. He would never again have to filter a decision through the egomaniacal brain of Joe Kennedy.

He was finally, truly, president of the United States.

Robert Kennedy understood exactly what was happening. He, too, had changed his modus operandi.

Robert Kennedy was now the attorney general of the United States instead of his father's attorney masquerading as the people's attorney.

John and Robert Kennedy could now set their own agendas.

John Kennedy had a new passion.

In 1962, the United States still lagged behind Russia in space technology. The first man to orbit the earth was a Russian, not an American. Yuri Gagarin had electrified the world by rising to the heavens and safely returning in April of 1961.

It was a blow to Kennedy. He wanted the first man in space to be an American. Astronaut Alan Shepard was in the bullpen, but mechanical delays resulted in five postponements. Gagarin just beat him out by weeks.

One month after Gagarin's epic adventure, Shepard made a suborbital flight and safely returned to earth. It was not nearly as spectacular as Gagarin's orbital flight, but Kennedy grabbed at the straw.

He decided to go big.

Standing in front of a joint session of Congress on May 25, 1961, Kennedy said America was going to the moon. In this decade.

It mattered not that the goal was nearly impossible. Kennedy believed the United States could make it happen.

Kennedy was just weeks past the disastrous Bay of Pigs. He needed to change the subject. He succeeded.

His father told him the pivot was brilliant.

Now Kennedy had to back up his big promise. By 1962, America still trailed the Russians.

From 1957 to 1962, Russia kept beating America in the "we did it first" category. First satellite in space. A Russian. First woman in space. A Russian. First spacewalk. A Russian.

Now it was late January 1962. John Kennedy believed the United States was about to take a giant step forward.

Astronaut John Glenn was picked to be the first American to rise above the atmosphere and circle the planet.

His orbital flight had been canceled five times. It usually involved fuel leaks. Leaking fuel could cause a disaster, and Kennedy understood the need for caution.

But Kennedy was chomping at the bit to get Glenn into space. He believed if Glenn's flight were successful, it would mean parity between Russia and the US.

There was another powerful Kennedy in Washington with grand ambitions.

Robert Kennedy wanted to step up his campaign against organized crime. Not that the current campaign was listless.

Kennedy wanted to turbo-charge his investigators and lawyers. Kennedy commanded the heads of the Mafia be put in the dock. Not just the underlings.

He also wanted their lifestyles truncated. Kennedy told his FBI men to walk in lockstep with mobsters.

When Sam Giancana visited a restaurant bathroom, standing next to him was an FBI agent.

A mobster on a golf course might be shadowed by FBI men for the entire eighteen holes.

The government men did not hide their presence. They advertised it.

There was an explosion of wiretapping under Robert Kennedy. Some of it was legal. Some not.

Kennedy was getting results. Prison doors were slamming shut behind a slew of wise guys.

Telephone lines were burning up nationwide.

Mobsters were screaming about the harassment. Not to mention the duplicity.

On one hand, the government was asking the Mob to help the CIA kill Fidel Castro.

The next moment the government was ordering the arrest of these same men.

Complicating everything was the fact Joe Kennedy had never told his sons that he had gotten in bed with mobsters in order to secure electoral victory.

These facts were creating a dilemma that could not go on unresolved. Something had to give.

Sam Giancana and Carlos Marcello were now communicating mainly by using pay telephones. Each man knew their household lines were probably compromised.

When Marcello came back from Guatemala, he was hellbent on shooting one, or both, of the Kennedy boys.

Giancana was the mobster trying to suppress those inclinations. As the months rolled by in 1962, Giancana was losing the argument.

Still there was one huge obstacle. How does one kill a United States president and get away with it?

Giancana told Marcello, "Until we figure that out, we have to sit and wait."

Chapter 39

Stuart Dunleavy loved his job.

It was now July of 1962. He was settled in at the NSA. He was the agency's golden boy because of his relationship with the president.

Curt Holmes also had the same exulted status. Laurence Frost, the man who ran the NSA, had to accommodate this reality. He did not like it.

Holmes and Dunleavy were supervising two projects at the NSA.

One involved Robert Kennedy's request that telephone traffic between gangsters was to be monitored. Not for content. Just for patterns.

The other project involved the Russians and their nuclear weapons. Tracking Russia's nukes was the agency's highest priority.

The NSA and the CIA were not too concerned when the Russians moved their nukes around the interior of the country.

A Russian nuke moving into or close to a port city caused eyebrows to rise inside America's intelligence agencies.

A port city destination might mean the weapons were going to be shipped overseas. This kind of information was deemed the highest priority.

Dunleavy and Holmes back in January told Frost he needed to schedule a meeting with the president.

Holmes's hunch about Sevastopol had proven prescient.

Security around Sevastopol had quadrupled. Not only Russian soldiers but KGB men were pouring into the city.

The CIA ordered ten assets to quietly move out of their current stations in Russia and take up residence in Sevastopol.

Something was moving from the docks to transport ships. This something was heavily shrouded. But the dimensions of the cargo appeared to coincide with the length and width of a Russian mid-range nuclear weapon.

The ships were then tracked minute by minute to their destination. And a great number of ships were stopping in Havana, Cuba.

Russian ships going to Cuba was not unusual. Castro had turned the country into a Soviet ally.

It was expected that the Russians would be handing over tanks, trucks, and ammunition to the Cubans.

Nuclear weapons were a whole different ballgame. John Kennedy knew he could not allow this to happen.

He also knew his behavior in 1961 might have convinced Khrushchev he could get away with a stunt of this magnitude.

The United States had an ace up its sleeve—the Lockheed U-2 spy plane.

The plane was first proposed in 1953. The concept involved building a plane that could fly at seventy thousand feet.

At that height, enemy missiles could not reach the intruder. America had in addition developed cameras that were so sophisticated they could see down from great heights and take accurate photos.

John Kennedy in the spring of 1962 ordered the CIA to start overflying Castro's Cuba.

The U-2 cameras picked up activity that was highly suspicious. Workers were using daylight and nighttime hours to build infrastructure that certainly looked military oriented.

Kennedy desperately needed to know if these were launch pads.

One man Kennedy was no longer consulting was CIA Director Allen Dulles. Kennedy had fired Dulles in November of 1961, one day after he had given Dulles a medal for exemplary service.

This jarring dichotomy left Dulles angry and resentful.

Kennedy was enraged at Dulles and his ilk.

In April of 1961, Kennedy was the new kid in town. His father instructed him to listen to his elders.

Kennedy agreed with Stuart Dunleavy and Curt Holmes that Operation Zapata was fraught with danger and should be abandoned.

Dulles told Kennedy the plan would work.

It was a spectacular failure. Kennedy became a worldwide figure of derision. The bad advice that Dulles and other Washington wise men had provided caused Kennedy to gnash his teeth.

Kennedy also got rid of the number two man and number three man at the CIA. These were Dulles's loyalists named Richard Bissell and Charles Cabell.

In one day, Kennedy had created three powerful establishment enemies. Men with long memories.

Dulles, of course, blamed Kennedy for the Bay of Pigs disaster. He said, "Kennedy did not have the backbone of his predecessor." That man was Dwight Eisenhower.

Under Eisenhower's watchful eye, Dulles had eliminated two communist threats, Mossadegh in Iran and Arbenz in Guatemala.

Each of these CIA operations had moments when it looked like failure was inevitable.

In each case, Dulles saved the day, but only because Eisenhower gave him unqualified support.

Dulles said Kennedy caved under pressure and embarrassed himself as well as the country.

Kennedy now had his own man at the CIA. His name was John McCone.

Lyndon Johnson took judicial notice of the humiliation Kennedy inflicted on Allen Dulles.

Johnson invited Dulles over to his office for a drink. Johnson did not clear the meeting through the White House. Some things are better left unadvertised.

Inside this political milieu, Holmes and Dunleavy were carrying on. Dunleavy knew he was doing something important with his life. He was going after gangsters both domestic and international.

Dunleavy's wife was dying to know what her husband was up to at work, but he could not tell her.

She could tell he was happy. He would come home late, eat a light dinner, have one cocktail, and then attack her like a wolf.

His testosterone rampages were frequent enough for her to know he was not seeing other women.

Arlene Dunleavy was now an insider in the most coveted club in the world—the Kennedy social circle.

She loved Jack Kennedy the statesman. She did not love Jack Kennedy the husband.

Married men fooling around in the Kennedy administration seemed to be ubiquitous.

John Kennedy's indiscretions were common knowledge. Arlene liked Jackie Kennedy, and she felt sorry for her situation.

Arlene Dunleavy was not a woman who would tolerate betrayal. And she was not shy about making that fact known to her husband.

"Don't worry, honey," he would say. "My bad boy days are over."

"They better be, babe," she retorted. "I'm a lifelong member of the NRA."

Chapter 40

The sun beat down on the tanned face of the president of the United States.

John Kennedy was in his element. He was addressing a large crowd at Rice University in Houston, Texas.

The date was October 9, 1962.

Eight months earlier John Glenn had successfully orbited the earth and returned unharmed. This was the mission that had to succeed if John Kennedy wanted to move forward in space.

Glenn's flight turned out to be a harrowing experience. It was cut short. A sensor in Glenn's capsule told ground support that his heat shield might have come loose from the vibration of the launch.

Mission control ordered Glenn to return home after three orbits around the planet. Glenn plummeted to earth while the front of his capsule reached three thousand degrees Fahrenheit.

Had the shield been damaged Glenn would have died a horrible death with a hundred million people watching on television.

John Kennedy would not be in Houston outlining a bold new endeavor. It was the sensor, not the heat shield, that was faulty.

Glenn was given a ticker-tape parade.

Kennedy's call for a moon program radiated through the country like an electric shock.

He was going to Rice University in Houston, Texas, in October to reconfirm his moon speech a year earlier in front of Congress.

He invited Curt Holmes and Stuart Dunleavy to accompany him on Air Force One for the flight to Houston.

Each man was happy to go. Not only was it a profound honor, but the trip would allow them to brief the president on the intelligence they had been gathering for nearly a year.

The news was explosive. So explosive they decided to wait until Kennedy had delivered his speech.

They did not want to depress his mood prior to this important address.

Kennedy basked in the warmth and affection of the crowd. When it was time to go, he bolted up the steps leading to Air Force One.

Holmes and Dunleavy waited for the president to finish all the handshaking that was a requirement of the job.

When it was their turn to grab the flesh of the leader of the free world, they asked if they could see him in private.

He agreed without hesitation. "What's up, boys?"

Holmes was the higher-ranked bureaucrat, so he started off the briefing. "Mr. President, Admiral Frost has given me permission to update you on the extent of Russian activity regarding arms shipments to Cuba. The NSA and the CIA have been tracking the movement of nuclear weapons inside the Soviet Union. We are convinced that atomic warheads and their attendant launch vehicles are in Cuba."

Kennedy was not completely surprised. This was not like the attack on Pearl Harbor, which no one saw coming.

Kennedy had been briefed about the possibility of nuclear arms in Cuba, but always there was a doubt about the veracity of the claim.

Now he was being told there was little or no doubt. Kennedy leaned back in his leather chair, the one with the seal of the president emblazoned on it. "Well, gentlemen, when we get back, we are going to have a lot of work to do."

The president was now just two weeks away from the most dangerous crisis humanity would ever face.

On October 15, 1962, John Kennedy and his national security team known as EXCOMM were looking at pictures supplied by the National Photographic Interpretation Center (NPIC). The photos were captured by U-2 pilots. The spy planes were being used relentlessly in a campaign to nail this issue to the wall.

America had another intelligence vehicle. This was a human asset.

His name was Oleg Penkovsky. He worked for the Russian security agency GRU, but he spied for the United States.

Penkovsky told his American handlers he was 99 percent certain Russia was shipping nukes to Cuba.

By October 17, Kennedy was sure the missiles were there. He alone had the authority to decide how to get rid of them.

Allowing them to stay was not an option.

Kennedy stood up from a long rectangular table. Sitting at the table were fifteen of the most important security members of the government. "Gentlemen, I will want a series of recommendations by noon tomorrow."

He left and strolled despondently back to the Oval Office.

He told his secretary to locate Bobby. The attorney general of the United States did not automatically have a role in a national security issue.

John Kennedy did not care. He wanted his brother at his side for every second of this crisis.

Twenty-four hours later, the recommendations were given to Kennedy in a memo.

Option one: Do nothing. The missiles did not change the balance of power.

Option two: Use only diplomacy and, if necessary, bribery to get the Russians to remove the missiles.

Option three: Consult Castro without telling the Russians. Tell him to get the missiles out or face an invasion.

Option four: A full invasion of the island and the arrest or killing of Fidel Castro.

Option five: Blockade. Nothing goes in or out without a US naval inspection.

The joint chiefs of staff recommended the most brutal of the potential responses: Send in the Marines immediately. Get rid of every communist on the island.

Kennedy asked the chiefs what they thought Khrushchev might do in response. The chiefs said Khrushchev was not crazy. He would just accept it.

"What about West Berlin?" Kennedy asked.

The chiefs again said Khrushchev would bluster but back down.

Kennedy was highly skeptical. Russia could conquer West Berlin in one day.

But not without killing hundreds of American troops.

In 1945, it might have made sense to position an enclave of freedom one hundred miles behind Russian lines. That enclave was the city of West Berlin.

In 1962, that decision looked like a tinderbox that could ignite WWIII.

Kennedy was also operating under severe time constraints. His experts were telling him the missiles could be operational in two weeks.

Complicating matters were Kennedy's 1960 campaign statements that the United States was suffering from a "missile gap" that favored the Russians.

This was blatant mendacity. In 1960, the US had five thousand nuclear weapons and rockets to deliver them.

The Soviet Union had three hundred. The missile gap nonsense was designed solely to make Kennedy look tougher than Nixon.

Once again, John Kennedy was a prisoner of one of his father's brilliant ideas. "Just make stuff up, son. Nobody will check it."

On October 18, Kennedy met with Soviet Minister of Foreign Affairs Andrei Gromyko.

Gromyko was a stone-faced survivor of Joe Stalin's genocidal regime. He learned early on that the Soviet system valued lying above all other human traits.

Communists regarded lying as a moral imperative because the ends always justified the means.

Gromyko told Kennedy that all Russian military aid to Cuba was for "defensive purposes only." There were no nukes in Cuba. Nor would there ever be.

Kennedy constrained himself. He stared at Gromyko like he was a tarantula climbing up his shower wall.

Kennedy dismissed Gromyko without telling him about the U-2 photos he had in his possession.

On October 21, John Kennedy went around the room at an EXCOMM meeting and asked each attendee for a recommendation.

Kennedy was annoyed at the number of experts who favored a full invasion of Cuba. He asked his brother to meet with him alone in the Oval Office.

Bobby Kennedy had a reputation as a reckless and aggressive individual. But at the height of the Cuban Missile Crisis, he was a voice for moderation.

"John, you can't push Khrushchev into a corner." In official Washington, only Bobby referred to the president as John.

"What's your recommendation, Bobby?"

"A blockade. Except we do not call it a blockade. In international law, a blockade is recognized as an act of war. We call it a quarantine instead."

"What's the difference between a blockade and a quarantine?"

"There isn't any. Except the word 'quarantine' has a softer connotation. This could be just the fig leaf we need to give Khrushchev some wiggle room."

Kennedy loved the idea. A quarantine provided Kennedy with the one thing he valued more than any other—time.

Kennedy believed a world facing nuclear annihilation deserved leaders who would explore every other possibility before resorting to the button.

Kennedy told Secretary of Defense Robert McNamara to begin setting up a line of ships surrounding Cuba.

Now he had to write a speech telling every American about the danger they faced.

At 7:00 p.m., on October 22, Kennedy appeared on all three networks. He outlined what his intelligence people had discovered in Cuba.

Then he issued this ultimatum: "It shall be the policy of this nation to regard any nuclear missile launched from Cuba against any nation in the Western Hemisphere as an attack by the Soviet Union on the United States, requiring a full retaliatory response on the Soviet Union."

In the middle of the speech, the US Navy went to DEFCON 3.

In Moscow, Khrushchev was bewildered. He had guessed wrong about John F. Kennedy. Now he had to respond in equal measure. Khrushchev lived in a world where Boy Scouts were eaten alive by predators. Weakness could cost Khrushchev his life.

In 1962, there was no hot line between Moscow and Washington. Kennedy and Khrushchev had to communicate using intermediaries. This was dangerous.

Khrushchev had to make a decision. There were Soviet ships on the high seas heading toward Havana. In twenty-four hours, the leading cargo ship would collide with the US Naval quarantine.

"What orders do I give to the captain? Tell him to run the blockade? Tell him to submit to an inspection? Tell him to turn around?"

A wrong decision could turn a confrontation into a war. Khrushchev had to worry about the men who comprised his top military command.

If they deemed him weak, he could be deposed. Even killed.

In March of 1953, when Stalin died, the head of the Soviet secret police was a man named Lavrentiy Beria. Beria assumed he was going to inherit Stalin's throne.

His reputation for rape and mass murder was so pronounced the Red Army said no.

Khrushchev and a cabal of Red Army generals ambushed Beria and put him in prison. He and five of his acolytes were convicted of treason. Each one was shot in the back of the head.

This all happened in the very recent past. Khrushchev knew he had to keep his military on his side.

And that meant not kowtowing to the Americans.

John Kennedy was not worried about his generals arresting him. He was worried about a Congressional impeachment trial if Cuba turned into an existential threat.

Kennedy and Khrushchev were both in a box. Each man had to walk a tightrope without falling off.

The mythical doomsday clock was ticking. It was five minutes to midnight.

Diplomats in dozens of countries were working overtime, trying to find a way out of this disaster without a war.

In the end, war or peace would be decided by two men. The president of the United States and the general secretary of the communist party of the Union of Soviet Socialist Republics.

All other men were bit players.

Robert Kennedy was a bit player. But it was he who would direct his brother down a road that led to peace instead of war. Kennedy was bombarded with advice from men who regarded themselves as peerless experts.

Most of the advice centered around the concept of "Don't show weakness. Stand your ground.'

Robert Kennedy was always the last man John Kennedy spoke to during the entire crisis. Robert Kennedy repeatedly told his brother, "You have to give Khrushchev something. He cannot simply back down. He has to look his generals in the eye and declare some kind of victory."

John Kennedy was being told by his brain trust that giving Khrushchev anything in return for a missile withdrawal would be a mistake.

But John Kennedy was more and more leaning toward his brother's argument. Kennedy was forced to put himself in Khrushchev's shoes.

Every decision Kennedy made during the crisis was designed to keep the clock running.

He was being whipsawed by men such as Air Force General Curtis LeMay. LeMay was the man who firebombed Japan into submission in 1945.

He was the leader of the "invade now" wing of EXCOMM. LeMay was also speaking ill of Kennedy behind his back. More than a few of his brother officers shared his opinion of Kennedy.

Kennedy knew that Khrushchev was probably facing the same level of enmity from his generals.

The difference was that there was no Constitution in Russia prohibiting the military from taking independent action.

There were four Russian submarines heading for Cuba. They were ordered to get to Cuba without being detected. In order to accomplish this mission, they stayed submerged most of the time.

This also meant they were out of radio contact with Moscow for most of the journey.

There were many close calls during the missile crisis, but the most dangerous moment occurred when one of these submarines encountered a US Navy destroyer.

This would go down in history as Black Saturday. A US destroyer using sonar found submarine B-59. It decided to signal the sub to surface for inspection.

The captain of B-59 was Valentin Grigorievitch Savitsky. Savitsky could only contact Moscow when he was riding the surface of the ocean.

The sub had to surface in order to charge its batteries. During its last sojourn above the water line, Savitsky was told by Moscow that the situation was "extremely grave" and that war could break out at any minute.

A glum Savitsky closed his hatch and resumed his travel to Cuba.

Now Savitsky's radarman was telling him there was an American ship right above him. Seconds later, Savitsky and his men heard explosions. They assumed the explosions were caused by depth charges.

This could only mean that war had been declared.

Except the explosions were not depth charges. They were specially designed signaling devices that looked exactly like hand grenades.

The explosions were not lethal. They were created to signal a sub to come to the surface.

The commander of the US destroyer assumed the Russians would know the difference. The commander was wrong.

Savitsky had one nuclear-tipped torpedo aboard his sub. He wanted to use it to take out the destroyer.

Russian military doctrine mandated that a decision to use a nuclear weapon at sea required the consent of the captain and two lesser officers.

One of Savitsky's officers said go with the torpedo. Savitsky said, "I agree."

The third officer, a man named Vasily Arkhipov, said no.

The stress of the moment was enormous. It took unbelievable courage for Arkhipov to stand up to a superior officer under these conditions.

Perhaps the hand of God was operating inside submarine B-59 that Saturday.

Had a US destroyer been taken out by a nuclear weapon, war would have been inevitable. Nuclear war.

Savitsky brought his submarine to the surface. Only then did he learn the Americans were trying to signal him, not kill him.

The lives of thirty million human beings were saved.

The longer the missile crisis lasted, the greater the danger a mistake would trigger Armageddon.

John Kennedy told his brother, "There is always one son of a bitch who doesn't get the message."

Ten days into the crisis Kennedy had had enough. Nearly all of Kennedy's advisors told him not to swap military assets with Khrushchev in order to bring the crisis to an end.

It would set a bad precedent.

Kennedy believed this line of thinking, if allowed to continue, would guarantee a nuclear war. He decided to send his brother on one last desperate mission to avoid conflict.

Bobby Kennedy drove to the Russian embassy and met with Ambassador Anatoly Dobrynin.

Dobrynin told Kennedy that the US promise not to invade Cuba was insufficient to bring the crisis to an end. "You've got to get those missiles out of Turkey!"

Dobrynin was referring to the nuclear-tipped Jupiter missiles that NATO had stationed on a landmass that bordered the USSR.

Russia's leadership believed the United States was being hypocritical. Why was it okay for NATO to station nuclear weapons on Russia's borders, but the Soviets were not allowed the same privilege in Cuba?

John Kennedy saw the logic in it. So did his brother.

Men such as Curtis LeMay saw the argument as appeasement. He was not alone.

The doomsday clock was at one minute to midnight when Robert Kennedy stood up and addressed Dobrynin.

"Mr. Ambassador, I have been authorized by the president to make one more concession, but only one."

"I am listening, Mr. Kennedy."

"We will take our missiles out of Turkey, but not for six months. In addition, this proviso must be kept secret. If one word leaks out, the deal is off."

"I will take your offer to my superiors in Moscow. Thank you for coming, Mr. Kennedy."

Khrushchev took the deal. He told Castro the missiles were coming back to Russia.

Castro howled like a newborn baby. Khrushchev told his generals they had won a victory. They just could not talk about it.

This presented a huge public relations problem. The Russian people could only come to one conclusion. Their leader had backed down.

John Kennedy did not face the same criticism. Worldwide press coverage stated Kennedy had emerged from the crisis as a hero and as the "winner."

He truly was the king of Camelot.

It was weeks before Khrushchev recognized he had been played.

He was weaker now, and in one sense, more dangerous because of it.

Chapter 41

Eight months had gone by since the United States and Russia escaped Armageddon by a mere whisker.

The year 1963 was a happy one for the man from Massachusetts. He was cruising toward a second term.

John Kennedy's gravitas had soared following the Cuban Missile Crisis.

It appeared to reporters in July of 1963 that the Republicans might nominate Senator Barry Goldwater of Arizona as their standard-bearer in 1964.

Kennedy believed he could easily defeat Goldwater. The main reason for Goldwater's candidacy was his rabid anti-Communism. But following the Cuba crisis, Kennedy no longer believed he could be outflanked on the right by any politician.

Kennedy's political wise men believed everything was coming up roses. The economy was booming. On the horizon was a plan for a significant tax cut for the American people.

As much as Americans love government largesse, they love tax cuts even more.

In 1963, Kennedy created the Peace Corps, a program that was certain to delight liberals.

On the international stage, he created the Alliance for Progress, a formula to enhance trade between the United States and the countries of South America.

Pending was a nuclear weapons pact between America and Russia. This was the birthchild of the near disaster of 1962.

Kennedy wanted to pass a civil rights bill, but Southern Democrats stood like a stonewall against the concept.

It still did not hurt that Kennedy supported the bill. In the eyes of most Americans, Kennedy was the good guy, and the old bulls in the Senate were the bad guys.

It seemed to many that Kennedy was the right man at the right time in history.

It is almost impossible to beat a sitting president when there is peace and prosperity. Kennedy had supplied both of those coveted results.

Kennedy did have one major decision to make that might be problematic.—what to do about Lyndon Baines Johnson.

Robert Kennedy was begging his brother to unload Johnson.

John Kennedy did not despise Johnson with the same ferocity as his brother, but he was not fond of the man, and their three years together did not enhance Johnson's status.

Johnson's obsequiousness irritated Kennedy. He understood the reason for it. Johnson wanted the 1968 presidential nomination. If he had to grovel for eight years, he would.

Kennedy did not know how much Johnson hated his self-imposed servile behavior. He would do anything to escape this trap.

Kennedy no longer believed Johnson was necessary for the Democratic ticket to carry Texas. He had only recently come to this conclusion. But once Kennedy crossed this mental threshold, Lyndon Johnson's days were numbered.

Lyndon Johnson was no fool. He could see the arc of history trending away from him. People who knew Johnson well were amazed at his shrunken appearance.

Only four years earlier he had walked the halls of Congress as a giant. His position as Senate majority leader gave him power, and the title commanded respect from everyone, including Dwight Eisenhower.

Now he was a tiny sailboat in a marina filled with yachts.

The stress of being a permanent toady caused Johnson to lose a tremendous amount of weight. His skin was sallow, and his gait was uncoordinated, almost as if he suffered from a neurological disorder.

At the conclusion of the Cuba crisis, Kennedy sent Johnson fewer and fewer memos. He deliberately truncated his movements, especially when Johnson was overseas.

Bobby's taunts and humiliations reached a new level of cruelty.

Were one to make an analogy, it would be this: Kennedy was on a rocket ship headed for the moon, and Johnson was tethered to the *Titanic* headed toward an icy grave.

In the summer of 1963, two storms were headed in Johnson's direction. Each one held the potential for disaster. Combined, they meant certain political death.

The first storm involved a potential federal investigation into how Lyndon Johnson became rich while serving in Congress. Johnson grew up dirt poor. His father was a failure as a businessman.

Johnson did not want to follow his father's failed career.

At the age of twelve, Johnson told everyone he would one day grow up to be president of the United States.

His friends and neighbors may have scoffed, but Johnson was deadly serious.

Immediately after college, Johnson got a job as a Congressional aide. Then he ran successfully for a US House seat in Texas.

His first run in 1941 for the US Senate was sidetracked by crooked voting. Johnson reversed the outcome in 1948. He did it via voting skullduggery. But so what? It worked.

Johnson was not satisfied with power alone. He wanted money. Lots of it.

A politician possesses two attributes that are salable—influence and access.

Everyone knows this, which is why politicians are forbidden by law from selling their offices for pecuniary gain.

The great loophole, of course, is campaign donations. The law allows individuals to contribute to a political figure's campaign if the money is used solely for campaign purposes.

A politician can spend money on posters, television ads, salaries, cocktail parties, and anything else directly connected to advancing an election.

A politician cannot spend campaign donations on a condo in San Francisco or a gold necklace for a mistress.

Nor can a candidate blackmail a donor into buying something of value that belongs to that same candidate.

Early in Johnson's career, he obtained licenses for radio and television stations in Texas. These entities needed advertising dollars in order to survive.

A businessman seeking a change in a law can donate money to a politician's campaign in the hope that it makes a difference.

That same businessman cannot be told to buy advertising in return for a guaranteed favor. If the line between propriety and corruption seems blurred, it is by design.

Lawyers make a good living navigating these distinctions.

But for an aspiring politician, just having headlines about influence peddling can prove deadly.

Johnson was now facing this possibility. More than any other politician, Johnson had his ear to the ground.

He learned that reporters were sniffing around an indiscretion involving a man named Bobby Baker.

Bobby Baker held the title secretary to the United States Senate. He was a problem solver and a gofer to one hundred members of the Senate.

He was hired by Lyndon Johnson. The men became so close Baker was known by everyone as Lyndon's boy.

One senator stated, "There is no daylight between Bobby and Lyndon."

In the summer of 1963, Baker was named as a principal in a lawsuit. The allegation was that Baker used his influence to pressure a defense contractor to install vending machines in multiple factories.

The current vendor was expelled from the defense plants.

The vending contract was worth millions. The only leverage Baker had was his close access to Lyndon Johnson.

A lawsuit involves subpoenas, depositions, testimony, and documents being handed from one litigant to another.

Bobby Baker was involved in every aspect of Lyndon Johnson's life. He was not just called Lyndon's boy. He was also referred to as Little Lyndon.

Bobby Baker being trapped inside a legal rathole was a profoundly dangerous situation for a sitting vice president.

A civil trial could metastasize into a criminal investigation.

Human beings are weak. They are susceptible to pressure from prosecutors.

Baker might decide to save his skin by telling Bobby Kennedy's prosecutors everything he knew about Lyndon Johnson's business empire.

Baker could possibly testify he directed money from favor seekers into the bank account of the Senate majority leader.

Johnson had, in the past, deflected questions about his businesses. He told everyone that his wife ran everything.

Johnson said there was a Berlin Wall between him and Lady Bird when it came to details concerning the businesses.

Everyone knew this was laughable. Lady Bird Johnson might be in charge of the family kitchen, but that was all.

Over a ten-year period, Baker had run hundreds of errands and made thousands of calls directly related to Lyndon Johnson's empire.

Johnson's fate completely rested on Baker's ability to withstand pressure.

Lyndon Johnson was extremely nervous. The second storm bearing down on Johnson involved his number one nemesis.

Robert Kennedy was now projected to seek the presidency in 1968.

Five years is a long time. Anything can happen.

In five years, Bobby Kennedy would be old enough to seriously consider the office of president.

He might have a distinguished record to run on. Johnson knew that Bobby was at war with the Mob. If he succeeded in breaking the back of La Cosa Nostra, that would be one hell of a campaign issue.

John Kennedy would do anything for his little brother. John Kennedy's popularity among Democrats might easily be transferred to Bobby.

Lyndon Johnson knew he could not survive another five years of subservience. In 1968, Johnson would be an afterthought. No, a joke.

In 1968, he would be thirteen years removed from his near-fatal heart attack.

No one would remember his days as Senate majority leader.

Johnson was certain this newfound interest in his financial affairs came right out of the office of the attorney general.

Robert Kennedy had enough juice in Washington to secretly launch a smear campaign against Johnson.

It would not be necessary to have Johnson indicted. Bad publicity was all Robert Kennedy needed to slay this despised rival.

The walls were closing in. Something dramatic had to happen. And it had to happen quickly.

Johnson did have one powerful ally in his war with the Kennedys.

He picked up the phone and dialed a private number inside the office of J. Edgar Hoover.

Chapter 42

The titans of organized crime in America went to extraordinary lengths to mask their travel plans.

Santo Trafficante insisted they meet in his home state of Florida. Carlos Marcello wanted the gathering to take place in New Orleans, but Trafficante was obdurate on the subject.

In the summer of 1963, Sam Giancana, Johnny Roselli, Carlos Marcello, and Santo Trafficante found their way to a restaurant in Tampa owned by a Trafficante confidant.

It was a Sunday morning. Trafficante was the first one to arrive. He had with him an electronics expert. Trafficante paid the man one thousand dollars to sweep the restaurant for bugs.

Trafficante also had a confederate do nothing but circle the block looking for parked cars. Cars that might conceal FBI agents. A third man utilizing binoculars was on the roof of the closed restaurant.

Trafficante was not paranoid. He knew the Justice Department wanted his hide.

Next to arrive was Roselli. He was Giancana's closest friend in Chicago.

In 1962, the CIA recruited Roselli in a conspiracy to kill Castro. Roselli pretended to play along. Then he realized the government was guilty of the worst form of duplicity. One arm of the government, the intelligence part, wanted the Mob as an ally while another arm, the Justice Department, wanted the Mob destroyed.

This duality was the subject of debate among mobsters all over the country.

Giancana arrived twenty minutes after Roselli. Last to arrive was Marcello.

The four men made small talk for fifteen minutes. Trafficante waited for his motorized spy to come inside and tell him they were not under surveillance.

Trafficante produced a bottle of red wine. He filled four glasses and then sat down. "Gentlemen, we are here at the behest of our friend Carlos Marcello of New Orleans. Carlos, perhaps you should take the floor and outline the problem we are facing regarding the Kennedy Administration."

Marcello got to his feet and leaned on the table. "I am not as articulate as my good friend Santo. So, I am just going to lay it on the line. Those sons of bitches want us dead or in jail for life. You saw what they did to me. They kidnapped me and dropped me in fucking Guatemala. No money, no food, no water. Those FBI guys flew away hoping I would die in the jungle."

Marcello straightened up but did not stop his rant. "How many of our friends are in jail today? One hundred? Two hundred? I'm losing track. And you, Sam, you can't go to the bathroom without an FBI guy strolling in and taking a leak on your shoes!"

Marcello got nose to nose with Giancana. "Aren't you the guy who put John Kennedy in the White House! I told you that Joe Kennedy was a piece of shit! I have known the man for forty years! He would stab his grandmother for a sawbuck!"

Giancana lowered his eyes and nodded his head in affirmation.

Marcello sat down mumbling and cursing.

Trafficante turned and addressed Roselli. "John, what's up with you and the CIA?"

Roselli was a suave playboy who had a minor role in the making of two Hollywood motion pictures. He fancied himself as a producer which facilitated his main priority in life—seducing hundreds of young women.

Roselli locked his thumbs in his coat pockets. "They still think I am recruiting hitters to send to Cuba," Roselli said, laughing. "I'm spending their money and making up excuses for why we haven't hit Castro yet."

Trafficante continued. "John, what do you think they'll do when they decide you are useless?"

"They told me if I didn't come through, I could disappear or end up in Leavenworth."

Marcello shot to his feet. "Can someone explain to me the difference between how we do business and how the government does business?"

Trafficante wanted to answer. "There isn't any difference, Carlos. But you want a showdown with the Kennedys. I have a question for you. Between the government and the mobs, who has the biggest army?"

"Point well taken. Well, what do you want to do, Santo? Should we fold up and go out of business completely? If Kennedy gets reelected, he will be in power until 1968. Do you think we can hold out that long?"

"No, I don't, Carlos. I believe each one of us will be sitting inside a prison cell long before 1968. I have sources who have told me the Kennedys want my scalp as much as they want yours."

Trafficante got up and replenished the four glasses.

"Carlos, each man sitting here today wants the Kennedys gone. There are only two ways that can happen. John Kennedy can be defeated next year by a Republican, someone who is more concerned about issues not associated with La Cosa Nostra. I don't think that is going to happen."

"The other way to remove the Kennedy boys is by force."

Trafficante let that remark sink in.

"Before we move on, I want to tell you something. Yesterday I visited our local library, and I perused a book about a man named Abraham Lincoln. You may have heard that name before."

"Ninety-eight years ago, John Wilkes Booth shot Lincoln in the head. Two weeks later, the army found Booth hiding in a barn. A sergeant shot him in the neck and killed him dead. You notice they didn't bother to bring him in alive."

"Booth had co-conspirators. Each one was hanged less than one hundred days after Lincoln's assassination. One of the conspirators was a woman. It didn't matter. They strung her up with the others."

"My point is that the government takes the killing of a president rather seriously."

Marcello had to chime in. "Sounds like you are telling us to roll over and let the Kennedys have their way."

"Not necessarily. Booth's mistake was that he made no effort to hide his complicity. After shooting Lincoln, he jumped on the stage at Ford's Theater and made some dramatic statement in Latin. He wanted the whole world to know it was he who did the deed."

"Three presidents have been shot and killed while in office. In each case, the perpetrator was happy to take the credit."

"If we take down John Kennedy, we will have to bury our involvement under so much rock no one will be able to dig it out."

Giancana decided he had to get involved in the conversation. "That has been my biggest concern. I want our way of life to continue. It has been good for all of us. But I can't think of a more high-risk enterprise than killing a United States president. How do we get away with it?"

Marcello jumped back in. "We need a fall guy."

Trafficante agreed, but he had an addendum.

"Carlos is absolutely right, my friends. But this fall guy, this patsy, cannot under any circumstances survive the event. He has to be dead ten minutes after the president is hit."

Roselli was skeptical. "Santo, the FBI will investigate our dead patsy from the day he was born. How do we shield ourselves completely?"

"Under normal circumstances, it would be very difficult. But there might be a way."

Trafficante fixed his dark black eyes on Marcello. "Carlos, you know Lyndon Johnson. How badly does he want to be president?"

"He'd give both arms and a leg for the chance. But help us in a murder plot against his boss? I don't see that happening."

"I agree. But there might be a way of recruiting Johnson without actually recruiting him."

Marcello threw his palms open and said, "I don't know what that statement means."

Trafficante pushed on. "Let's send a guy to see him. Someone who is as clean as a hound's tooth. This guy asks Johnson a bunch of hypotheticals, questions that could be construed as academic in nature. A skilled interrogator could learn a lot just by being obtuse."

"The trick is to make certain Johnson is in charge of any investigation involving the death of John Kennedy."

"What about Hoover?" It was Giancana who posed the question.

Trafficante shrugged. "Hoover and Johnson are tighter than two peas in a pod. And they both hate the Kennedy family. This could work."

Trafficante stood and wagged his index finger. "But it is absolutely critical the fall guy never sees the inside of a courtroom! If he does, we are all going to hang!"

Suddenly Marcello's eyes widened to the size of coffee cups. "Wait a minute! What if the fall guy is so radioactive the government will move a mountain to hide the truth!"

Giancana, Roselli, and Trafficante stared at each other. What was Marcello talking about?

"What if the fall guy was a communist who betrayed his country and then came crawling back to the United States in disgrace? What if this traitor had ties to the CIA? Do you think the government might be interested in burying the truth along with the assassin?"

Roselli asked, "Where do we find such a guy?"

"We don't have to find him. I know where he is. He used to work for one of my bookies. He quit the Marines and went to Russia. He's perfect. Everyone hates his guts."

"Who is he?"

"His name is Lee Harvey Oswald. He used to call me Uncle Carlos. He will do whatever I ask him to do."

"How do we get Oswald in the same proximity as Kennedy?"

"You guys need to read the papers more often. Kennedy is coming to Texas in November. One of his stopovers is in Dallas."

Trafficante smiled. "Carlos, don't you have influential friends in Dallas?"

Marcello chuckled. "I know a few people."

Trafficante motioned for everyone to stand up. "Does anyone in this room believe we can survive eight years of John and Robert Kennedy?"

All three men shook their heads no.

"Well, gentlemen, the only issue left on the table is this: do we have the *coglioni* to pull this off? If the answer is yes, take my hand."

There were handshakes all around.

Chapter 43

Marcello and Trafficante waved at Roselli and Giancana as the two men boarded a flight back to Chicago.

"Santo, let's go have a drink."

Trafficante and Marcello found an airport lounge with a quiet table far from any potential curious listeners.

Neither man spoke until a waitress had delivered two bourbons. She walked away with a ten-dollar tip.

Marcello turned to Trafficante. "Santo, is there some way for you to locate the Cobra?"

Trafficante knew immediately where Marcello was headed. Killing a US president would require the best in the business.

No one had dispatched more human beings with a rifle than the Cobra.

The Cobra was an Englishman. In 1939, he was sixteen years old. In order to get into the Army, he changed his name and date of birth.

Two years later. he was in North Africa fighting with the British Eighth Army.

It was said he had eyesight that would make an eagle envious. His commanders gave him a rifle with a scope and told him to get to work.

Field Marshal Erwin Rommel took notice of a mysterious but never-seen nemesis who was killing his men by the boatload.

There would be no warning. One minute, a German soldier would be chatting up a comrade. A second later, he would fall down. Half his head would be missing.

No matter how thoroughly the Germans searched for this sniper, they always came back with nothing.

The Germans gave him a name—the Cobra.

The English found out about the nickname and decided to adopt it.

In April of 1945, the Cobra was still at it. He was on German soil killing SS men with abandon.

One hundred and sixty-two men met a premature death at the hands of the Cobra. He should have been knighted. Except two days after Adolph Hitler committed suicide, the Cobra kidnapped two sisters and raped them both. One was twelve. The other was ten.

Now the British Army had a problem. On one hand the Cobra was a potential national hero. On the other hand, he had clearly become a sociopath.

He was cashiered. He was told to leave England and never to return.

The Cobra could not understand his fall from grace. Those were German girls. Who cared how old they were?

The British government gave him a passport with the name Thomas Harrison. He was told to disappear.

He took his umbrage and decided to make a living using the one talent he had—the ability to kill people at a great distance.

In 1945, the richest country on the planet was the United States. This was his destination. Follow the money.

In 1947, the Cobra found his way to Florida. He visited night-clubs in Tampa every night. He was trying to find out who the Mob bosses were.

One night, he met a man known in criminal circles as the first among equals. His name was Santo Trafficante Sr.

He convinced Trafficante to give him one chance to prove his worth. Trafficante brought along his son for protection. This mystery man wanted the three of them to go to the woods. One cannot be too cautious.

The Cobra put a paint can on a log. Then the three men marched five hundred yards in the opposite direction.

The Cobra braced his rifle and squinted into the scope. A second later the paint can exploded. One shot was all it took. He picked red paint for dramatic effect.

Trafficante hired him on the spot.

In 1950, the amount of money being made by the Trafficante family was attracting rivals. The elder Santo told them, "Don't even try." They did.

Bodies started turning up all over Tampa. Most of the victims died from clean headshots. Witnesses told police they never saw the assailant. They were not lying.

The Cobra was getting rich keeping the Trafficante family safe.

In 1954, Santo Sr. died. His son became boss of all Mob activity in Tampa.

Santo Jr. was no fool. His first order of business was making certain the Cobra stayed on his payroll.

In the mid-1950s, Trafficante was investing millions of dollars in Havana, Cuba. That money went to two sources. The president of Cuba and the casinos popping up all over Havana.

The Cobra often accompanied Trafficante to Cuba. The women were beautiful. And authorities did not care if a man's proclivities favored very young girls.

Cuba before Castro was heaven on earth. Cuba after Castro was Dante's hell.

In 1959, Trafficante went to Cuba to try and make a deal with Castro. He ended up in jail. He did not bring the Cobra on this trip. He regretted it.

Jack Rubenstein of Dallas had to fly to Cuba with a suitcase full of money to get Trafficante out just days before his scheduled execution. Trafficante decided he was never going to fly solo again.

In 1961, newly elected President John Kennedy had a lot on his plate.

There was Cuba of course. But that was not the only Spanish-speaking country giving the United States a collective headache.

The nearby Dominican Republic was ruled by a brutal despot named Rafael Trujillo.

He first came to power in 1930. With the exception of four years, he ran the Dominican Republic for three decades.

In 1916, the United States occupied the Dominican Republic. The US established a local National Guard.

Seeing an opportunity, Trujillo joined in 1918. He impressed his overlords, and he rose through the ranks.

He went from a cadet to commander-in-chief in only nine years.

In 1930, Trujillo launched a coup against President Horacio Vasquez. In a laughable attempt at electoral legitimacy, Trujillo ran for president. He received 99 percent of the votes.

After only six years in power, Trujillo lost all conception of humility. He started naming buildings and even cities after himself. He ruthlessly attacked all political opposition. The sound of prison doors slamming shut and bullets winging through the air were common.

Trujillo made his country a safe haven for Jews. He also favored whites over blacks in immigration. He followed both policies because whites and Jews brought immediate economic gain while other races were deemed to be a burden.

In 1937, Trujillo accused Haiti of harboring his political enemies. He unleashed his army.

In what became known as the Parsley Massacre, twenty thousand Haitians were killed. Many were hacked to death by troops wielding machetes.

Trujillo bought himself some goodwill by siding with the Allies in WWII.

At the conclusion of the war, he resumed his totalitarian methods and turned the entire country into a prison camp.

The decade of the 1950s saw Trujillo acquire tremendous wealth. The entire nation existed only to feed his interests.

Trujillo was not the kind of a man who could bond with a John F. Kennedy.

In 1961, relations between the US and the Dominican Republic plummeted.

Trujillo was torturing and butchering his opponents, and he did not even try to hide the depravity of it all.

He crossed a line a year earlier. In June of 1960, Trujillo attempted to kill the president of Venezuela, Romulo Betancourt.

President Betancourt was Trujillo's loudest and most persistent critic.

Agents working for Trujillo placed sixty-five kilograms of TNT in Betancourt's car. The bomb went off. It killed one of the car's occupants. Betancourt suffered severe burns but survived.

South American leaders roundly condemned the incident.

In November, right about the time John Kennedy was winning his presidential race, Trujillo went after three very pretty women who had committed the crime of opposing his rule.

The victims were Patria, Minerva, and Maria Teresa Mirabal.

The women were visiting their incarcerated husbands in a prison. On the way home, they and their driver, Rufino De La Cruz, were stopped by Dominican soldiers.

Cruz and the women were beaten and then strangled to death. Their bodies were put in a jeep, and the vehicle was pushed off a cliff. It was a crude attempt to make the deaths look accidental.

No one was fooled. Least of all the Kennedy Administration.

Something had to be done about Rafael Trujillo.

South American leaders told John Kennedy only the United States can pull this off. Kennedy told the CIA director Allen Dulles his agents should do "everything they can to aid and abet the removal from power" of one Rafael Trujillo.

It was exactly the same time frame the government was recruiting mobsters in a joint attempt to get rid of Castro.

Now they had a second mission—organize a hit on Trujillo.

Santo Trafficante was already part of the Castro plot. Maybe he could help the government in the Trujillo matter?

In early 1961, Trafficante still believed he could curry favor with the Kennedy administration and thus hold law enforcement at bay.

Trafficante told the CIA he knew a man who could guarantee any attempt on Trujillo would be successful—the Cobra.

"He doesn't come cheap," Trafficante warned.

Agents scoffed. "Just get him there," they said.

On May 2, 1961, the Cobra was on an airplane headed for the Dominican Republic.

The disaster of the Bay of Pigs was only two weeks earlier. The Cobra was not impressed. He wondered what kind of a man was sitting in the Oval Office.

The Cobra decided he needed a plan B exit strategy in case the CIA abandoned him the way it abandoned those patriots on the beaches of southwest Cuba.

The CIA introduced the Cobra to the men who would be in charge of ambushing Trujillo.

His co-conspirators were General Juan Tomas Diaz, Pedro Livio Cedeno, Antonio De La Maza, Amado Garcia Guerrero, General Antonio Imbert Barrera, Luis Amiama Tio, and General Jose Rene Ramon Fernandez.

The attack on Trujillo was still weeks away. The Cobra demonstrated his skills with a rifle. One by one melons with painted faces blew up in a remote section of jungle while seven men looked on awestruck.

The conspirators put him in charge of the actual assassination.

The Cobra wanted just one assistant, a man with a radio and a fast jeep. The Cobra was told that after the hit, he was to get on an airplane and just fly away. The CIA would facilitate his exit from the country.

If only life were that simple. He thought about those abandoned Cuban patriots.

The Cobra rented a motor craft and hired a man to be ready if called—plan B.

On May 30, 1961, Rafael Trujillo was driving a 1957 Chevrolet Bel Air on a road outside the Dominican capital.

He had only three bodyguards. This was reckless for a man as unpopular as he was at this stage of his life.

Trujillo neither saw nor heard the missile that ended his life. He was dead instantaneously.

The bodyguards exited the car in great haste. In five seconds, all of them were dead.

The Cobra was just one hundred yards away.

A hundred yards. Child's play.

The Cobra and his lookout hopped in a jeep and headed for the Capital of Santo Domingo. The Cobra was supposed to meet his CIA handlers at a safe house.

He opened the door. No one was there. Every stitch of clothing was gone.

The Cobra knew immediately what was going on. The CIA had been told the assassination was a success. So, they pulled out.

Trujillo's body was discovered twenty minutes after he had been killed. The country's security agencies went into overdrive.

The airport was shut down. Men with submachine guns were everywhere.

The Cobra calmly walked to the docks and got inside a fast boat.

In three hours, he was in Haiti.

The men who plotted against Trujillo did not do their homework. They failed to take over the security apparatus of the state.

It was the same mistake German conspirators made in July of 1944 when a bomb, placed in close proximity to Der Führer, failed to kill him.

With one phone call, Hitler flipped the allegiance of the Home Army.

Five thousand people were arrested. Many of them were hanged with piano wire wrapped around their necks.

The men who sought to rid the Dominican Republic of a tyrant faced the same consequences as the men who sought to kill Hitler.

They were all shot. The Cobra survived.

It took two weeks for Trafficante to smuggle the Cobra back into the United States.

When the Cobra walked into Trafficante's house, he grabbed the Mob boss by his shirt and pulled him toward his face.

"Why are you in bed with the US government? They are all a bunch of backstabbing sons of bitches!"

Trafficante did not have a good answer.

Carlos Marcello knew all the details concerning the Cobra's escape from the Dominican Republic. He figured correctly that the Cobra had little love in his heart for John Kennedy and his administration. The perfect assassin.

Chapter 44

"Curt, do you have a minute?"

Curt Holmes always had time for his favorite analyst. Holmes and Dunleavy had become extremely close.

It was Thursday, November 21, 1963. Holmes and Dunleavy were in charge of two very important and highly classified missions.

They were tracking Soviet missile deployment. Along with the CIA, they were put in charge of making certain the Soviet Union honored its commitment to remove its missiles from Cuba.

Their second mission involved tracking phone calls between mobsters. They were not allowed to wiretap. Their job was to look for patterns.

For many months, FBI agents surveilled the nation's most notorious crime lords. To no one's surprise, the bosses and their underlings were taking advantage of Ma Bell's extensive pay telephone system.

No sane mobster would discuss criminal activity from a home phone. Although some did.

The FBI would wait for a boss to finish a conversation and drive away. An agent would then enter the phone booth and write down the number.

The phone company would then trace the number and the time of the call.

The recipient of the call was another Mob guy who was also under surveillance.

In a six-month period, the NSA had identified those phone booths that were conduits for gangsters seeking to hide their affairs.

These call patterns were sent over to Robert Kennedy. It was the attorney general's job to convince a judge that these phone calls met the threshold of a warrant.

A warrant would enable the FBI to listen in on the crooks. Judging by the number of bad guys being sent to prison, Holmes and Dunleavy could only conclude their mission was a success.

Dunleavy was a little confused that certain mobsters seemed to elude the government's net. Those men were Carlos Marcello, Santo Trafficante, John Roselli, and Sam Giancana.

The NSA knew that these four men were in constant contact with one another.

Where were the wiretap warrants? Holmes did not have an answer.

Neither Holmes nor Dunleavy was aware of the secret CIA plan to recruit La Cosa Nostra members to kill Castro.

It was this partnership that shielded the four men from arrest.

Robert Kennedy knew about the alliance. He was instructed by his brother to discuss it with no one.

Dunleavy had ascertained some new facts he thought Holmes should address immediately. "Curt, here's the latest intelligence on our boys with broken noses."

He handed Holmes a folder labeled top secret.

"Can you give me a quick synopsis, Stuart?"

"Yeah, these phone numbers are used by Giancana, Marcello, Roselli, and Trafficante. Back in July, they only communicated once or twice a week. That number held until early November. Then the four of them started speaking to one another once a day."

"I know. We discussed that two weeks ago."

"Well, in the last two days, the number of conversations between these four hoods has exploded. In the past forty-eight hours, they have literally spoken to each other five times a day."

Holmes looked at Dunleavy like an owl about to pounce on a rodent. "Stuart, does the DOJ have warrants on these characters?"

"No. And that's another thing I don't understand. These are big fish. They would make great trophies. Why isn't Bobby moving on them?"

Holmes shrugged. "I'm certain he has his reasons. I'm going to call Bobby and see if he will meet with us. What's your schedule?"

"I'm taking Arlene to the doctor tomorrow."

"Anything wrong?"

"Yeah, she's pregnant. So, I'm going to need a raise."

"It's about time you squeezed out a kid. How old are you? Forty?"

"Jack Benny said a man should stop counting at thirty-nine. I am going to take his advice."

Holmes stood up and put his right arm around Dunleavy. "Listen, the president is in Texas. Does he know about Arlene?"

"You are the first one. You should be honored."

"I suppose I will be buying toys for the next five years."

Each man laughed. Dunleavy took two steps toward the door. He stopped abruptly. "Curt, isn't the president going to be in Dallas tomorrow?"

"Yes, he is."

"Isn't that Marcello's territory?"

Holmes froze for a quick moment. Marcello was boss dog in New Orleans, but he also had huge sway in Dallas. "Yes, it is, Stuart. Yes, it is."

"I heard a rumor that two years ago Bobby had Marcello picked up and then he had him dumped in a jungle somewhere in Central America."

"I believe that story is true."

Dunleavy moved forward and put two hands on a chair. "Should we make a call?"

"And say what? Stuart, we don't have any actionable intelligence that something is about to happen."

"I guess you are right, Curt. But I am going to be awfully happy when Air Force One takes off and leaves Texas behind."

At the exact moment Holmes and Dunleavy were brainstorming in Washington, Carlos Marcello was meeting with Lee Harvey Oswald.

The meeting took place in a small diner fifteen minutes from Oswald's house in Dallas. Two of Marcello's security people stood watch outside the diner in case the FBI was in the neighborhood.

Oswald once worked for a bookie. The bookie answered to Marcello.

Marcello stirred his coffee while Lee sucked on a straw embedded in a milkshake.

"So, Lee, how's it going?"

"How do you think it's going, Uncle Carlos? My marriage stinks. My job stinks. And my bank account is empty."

"I might be able to help you with one of those three problems, Lee."

"What do you have in mind?"

"How would you like to receive ten one-hundred-dollar bills for doing me a small favor?"

A thousand bucks sounded pretty good to the ever-pecunious former Marine.

"Sure, Uncle Carlos. Anything!"

"We want that rifle you purchased back in March."

Oswald was confused. There was no shortage of high-grade weaponry in the Marcello organization. "Uncle Carlos, you want my piece-of-crap Carcano rifle? The one I bought for twenty bucks? What the hell for?"

"We need a weapon that can't be traced."

Oswald knew the significance of that statement. Marcello was going to kill someone who had trespassed him in some manner.

Months ago, Oswald answered an ad in a newspaper. Klein's Sporting Goods in Chicago was offering a Carcano 6.5-mm rifle for twenty dollars. It offered a scope for an additional seven dollars.

Oswald's perpetually depleted bank account made the purchase of a quality weapon impossible. At least it was something.

Oswald purchased the weapon under the name, "A. Hidell."

Marcello continued his phony narrative. "We know you didn't use your real name when you ordered that rifle. That's the beauty of it. It can't be traced."

Oswald knew he should not ask this question, but he couldn't help himself. "Who's the target?"

Marcello cocked his head and gave Oswald a "Come on, Lee" look. "Lee, you know better than to ask that. Let's just say that when a man steals from his friends, he has to pay a price."

Oswald knew that Marcello did not tolerate rats in his organization. Pocketing as little as a hundred bucks could bring down the godfather's wrath.

"You want to send someone over to my place and pick it up?"

Marcello knew he had to answer this question using perfect logic. "Lee, you know the government is not too fond of you. There is a really good chance they have your place under surveillance. In fact, I know they have. Let's do this. Wrap the rifle up in paper. Bring it to work tomorrow. If anyone asks what you are carrying, tell them you just bought curtain rods because your wife has been bugging you about redecorating. Take the package up to the sixth floor. I will have Tito retrieve it."

Tito Bendado was Marcello's chief gofer. He had a low ranking in the organization and usually his most important job was getting Marcello's laundry.

Oswald swallowed Marcello's story hook, line, and sinker.

Oswald made no connection to Marcello's request for a rifle and the fact that the president of the United States was coming to town Friday.

He did not know the true history of the bad blood between Marcello and the Kennedy family.

Oswald's radar was also dimmed by the promise of a thousand dollars for virtually no work. Oswald's job did not pay enough to support a bachelor, let alone a married man with children.

One thousand dollars. That was enough money to keep his wife quiet for maybe two weeks.

Stuffing a rag in the mouth of his hectoring wife was all that Oswald thought about.

Fifteen hours later, Oswald walked into the Texas School Book depository carrying curtain rods.

It was Friday morning, November 22, 1963.

Chapter 45

John Kennedy was in Texas for three reasons.

He wanted to kick off his 1964 presidential run. He bestowed that honor on the people of Texas, in part because a majority of voters in that state had chosen him and Lyndon Johnson over Richard Nixon and Henry Cabot Lodge.

Kennedy also wanted to cement his relationship with donors. A fundraiser was scheduled for Austin.

Kennedy wanted to repair a rift among bigshot Texas Democrats which could threaten unity in the state. The new governor, John Connally, was feuding with Ralph and Don Yarborough, the leaders of the liberal wing of the Democratic Party.

There was an unspoken fourth reason for sojourning to Texas. Kennedy wanted to powwow with Texas Democrats about the future of Lyndon Johnson.

This had to be done in a very clandestine fashion. Lyndon Johnson was accompanying the president to Texas.

November of 1963 was the nadir of Johnson's term as vice president.

He was under investigation for influence peddling. The news media was picking around in his personal and business life to see if anything smelled bad. They would, of course, find something. They always do.

Government officials were also poking around Johnson's relationship with Bobby Baker, the secretary of the United States Senate.

Baker was an encyclopedia of knowledge pertaining to all aspects of Johnson's life.

Johnson knew how the game was played.

The government would threaten Baker with a battery of criminal charges. Facing off against the US government meant spending tens of thousands of dollars on legal fees. The government would, of course, offer Baker a reduced sentence in return for his cooperation.

The only ace Baker possessed was his knowledge of Lyndon Johnson's business empire.

When a man is facing twenty years in prison and he is offered two or five years, logic dictates the outcome. Baker would become a rat.

Johnson was absolutely convinced Robert Kennedy was behind this mess. He was now thoroughly convinced Robert Kennedy would seek the 1968 presidential nomination.

That meant Lyndon Baines Johnson had to go. A sitting vice president who is kicked off a thriving ticket is a man whose time is up.

Johnson's assumption that Kennedy was going to dump him was dead-on accurate. Kennedy a month earlier had told his secretary Evelyn Lincoln that Johnson would not be on the ticket in 1964.

Joe Kennedy might have been able to save Johnson. But that ship had sailed. The once all-mighty patriarch was now a stammering husk of a man sitting in a wheelchair and cursing his fate.

Doors were shutting all over Johnson's world.

Only one door remained open—John Kennedy's untimely death.

Johnson joined the ticket believing Addison's disease might do the trick. But modern medicine had greatly reduced the lethality of that illness.

John Kennedy had never looked healthier. That left only the possibility that an external force might violently remove Kennedy from the White House.

John Kennedy was now on Lyndon Johnson's home turf.

The lords of La Cosa Nostra also knew the clock was running on their time at the top. A reelected John Kennedy would mean the end of the Mob.

His brother would certainly redouble his efforts if for no other reason than to buttress his 1968 presidential prospects.

The choice was clear—life in prison or fight back.

The clock was also ticking for J. Edgar Hoover. His only purpose in life was to die as head of the FBI.

Hoover had enough information on the entire Kennedy clan to cause all kinds of hell. This was a ton of bricks Hoover intended to drop on John Kennedy.

A reelected John Kennedy might not be afraid of the tyrannical Hoover.

Kennedy might be emboldened enough to send a small army of prosecutors over to Hoover's office and seize his secret files.

Hoover's only power lay inside that highly protected office, where blackmail documents accumulated over thirty years were stacked floor to ceiling.

Robert Kennedy wanted Hoover gone. He despised him as much as he did Lyndon Johnson.

Hoover's only guarantee of power resided in the personage of the vice president of the United States. Lyndon Johnson had to become president. Quickly.

Lee Harvey Oswald knew nothing of the machinations of powerful men in faraway Washington, DC. His life revolved around keeping his wife from leaving their marriage.

The money Carlos Marcello promised him was coming at a most propitious time. The talk among employees of the Texas School Book Depository centered on the arrival of President Kennedy.

Air Force One was on the ground at Love Field. A caravan of cars was heading toward Dallas.

The assemblage included John Kennedy and his wife, Jackie. Lyndon Johnson and his wife, Lady Bird. Governor John Connally and his wife, Nellie.

There was a buzz of activity at the depository. Kennedy's caravan was due to pass by in less than twenty minutes.

The president of the United States was going to be no more than fifty feet from the front door of the book depository.

Oswald could have cared less. He was instructed to wait for Tito Bendado to arrive. If anyone questioned his presence, Oswald was supposed to vouch for him.

Oswald was in the third-floor lunchroom when he spotted a new man on the premises.

The man was wearing a uniform with the word "Security" written right above the left shirt pocket.

He had a .38 caliber pistol on his hip.

He sat at Oswald's table. The guard nodded in Oswald's direction.

Oswald thought the man looked edgy, even nervous. Suddenly, Oswald spotted Bendado walking up the steps toward the sixth floor. Oswald had briefed him on where the rifle was hidden.

Oswald was surprised Bendado did not even acknowledge him. Marcello had probably told him not to have contact unless circumstances dictated it.

Oswald expected Bendado to return any second. Bendado did not return. Oswald figured he was having trouble locating the rifle.

If he were not down in ten minutes, Oswald would go upstairs and help him.

Suddenly the security guard got up from the table. He gave Oswald a five-second terrified glance. Then the man hurried out the door.

Oswald found this behavior to be pretty weird.

Voices inside the depository were elevating in tone. The president was approaching.

All eyes were cemented inches from glass panes in a collective effort to catch a glimpse of the chief executive. There was loud clapping and cheering.

Oswald was still at his table waiting for Bendado to come down.

Suddenly Oswald heard three sharp noises.

They could only be firecrackers. Or gunshots.

The noisy book depository was suddenly very quiet.

Something big had happened.

Oswald saw Bendado running down the steps. He did not give Oswald so much as a sideways glance. He was out the door in a flash.

Sixty seconds elapsed.

Then came a loud voice. "The president's been shot!"

Thirty seconds later, a Dallas policeman came running into the lunchroom. He had his service revolver out. He pointed it right at Oswald. "Who's he?" the patrolman asked a janitor.

"He works here." The response was enough to get the patrolman to holster his weapon and continue his search.

Soon there was chaos in the building.

Ten seconds after the patrolman had exited the room, Oswald had an epiphany.

The president had been shot. Oswald had brought a rifle into the book depository. Tito Bendado had gotten away clean as a whistle.

He wasn't carrying anything.

The rifle was still on the premises. Its provenance would be easy to trace.

"They set me up!" Oswald spoke under his breath. He knew he absolutely had to get out of the book depository.

Oswald walked out. Running away certainly would attract the attention of the police who were starting to surround the building.

He got away without being interrogated. His day was far from over.

John Kennedy's head was in his wife's lap. His convertible was speeding toward Parkland Hospital.

A large section of Kennedy's head was spread out on the trunk of the car.

Tito Bendado had done his job. He was instructed to fire three shots in the general direction of the president's car. It did not matter if the bullets found their mark.

The real assassin was at ground level. He was behind a fence in front of the soon-to-be famous grassy knoll.

By some miracle, Bendado's first shot hit the president in the neck.

The other two shots struck the roadway. Bendado aimed the first shot but not the next two. He just wanted to get out.

The man behind the fence was as calm as a bored librarian. The Cobra.

While John Kennedy was clutching his injured throat, the Cobra inserted his rifle barrel five inches over the fence.

Kennedy was so close there could only be one outcome.

A speeding bullet smashed into Kennedy's forehead. Crimson red sprang out in all directions. The bullet exited the rear of the skull, leaving a large hole.

The Cobra was inside his getaway car at the very same moment Jackie Kennedy was climbing out on the trunk to retrieve her husband's demolished flesh.

Left behind was a Marcello associate. He was dressed in a blue suit. He had on cop shoes and a cop tie. He also had a phony Secret Service badge.

Fifty people who had been on the grassy knoll were still lying on the ground.

They had all reacted rationally. Each man, woman, and child had heard the report of a rifle immediately behind them.

Survival instincts kicked in. Mothers covered their children. Fathers covered their wives.

"He's behind the fence! He's behind the fence!"

Police were being told a gunman had used the grassy knoll fence as cover. A patrolman ran to investigate.

He found a well-dressed man who instantly produced a Secret Service badge.

"The only people back here are US government employees!" The man spoke with authority and clarity.

The patrolman retreated. He did not write down the man's name.

Having nailed his acting job, the phony Secret Service man disappeared.

Three minutes after the president was shot, Oswald walked out of the depository building. He caught a city bus. He went a few blocks and summoned a taxi.

He knew the danger he was facing. A high-profile assassination requires a patsy. Marcello's phony script was designed to get Oswald to fall into a trap.

To be successful, an assassination protocol mandates that the patsy die at the scene.

Oswald now knew the security guard was there to shoot him.

He got cold feet instead. The magnitude of the moment over-whelmed him. Oswald knew Marcello would deal harshly with the security guard.

Now for the plan to work, two men had to die. And die quickly.

Oswald told the taxi driver to take him to a boarding house in the Oak Cliff section of Dallas. He was staying there because his wife had ordered him out of their house.

Oswald bolted inside the boarding house. He entered his room. He grabbed a coat and a .38 caliber pistol.

Oswald started walking aimlessly. He had to come up with an escape plan. He had no money, and now he knew he had no friends.

Oswald found himself walking in front of the W. H. Adamson High School. This was the school Oswald had abandoned at age seventeen in order to join the Marine Corps.

Oswald heard the wails of police sirens. The city of Dallas was comparable to a beehive that had been hit by a broom.

Fate would have Oswald meet Dallas Policeman J. D. Tippit in this location. Tippit was parked in his patrol car. His radio was blazing with information about the shooting of the president.

At the intersection of Tenth Street and Patton Avenue, Tippit's short life would come to an end. He spotted Oswald walking with his head down. He decided to question this strange sojourner.

Oswald's paranoia caused his brain to go to a dark place. Maybe Tippit was on Marcello's payroll.

Tippit and Oswald had an angry exchange. The shouting match attracted the attention of twelve people in the immediate area.

Tippit sealed his fate when he opened his door to exit. Oswald pulled his .38 and shot him dead.

He fled like the furies of hell were behind him. In fact, they were.

Oswald ran to a commercial neighborhood near Jefferson Boulevard in Dallas. He ducked into a movie theater. But his running had attracted the attention of a shoe store manager named Calvin Brewer. Brewer watched Oswald and noticed his final destination.

Brewer waved down a patrolman named Nick McDonald. He told McDonald a possible suspect was inside the Texas Theater.

The theatre was showing the movie *War Is Hell*. It was narrated by Oswald's hero, Audie Murphy.

Oswald was slumped in his seat. McDonald and two other officers told the manager to turn on the lights.

Oswald knew he was cornered. "This is it!" Oswald stood up and pulled his pistol. McDonald jumped him and managed to keep the suspect from discharging the weapon.

Oswald slugged one of his attackers. The police officer retaliated and left Oswald with a huge black eye. Police kept Oswald pinned to his seat for twenty minutes.

When they escorted him out, a crowd of people shouted, "Kill him! Kill him!"

Had the enraged citizens stormed the police and killed Oswald, it would have made Carlos Marcello very happy.

The mobster heard on the radio that a suspect in the killing of John F. Kennedy had been captured alive.

Now Marcello had a huge problem. The security guard who got cold feet was responsible for the potential unraveling of the entire conspiracy.

Marcello decided that when found, the guard would be stuffed into a fifty-gallon drum and buried alive.

Now Marcello had to go to any lengths to silence Lee Harvey Oswald. A talkative Oswald would destroy the Mob nationwide.

Lyndon Johnson would have no choice. He would as a matter of political necessity go after the Mob with the full weight and power of the government.

Johnson was at Parkland Hospital. He and his wife were together in a room heavily guarded by Secret Service agents.

John Kennedy was dead.

The bullet that passed through his neck continued on its flight, and it struck Governor John Connally. Connally was three feet away from Kennedy in the front seat of the convertible.

Doctors were fighting to save Connally. They would succeed.

People who saw Johnson at Parkland Hospital said he was completely calm.

Kennedy died a split second after the Cobra's bullet hit his skull. Doctors at Parkland were simply going through the motions of attending to him. It would not look good if they pronounced him dead without taking any restorative medical action.

Johnson had to remain immobile until Kennedy was officially declared dead. The announcement came sixty minutes after the shooting.

In an instant, Johnson shed his obsequious demeanor. He dispensed with his slouch and hangdog expression. He was once again the towering figure who had run the Senate as though it were his fiefdom.

At 1:00 p.m., on November 22, 1963, Lyndon Baines Johnson was president of the United States.

Johnson's first act was to mediate a dispute between the Dallas Police Department and the Secret Service.

Under Texas law, John Kennedy was a murder victim who had expired in the city limits of Dallas.

The police wanted Kennedy's body to remain in Texas. They wanted the autopsy performed in Texas. They wanted the gunman tried in Texas.

Johnson desperately wanted Kennedy's body taken to Air Force One. He wanted the autopsy performed under federal jurisdiction.

His main ally in this endeavor was Jackie Kennedy. She wanted to leave the state of Texas as soon as humanly possible. She would not leave without her husband's remains.

There was an actual shoving match inside Parkland Hospital with the police on one side and the Secret Service on the other. The mortal remains of John Kennedy were being manhandled by competing law enforcement agencies.

The gurney carrying Kennedy's body was almost knocked over.

A Secret Service agent threatened to pull his gun unless the bickering stopped. He and his fellow agents pushed aside the police and took Kennedy's body away.

Johnson's next task was to assuage the shattered widow. Jackie Kennedy refused to take off her bloody clothes. She wanted the world to see.

It would be an absolute public relations disaster if the widow refused to endorse the transfer of power.

Lady Bird was assigned the duty of placating Jackie Kennedy. There would be no placating the attorney general.

Robert Kennedy; his wife, Ethel; United States Attorney Robert Morgenthau; and Morgenthau's deputy Silvio Mollo were all at the Kennedy compound at Hickory Hill. They were having lunch.

The phone rang. Ethel got up to answer it.

It was J. Edgar Hoover. Ethel handed the phone to Bobby.

"Your brother has been shot," Hoover said. "It might be fatal."

Kennedy slapped his hand over his mouth. Ethel was stunned by his changed demeanor.

Kennedy raced inside the house to turn on the television. Two seconds after Hoover concluded his conversation with Kennedy, he ordered his secretary to come inside his office.

"Get rid of that damn red phone! Now!"

The hated direct conduit between Robert Kennedy and J. Edgar Hoover disappeared, never to be seen again.

Kennedy's enemies were not done torturing him.

Minutes after Hoover's call the phone at Hickory Hill rang again. It was Lyndon Johnson.

Paralyzed with grief, Kennedy could hardly speak. Johnson wanted clarification on the protocols for a transfer of power.

"As the chief law enforcement officer of the land, only you can to speak to this issue," Johnson said.

The statement was utter nonsense. There were hundreds of people Johnson could have called for this information.

Johnson had been humiliated for three years by Robert Kennedy. Now it was his turn to twist the knife.

Air Force One was kept waiting on the tarmac while US District Judge Sarah T. Hughes was located.

Johnson insisted that only Hughes be allowed to give the oath of office. She was an old family friend who had once been humiliated by the Kennedy family.

Jackie Kennedy finally found the courage to stand next to Lyndon Johnson as he took away all the power and trappings of the office of president of the United States.

Johnson got what he wanted—a photo of Jackie Kennedy standing just six inches away from his left shoulder.

The swearing ceremony was completed. Air Force One was now taxing down the runway.

Next stop was Washington, DC. Johnson steeled himself for the inevitable encounter with Robert Kennedy.

This would be an eyeball-to-eyeball confrontation. Johnson was told that Robert Kennedy was on his way to Washington, and he would be there when Air Force One arrived.

When a scorpion meets a tarantula, the encounter is never a lovefest.

The world's deadliest sniper was now far removed from his victim. Four hours after the assassination, the Cobra was in Mexico. He was a million dollars richer.

His final destination would be Brazil.

He decided he was going to retire.

Chapter 46

Stuart Dunleavy and Curt Holmes could barely speak to one another.

Each man was glued to the television set in Holmes's office. All constructive work inside the National Security Agency building in Washington, DC, had come to a stop.

Men and women were crying, hugging, and standing in clusters.

Air Force One was winging its way back to Washington with the mortal remains of John Kennedy on board.

After ninety minutes, Holmes broke the silence. "Want some coffee?"

The answer was immediate and abrupt. "No!"

Holmes did not take offense. He knew his friend was about to explode.

Holmes had his back to the television set when Dunleavy shouted, "Curt! Come back! They might have made an arrest!"

The sonorous voice of Walter Cronkite was reporting that the Dallas police had a man in custody.

Holmes spilled hot coffee on his right hand running back to his seat. He did not even notice the pain.

Cronkite said there had been a violent confrontation in a Dallas movie theater. A suspect was dragged out in front of a screaming crowd.

Fifteen minutes later Cronkite announced, "We have a name. The Dallas police just announced that Lee Harvey Oswald has been charged in the shooting death of a patrolman. Authorities stated that Oswald is the primary suspect in the assassination of the president."

Holmes rocketed out of his chair. He grabbed a telephone.

"Margaret, I want you to find out everything we have on a man named Lee Harvey Oswald. Recruit as much help as you need!"

Dunleavy rose from his chair. "Curt, you and I need to take over this investigation right now!"

"I could not agree more. Let's go see Frost."

At 3:00 p.m. on Friday, November 22, 1963, two very determined men marched down an NSA hallway looking for a man who was nominally their boss.

Neither Holmes nor Dunleavy was going to accept no for an answer.

Frost kept them waiting for thirty minutes while he fielded one phone call after another from high-ranking Washington big shots. Everyone wanted a piece of the action.

Frost finally told his secretary to give him fifteen minutes of uninterrupted time.

"Gentlemen, what's on your mind?"

Holmes was about to speak, but Dunleavy violated protocol and spoke first. "Mr. Director, we are uniquely qualified to help law enforcement. This building houses infrastructure that is not available anywhere else in the world."

Holmes said, "I concur."

In a split second, Frost realized he was now the actual man in charge of the NSA. For two years, he had to walk on eggs around Holmes and Dunleavy.

He sat back in his leather chair and reveled in his new status. "Gentlemen, the NSA stands ready to do everything in its power to aid and abet the capture and incarceration of all persons found to be connected to this heinous crime. That is a given."

He leaned forward and folded his hands. "We now have a new president. His name is Lyndon Johnson."

Frost let the power of that statement sink in. It hit Holmes and Dunleavy like a fist in the stomach. "I need to have a conversation with the president before I commit resources. I am sure he will greenlight our participation, but I still need to go through the chain of command."

"May I suggest we operate on the assumption the president will demand our full cooperation?" Holmes's delivery was very soothing.

"You will not make any assumptions. The president might put J. Edgar Hoover in charge of the investigation. If that happens, Hoover will insist that all other federal agencies answer to him."

Dunleavy felt the muscles in his stomach tighten.

He understood Hoover was no fan of the Kennedys. Dunleavy was a Kennedy insider. He knew Robert Kennedy enjoyed bossing Hoover around. Bobby used to joke about how much Hoover hated that red telephone and how much he enjoyed making him dance to his tune.

Dunleavy was positive that Hoover was at this moment smiling, not crying. "Director Frost, when do you plan on speaking to the… president?" Dunleavy could barely get the word out of his mouth.

"I will make every effort to speak to President Johnson on Monday."

"Wouldn't tomorrow be better?"

Dunleavy was getting dangerously close to crossing a line. The remark sounded snarky.

Holmes immediately realized that he and Dunleavy no longer had any friends in the White House. "Mr. Director, Stuart and I are, of course, very emotional about today's events. We will leave you alone now. I am certain you will be answering phone calls from now until midnight. Thank you, sir!"

Dunleavy shot out of his chair and darted out the door. Holmes managed to look back at Frost and smile.

Frost did not smile back.

Robert Kennedy's trip from Hickory Hill to Andrews AFB in Washington was a nightmare. In the three years John and Bobby had worked together, they had become as close as any two brothers on earth.

Bobby was the first man John Kennedy saw in the morning and the last man he saw at night. John Kennedy was dead. Murdered. In Lyndon Johnson's home state.

Bobby could not push those thoughts out of his mind.

There would be time for speculation later. Now, he had to get his brother's mortal remains as far away from Lyndon Johnson as possible.

Bobby had spoken with Johnson twice since the assassination. Johnson's condolences were hollow, unemotional, robotic.

Bobby beat Air Force One to Andrews AFB by half an hour.

The giant plane came to a stop. Movable stairs were pushed up against the aluminum frame. A door opened. Bobby ran up the stairs. The plane was crowded. He did not stop for a second.

He pushed his way past the passengers, saying, "Excuse me. I have to get to Jackie."

He did not look right or left or acknowledge anyone. He pushed past Lyndon Johnson without saying a word.

Bobby ordered Secret Service agents to begin moving the coffin to the rear of the plane. He told Jackie, "We are leaving now!"

He pushed past Johnson a second time. Not a word or even a glance in the president's direction.

The Kennedy people and the Johnson acolytes behaved as if a wall separated them.

There was an uncomfortable silence. A forklift found its way to the plane. Only Kennedy people got on the forklift.

Johnson and Lady Bird watched, expecting they would be invited to ride with the dead president. They were wrong.

The coffin was lowered to pavement level. It was placed in a hearse. Bobby opened the door for Jackie. He immediately got in beside her.

"Let's go!" The hearse sped away.

The attorney general of the United States had just given a symbolic middle finger to the president.

Johnson faced the cameras and spoke only a few sentences. He and Lady Bird then headed for the Executive Office Building. Under no circumstances was Lyndon Johnson going to move into the White House until John Kennedy's body was in the ground.

Johnson had no time to stew over Bobby Kennedy's deliberate humiliation of the most powerful man on the planet.

He had to organize a government. And he had to do it in record time.

While Air Force One was in flight from Dallas, Johnson had heard the police had made an arrest. The name Lee Harvey Oswald sounded vaguely familiar.

He asked his aides to research the man. In no time at all, Johnson learned that Oswald was a disgraced former Marine who spent two years in Russia.

"Was he a communist?" Johnson asked.

"Yes, sir, he was."

Johnson's radar for trouble immediately kicked in. Did the Russians order the assassination of John Kennedy?

The ramifications of that thought were astoundingly dangerous. Halfway to Washington, Johnson was told that Russian forces worldwide were on alert.

Johnson had no choice but to respond in kind. And he had been president all of two hours.

Johnson and Lady Bird walked to a limousine at Andrews AFB. Just before entering the vehicle, Johnson turned to a trusted aide.

"Find Allen Dulles. Tell him to wait by the phone."

"Yes, sir, Mr. President."

Chapter 47

Like 90 percent of America, former CIA director Allen Dulles was glued to his television set.

At 9:00 p.m. on that terrible Friday, the phone rang in Dulles's study.

An aide to Lyndon Johnson said, "Please do not leave the house, Mr. Dulles. The president will be calling you tonight."

Dulles waited ninety minutes. His phone rang a second time.

"Please hold for the president of the United States."

It took another five seconds for a voice laced with Texas twang to come on the line. "Allen, this is Lyndon Johnson. It has been a long time. It is nice to speak to you again."

Allen Dulles had been fired by John Kennedy. He immediately became persona non grata in Camelot. Johnson stayed away from contact with Dulles out of fear of antagonizing the president.

"Mr. President, it is great to hear your voice again. This is a terrible, terrible day. I can only say that I am greatly relieved that it is you who have taken over the mantle of power at such a critical time in history."

"Thank you, Allen. Mrs. Johnson and I are devastated. We were there when it happened, you know."

"The country should be grateful that a man of your experience was there to take the reins and prevent chaos."

Dulles was deliberately laying it on thick as syrup. He might find redemption in a Johnson administration.

"Allen, the country needs you and your expertise. Can I count on it?"

"Every minute of every day, Mr. President."

There was a pause. Dulles could hear the president ask an aide if the line he was using was indeed a secure line. The aide gave an affirmative response. Johnson then asked the man to leave the room.

"Allen, I am in the Executive Office Building. The Secret Service is everywhere, but right now there is no one else in this room. Is that clear?"

"Yes, Mr. President."

"Right now, the Russians are on high military alert. So are we. The situation is very dangerous."

"Don't read too much into it, Mr. President. The violent death of an American chief executive would automatically trigger an enhanced military alert."

"That's not what concerns me. Are you aware the Dallas police have arrested a man they claim shot John Kennedy?"

"I am aware, Mr. President."

"Are you aware this man is named Lee Harvey Oswald, that he is a former Marine who defected to Russia, and that he is for all intents and purposes a full-fledged communist?"

"His background is familiar to me, yes."

"Tomorrow, I am going to be on the hotline with Nikita Khrushchev. I cannot have that conversation unless I am totally briefed on all the facts. Do you understand?"

"I do, Mr. President."

"Was Oswald one of ours or one of theirs?"

Dulles hesitated. He did not want to go down this road.

"Allen, this is no time for procrastination. You must tell me!"

"He was one of ours, Mr. President."

"Okay, Allen, now tell me how this all came about."

The only man speaking for the next ten minutes was Dulles.

He told Johnson Oswald was a high school dropout who had an amazing affinity for foreign languages. The Marine Corps taught him Russian in just six months.

Almost all Marines lean to the right politically. Oswald was different. He leaned left. Oswald was also a screwup who was facing a third court-martial.

Dulles told Johnson these confluence of events made Oswald a perfect candidate for recruitment.

"Mr. President, we had very little to lose and much to gain. We facilitated his trip to Russia."

Johnson was stunned. "Allen! What did you think the Russians were going to do with this guy? Put him in charge of a defense plant?"

"We weren't certain. We speculated they might believe Oswald's assertion that he was a genuine communist who wanted to leave his home country and serve the cause."

"How did that assumption work out?"

"They put a blanket over him. They watched him twenty-four hours a day, seven days a week. They did not watch him from a distance. They were right on top of him. After a year we gave up. We finally found a way to slip him a note and told him he could come home."

"I remember reading about Oswald returning. I wondered how a traitor could get back into the United States."

"We paid his travel expenses, Mr. President. Remember, he was a pretend traitor."

"Allen, we have a fine mess on our hands. The newspapers are going to report to the American people that the man who shot their president was a communist who spent two years in Russia. The American people are going to rationally conclude that Russia ordered the death of John Kennedy."

"That is a very real possibility, Mr. President. However, there is another scenario that is equally devastating. Some enterprising newspaperman might find out that Oswald was a CIA plant who came home as a failure. John Kennedy blamed the CIA for the Bay of Pigs. He spoke publicly about breaking the CIA down and rebuilding it. What if the American people were told that the CIA killed John Kennedy in retaliation for his threats of dismemberment?"

Johnson had not seen that one coming. "Allen, it appears to me that Lee Harvey Oswald is a stick of dynamite that could explode right in our faces."

"A more apt analogy is that Lee Harvey Oswald is a nuclear bomb waiting to go off and destroy everything."

Johnson thought for a second. Yes, that was a better analogy. "Allen, do you have any recommendations?"

"Mr. President, I believe it is manifestly in everyone's best interests that Mr. Oswald never sees the inside of a courtroom."

"Are you saying what I think you are saying?"

"Lee Harvey Oswald above ground could tear apart your administration before it even gets started. If, by some miracle, he could be put under the earth, we could control the narrative."

"You want me to arrange his death? I cannot take that kind of risk."

"You won't have to. I believe there are men in Louisiana and Texas who are upset that Mr. Oswald is still alive. If we could get word to them that the deed would not be honestly investigated, we might have a chance of surviving this calamity."

"Allen, do you know a name of someone who can handle this?"

"I do."

"Can you make the call?"

"I can. But I need you to tell me right now this is what you want, and come all the furies of hell you will never discuss this conversation."

Johnson did not respond.

Dulles waited patiently on the phone. He knew Johnson was weighing the risks. Best to let him sort it out without pressuring him.

"Allen!"

"Yes, Mr. President."

"Do what you think is in the best interests of the United States."

The line went dead.

Chapter 48

Mobsters in Tampa, New Orleans, Chicago, and Dallas were burning up pay telephone lines on Saturday, November 23, 1963.

The heavyweights in La Cosa Nostra had a serious problem.

The men sweating bullets on that day were Carlos Marcello, Sam Giancana, John Roselli, and Santo Trafficante.

Phase one of their conspiracy had been a success. John Kennedy was dead. Robert Kennedy would soon be neutered by Lyndon Johnson.

But the one man who absolutely had to die along with John Kennedy was not dead. He was housed inside the Dallas Police Department.

His name was Lee Harvey Oswald. He was a skinny twenty-four-year-old man who had the potential to tear down the entire edifice of organized crime in America.

And he was talking. He denied killing John Kennedy. He asked for legal representation. He used the word "patsy" in describing his involvement in the assassination.

So far Oswald had not named names. The high lords of crime knew it was only a matter of hours before he did.

Two days earlier Carlos Marcello believed he had covered all his bases. He had put in place two scenarios concerning the demise of Oswald.

First, there was the bogus security guard. He panicked at the critical moment and disappeared, allowing Oswald to walk out of the depository.

Marcello did not want all his eggs in one basket. Dallas Patrolman J. D. Tippit was on his payroll.

Tippit was instructed to take care of Oswald should he escape from the book depository.

Tippit left his normal patrol zone and waited near the boarding house that was Oswald's temporary abode.

Tippit did not intercept Oswald before he got to the boarding house. That was unfortunate. Had he done so, Oswald would not have had a gun in his coat pocket.

Tippit found Oswald after the suspect had armed himself. Tippit did not know Oswald was fortified with a handgun. That is why Tippit exited his patrol car with his gun still holstered.

Goodbye, Officer Tippit.

The men who arrested Oswald at the movie theater were not on Marcello's payroll.

Oswald pointed his gun at them. They could have blown him away. They instead brought him in with only a black eye.

Marcello had just one more card to play. It had to work. It had to work quickly.

The instant Oswald was booked into the Dallas Police Department, Marcello went to a pay telephone and called Jacob Leon Rubenstein, a.k.a. Jack Ruby.

Ruby owned the Carousel Club in Dallas. This was a hangout for gangsters and cops.

Ruby bought the loyalty of Dallas police officers by buying them drinks, and he would order his strippers to provide the lawmen with sex on demand.

Ruby was Jewish. This prevented him from becoming a made man in La Cosa Nostra. But he was a recognized associate of Marcello's Mob.

Marcello was Ruby's boss. Ruby could not make a move in Dallas without first asking Marcello. Now Marcello was telling the nightclub owner he had to take charge.

"Jack, you've got to kill the little bastard. We don't have a choice."

Ruby did not want to do it. The deed would have to be done in front of millions of people. The entire media world was in Dallas covering the assassination.

Marcello put the best spin possible on the situation. "For Christ's sake, Jack! You will be killing the man who shot John Kennedy! They might give you a medal."

Ruby did not buy that line, but it was in Marcello's interest to spin the crisis the best way possible.

"Look, Jack, you might have to spend a year in jail, maybe two. The organization will be working night and day. You know if we spread enough money around, we will get you out! And when you do get out, there will be a half a million dollars sitting in a bank in the Cayman Islands. And the mortgage on the Carousel Club will be paid off."

Ruby was trapped. He knew in the end he would have to accede to Marcello's importuning.

Marcello had the power to order a hit on Ruby. And he would do it because the situation with Oswald was critical.

Ruby also knew he was the logical choice for the job. He was so well known he could wander around the Dallas Police Department without drawing any attention.

Half the department had consumed Ruby's liquor and enjoyed the company of his women.

There was a press conference in the Dallas Police Department just hours after Oswald's arrest. District Attorney Henry Wade was briefing reporters. Ruby pretended to be a newsman. He had a snub-nosed .38 caliber revolver in his coat.

Had police made Oswald available, Ruby would have shot him on the spot. Oswald was not there.

Sunday, November 24, 1963, was sunny and warm.

At 11:17 a.m. Ruby was at Western Union. This was no accident. The building was one block from the Dallas Police Department.

Police were going to transfer Oswald from the police station to the county jail. In an abundance of caution, they were going to use an armored car to facilitate the move.

Ruby sauntered over to the police station and used a ramp to access the basement. He knew all about the transfer. The police were not circumspect in telling the whole world about Oswald's schedule.

There were dozens of cops and reporters in the basement. Ruby fit in like a piece of furniture. No one challenged his presence.

Oswald was manacled between two detectives. He should have been as safe as a baby in the womb.

Except the Dallas Police Department basement that Sunday morning was not a womb. It was a snake pit.

Ruby lunged at Oswald. He fired one shot at point-blank range. The bullet damaged his spleen, stomach, aorta, vena cava, kidney, liver, diaphragm, and a rib.

Oswald buckled over in pain. The two detectives looked as if they had seen a werewolf.

Ruby only expended one bullet. This was a risk. Had the bullet missed all the vital organs, Oswald might have survived.

It would have been a nightmare. Oswald certainly would have sung like a canary in order to destroy his tormentors.

Marcello and Ruby got lucky. A single bullet did so much interior damage Oswald was dead in two hours.

He died at Parkland Hospital, the same hospital that treated John Kennedy two days earlier.

Jack Ruby instantly replaced Lee Harvey Oswald as the most famous person ever to be arrested in Dallas.

Lyndon Johnson that Sunday morning was on the hotline with Nikita Khrushchev.

It was inevitable that the leaders of the planet's only two superpowers would communicate. Each side had enough nuclear weapons to destroy the human race. Johnson immediately told Khrushchev that Oswald was an American asset sent to Russia in a silly attempt to penetrate some unidentified Soviet defense or military installation.

Khrushchev fired back that his people were never fooled. "We watched him day and night."

Johnson said he personally had nothing to do with the Oswald spy effort. "I was in the Senate when he defected," Johnson explained. "President Eisenhower did not normally inform Senators about such things."

Khrushchev said he was not concerned about Oswald's mission. "You spy on us, and we spy on you."

What did bother the Russian leader was any perception in America that Oswald was a Russian asset sent here to kill an American president.

"You must squash this misinformation in its cradle!" Johnson could hear the Soviet premier hit a table with his fist.

The man speaking to Johnson was a translator. Johnson also had his own translator sitting next to him.

Midway through their conversation, Johnson could hear the Russians speaking amongst themselves. He could hear chairs being pushed back and the sound of feet shuffling over a carpet.

Seconds later the Soviet translator explained what was going on.

"Mr. President, the premier has cleared the room of all military and intelligence people. It is just the two of us. He wishes to discuss some matters of a highly personal nature."

Johnson was intrigued. "Go ahead."

"I will attempt to translate simultaneously as the premier speaks. Please bear with me."

"I understand."

"The premier wants you to recall that it was only a year ago our two countries came within a whisker of going to war. A single miscalculation could have triggered what you in the West call Armageddon."

"Tell the premier I recall those days most vividly."

"In order to achieve peace, each side had to give way. We took our missiles out of Cuba. You took your missiles out of Turkey. Herein lies the problem. Our dismantling of missiles in Cuba was reported across the world. But John Kennedy insisted the removal of missiles from Turkey had to remain a secret. The entire world was told America had 'won' the Cuban crisis. I believe one of your statesman said, 'We went eyeball to eyeball with the other side, and they blinked first.' This was a terrible blow to Russian pride and prestige. To this day my military and intelligence people are seething. And who do you think they blame? They blame me.

"Mr. President, since October of 1962, my position in my own country has become tenuous. I cannot under any circumstances appear weak in the face of American pressure for a second time. Mr.

President, if your news media accuses my country of organizing the death of John Kennedy, I will have to respond. I will order my army to seize West Berlin."

Johnson felt a chill go up his back. A Soviet move on West Berlin would mandate an American military response. No ifs, ands or buts.

In a matter of hours, the missiles would be flying east and west and human civilization would come to an ignominious end.

Johnson's mind was spinning like a top. At that very moment, there was a loud knock on Johnson's office door.

This could not be good news. Johnson had ordered that he was not to be interrupted while he was speaking with the Soviet premier. Only something sensational could negate his edict.

Johnson covered the telephone receiver with his hand. "What is it?"

John Kennedy's press secretary, Pierre Salinger, was in the doorway. "Mr. President! Lee Harvey Oswald has been shot!"

Johnson forced himself to remain calm. He took his hand away from the receiver. "Premier Khrushchev, we just had a development that changes everything. May I call you back in one hour? One more thing. You might want to turn on your television set."

Chapter 49

Curt Holmes and Stuart Dunleavy were both at their desks at 6:00 a.m. on the morning of Monday, November 25, 1963.

Three days earlier each man had received the shock of a lifetime.

John Kennedy was dead. All work at the NSA came to a stop. Dunleavy sat in Holmes's office glued to the television set.

They watched the televised images of Parkland Hospital. The reporters, the doctors, the Secret Service men running in and out of the building.

Then came the arrest of Lee Harvey Oswald.

Saturday saw the two men back together at the NSA. Once again Holmes's television set kept them occupied for hours.

"Curt, we have to jump on this immediately!"

"I couldn't agree more, Stu. We need to find out everything there is about this Oswald character. But let's wait until Monday. My family needs me. I'm sure Arlene wants you home too."

"She does. Okay, Monday. I'll be here before the sun comes up."

John Kennedy's body was lying in state at the Capitol Rotunda. Thousands of people were filing by the flag-draped coffin.

Holmes and Dunleavy that Monday morning believed they had a higher mission to perform. As much as they wanted to pay their respects, they felt compelled to stay at their desks garnering information.

Oswald's death a day earlier had triggered an investigative urge in each man.

Holmes and Dunleavy believed Oswald was shot for a very obvious reason—to silence him forever.

Now, a man named Jack Ruby needed to be investigated from the day he was born until this very moment.

Normally this was not something the NSA would do. It was Robert Kennedy who changed the mission of the NSA when he asked for help in tracking the actions of gangsters.

Holmes and Dunleavy believed Robert Kennedy would want them to dive into this calamity and help in any way they could.

Neither man realized that the political dynamics had changed one hundred and eighty degrees.

NSA Director Laurence Frost telephoned J. Edgar Hoover Monday morning. Frost told Hoover his agency stood ready and eager to help. Hoover immediately called Lyndon Johnson. Johnson then called Frost.

For ten minutes, Johnson did all the talking. Frost was permitted to say, "Yes, Mr. President," about five times. Johnson then abruptly hung up.

Frost was stunned by Johnson's tone. It was harsh and definitive. Frost summoned Holmes and Dunleavy into his office immediately after concluding his phone call with Johnson.

"Gentlemen, please have a seat."

Dunleavy could not contain himself. "Curt and I have been—"

Frost cut him off. "Mr. Dunleavy, I just got off the phone with the president of the United States."

Frost let that statement sink in. Then he continued, "The president said the FBI is going to be the lead agency in the investigation of the death of Mr. Kennedy."

Dunleavy took umbrage that Frost said "Mr. Kennedy" instead of "President Kennedy." He did not believe the slight was accidental.

"The president said the NSA is to stand down and not engage in any investigative activity without the consent of the FBI. I am suspending Robert Kennedy's program of tracking the phone calls of mobsters until and unless I hear from J. Edgar Hoover."

Holmes felt he had to interject. "Director, we are uniquely situated to help catch the people who killed our president."

Frost raised his eyebrows. "You said 'people.' The president told me there is a high probability Lee Harvey Oswald acted alone."

Dunleavy shot to his feet. "How could he possibly say that? Oswald was shot and killed just twenty-four hours ago! There are hundreds of people who need to be interviewed and thousands of hours of tape that have to be analyzed."

"Sit down, Mr. Dunleavy. Getting agitated will not advance your argument."

"Excuse me, Mr. Director. You haven't seen me agitated!"

Holmes grabbed Dunleavy's arm and gently pulled him back into his seat. "Director, Stuart and I have a year's worth of investigative material concerning individuals who might have a motive for harming the president. What do you want us to do with it?"

Frost leaned back in his chair. "We are going to turn it over to the FBI. That is a direct order from the president."

Dunleavy again stood up and put his hands on Frost's desk. "Are you ordering us to take no further action unless J. Edgar Hoover deigns to give us the time of day?"

Frost leaned forward into Dunleavy's face. "I thought I made that obvious."

Fearing Dunleavy might punch Frost, Holmes got up and pulled his friend back.

Frost debated firing Dunleavy on the spot. He decided to issue a warning instead. "Mr. Dunleavy, the political world of Washington has changed completely. You would be well advised to adjust to the new reality."

Frost watched Dunleavy spin on his heels and exit his office. It was not the first time he had seen this form of insubordination from Stuart Dunleavy.

Holmes decided to calm the waters. "We have forty-two files connected to Robert Kennedy's investigation," Holmes said. "Do you want them all photocopied, and we will keep the originals on site?"

Frost gave Holmes a hard stare. "Give the FBI the originals. I want them out of this office by noon Wednesday."

"Yes, sir."

Holmes turned and exited Frost's office in a more respectful manner than Dunleavy's brusque departure.

It took him fifteen minutes to find Dunleavy. His friend was in the NSA lunchroom pacing back and forth. "Stu, you have to be careful around Frost. I am going to be very upset if you get fired."

Dunleavy was not assuaged. "Curt, I smell a rat! Does it bother you at all that our president was killed in Texas? There are fifty states, but John Kennedy dies in the one state where Lyndon Johnson holds sway."

"Stu, I don't mind you speculating when it is only the two of us. But be careful about spouting off when someone else is around."

"Curt, what the hell are we going to do about this?"

"You and I are going to start a two-man cabal. Call it Holmes and Watson. There is a lot we can do clandestinely, but we have to be careful!"

"I am all in. I am not going to sit idly by."

"The president is going to be buried today. I want to be there. I know you do. Let's take a week off from investigating the death of John F. Kennedy."

Dunleavy took two steps toward Holmes and looked him straight in the eye. "Curt, do you have the stones to take this no matter where it leads?"

Holmes was not offended. It was a legitimate question. "Stu, I loved the man as much as you did. I will not allow the men responsible for this to get away with it."

Dunleavy decided to end the discussion with some gallows humor. "You and I should invest in two bulletproof vests. We might need them."

Chapter 50

Lyndon Johnson prowled the White House like a gold miner on a riverbank in the Klondike. It was finally his house. A prediction he made at the age of twelve had become a reality.

He was still a trespasser. His acquisition was not the result of an electoral mandate, but it reached fruition from the barrel of a rifle.

It was now seven days since that terrible afternoon in Dallas. John Kennedy was in the ground. The country he left behind was roiling.

Both the House and the Senate were planning on creating special commissions to investigate the assassination.

The Dallas Police Department was still looking into a homicide that occurred on its territory. Authorities in Texas were angry about the body being shipped out of their jurisdiction.

And there were thousands of investigative journalists who might smell Pulitzer in solving the death of John F. Kennedy.

Finally, and most importantly, the Russians were hauling ammunition and trucks up to the border of West Berlin.

Johnson had to put a stop to all of this. And he had to do it quickly. The master of the Senate had a perfect solution—a bipartisan, blue-ribbon commission to examine the matter.

The commission had to be comprised of only the most sterling Americans. The blood running through the veins of these commission members had to be perfectly blue.

The most important criterion was the assurance that these men were persuadable. Johnson had to sell them on a narrative. If the narrative conflicted with the facts, then the facts must suffer.

Executive Order No. 11130 came into existence on November 29, 1963. It called for the creation of a national seven-member commission to explore "the assassination of President John F. Kennedy."

Johnson ordered that the commission's powers "superseded all other investigative agencies."

The chairman of this commission had to be a superstar in the Pantheon of Olympians who roamed the halls of Congress, the White House, and the Supreme Court.

Johnson decided the chairman would be Supreme Court Chief Justice Earl Warren. Warren was a Republican and a liberal. Hollywood could not have done a better job of casting.

One problem. Warren did not want the job. He believed justices serving on law enforcement commissions presented all kinds of problems. Warren was also leery of Lyndon Johnson and his motives.

He told Johnson he would not take the job.

Lyndon Johnson in 1963 was the world's unsurpassed cajoler and convincer. He would not take no for an answer. He played his best card first.

"Earl, the Russians are gearing up to take over West Berlin. One hint that we are going to blame them for John Kennedy's death and it is game over. You are going to be the man who goes down in history as saving hundreds of millions of lives."

Warren was trapped. He consented to the assignment.

The next man Johnson had to recruit was Richard Russell of Georgia. Russell's prestige was so immense he could singlehandedly quell investigations in both the House and the Senate.

Russell was adamant. He would not serve. He was suffering from emphysema, and the stress of the work on the commission might shorten his life.

He told his friend Lyndon Johnson he would not serve "under any circumstances."

Johnson did not blink. He ordered reporters to convene in the White House. He told them Richard Russell had agreed to serve.

The reporters of course published the information. Russell was incensed. He ripped Johnson a new one. Johnson kept his cool and said, "You are an old soldier, and I know if your president asks you to do something, you will not disobey."

Russell caved. His participation had the desired effect. Both the House and the Senate ended their assassination investigations.

Now that Johnson had the two biggest enchiladas in Washington, he had little trouble lining up the other five members.

Congressman Gerald Ford of Michigan did not protest for even a second.

John J. McCloy was an advisor to both Republican and Democrat Presidents. He signed up immediately.

Senator Sherman Cooper of Kentucky and Democratic Whip Hale Boggs of Louisiana also put up no barriers.

The last man Johnson wanted on the commission was going to be problematic. Allen Dulles had been fired from the CIA by John Kennedy.

Dulles's brain was a Fort Knox of information about clandestine operations worldwide. He also was aware how the Kennedy boys operated when they had power. And he knew all their skeletons.

Johnson believed he would have to get Robert Kennedy to sign off on the commission and its members. And that included Dulles.

Johnson had just the man to bring Robert Kennedy around—J. Edgar Hoover.

The relationship between Kennedy and Johnson was so toxic the president did not want to be alone with the man. They truly hated each other.

Robert Kennedy was also no fan of J. Edgar Hoover. The feeling was mutual.

Johnson telephoned Hoover. He told the FBI director that Robert Kennedy "had to be corralled and broken."

Hoover smiled into the phone. "Yes, sir, Mr. President."

Hoover had waited three years for this opportunity. Robert Kennedy was still his boss, but his brother's death had knocked the arrogance out of him.

Hoover was determined to bring him to his knees. He had the ammunition to accomplish this goal.

Robert Kennedy buried his brother on Monday. He could not bring himself to set foot in the Justice Department until Thursday.

The first thing he noticed was his direct line to Hoover was disconnected. He called Hoover's secretary to ask about it.

"Mr. Hoover ordered it be taken away," she said.

"When?"

"The day your brother died." The woman did not sound like she was afraid of any response Robert Kennedy might throw in her direction.

For a split second, Robert Kennedy almost said, "Get that son of a bitch on the line right now!"

He held back. J. Edgar Hoover had a new boss. His name was Johnson.

Robert Kennedy's ability to push around J. Edgar Hoover ended at 1:00 p.m., Friday, November 22, 1963.

Kennedy said, "Thank you," and he hung up.

The next day Hoover asked Robert Kennedy to come down to his office. For three years, it was Hoover who had hoofed it over to Kennedy's office.

Hoover's secretary did not say, "Good morning, Mr. Kennedy" or "I'm so sorry about your brother."

She merely said, "The director will see you now."

Hoover did not rise when Robert Kennedy entered his office. "Please sit down…Bobby."

The world had indeed turned. Hoover had never dared refer to the president's brother by his first name. And he did not even say Robert.

Kennedy eased himself into a leather chair directly opposite the unappealing face of J. Edgar Hoover. "Bobby, our country needs you now more than ever."

Kennedy had expected at least a half-hearted condolence over his brother's death, but that clearly was not forthcoming. "What can I do for you…J. Edgar?"

Hoover would have fired any agent who used such familiarity, but he understood Kennedy was merely counterattacking one insult with another. "Bobby, the president asked me to brief you on his decision to appoint a blue-ribbon commission to examine your brother's demise."

Kennedy thought, *Demise! He was murdered!* But he did not express his viewpoint with Hoover. He just said, "Go ahead."

"We cannot have eight or nine individual criminal investigations nationwide. We have to contain this situation right here in Washington."

"I want the men responsible for my brother's death found and punished to the full extent of the law!" Kennedy had risen halfway out of his seat.

"We all want that, Bobby. Your brother deserves justice. But that is not the only issue President Johnson must contend with."

"It is the only issue that really matters, J. Edgar. The American people will demand the truth!"

"Bobby, earlier this week, the president was on the hotline with Soviet Premier Nikita Khrushchev. The premier told President Johnson that Lee Harvey Oswald was not a Soviet agent. President Johnson told the premier he believed him. That did not put an end to the issue."

Hoover continued, "Khrushchev told the president he was prepared to move on West Berlin if there were accusations in the Western press about Russian complicity in your brother's death."

"I find that hard to believe."

"I will tell you why it is true, Bobby. Remember a year ago when you were at the Russian embassy negotiating an end to the Cuban Missile Crisis?"

"Of course, I remember."

"You agreed to give up our Jupiter missiles in Turkey in return for a Russian promise to remove their missiles from Cuba. Correct?"

Kennedy hesitated. "Yes."

"You demanded the removal of the Jupiter missiles had to remain a secret. But the removal of the Russian missiles was on the front page of every newspaper in the world. Khrushchev was embarrassed and humiliated. That is never a good look for a man who heads a totalitarian regime."

Kennedy rubbed his chin and pondered Hoover's analysis. He decided it might have merit. "Listen, J. Edgar. I am prepared to believe the Russians might not be involved in my brother's death. That does not mean Oswald acted alone. I have a pretty good idea who ordered my brother's death. Their names are Marcello, Trafficante, Roselli, and Giancana. And I would not exclude James Riddle Hoffa from this group."

"Well, Bobby, that brings up another set of problems. If we go after these unsavory characters, we might all get burned. Right now, you should be concerned about your brother's legacy."

"How can the prosecution of these scumbags hurt my brother's legacy?"

"Give me a minute, Bobby."

Hoover stood up, walked to his office door, opened it, and told his secretary to bring in the boys.

Hoover returned to his chair and folded his hands in front of him. He and Kennedy just stared at each other for thirty seconds.

Three FBI agents entered Hoover's office. Each one had a dolly. On each dolly were boxes stacked five feet high. The agents slid the boxes off the dollies.

"You may go, gentlemen."

The agents filed out and closed the door.

Kennedy was confused. "What's all this?"

"This is your life, Bobby. This is also your father's life. And your brother's life. It is the story of the Kennedy clan going back to the days of Prohibition, right up to the year 1963."

Kennedy knew immediately what Hoover was about to do. Blackmail. "What do you plan on doing with all this material, J. Edgar?"

"Hopefully, nothing. It is my desire to cart all of this right back into the bowels of this building and let it all continue to collect dust."

"Then why bring it out and show it to me?"

"To let you know what might happen if there are a dozen criminal trials connected to your brother's death."

"Nothing in those files is more important than bringing these men to justice!"

"Really? May I give you a tutorial about what might be exposed if we don't contain this situation?"

"I suppose I can't stop you."

"Bobby, in 1919, your father was worth less than a million dollars. Fourteen years later, he was the fourth richest man in America. What happened between 1919 and 1933?"

"I suppose you are going to bring up that old canard about my father and bootlegging."

"It's not a canard, Bobby. It's all in here."

"No one cares what my father did forty years ago."

"Okay, but I'm just getting started. Do you know who first asked me to start a file on your father? It was Herbert Hoover. The year was 1929. He had heard stories about your dad. You know what saved your father? The stock market crashed that year. Hoover had more important things to do than chase after Joseph Patrick Kennedy."

"Your father was spared the embarrassment of an income tax investigation concerning all the money he made in a decade and a half. Remember what happened to Al Capone? He got eleven years for not paying his taxes."

Kennedy shuffled uneasily in his chair. "I suppose there is more."

"Oh, yes. In 1933, Roosevelt asked me to come to the White House. He and your dad were friends. But that did not stop good old Franklin from ordering a thorough investigation of everything Kennedy. Surveillance, wiretaps, photos, witness statements, we got it all. Once a month I would brief Roosevelt on your father's activities. He could not get enough."

Kennedy started to counterattack. "If Roosevelt had so much dirt on my father, why did he pick him to become ambassador to England?"

"To get him out of the country. Roosevelt was going for a third term. He knew your father wanted to be president in 1940."

"You sound pretty sure of yourself, J. Edgar."

"I should be. Roosevelt instructed me to send two FBI agents to England to monitor your dad's behavior. What a character your dad turned out to be! Did you know your dad hung out with the most vicious anti-Semites in England? Would you believe me if I told you we have audiotapes of your dad telling his friends that whatever happened to the Jews in Germany they had it coming?"

"I don't believe you."

Hoover stood up and walked over to the boxes. He pointed to one and said, "I believe those tapes are in here. Should I pull them out?"

Kennedy started to squirm.

"Bobby, how is your sister Rosemary doing?"

Kennedy could not understand why Hoover was mentioning his mentally impaired sister. She certainly had no dark secrets. "She is in Wisconsin. She is institutionalized. Why on earth are you bringing this up?"

"I'll bet your dad told you she was mentally retarded, correct?"

"Yes."

"She was never mentally retarded. She was depressed. Your father found her irritating. He was afraid she might disgrace the perfect family. So, he had her lobotomized."

"That's a lie!"

"No, it isn't. I have an affidavit from the doctor who performed the operation. Would you like to see it?"

"No!"

"A man who deliberately incapacitates one of his own children could be construed by the American people as a monster, don't you think so?"

"The American people will not punish my brother's memory because of the alleged sins committed by our father!"

Hoover smiled. "Let's talk about your brother." He returned to his seat.

Kennedy saw an opening. "If you want to talk about my brother the war hero, by all means, let's proceed."

"Your brother became a war hero in 1943. I'd like to talk about what he was doing in 1941 and 1942."

Kennedy did not know where Hoover was going. "Adolph Hitler declared war on America on December 11, 1941. Your brother was in Washington cavorting with a woman named Inga Arvad. Does this ring a bell?"

Inga Arvad. The Danish beauty queen who captured John Kennedy's fancy.

In the 1930s, Arvad was a journalist. Her beauty came to the attention of Der Führer. He invited her to attend the 1936 Berlin Olympics. He granted her three interviews, something no other female correspondent ever accomplished. She may have slept with the Chancellor of Germany.

Naval officer John Kennedy was sleeping with a woman who wrote glowing stories about Germany under Hitler's guidance.

Hoover believed she might have been a spy. He assigned agents to monitor her every movement in America. There were photos and wiretaps of intimate moments.

"Your brother lived quite a ribald lifestyle, Bobby."

Robert Kennedy knew all about the relationship. "They never proved she was a spy," he said defensively.

"Sure. Sure. But your brother insisted on seeing her even after we warned him about her potential threat."

"Anything else, J. Edgar?"

"I'm just getting warmed up. Two days after your brother returned from his honeymoon, he had an assignation with a buxom blonde. She threatened to spill the story. Your dad wrote her a check for ten thousand dollars. Her witness statement is somewhere in those boxes."

"My brother nearly died in the South Pacific. Then he took a bullet to the brain while serving his country as president. The American people will forgive his infidelities."

"They probably will. But it will still be a dark stain on his record."

"If this is all you've got, J. Edgar, then I am not impressed."

"Bobby, please look at those boxes. Each box contains dozens of files. Each file is a hand grenade waiting to go off. Do you want to hear the good stuff?"

Kennedy did not answer. He just nodded in the affirmative.

"In 1960, your dad was worried about a close election. He was right to be worried. He wanted an insurance policy. The state of Illinois was key. Your dad contacted a man who had a lot of pull in the city of Chicago. This man manufactured votes for your brother, enough votes to give him the election. That man was Sam Giancana."

Kennedy had a one-word answer. "Bullshit!"

"Oh, your dad didn't tell you, did he? Not surprising. You and your brother had spent years trying to get Giancana and his friends behind bars. Your dad probably thought the two of you would not understand the necessities of politics. Well, I am telling you he did make that deal."

Kennedy started to wonder if Hoover knew the rest of the story. Did Hoover know that following the Bay of Pigs, John Kennedy's CIA recruited Giancana, Roselli, and Trafficante in a plot to kill Castro?

Hoover read Kennedy's mind like it was an open book. "Yeah, I know all about Operation Mongoose. You and your brother recruited gangsters to kill Castro because you did not have the stones to do it the first time you had a shot at him. Imagine what the American people would think of these shenanigans.

"And here's the best part of this story, Bobby. Your brother was banging Sam Giancana's girlfriend. In the White House. Do you think maybe he might have spilled some state secrets during those assignations? Do you think the girlfriend kept Kennedy's ruminations quiet or did she tell Sammy Boy all about them?"

Kennedy knew this story was true. The woman's name was Judith Campbell. She was a stone-cold fox. It was Robert Kennedy who told his brother he had to stop seeing her.

"You seem to be a volcano of information, J. Edgar."

"I have hundreds of the world's best investigators at my beck and call. Of course I know a great many things."

Kennedy was not ready to fold. "Are you going to help me track down my brother's killers?"

"We know who killed your brother. His name is Lee Harvey Oswald. And he acted alone."

"I can't accept that!"

"Okay, Bobby. I forgot to mention the file we have on someone who is, or was, more famous than you or your brother."

Kennedy froze. There was only one person who fit that criteria—Marilyn Monroe.

Hoover again read Kennedy's eyes and knew what he was thinking. "That's right, Bobby. It was just a year ago Ms. Monroe left us at the tender age of thirty-six. Did you know we had been tracking Monroe ever since she married that commie writer Arthur Miller?

We bugged her no matter where she went. Even after she divorced Miller."

Hoover was getting revved up. "That woman slept with more men than any hooker who ever lived. Famous men. Actors, singers, composers, and of course, politicians."

Kennedy stared at Hoover as if the man were a spider crawling across his pillow.

"Then we noticed Ms. Monroe was making telephone calls to the White House. And guess who stayed overnight multiple times when Mrs. Kennedy was out of town? Ms. Monroe was not shy. She bragged about her affair with the world's most powerful man. She was so high on drugs and alcohol she no longer had the capacity for rational thought. That's when I had a conversation with your brother. I told him he had to cut her loose. Immediately!"

Hoover now leaned in for the kill. "He cut her loose, all right. He handed her off to you. My surveillance team laughed their heads off when they heard you and Marilyn going at it like dogs."

Hoover again got up and walked over to the stacked files. "I believe that tape is…hmmm, oh yeah, it's in this box."

He put his index finger on a brown storage box. He also grinned. Hoover returned to his desk.

"I believe you were in Los Angeles no more than a mile away from Ms. Monroe's bungalow the night she died. Am I correct?"

Kennedy was beaten. It was all true.

He was a married man with eleven children. He had an affair with a woman his brother had tossed aside. A very famous woman.

A nut job was threatening to tell the whole world about how the Kennedy men treated women.

Bobby had many conversations with Marilyn that could only be described as sexually prurient. If Hoover had these conversations on tape, it was game over.

From this point on it was no longer "J. Edgar." "What is it you want me to do, Mr. Hoover?"

"The president and I want you to endorse the Warren Commission and every man selected to serve on it. When the commission releases its findings, you will stand next to the president and state you support its conclusions. We want you to stand in front of the media and tell the world you want Allen Dulles to serve on the commission. Is that clear?"

Kennedy shrunk into his seat. "Yes."

"You are doing the right thing, Bobby."

"Then why do I feel like shit?"

Hoover decided to placate Kennedy, if for no other reason his victory was so complete. "Bobby, Lyndon Johnson is going to run for president in 1964. He will probably be facing Barry Goldwater of Arizona. Johnson will clobber Goldwater."

"He can lawfully run again in 1968. When he completes his second term in 1972, you can run. You will still be a young man."

Hoover stood up and walked over to the boxes. He spread his arms wide as if to encompass all the awful material that threatened the future of Robert Kennedy and his brother Teddy.

"None of this ever has to see the light of day, Bobby. I intend to die sitting in that chair. When that happens, my secretary is under orders to incinerate everything I keep in a very special room here in this building. You will be able to build your own legacy. And you will have protected your brother's legacy for all time. Have a nice day… Bobby."

Robert Kennedy marched out of Hoover's office with hunched shoulders and a hangdog face. In one week, he had lost the two things he treasured most of all. His brother. And then his dignity.

Chapter 51

Curt Holmes and Stuart Dunleavy went about their business at the NSA like they were robots. All the passion had been drained from the two men.

The year was 1964. It was the early spring. The cherry blossom trees were once again in full flower and the cavalcade of color dazzled tourists.

Two months earlier, Robert Kennedy asked Holmes and Dunleavy to meet him in his office at the Department of Justice.

Each man was shocked by Kennedy's countenance. The vibrancy was gone. Kennedy's face was permanently morose.

His personality once filled the office with strength and determination. Now he was a crushed bug, scrunched back in a leather chair that seemed to consume him.

Holmes and Dunleavy naturally assumed his demeanor was directly related to the loss of his brother.

That was only part of the answer. What Kennedy could not tell them was that there were two knives in his back, not just one.

Kennedy could not explain the real reason he was shutting down the NSA surveillance program aimed at the country's criminal class.

He could not tell his friends that J. Edgar Hoover had a warehouse full of information that would sink the Kennedy family forever if it saw the light of day.

Kennedy told the two men, "Please cease and desist the surveillance program unless you are directly asked to continue by the FBI." Kennedy said he was committed to allowing the Warren Commission enough time to complete its report.

Kennedy then handed Holmes and Dunleavy two photocopies of a memorandum. It had been written by his close friend, Nicholas

Katzenbach. Katzenbach was Kennedy's deputy attorney general. He was a staunch Kennedy acolyte.

That was why the language in the memo absolutely floored Holmes and Dunleavy.

The memo was written Sunday, November 24, 1963. Katzenbach had put pen to paper as soon as he heard that Lee Harvey Oswald was dead.

The memo was transcribed the next day and sent to Lyndon Johnson's aide Bill Moyers.

The essence of the memo was simple. It recommended that the entire weight of the federal government be directed in only one direction. Lee Harvey Oswald acted alone, and there was no conspiracy.

The Russians were not involved. The Mob was not involved. The CIA played no role in the president's death. Neither did any right-wing militia groups. The Cubans were not involved. Nor were any leftwing domestic groups involved.

It was only Oswald.

Wrote Katzenbach: "The public must be satisfied that Oswald was the assassin, that he did not have confederates who are still at large, and that the evidence was such that he would have been convicted at trial."

He continued, "Speculation about Oswald's motivation ought to be cut off."

The memo was two pages long, but the narrative never varied.

Holmes and Dunleavy were flabbergasted. The death of John Kennedy was the most important homicide worldwide in a hundred years.

It was inconceivable that the number two man in the DOJ was making such a foundational statement forty-eight hours after the assassination.

A proper investigation would take a minimum of six months. Hundreds of interviews would have to be arranged. A careful collection of forensic evidence was mandatory before any conclusions could be drawn.

Dunleavy could not contain himself. "Bobby, what the hell!"

Kennedy just put his chin on his chest. He could not look at his friends.

Holmes felt compelled to give his friend the attorney general the benefit of the doubt.

"Bobby, I know there have to be important reasons for this. I am not going to pressure you to explain. You loved your brother more than your own life."

"Thank you, Curt." Tears started to form in Kennedy's eyes.

Dunleavy was not pacified. "Dammit, I loved your brother too! We all did! This was a crime of staggering magnitude! We have to find out if there was a conspiracy!"

"Stuart, I am asking you as a friend to let the Warren Commission do its work. Can you just trust me on this?"

Dunleavy saw the pain in Kennedy's face. He felt for the man. "Okay, Bobby. I will back off. I just pray the commission is not being controlled by some sinister forces seeking to corrupt the investigation."

Holmes stood up. "Okay, Stu. Time for us to go."

Each man exited Kennedy's office with a different demeanor. Holmes was dejected. But Dunleavy's face was red. He was furious.

The two men walked to their cars to drive back to the NSA.

Dunleavy's fists were balled up like a boxer. Had someone brushed his shoulder on the sidewalk, Dunleavy might have turned and pummeled the unsuspecting pedestrian.

"Curt, what the hell is going on? I didn't realize that detectives looking into a murder started with a conclusion and then proceeded with an investigation!"

Holmes did not have a cogent answer. "There has to be a reason, Stu. God knows I wish I had the answer."

"What are we going to do? Stand down? Do nothing?"

"Stu, Frost told us we are not to lift a finger unless the FBI asks us directly to get involved."

"It seems to me that day is never going to come!"

"What can we do, Stu? We are two tiny cogs in a giant machine."

"All right, Curt. I'll back off. I'll wait. When the Warren Commission completes its work, I will read it cover to cover. But if I believe it is all a bunch of crap, I won't just take it."

"Seriously, Stuart. What can you do?"

"I don't know. I just know I am not going to roll over."

They drove in separate cars until they reached the NSA.

Stuart was handed a slip of paper by Frost's secretary. It was a request that he call his mother.

This could not be good. He dialed his mother's number in West Palm Beach.

Mike Dunleavy was dead.

Mother and son spoke for twenty minutes.

Dunleavy hung up. He was sad. But he also saw an opportunity. Dunleavy asked Frost for some time off. He was not teary-eyed.

"Director, I would like to take off for an entire month. There is going to be a funeral, and then I have to help my mother settle my father's affairs."

Frost was inclined to grant an extended leave of absence. He looked forward to an entire month without Stuart Dunleavy. "Son, I am sorry for your loss, and yes, you can take all the time you need."

"Thank you, Director."

Curt Holmes was now doubly depressed. They had just left Bobby Kennedy's office, and now this calamity. "Stu, I have some time saved up. I would be honored to accompany you to Florida."

"God bless you, Curt. But I don't want you wasting your vacation time on a funeral."

"It wouldn't bother me one bit."

"Do me a favor. Stay in Washington and keep an eye on Bobby."

"Okay, Stu. Just don't forget to use the telephone."

Dunleavy spent the rest of the day speaking with his wife and his siblings. He ordered two plane tickets for the following day.

He had a plan. He would honor his father. He would spend two weeks in Florida.

Then he would again hop on an airplane. Except his destination would not be Washington, DC.

Stuart Dunleavy would take a direct flight in the opposite direction.

He was going to spend the remainder of his leave time in Dallas, Texas.

Chapter 52

Stuart Dunleavy had mixed emotions as the wheels of a United Airlines jet hit the pavement at Love Field in Dallas.

It was late April 1964. Less than six months earlier, Air Force One had landed at this same airport. It brought a live president to Texas. It left with a dead one.

Stuart and his very pregnant wife had flown to Florida to bury seventy-seven-year-old Mike Dunleavy.

After fourteen days in West Palm Beach, Arlene Dunleavy went back to Washington. Solo.

She did not want her husband heading to a different location. She wanted Stuart to stick to his job and keep his nose out of the Kennedy assassination.

It took twenty-four hours of debate and argument before Stuart convinced his wife this was something he had to do.

"I hope I don't give birth to this child alone, Stuart!"

Dunleavy felt a pang of regret, but he stuck to his guns. "I will call every night, I promise."

In the end, she kissed him at the airport. "Be careful Stuart. You are poking your nose where no one wants you."

Dunleavy hugged his wife for a long time.

Now he was in that awful state that housed men who had the capacity to kill an American president.

Dunleavy did not want to check into a first-class hotel. The staff of the Warren Commission was all over Dallas. He was certain to bump into someone in some swank digs who knew him from Washington.

Dunleavy found a second-rate hotel called the Cranston. It had running water and heat, which was all he cared about. He unpacked his suitcase. He had five pair of pants and an equal number of shirts.

He also had his military edition 1911 Colt .45, the same weapon that helped to keep him alive in the South Pacific.

He had to wear a jacket every day regardless of the temperature. The jacket would hide his shoulder holster.

He spent the day mapping out his strategy. Day 1 would see him visit the infamous Texas School Book Depository.

Dunleavy decided he would use his NSA identification on civilians. He could easily pass himself off as a Warren Commission staffer. That strategy, of course, held risk. If he was caught, NSA Director Frost would probably fire him.

It was a calculated risk he was willing to take.

Dunleavy stayed in his room the entire first day. He spent an hour on the telephone with his wife. He succeeded in calming turbulent waters. He debated calling Curt Holmes. He decided against it. Curt had enough on his plate besides worrying about his best friend, who was in the middle of a clandestine intelligence operation.

Dunleavy poured himself a stiff bourbon. He turned on the news. Three bourbons later he was sound asleep.

At the crack of dawn, Dunleavy was showered and shaved. He walked two blocks to a breakfast joint. He downed three eggs, four strips of bacon, an English muffin, and two cups of coffee.

A taxi was parked out front. "Dealey Plaza," Dunleavy told the driver.

"I can find it blindfolded," the driver responded. "I cannot count the number of people I have driven to that godforsaken address."

Dunleavy stepped out of the cab one hundred feet from the Texas School Book Depository. For sixty seconds, he just stared up at the sixth floor.

He was not alone. Hundreds of tourists were lining the streets to experience the history that occurred there.

Dunleavy walked through the front door. He was glad to see dozens of other people roaming about the premises.

He would use their numbers as cover. He wanted to find someone who was working at the depository in late November.

It did not take long.

Henry Jackson was a fifty-five-year-old black custodian. He had been hired three years earlier to keep the book depository clean. Dunleavy introduced himself. He lied and said he was officially connected to the Kennedy assassination investigative team.

Jackson was hostile. Dunleavy could not understand why.

"Are you with the FBI?" Jackson glowered at Dunleavy.

"No, I am not."

"Good. Because I have had it up to here with the F…B…I."

"I don't have any preconceived notions, Mr. Jackson. Can you tell me what happened?"

"Sure! Two days after Mr. Kennedy was killed, I was called into the Dallas FBI headquarters. They grilled me hard. I guess they wanted to make certain I wasn't in on it."

"I told them I saw Lee Harvey Oswald that day. But he was not on the sixth floor when those shots rang out. He was on the third floor, in the lunchroom, with me. Those FBI guys, they didn't want to know nothing from nothing. They kept telling me I had to be wrong. I told them 'Hey, were you there? No. I was there.' They kept shaking their heads and telling me I was mistaken. Finally, they got nasty. They said I could get into real trouble if I kept telling that story. I didn't want to tangle with the federal government. So, I shut up. Until now."

Dunleavy asked Jackson, "Did you see anyone you didn't recognize that day?"

"Yeah. I did. But only for a few seconds. I saw him climb the stairs. White guy. Short. Looked Hispanic or Italian."

"Did you see him leave?"

"No. But I told the FBI about the guy. They showed no interest in him at all."

"Has the FBI called you in for any follow-up investigation?"

"Nope. And I haven't been called by the Warren Commission either. Can you tell me what the hell is going on?"

"I'm trying to find out myself, Mr. Jackson. Thank you very much."

Dunleavy was about to leave but he stopped himself. "Would it be possible for me to see the sixth floor?"

"Sure. Go right up those stairs."

Dunleavy easily traversed the steps that led to his destination, the infamous sixth floor of the Texas School Book Depository.

Now he was standing at the very window where, the government maintained, Lee Harvey Oswald fired three shots.

Those bullets left the barrel of a Mannlicher-Carcano 6.5×52-mm Italian sniper rifle, a weapon Oswald had purchased for twenty dollars.

Months earlier, Holmes and Dunleavy had researched the provenance of the Mannlicher-Carcano. It was a bolt-action rifle with a reputation for inaccuracy. No army on the planet used the rifle for sniping or for any other purpose.

Dunleavy stared out the window. It was possible the first shot could have been fired with accuracy. The shooter would have had several seconds to take careful aim.

After that, forget it. A large oak tree intruded itself into the flight path of a second shot. Activating the bolt would have interrupted the flow of the second and third shots, which according to witnesses, came in rapid succession.

Completely impossible? No. Probable? Also no.

Dunleavy stayed ten minutes at the window. He knew his next destination—the so-called grassy knoll.

The book depository building was located at the intersection of Elm Street and North Houston Street. The grassy knoll was perhaps fifty yards away from the book depository. It was on Elm Street where John Kennedy was shot.

Dunleavy walked slowly to the fence where witnesses said they heard the report of a long-barreled firearm.

From the fence to the street was maybe a hundred feet. The worst sniper on the planet could not miss from that distance. A man in a slow-moving vehicle would not have a chance.

Dunleavy came to this spot fortified with information that the general public did not have. Months earlier he and Curt Holmes had spent an entire day reviewing the Zapruder film.

Abraham Zapruder was a clothing manufacturer in Dallas. The Ukrainian immigrant was a staunch Democrat. He owned a Bell &

Howell 8-mm Zoomatic camera. He wanted to catch the president on film for his family archive.

Except it rained that morning and Zapruder left his camera at home.

Then the clouds parted, and the sun came out. His assistant, Marilyn Sitzman, goaded him into going home and bringing the camera to Dealey Plaza. At 11:00 a.m., he was on Elm Street.

Sitzman helped steady Zapruder as he stood on a concrete abutment. He took twenty-six seconds of film. Four hundred and eighty-six frames. It would be the most famous news footage of all time.

It showed John Kennedy waving at the crowds. His beautiful wife sitting next to him. John and Nellie Connally were immediately in front of them along with the limo driver.

The film showed Kennedy coming out from behind a street sign. He was holding his neck. Jackie Kennedy looked at him in horror.

Seconds later, John Kennedy's head exploded. Mrs. Kennedy climbed out of her seat and tried to recover something. It was her husband's brain matter and a piece of his skull. A Secret Service agent jumped on the car.

The Zapruder film was shown on national television a thousand times.

Holmes and Dunleavy decided to enhance the film, using the resources of the NSA. This had to be done clandestinely. Director Frost had explicitly told both men to stand down from investigating the death of John Kennedy.

Each man repeatedly watched the enhanced version of the film. After twenty viewings, Dunleavy was convinced.

"That's a head shot from the front," he told Holmes.

"I am afraid I have to agree," Holmes put his head in his hands.

"If Kennedy had been shot from the rear, his brain matter would have been all over the limo driver, the governor, and his wife."

"The laws of physics would mandate it," Holmes added.

"Curt, there were lots of people on the grassy knoll. Dozens have stated they heard a rifle report from behind. Are they all delusional? And they all hit the ground at the same time. Some of them landed on their children to protect them. Were their brain neurons connected telepathically? They all did the same thing instantaneously. There is only one explanation!"

"Stu, you are preaching to the choir. There was a man with a rifle behind that fence, no question."

"So why are these witnesses being told to shut up? I have a sick feeling in my stomach that some kind of fix is in the making. But why? When Abraham Lincoln was shot, the government moved heaven and earth to catch the guilty parties."

"Stu, maybe we should approach Frost and demand that we get back into this investigation."

"And what do you think his answer is going to be?"

Holmes knew it was futile. Frost was not about to contradict Lyndon Johnson and J. Edgar Hoover.

Dunleavy stood on the grassy knoll thinking about the hours he and Holmes had dedicated to reviewing the Zapruder film.

Why did so many experts fail to see the obvious?

Dunleavy shook his head. Then he hailed a cab. His next destination was Parkland Hospital.

It took only a few minutes for the cab to arrive at what was now America's best-known medical center. He walked into the emergency room. He wanted to see where the fight for John Kennedy's life took place.

He found a nurse sitting behind a counter with a sign that read "Admitting."

He flashed his NSA credentials. Most civilians never question an authority figure when they flash identification. They just accept it.

The nurse had a name tag. It read "Barbara."

"Hello, Barbara, my name is Stuart Dunleavy. I am with the Warren Commission. Are there any physicians working today who were present when John Kennedy was brought in for treatment?"

"Just one. Dr. Joe Goldstrich. He's in the breakroom right now."

"How would I find out the names of all the doctors who treated the president."

"I have a list. We keep getting asked that question." She reached under her desk. "Here."

Besides Goldstrich, the list contained six names: Donald Seldin, Robert McClelland, Ronald Jones, Peter Loeb, Kenneth Salyer, and Lawrence Klein.

"Would it be an imposition for me to visit the breakroom and speak with Dr. Goldstrich?"

"I don't think he would mind."

"Thank you."

Dunleavy had no trouble isolating Dr. Goldstrich. He was the only person in the breakroom.

Out came the NSA identification. "Dr. Goldstrich. May I speak with you for a second?"

"Was that FBI identification you just showed me?"

"No, Doctor. I work for the NSA. We have been asked to coordinate with the FBI."

"I hope you have a more open mind than those FBI guys!"

"My mind is completely free of prejudice in this matter, Doctor."

"Good! Because I am tired of people who do not possess medical degrees telling me I'm wrong!"

"I am well familiar with the FBI scenario. They insist President Kennedy was hit twice from the rear." Dunleavy wanted to appear calm and diplomatic.

"He was hit one time from the rear. The bullet entered his neck and tore apart his trachea. But the bullet that ended his life came from the front. I have treated headshots in this hospital for years. I know what to look for!"

"And you so informed the FBI?"

"Of course. They countered my argument with photos from the president's autopsy at Bethesda Hospital. As God is my witness, those photos were doctored." Goldstrich leaned forward. "Naturally, the easiest way to ascertain the truth would be to track the bullet through the president's brain. Now here is where it gets interesting, Mister…what's your name?"

"Dunleavy, Stuart."

"Mr. Dunleavy, I told the FBI the brain would establish the bullet's track once and for all. You know what they told me? The president's brain has disappeared."

Dunleavy was shocked. "They lost the president's brain?"

"Can you believe it? History's most important homicide and they lose the one human organ that can confirm or contradict a conspiracy theory."

Dunleavy took five seconds of silence to comprehend this information. If true, he did not believe the missing brain was an accident.

Now more than ever he knew something was terribly remiss in the investigation of the events of November 22, 1963.

"Doctor, I want to show you something." Dunleavy produced the list Barbara the nurse had given him. "Doctor, besides you there are six names on this list. Can you name just one of these doctors who disagrees with your interpretation?"

"No. We are all in agreement. And not one of us can understand the FBI's intransigence in this matter. Can you explain it?"

"No, I cannot. But I want to tell you that I believe you, Doctor."

"You are an outlier, Mr. Dunleavy. You are the only member of the Warren Commission who has treated me like someone who knows a thing or two about medicine."

Dunleavy left the hospital and decided to call it a day.

Tomorrow he would visit the local library. He would research newspaper articles from November 23 through November 28.

The names of people who were at the grassy knoll that terrible day would be his target. He would not have to interview all of them. Five or six would do.

Chapter 53

Two days after Stuart Dunleavy returned home, his wife gave birth to a beautiful eight-pound baby boy.

Dunleavy did not spend two weeks in Dallas. He spent four days. His wife told him she was going to give birth at any moment.

Dunleavy weighed his options. He decided not being there for the birth of his first child would later haunt him. And it could cause a rift in the marriage.

He did not need to spend two weeks in Dallas. He spoke with four people who had been on the grassy knoll.

What they told him was definitive. Each of the four said they hit the dirt because a rifle report rang out clear as a bell right behind them.

Two of them managed to see the president's head explode.

One witness, Amanda Johnson, said she flagged down a Dallas motorcycle cop. "I told him there was a man with a gun behind the fence! He went and had a look-see."

Dunleavy asked, "Did you have any interaction with this patrolman after that?"

"Yeah, he was only behind the fence for sixty seconds. He said there was no gunman. Just a Secret Service agent."

"A Secret Service agent?"

"Yeah, and the agent told the cop he was ordered that morning to secure the fence line."

"How certain are you that the noise you heard was a rifle shot?"

"Is one hundred percent certain strong enough?"

Dunleavy heard the exact same story from the other three witnesses. It was enough. Time to go home. Time to ponder the significance of it all.

Twenty-four hours after the birth of his son, Dunleavy was visited by Curt Holmes. Holmes found Dunleavy in a hospital room cradling the infant while his spouse packed up her things.

The first words out of Holmes's mouth were "Thank God he looks like your wife."

Holmes kissed Arlene. Then he was offered the singular honor of holding the unnamed child. "You haven't given this bundle of joy a name yet?"

Dunleavy laughed. "We have been arguing about it for three hours. I have a feeling she is going to have the final say."

Arlene chimed in. "After leaving me in Washington, you are lucky you have any say at all!"

Holmes saw an opportunity and jumped in. "Arlene, I am just dying to hear about Stu's visit to Dallas. Could I borrow him for twenty minutes?"

"Only if you watch over the most important thing in my life! If you drop that baby on his head, there is no country on this planet where you can hide!"

Each man roared with laughter. "Stu, you better take him back. My arms are turning to jelly!"

Dunleavy kissed his wife. "The nurse said she has to push you in a wheelchair until you are off the premises. I will meet you in the lobby."

Arlene could not help herself. She kissed her son, and she gave her husband a look that said, "Guard him with your life!"

Holmes, Dunleavy, and the baby found an elevator. They landed on the lobby floor and found a coffee shop.

"My treat," Holmes said.

The two men deliberately found a table away from other patrons. Dunleavy squeezed his son close to his chest, and he pulled out a chair.

"Stu, your wife is going to be down here in about thirty minutes. There is no time for idle chatter. Did anyone recognize you in Dallas?"

"I'm positive no one did."

"That was a heck of a chance you took. Frost would certainly look at your trip with shall we say…an evil eye."

"I knew I was taking a chance, but I am damn glad I did. Do you want to hear what I found out?"

"More than anything."

Dunleavy then monopolized the conversation for twenty minutes. He told Holmes about the custodian in the book depository. He described the sixth-floor window and the absence of a clear shot at the president.

He hit hard on the conversation he had with a physician who was hands-on during the battle to save the president's life.

Holmes nearly fell down when he heard the president's brain might be missing. He discussed at length the conversations he had with four people who were on the grassy knoll.

"Curt, everyone I spoke with was firm and confident. I did not get any wobbly answers. These are American patriots, and they just wanted to do the right thing. And yet each one of these witnesses said the FBI gave them a hard time."

Holmes put his coffee down and shook his head. "I don't get it. I just don't get it."

"Curt, we need to see Bobby. We have to let him know that an investigation controlled by Lyndon Johnson is not acting in good faith!"

"I spoke with Bobby while you were out of town. I mentioned he might want to use his family's wealth and hire a team of independent investigators. He wouldn't hear of it."

"Why? For God's sake, why?"

"Stu, I wish I could give you an answer. But I cannot."

Dunleavy stood up. "I am convinced the Warren Commission was given marching orders from the day it was conceived. And those orders state that no matter what the evidence actually reveals, the final report will find that Lee Harvey Oswald acted alone."

Holmes rapped his fingers on the table. "I wish I could hit you with an opposing argument, but I cannot."

Dunleavy sat down. "There is just one more loose end I need to nail down before I am absolutely convinced. Do you have any friends at the Secret Service?"

Holmes thought for only a second. "Yes, one."

"Do you trust him?"

"We go back a long time. What do you have in mind?"

"When I was in Dallas, I spoke with a woman who was on the grassy knoll. She said she was absolutely certain there was a sniper behind her. She found a motorcycle cop and told him to check out the area behind the grassy knoll fence. He did. When he came back, he told the woman there was no gunman, just a Secret Service agent. I believe her story. I also believe the man behind the fence was impersonating a Secret Service agent. Ask your friend if the Secret Service assigned anyone to guard that fence. If the answer is no, then the conspiracy is real."

At that instant the elevator doors opened, and a very anxious new mother was wheeled into the lobby. When she saw Dunleavy, she beamed in delight.

Both men stood up in perfect synchronization. Dunleavy cradled his son a little too tightly. "Will you do it, Curt?"

Holmes grabbed Dunleavy's one free arm and squeezed. "Yes, I will. And damn the consequences!"

Chapter 54

Everything the government did in 1964 cemented Dunleavy's conviction that skullduggery was afoot in the matter of John Kennedy's death.

In March, Jack Ruby went on trial for first-degree murder. There was no change of venue. Ruby would face jurors who lived in Dallas, Texas.

Ruby had a high-profile defense attorney named Melvin Belli. He was nationally known well before Jack Ruby hired him.

Belli could not get trial judge Joe Brown to give him the time of day. Belli saw motion after motion go down the tubes. Belli's frustration boiled over, but Judge Brown did not seem to care.

The trial of Jack Ruby was certainly not a whodunit. Ruby shot Oswald on national television. There were potentially one hundred million eyewitnesses for the prosecution.

Police had the murder weapon. And fingerprints. No murder case in history was so one-sided in favor of the state.

Belli put Ruby's mental state into play. Jurors in Texas were traditionally not inclined to cut a defendant any slack for presumed mental illnesses. That was something squishy liberals in New York might do, but not the good people of the Lone Star state.

And what was Ruby's motive for shooting Lee Harvey Oswald? Ruby's own explanation was so ludicrous it caused Dunleavy to grab his head with both hands and exclaim, "You have got to be kidding."

Ruby told the news media he shot Oswald "to spare Mrs. Kennedy the pain of returning to the state where she lost her husband."

Dunleavy told Holmes, "As if a gun-running, Mob-affiliated hood was capable of such empathy!"

Dunleavy knew exactly why Ruby pulled the trigger. It was to make certain Oswald never saw the inside of a courtroom and a chance to tell his side of the story.

Dunleavy was positive Ruby was acting under orders. And the man who issued those orders was probably Carlos Marcello.

Oswald was silenced forever. But what about Ruby? What if he decided to come clean? Marcello had to shut that door just as tightly as he did on Oswald.

Here is where the common interests of Marcello and the US government melded together.

Neither Marcello nor the federal government wanted Jack Ruby selling his story to *Life Magazine* or any other publication.

He was kept under twenty-four-hour surveillance. His cell was bugged.

Marcello had told Ruby he might be convicted of manslaughter and he might have to serve a couple of years behind bars.

Ruby was stunned when the jury found him guilty of murder in the first degree. Equally astounding was the sentence Judge Brown handed down.

Death.

A hangman's noose was now right above the balding skull of Jack Ruby.

Dunleavy smelled a rat. The man who killed the man who killed the president of the United States is given the ultimate punishment?

Dunleavy told Holmes, "They want to have leverage over him. Keep quiet. If you do not, we can move up your execution date."

Holmes shook his head. "Just once I wish I could disagree with your interpretation, but I cannot."

Absolute proof of the veracity of Dunleavy's analysis came in June of 1964. Jack Ruby knew he had been had. His friend Marcello had sold him up the river.

Ruby decided it was time to tell the truth. He could still win the day with an honest exposition of the facts.

How wrong he was. Both the Mob and the federal government had Ruby by the scruff of the neck, and they weren't going to let go.

Ruby told his jailors to contact the Warren Commission. He told them he wanted to make a statement. Two days later, Ruby received word the Warren Commission did not have time to meet with him.

Ruby was floored. The Warren Commission did not have time to meet with a central player in the John Kennedy investigation?

Ruby got hold of his sister, Eileen. She started a letter-writing campaign aimed at Earl Warren and his staffers. Still no affirmative answer.

Eileen contacted the news media and told any reporter who would listen that her brother was being stonewalled.

This did the trick. Earl Warren and Gerald Ford agreed to meet with Ruby inside the Dallas County Jail. At the last minute, two other commission members decided to tag along.

Ruby was surrounded by law enforcement officers. He asked that they be dismissed so he could speak with the commission in private.

Earl Warren said no.

A very nervous Jack Ruby then told Warren and his fellow members, "I want to make a statement. I want the truth to come out. But I do not feel safe here. Can you take me to Washington?"

Earl Warren then made a statement so patently absurd it would resound through history as a giant, "What the hell?"

"Mr. Ruby, I do not have the legal authority to take you out of this jail. I have no police powers, and I could not protect you. Public scrutiny of your move to Washington would be too intense."

Now Ruby knew for certain his goose was cooked.

Of course Earl Warren had the power to move Ruby. He could snap his fingers and it would be done.

Of course Warren had the authority to order the FBI to guard Ruby from Dallas to the Capital. He headed a presidential commission that superseded all other investigative agencies in the United States.

Earl Warren was telling Ruby that his only option was to keep quiet. Ruby got the message loud and clear.

So did Dunleavy and Holmes.

"Curt, I am not even going to bother reading the Warren Commission report when it is released."

"Stu, unless Bobby orders me to read it, I am going to use it as a doorstop."

It was a funny line, but neither man felt like laughing.

Chapter 55

Bobby Kennedy could no longer handle his status as a member of Lyndon Johnson's cabinet.

He was attorney general in name only. He drifted in a fog through the obligatory functions of the office.

He and other Kennedy loyalists stayed on simply to satisfy the country's need for continuity. President Johnson begged all of John Kennedy's people to remain at their jobs.

Most of them did. But all the joy of public service was gone. Each one looked for the earliest possible exit. Secretary of State Dean Rusk was the outlier. He loved his job and did not want to leave.

Lyndon Johnson spent the spring and summer consolidating his position as head of the Democrat Party.

Johnson was terrified of what Bobby Kennedy might do. Johnson knew the emotional heart of the party lay inside the Kennedy camp.

If Bobby decided to run, it would be ruinous for Democrats. The convention would be a bloodbath.

But Bobby Kennedy was still too shattered by his brother's death to contemplate an all-out war for the presidency.

In August of 1964, Bobby Kennedy decided he was going to attempt a jailbreak from Johnson's insufferable embrace. He would challenge Republican incumbent Kenneth Keating of New York for one of the two Senate seats in the Empire State.

Kennedy was a carpetbagger. He was a Massachusetts man. Keating hoped that a charge of poaching would prove crippling to Kennedy's efforts.

Keating was wrong. The public loved John Kennedy when he was alive. His death elevated him to a God-like status. Bobby Kennedy would reap the benefits of this emotional attachment.

In November 1964, Kennedy defeated Keating. The vote tally was 3,823,749 for the Democratic ticket. Keating received 3,104,056.

Kennedy was free. He no longer had to pretend to like Lyndon Johnson. Kennedy was now a member of a co-equal branch of government. He could speak his mind.

In July 1964, Johnson was on a roll. He had heard rumors that Kennedy would run for the Senate in New York State.

Johnson would naturally endorse this effort. It would remove the Kennedy threat once and for all.

Johnson's ebullience was premature. The Democratic Convention was held in Atlantic City beginning August 24 and ending August 27.

Johnson received the nomination. He chose Hubert Humphrey of Minnesota as his running mate. He was wise to insist that Bobby Kennedy address the convention on its final day.

Had Kennedy been allowed to address the convention on day 1, history might have gone in a different direction.

When Kennedy took the podium on August 27, his reception was unparalleled in American political history.

The applause would not stop. No matter how many times Kennedy said, "Thank you, Mr. Chairman," the convention delegates just kept going.

For twenty-two minutes, Kennedy waited for the crowd to cease and desist. His eyes began to water.

The thunderous ovation was a deadly reminder to Lyndon Johnson that he might have the title, but he did not have the soul of the party.

Had Bobby Kennedy appeared on August 24, it is conceivable an emotional title wave could have landed him the nomination.

The very instant the convention ended, Kennedy was bound by political necessity to give his unqualified support to Lyndon Johnson. Lyndon Johnson's opponent in 1964 was Barry Goldwater of Arizona.

Goldwater picked the wrong time to try to launch a conservative movement in America.

Liberalism was in its heyday. America had both peace and pros-perity. A booming economy allowed Progressives the opportunity to expand the government exponentially.

Lyndon Johnson dreamed of surpassing Franklin Roosevelt in the arena of government activism.

He was sure he would beat Goldwater. But he wanted a blowout in order to command the political capital to push through his agenda.

Exactly one month after the start of the Democrat Convention, Earl Warren marched into the Oval Office and handed Lyndon Johnson the final report on the death of John Kennedy.

It was 888 pages long. It was beautifully embossed. It had facts and figures, and it contained the collected wisdom of the FBI.

It stated that Lee Harvey Oswald killed John Kennedy. He had no confederates. No foreign governments or domestic criminal enterprises were involved.

John Kennedy was put in his grave by a grievance-driven nut with a rifle.

Johnson's strategy had worked perfectly. While it was in oper-ation, the Warren Commission suppressed speculation about the assassination.

Everyone, including the news media, was willing to give the commission members time to do their work.

Time was what Johnson wanted most of all.

The Russians needed time to see what the Americans were going to do. By June of 1964, Khrushchev was convinced his country was not going to be blamed for John Kennedy's death.

Khrushchev told his military commanders that a move against West Berlin was postponed indefinitely.

This was the real reason Johnson created the Warren Commission—to prevent thermonuclear war between Russia and America.

Johnson felt that the truth was vastly less important than pre-venting a civilization-killing war. This argument had merit.

But there is always a downside. Lying in the name of a good cause is still lying. It was inevitable the Warren Commission findings would come under attack.

All Johnson wanted was quiescence until the elections were over in November.

He got it.

Lyndon Johnson beat Barry Goldwater by a margin of fifteen million votes. He won forty-four states. Goldwater carried Arizona and five states in the Old Confederacy.

The Republican Party was wiped out in both the House and the Senate. Democrats held all the levers of power.

Lyndon Johnson was master of the universe.

Curt Holmes and Stuart Dunleavy did not quit the NSA to help Bobby Kennedy run for the Senate.

Kennedy asked them to stay put. He wanted some separation from the two men. He did not want them in close proximity, because then he would have to explain his bizarre support for the Warren Commission findings.

Kennedy could not tell them he was being blackmailed by J. Edgar Hoover. His father had created a family dynamic of reckless behavior that made blackmail possible. The sons had learned this behavior at Joe Kennedy's knee.

Dunleavy and Holmes broke their own injunction about reading the Warren Commission report. They could not help themselves.

When each man had finished the report, they got together in Holmes's office.

"See anything that changed your mind, Stu?"

"Not one damn paragraph."

"Well, this crap is now the official government position on the death of John Kennedy. How long before cracks start to appear and this ship sinks to the bottom of the ocean?"

"It could be decades, Curt. The government is going to fight to protect its handiwork. It is going to label dissenters as nuts and conspiracy theorists."

Holmes stood up and put his hands in his pockets. "Well, we can't bring the man back to life, Stu. Sometimes in life, you just have to roll with it."

Dunleavy stood up just so he could bore into Holmes's eyes. "I am not ready to throw in the towel, Curt. A huge lie is being perpetrated. I do not know why. I just want to know the name of the man who put a bullet in my president's brain."

"Don't do anything rash, Stu. You have a son and a wife. Just think carefully before you do anything."

"Sure, Curt. That's very sensible advice."

Dunleavy started for the door. He turned at the last second. "Sometimes being sensible just doesn't cut it."

Chapter 56

The years 1964–1965 saw triumphant Democrats put their stamp on history.

Johnson wanted his administration to have a name commensurate with its pending greatness. Ergo the word "great" had to be part of it.

With typical Johnson humility, the appellation Great Society was adopted. The phrase would incorporate all the pending legislation Democrats intended to push through Congress.

No one could stop them. The party in late 1964 held super majorities in the House and Senate. Prior to that, the party employed the memory of a beloved dead president to force through legislation.

The main issues were the economy, Medicare, Medicaid, civil rights, and voting rights.

John Kennedy's proposed tax cuts became law. This supercharged the economy. Prosperity opened the door for Johnson's other priorities.

Johnson used the emotional trauma of John Kennedy's death to get the landmark Civil Rights Bill through Congress even before the 1964 election blowout. In the spring of 1964, the Senate followed the House in passing the legislation.

In one of the great ironies of history, Democrats reaped the benefits of the passage of civil rights even though it was the Democrat Party that tried to scuttle it.

Sixteen Democrat Senators voted against the bill. Only two Republicans cast a similar vote.

Johnson had pleaded with Republican Senate Minority Leader Everett Dirksen of Illinois for help. He needed a vote to end a filibuster. Southern Democrats had used this ancient tactic for one hundred years. It was a surefire method of killing civil rights legislation.

With Republican help, a cloture vote ended a filibuster on the Civil Rights Bill. Southern Democrats were routed.

This was the last straw for Georgia Senator Richard Russell. First Lyndon Johnson dragooned him into serving on the Warren Commission. Then he tossed aside his thirty years of loyalty to the Old South. He championed civil rights, a concept Russell had spent his entire life opposing.

In an emotional meeting, Russell told Johnson, "You just handed the South to the Republicans for the next generation."

Johnson did not care. He was on a political sugar high. It was he, not Russell, who would inherit the title Great Man of History.

A year later that exact same formula worked to pass the 1965 Voting Rights Act.

Again, Republicans overwhelmingly supported the bill. Russell and his Southern cronies opposed it.

A title wave of moderate Democrats and Lincoln Republicans got the job done.

After 1965, Democrats owned the African American vote. This only happened because the titular head of the Republican Party was Barry Goldwater. And Goldwater came out against both the Civil Rights Act and the Voting Rights Act.

It mattered not that House Republicans and Senate Republicans supported both pieces of legislation by huge majorities.

Goldwater's opposition became the only thing that mattered. One would think that a president who had just won an election by fifteen million votes would have a lock on the presidency for eight years. The vagaries and vicissitudes of American politics allow for no such guarantee.

Great victories have a tendency to produce hubris in mortal men. This truism applied to Lyndon Johnson more than other applicants for historical greatness.

One reason Bobby Kennedy hated Johnson so intently was Johnson's propensity for lying. "He lies about everything," Kennedy said. "He lies when he doesn't have to."

People who knew Johnson going back to his high school years saw this flaw clearly. Again, this is why they gave him the nickname Bull Johnson.

In the 1930s and the 1940s, mass communication did not exist. A politician could take one position in West Texas and completely reverse himself in East Texas.

The ability to instantly fact-check was nearly impossible. Johnson used this reality to say whatever he had to say to win elections. He was not alone in practicing this tactic. But he refined it better than any man alive.

Johnson's lifelong habit in favor of perverting the truth was about to collide with a foreign policy issue of galactic importance—the civil war in Vietnam.

In the 1950s and early 1960s, Communism was on the march. It was greatly aided by Western intellectuals who fell for the rhetoric of Marxism while ignoring its reality.

In 1964, the Communist Viet Cong was making great strides. Ho Chi Minh was being lavishly supplied by both China and Russia.

A political theory called the domino effect was very much alive in the Pentagon and the US State Department.

The theory held that the loss of South Vietnam would trigger an avalanche of failure amongst free states in Asia.

A fully united Communist Vietnam would quickly bring with it the downfall of Cambodia, Thailand, Burma, perhaps even India.

The issues were immense. The subject matter was nothing short of the difference between slavery and freedom.

The gravity of the situation required a statesman of great moral fortitude.

Lyndon Johnson was not that man. Johnson was a man who knew how to prioritize.

Priority number one in the fall of 1964 was winning an election. Not just winning. Crushing the opposition.

The issue of how much force to use in Vietnam was going to be critical to the outcome of this election.

Goldwater was a ferocious anti-communist. To his credit, he did not attempt to hide the costs of keeping Vietnam out of the hands of

Marxists. Goldwater said he would put troops on the ground to keep this from happening.

Lyndon Johnson understood America was not in the mood for a land war in Asia. He knew he was in no danger of losing votes if he adopted the peace platform.

"I believe an Asian war should be fought by Asian boys." He stated this over and over.

Johnson ran a television ad showing an atomic bomb exploding. The implication was this is what would happen if Goldwater ever sat in the Oval Office.

Goldwater did not hide from his war posture. He embraced it. The end result was the biggest political shellacking in American electoral history.

On election night, Johnson strode the planet like the colossus of Rhodes. In his entire life he had never once paid a price for using the English language to obfuscate rather than enlighten. This had served him well for thirty years. Why stop?

Except the presidency is unlike any other office in the world. Everything a president does receives ten times the scrutiny of a lower-ranking politician.

Johnson could no longer say one thing in San Francisco and another in New York. An army of reporters now traveled with him no matter where he went. Johnson never saw the trap he had fallen into by seeking the presidency.

All presidents basically have two options: Tell the truth. Or say no comment. All other options are landmines waiting to explode.

Johnson was proud of the way he had handled the investigation into John Kennedy's death. The Warren Commission had silenced critics for ten months. Its findings were initially accepted by all the good people—people who mattered.

Except it was a lie. And Johnson knew it was a lie.

The murder of Lee Harvey Oswald two days after Kennedy's death just screamed of a conspiracy. A Mafia henchman shoots the man who had shot the man who had declared war against the Mafia.

And no one is supposed to notice?

People did start to notice.

For two years questions about Kennedy's death remained underground.

In 1966, American lawyer Mark Lane broke the dam. He wrote *Rush to Judgment.* The book excoriated the Warren Commission. A year later Lane was on television with a documentary about all the contrary evidence to the single assassin theory.

Eighteen witnesses appeared on the show to contradict the accepted wisdom of Earl Warren and his staffers.

Stuart Dunleavy and Curt Holmes both read the book. They both watched the documentary. Together.

Holmes was philosophical about the whole issue. "Stu, we will probably be in our late eighties before the truth comes out."

Holmes poured his friend a bourbon. He noticed Dunleavy's eyes did not leave the television even though the show was over, and the credits were running. "I don't think I can wait that long, Curt."

Chapter 57

Lyndon Johnson was inaugurated on January 20, 1965. It took him all of six weeks to break his promise to the American people.

By March of 1965, the peace candidate was explaining to the voters why he was sending combat troops to Vietnam.

He did not ask the Congress for a declaration of war. He did not believe he had to ask.

In August of 1964, North Vietnamese patrol boats purportedly fired missiles at two American destroyers. The destroyers *Maddox* and *Turner Joy* were in the Gulf of Tonkin helping South Vietnamese combat operations.

A nighttime raid by North Vietnamese naval personnel did not produce any damage. If they fired on the two American ships, they missed.

This was not Pearl Harbor where the bomb damage was evident to a blind man.

The raid might have been a concoction of US intelligence. But it was enough to stir the patriotic impulses of 95 percent of the Congress of the United States.

Lyndon Johnson asked for, and received, permission to use lethal force to protect United States military personnel in Southeast Asia.

The Gulf of Tonkin Resolution became law on August 10, 1964.

Lyndon Johnson retaliated with one bombing raid over North Vietnam. That was it. He stopped. The election was three months away. Once the Republican Party was completely routed, Johnson felt emboldened. But still he held back.

He did not want to mar his inauguration with news stories about American troops dying in Vietnam. He waited.

By the first week of March 1965, half of South Vietnam was under communist control.

Suddenly Lyndon Johnson became Barry Goldwater. His speeches were laced with terms such as "Red tide" and "the light of freedom being extinguished in all of Asia."

The situation was ready-made for an address to Congress. Lay out the danger for all to see. Ask for a real declaration of war instead of a resolution.

Lyndon Johnson was not that man. His massive insecurities and lifelong habits were about to destroy him.

In 1941, Franklin Roosevelt told the American people they were going to have to give up butter for guns. He asked for real sacrifice. The American people came on board by the tens of millions.

The results of this kind of commitment were astounding. In just thirty-six months, America and its allies routed three fascist empires and sent the overlords of this tyranny into the dustbin of history.

In 1941, Roosevelt rose to the moment. In 1965, Johnson shrank from it.

Johnson wanted guns and butter. He wanted to massively expand domestic and military spending. And he did not want to raise taxes to accomplish these twin goals.

He deliberately hid his true intentions.

In early 1965, the United States had sixteen thousand military advisors in Vietnam. The job of these men was to train and supply South Vietnamese forces.

Now there were United States Marines landing at Da Nang Air Force Base. These were not advisors. They were warriors who could launch offensive military operations.

In no time at all, the self-defense mission would expand to include everything under the sun.

Johnson appointed Army General William C. Westmoreland as Supreme Allied Commander in South Vietnam.

Westmoreland accepted the assignment without asking Johnson the one question any competent military man would have demanded to know. "Mr. President, how do you define victory?"

By failing to ask this question Westmoreland consigned himself to defeat and ignominy.

Westmoreland allowed Johnson not to define victory. This was a path the president happily chose to traverse.

Johnson adopted a strategy of incrementalism. Under this philosophy, America would slowly ramp up the pressure until North Vietnam would quit.

Johnson also made it clear there would be no land invasion of North Vietnam. He told his enemies they would have a safe haven. So why should they quit?

Johnson seldom read books. He always said he did not have time. Had he bothered to research the subject, he would have learned that China occupied Vietnam for more than one thousand years.

During that entire period, the Vietnamese resisted.

From 1965 until 1968, the United States slowly added troops to the conflict. Eventually there would be half a million.

During this agonizing slow buildup, support for the war plummeted.

And the most vociferous opposition came from Democrats.

The opposition party came roaring back. In 1966, Republicans picked up forty-seven House seats. The GOP won three additional seats in the Senate.

Democrats still controlled both houses and the presidency. Thus, the wrath of the anti-war movement continued to rain down on Democrat officeholders.

All his life Lyndon Johnson had accomplished things by operating in the dark. He tried to win a war by using the same method. It did not work.

By late 1967, Johnson's three-year-old fifteen-million-vote victory margin had evaporated.

In the spring of 1968, there would be presidential primaries coming along. Half the Democrats in America were prepared to abandon Johnson. Their first choice as a successor was Robert Kennedy.

Bobby Kennedy was feeling the pressure. His New York office was safe. In 1970, he would have to run again for the Senate, but no one believed he would lose.

But millions of Democrats wanted action now. They wanted a choice.

Kennedy waffled. He feared a Johnson-Kennedy race would be a bloodbath.

Eugene McCarthy was a United States Senator from Minnesota. He became leader of the anti-war movement in Congress.

He asked Bobby Kennedy to challenge Johnson in the New Hampshire Primary scheduled for March 12, 1968.

Kennedy declined. McCarthy then asked Kennedy, "Would you have any objections to my entering the race?"

Kennedy believed Johnson would trounce McCarthy. Kennedy greenlighted the Minnesotan to give it his best shot.

McCarthy then asked, "You won't get in under any circumstances?"

Kennedy hesitated. He was boxed in by the question. "No, I'm not going to get in, Gene. Good luck!"

Bobby Kennedy would later pay a price for that promise. But all that was in the future.

For three years, the Johnson administration told the world that US, South Vietnamese, and other Allied forces were winning the war.

In early January 1968, the argument appeared to have merit. The war seemed to be slowing down.

The war was far from over. The communists were husbanding their forces. A huge escalation was on its way.

On January 30, 1968, the Viet Cong launched a nationwide offensive. They completely abandoned their ambush tactics. They went in for the kill.

Every major city in South Vietnam was hit. The city of Hue was captured. The American Embassy in Saigon was overrun.

For two weeks, Communism seemed to be transcendent. Lyndon Johnson got out of bed every day to bad news.

Young people in America were marching and shouting, "Hey, hey, LBJ, how many kids did you kill today?"

Johnson hated that verse. But he had no rejoinder. Truth be told, American commanders were glad the Viet Cong had rolled the dice.

For three years Americans had fought an enemy that lived underground. The communists would throw a punch and then immediately back away.

Now they wanted to brawl out in the open. Stand toe to toe.

One month after the initial offensive, the communists were taking it on the chin. Day by day, cities they had conquered were returned to South Vietnamese sovereignty.

The more ominous reality lay in the body count. The Viet Cong lost eighty thousand fighters. Strategically, they had gained absolutely nothing.

But politically they had gained a treasure trove of good news.

Ho Chi Minh and his successors knew they were not going to beat America on the battlefield. They were going to beat Lyndon Johnson on the streets of New York, San Francisco, Chicago, and thousands of other large and small cities.

The Tet Offensive was worth its weight in gold to Eugene McCarthy.

Every day Americans saw bloody fighting on their television sets. It mattered not that the entire Viet Cong army had been wiped out. The images of handsome young Americans being injured and killed in an undeclared war were all that mattered.

Support for Eugene McCarthy was rising. Bobby Kennedy took notice.

On March 12, 1968, the voters in New Hampshire went to the polls. Lyndon Johnson captured 49 percent of the vote. Eugene McCarthy won 42 percent.

In a normal year, that would have been a rout for Johnson. This was not a normal year. The news media lavished so much attention on McCarthy one would have thought the challenger had crushed the incumbent.

Johnson's supporters were morose. McCarthy's people were ecstatic.

The world was upside down.

Bobby Kennedy knew Lyndon Johnson was vulnerable. He could not stomach the thought of a lightweight such as Gene McCarthy entering the White House. This was now a real possibility.

Kennedy had promised McCarthy he would not enter the race. Now he knew he was going to have to pick up the telephone and call McCarthy and tell him he was "reassessing" the situation.

Kennedy also steeled himself for criticism that was certain to come from reporters. They would accuse him of double-dealing and political rapacity.

Kennedy also knew these same reporters would forgive him. He was John Kennedy's brother.

One day after the New Hampshire Primary, Kennedy picked up the phone and dialed the NSA. He asked Holmes and Dunleavy to join him in his office for lunch. Each man gladly accepted.

From 7:00 a.m. to 11:50 a.m., Kennedy was on the telephone calling supporters across America. He told them, "I am going to run."

Very few of them replied, "What took you so long?" Most were ecstatic.

There was now a chance Camelot would be reborn.

At 11:55 a.m. Holmes and Dunleavy entered Kennedy's office. There were handshakes and hugs. Kennedy bade his two friends to have a seat near his ornate Senate desk.

The conversation, of course, started around the subject of family, but Kennedy very quickly pivoted toward the main event.

"Gentlemen, in three days I will be announcing my candidacy for the presidency of the United States."

Each man stood and shook Kennedy's hand. Holmes and Dunleavy were exuberant.

"Stu, I want you to join the campaign. Curt, I am making you the same offer."

Holmes spoke first. "Senator, you know you will have my unqualified support. I have to decline. I love my job."

Kennedy smiled. "I know what I am asking is difficult. It will require you to quit your job. I will make you this promise, Curt. If I get elected, you will be running the NSA."

"I am flattered beyond all description, Senator."

"Stu, how about you? I can match the salary you are making now."

"I am all in, Bobby. I will quit the day you announce."

"Curt, you can resume your duties. I need to talk to Stu in private."

Holmes stood up and reached for Kennedy's outstretched hand. "God bless you, Senator. And I would not mind getting invited to one of the inaugural balls."

Dunleavy stood and shook Holmes's hand. "See you back at the office, Curt."

Five seconds later, Dunleavy and Kennedy were alone. "Stu, I want you to be in charge of my advance team."

Kennedy was slightly surprised by Dunleavy's response. He hesitated.

"Stu, did you hear what I said?"

"Yes, I did, Bobby. Would I be out of line if I made a counter suggestion?"

"Go ahead."

"Put me in charge of your security and give me a million-dollar budget."

Kennedy smiled. "Stu, I already have a plan in mind for security. I need you on my advance team. I saw how you did on my brother's Senate campaigns."

"Bobby, whatever plans you have for security, scrap them and put me in charge."

Kennedy was stunned by Dunleavy's forceful presentation. "Okay, Stu, what's bothering you?"

"The men who killed your brother are still out there. How happy are they going to be in seventy-two hours when you announce your candidacy for thee presidency?"

Dunleavy was entering dangerous territory. Kennedy could not explain to Dunleavy the reasons for his support for the Warren Commission. He could not tell his friend that J. Edgar Hoover was blackmailing him to keep his mouth shut.

Kennedy had to shut this inquiry down. "Stu, I made you a job offer. What do you say? Yes or no?"

Dunleavy's mind was racing. "Permission to make another suggestion."

"What?"

"Put someone you trust, like John Martin, in charge of your advance team. I will be his number two."

"You are asking for a demotion?"

"I don't see it as a demotion. This is an opportunity for me to have dual roles. Let Martin do the nitty-gritty work of the campaign so I can keep a close eye on you."

Kennedy's eyes started to moisten. The man cared deeply about the life and safety of one Robert Kennedy.

"Okay, Stu. Martin can have you fifty percent of the time and I will have you the other fifty."

"Thank you, Senator."

"Give my love to Arlene, will you?"

"Of course."

Dunleavy stood up in preparation to leave. He stopped at the door. "Senator?"

"Yes, Stu."

"Be careful."

Robert Kennedy very slowly nodded his head.

Chapter 58

On March 16, 1968, Robert Kennedy stood in front of a monstrous battery of television cameras and made this pronouncement: "I am today announcing my candidacy for the presidency of the United States. I do not run for the presidency merely to oppose any man but to propose new policies. I run because I am convinced this country is on a perilous course and because I have such strong feelings about what must be done, and I feel I am obliged to do all I can."

Lyndon Johnson watched the broadcast slumped in a chair and drinking a scotch. He was not a happy man.

The glory years of 1964 and 1965 were over. These were the years of agony.

The Oval Office had become a prison. Johnson's popularity had fallen so far he could not appear at rallies for fear of being shouted off the platform. He confined himself to addressing military men on military bases. At least these places were safe from "Hey, hey, LBJ…"

Johnson lived in terror of running against any man whose last name was Kennedy. More than anything, Johnson feared going down in history as a sitting president routed from power long before his constitutional term of office was over. He legally could sit as president until 1972.

Even if by some miracle he beat back Robert Kennedy's challenge, the nomination would be worthless.

He knew half the party would sit out the election. Johnson then faced the possibility of losing to Richard Nixon, the Republican Party's version of Lazarus.

Johnson emptied his glass and then quickly refilled it. He was fortifying himself. He was thinking the unthinkable.

Maybe he should quit. Quit the job he dreamed about since high school.

Too soon, Johnson thought to himself. *Wait a few weeks.*

There were other men in America equally unhappy about Robert Kennedy's announcement.

The titans of La Cosa Nostra were paying close attention. Telephone lines from California to New York were working overtime handling the traffic between the crime bosses.

John Kennedy's presidency had been a nightmare. A potential presidency involving Robert Kennedy was nothing short of apocalyptic.

A preview of what might happen took place a year earlier.

James Riddle Hoffa was sitting in federal prison. Robert Kennedy swore he would get him. And he did.

If a man as powerful as Hoffa could fall, what chance did they have?

Robert Kennedy as attorney general controlled only a small portion of the government. Robert Kennedy as president would control every inch of the executive branch.

Kennedy could declare the Mob was a national security threat. He could send in the Marines.

Not likely, but still theoretically possible.

At the very least, President Robert Kennedy would fire J. Edgar Hoover. And he would reopen the investigation into the death of his brother.

Everything was at stake. The money, the mansions, the power, the women. The ability to buy off judges and prosecutors. Everything.

Plans needed to be discussed. Not actionable plans. Too early for that. Contingency plans. It was too early to do anything drastic. Kennedy might fail in his bid for the presidency.

The bosses would wait and watch. If Kennedy won a string of primary races, a decision would have to be made—a decision every bit as important as the one made in 1963.

Planning for the worst-case scenario was absolutely critical.

Kennedy's first campaign stop was Kansas State University on March 18, 1968. Fourteen thousand five hundred students gave him a warm welcome.

That same day he traveled to the University of Kansas. The audience there was nineteen thousand.

The Kennedy aura was every bit as strong as it was five years earlier.

John Martin, Stuart Dunleavy, and about twenty other people had to lay the groundwork for upcoming primaries in Indiana; Washington, DC; Nebraska; Oregon; South Dakota; and California.

Each member of the advance team put his heart and soul into the effort.

Eugene McCarthy refused to drop out. He was furious. He believed Robert Kennedy broke his word. He vowed to fight Kennedy all the way to the convention.

In late March, Lyndon Johnson had an Oval Office meeting with his most trusted pollsters. The message was bleak. Johnson was told he would be clobbered by McCarthy in the state of Wisconsin. Only 12 percent of Democrats in Wisconsin wanted Johnson back in the White House.

This was the nail in the coffin. Johnson was scheduled to give a speech on the Vietnam War on March 31, 1968. Johnson asked the major networks to carry it live.

The body of the speech was mostly forgettable. It was the end of the speech that caused an earthquake. "I will not seek, nor will I accept, my party's nomination for another term as your president."

Countless people nationwide stood up from their couches and looked at their family members. "Did we just hear that correctly? He's out?"

A huge banner in Chicago caught the mood of the nation when it was unfurled the next day. "Thanks, LBJ."

The nation's crime lords did not take the news well at all. They were counting on Johnson and Hoover to continue to block Robert Kennedy's ambitions.

But there was now a new ray of hope. Johnson's withdrawal would certainly herald the coming of vice president Hubert Humphrey. Perhaps he could beat Kennedy and save the leaders of the syndicate from ordering yet another dangerous political murder.

Less than one week after Johnson's speech, all political calculations were overturned.

On April 4, 1968, a bullet left the barrel of a Remington Gamemaster 30.06 rifle. The projectile found the neck of the greatest orator in America.

Martin Luther King Jr. fell dead on the balcony of the Lorraine Hotel in Memphis Tennessee at 6:05 p.m.

News of King's death spread nationwide like a brush fire. Bobby Kennedy was campaigning. Told of the news, he did not hesitate.

Kennedy stood in front of a mostly black audience in Indianapolis. "I have bad news for you, for all of our citizens, and for people who love peace all over the world. Martin Luther King Jr. was shot and killed tonight."

There was an audible gasp from the gathering.

Stuart Dunleavy watched as Robert Kennedy put on a tour de force. He asked the crowd not to surrender to hatred and retaliation. He told them about his own brother and the pain his death had inflicted on his family.

He asked that everyone seize this moment to move forward toward a more just country. He did it all extemporaneously.

Dunleavy was now more certain than ever that this was the man who should be running the country.

Not everyone took Kennedy's advice. Protests broke out in every state with a significant African American population. Fires were set. Businesses were destroyed. Forty people lost their lives.

Lyndon Johnson ordered a national day of mourning. King's funeral was televised to millions.

One day after King's funeral, Stuart Dunleavy cornered Robert Kennedy. "You need to start wearing a bulletproof vest right now!"

Kennedy hugged his friend. But he did not heed his advice. Nor did he significantly increase his own personal safety infrastructure. This decision infuriated Dunleavy.

On April 12, 1968, Hubert Humphrey announced his intention to seek the presidency. King's death had prevented him from getting in sooner.

Humphrey was too late to enter the primaries. He would seek to win the nomination the same way Lyndon Johnson attempted to in 1960.

Humphrey relied on Democrat powerbrokers in each state not holding primaries to pledge their delegates.

For the next six weeks, Kennedy, Humphrey, McCarthy, and the usual assortment of lesser lights campaigned in the battleground states.

None of the candidates could pull ahead.

Unlike 1960, when John Kennedy won ten primary contests in a row, Bobby Kennedy struggled to crush McCarthy.

Kennedy's promise to back McCarthy six months earlier was now hamstringing him with voters who believed he was an opportunist.

Kennedy won in Indiana and Nebraska. McCarthy won in Wisconsin and Pennsylvania.

It was now the last week in May, and both candidates headed to liberal Oregon for a showdown. Kennedy was favored. He lost. It was a stunning development.

Now everything rode on the all-important California primary scheduled for June 4, 1968. The winner in California would almost certainly be the eventual nominee.

Carlos Marcello knew this. So did Sam Giancana. And John Roselli. And Santo Trafficante.

Marcello had one of his bodyguards drive him to a phone booth in the outskirts of New Orleans.

On the other end of the line, also in a phone booth, was Giancana. "It's time you laid down the law to the old man, Sam."

The old man was Nick Licata, head of the Los Angeles syndicate. Licata was the leader of an organization that had withered under his predecessor, Frank DeSimone.

The Los Angeles Police Department had been stung by allegations of massive corruption during the 1920s, '30s, and '40s.

Attempting to rehabilitate itself, the department went after organized crime, beginning with the reign of Mickey Cohen in the 1940s and 1950s.

It was a successful crusade. Cohen went to federal prison in 1961 for tax evasion. He made DeSimone his successor. DeSimone was harassed by police for his entire reign. The LA Mafia became something of a joke.

When DeSimone died in 1967, the syndicate was so crippled it took its lead from Giancana and Roselli. Giancana decided to give Licata a shot.

Licata was a puppet. He would take orders.

Giancana ordered his second in command, Tommy Borsino, to board a flight and get to Los Angeles no later than June 2, 1968.

Borsino had an enormous responsibility. He had to make certain everything was in place for the possibility of a cataclysmic event happening on June 4, 1968.

The event the Mafia feared most was the potential victory of Robert Kennedy in the California primary. Already the designated patsy was being primed for his role. Licata was ordered to find a foreigner of no social standing.

Licata found Sirhan Bishara Sirhan, a Palestinian stable cleaner who moved to Pasadena, California, in the 1950s.

Sirhan was born in Jerusalem in 1944. He was four when the state of Israel was born. He lost family members in the war between Arabs and Jews. He was a rabid Arab nationalist. He regarded Israel as an illegitimate state.

In June of 1967, Israel defeated five Arab armies in history's most one-sided war.

Sirhan was enraged and embarrassed at the magnitude of the defeat. He read Senator Robert Kennedy wanted to send fifty American Phantom jets to resupply Israel.

For an entire year, Sirhan told anyone who would listen Robert Kennedy should be killed. His diary was filled with anti-Kennedy hysterics.

This was precisely the kind of useful idiot organized crime was looking for if dramatic action became necessary.

Licata briefed Sam Giancana about Sirhan. Giancana told Licata to begin buttering up the Palestinian and reinforcing his prejudices.

When Tommy Borsino arrived in Los Angeles, he took control of Sirhan. For two days, he fed him a diet of LSD and alcohol.

Borsino told Sirhan that if he killed Kennedy, the syndicate would whisk him out of the country. He would return to the Middle East a hero, "on par with the great Saladin."

The Mob naturally had a backup plan. No way would an assignment of this magnitude be entrusted to an unskilled, mentally unstable foreigner.

Sirhan would have an accomplice. Sirhan would not even know he was being shadowed.

The accomplice would make certain at least one bullet was properly fired in case Sirhan's unskilled marksmanship proved ineffective.

Giancana gave Borsino very strict instructions. If Kennedy lost the California Primary, he would be allowed to live.

If he won, he had to die. "You have got to have that guy right there no matter how it goes!"

Borsino said, "Don't worry. I got this."

Licata loaned Borsino his best shooter. The man was not in the same class as the Cobra. But he was good enough.

On the morning of June 4, voters started streaming to the polls in California. The state's massive size made it a vital political target for any politician seeking higher office.

California as an independent nation would have the world's eighth largest economy.

Following his defeat in Oregon, Kennedy campaigned day and night. The race was neck and neck. The candidates had one televised debate. McCarthy may have lost the race when he said he would consider putting communists in a revamped South Vietnamese coalition government. Kennedy pounced hard on this gaffe.

In 1968, only presidents were afforded Secret Service protection. John Kennedy's death and Martin Luther King's death did not alter this policy.

Dunleavy was terrified of Robert Kennedy's reckless behavior. The young Irishman flung himself into crowds seeking out hands to shake.

Kennedy felt he had no choice. Losing California meant certain failure.

Borsino knew that the Ambassador Hotel was home to the Kennedy campaign team. If Kennedy won, the hotel would be awash in humanity. That was exactly what Borsino wanted to happen.

Borsino spent two days wandering around the hotel. He was trying to isolate a kill zone.

Marcello, Giancana, Roselli, and Trafficante spent the same two days sitting in close proximity to telephone booths.

They had no choice. On June 4, a very big decision was looming. The final decision might not be authorized until the very last minute.

Kennedy did not stop shaking hands until the polls closed. Dunleavy met with him in his hotel room at the Ambassador. "How are you feeling, Bobby?"

"God, I am tired. But I feel really good about our chances."

"Bobby, I am going to ask you one more time to put on a vest."

Kennedy smiled. "I'll think about it."

Dunleavy shook his head in disgust. "Besides me, who is going to be watching you tonight?"

"Bill Barry." Barry was a former FBI agent.

"Good man. Who else?"

"Rafer Johnson and Rosie Grier."

Johnson was an Olympic Decathlon gold medalist. Grier was a former National Football League player. The two African Americans were formidable physical specimens.

Neither of them, of course, knew anything about protecting high-profile individuals.

"For Christ's sake, Bobby, we need ten more men surrounding you tonight. This place is going to be a madhouse if we win."

"You mean when we win, don't you, Stu?"

"Don't change the subject. If what happened to King doesn't scare the pants off of you, I don't know what will."

"I've got you. What more do I need?"

Dunleavy walked over to Kennedy's bed. He pushed a chair up close and sat down. "After you give your victory speech tonight, you are going to be tempted to leave the podium and wade into the crowd. Do me a favor. Do not do it! Just wave and get the hell out of there!"

Kennedy smiled. "All right, Stu. I will give you this one. You can grab my arm and pull me off the stage."

"Don't think I won't do it. Now, try to get thirty minutes of sleep."

"You are a good man, Stu. See you tonight."

Dunleavy went to his own room. His wife and son were waiting for him. Arlene looked ravishing in a new cotton dress. "How's he doing, honey?"

"Well, if he wins, I believe I just left the room of the next president of the United States."

"So why the long face?"

"I don't know. I just have a feeling. I wish it would go away."

Chapter 59

Four-year-old Michael Thomas Dunleavy thoroughly enjoyed his trip to California with his doting parents.

The lad was old enough to understand some of the happenings he witnessed daily. It was exciting. His parents moved in elevated circles even if young Michael did not absorb the concept of social distinctions.

He saw that everywhere his father happened to be there was action and drama. A day earlier, Robert Kennedy had picked him up and kissed him. Michael observed how his father and mother beamed.

Now he and his parents were having dinner in a large hotel while television cameras and reporters and hundreds of people milled about. What a story he would have for his friends back in Washington.

Stuart insisted that only the three of them were to dine together. He wanted ninety minutes of quality time before the polls closed at 7:00 p.m. After that, Arlene and Michael would be shunted back to their room.

Stuart Dunleavy would be on full-time Bobby patrol.

Immediately at 7:00 p.m., people began to crowd around television sets. Talking heads would announce the voting results for the next six hours.

Stuart Dunleavy was inside Bobby's room. Access to this room on this night was a signal that the attendees had achieved a great status.

By 9:00 p.m., it looked like Bobby Kennedy might be pulling ahead. By 10:00 p.m., there was no doubt.

At 11:00 p.m., Bobby Kennedy was declared the winner of the California Democratic primary. The count was 46 percent for Kennedy and 42 percent for McCarthy.

There was more good news. At midnight, Kennedy was on the phone with South Dakota Senator George McGovern. McGovern told Kennedy, "The great state of South Dakota is yours."

Two victories in one day. Gene McCarthy was heading toward a city called Also Ran.

There was laughing, crying, shouting and backslapping in Kennedy's headquarters. The nomination was inching closer to reality.

Shortly after midnight on June 5, 1968, Kennedy left his room for the elevator that would take him to the embassy room inside the Ambassador Hotel.

Hundreds of supporters were waiting to see their champion.

Dunleavy rode down with Kennedy. Also close by were Barry, Grier, and Johnson. Dunleavy was determined to keep Bobby away from the adoring crowd.

He could not stop him from speaking, but he could prevent him from wading into a sea of humanity.

Dunleavy had no way of knowing that exactly two hours earlier Sam Giancana spoke into a telephone receiver to Tommy Borsino. "It's a go!"

That was the extent of the conversation.

Sirhan Bishara Sirhan was sitting in Borsino's car. They made a beeline to the Ambassador Hotel. Immediately behind Borsino's car was another vehicle. Inside was a very calm professional killer. His job was to enter the hotel and remain as inconspicuous as possible.

The plan to kill Robert Kennedy was now beyond the point of revocation.

Borsino's job was to make certain Sirhan did not lose his nerve. Again and again he whispered in his ear, "Your people will worship you."

His brain was spinning from the effects of psychedelic drugs. Sirhan was a loose cannon. Borsino kept looking at the car carrying his backup. His face said, "This might come down to you."

Sirhan had an Iver Johnson Cadet 55-A revolver. This was a .22 caliber weapon. It produced slow-moving bullets. But the Mob almost always used .22 caliber weapons when the assignment called for close contact with the victim. Unlike a .45 caliber gun, which sounded like a cannon, a .22 caliber weapon gave off only the sound of a firecracker.

Borsino's backup also had a .22 caliber revolver. It was critical all the contact wounds looked similar.

Bobby Kennedy walked onto a slightly elevated stage. "My fellow Americans…"

While Kennedy thanked a myriad of individuals, Dunleavy scanned the crowd looking for anomalies. He saw only happy, smiling faces.

Kennedy ended his speech with this line: "My thanks to all of you, and now it is on to Chicago. Let's win there!"

Kennedy planned to walk through the ballroom when his speech ended. Dunleavy was getting ready to attach himself to Kennedy's hip when suddenly a man spoke into the candidate's ear. "The news guys want to have a few minutes, Bobby."

It was campaign aide Fred Dutton.

Kennedy allowed himself to be directed away from the agreed-upon route.

"Damn." Dunleavy did not like unscripted actions.

The shortest route to the press area was through the hotel's kitchen. Dunleavy found himself thirty feet behind Kennedy. The candidate was surrounded by Johnson, Grier, Barry, and the writer George Plimpton. Hotel employee Karl Uecker was showing the pack which way to go.

There were dozens of other people in the kitchen. From a security protocol, this was a nightmare. Dunleavy decided he had to get closer to Robert Kennedy.

"Excuse me, excuse me…"

Then came those horrible sounds.

Bam! Bam!

Dunleavy knew instantly what was happening.

Then six more times. *Bam! Bam! Bam! Bam! Bam! Bam!*

Eight shots. Sirhan managed to empty the entire chamber.

Barry, Plimpton, and Grier grabbed Sirhan. The screams from the crowd were loud and from the soul. Barry was punching Sirhan.

All eyes were on Sirhan and the men seeking to subdue him. This was precisely the kind of chaos Borsino's backup was waiting for.

With a cool demeanor, he bent down and fired one shot into Kennedy's head. It was necessary. As feared, Sirhan's bullet barrage was wildly uncoordinated.

Only two of Sirhan's shots found Kennedy. Five other people were wounded. The final shot hit a wall.

Dunleavy raced to Kennedy's side. He passed a man heading in the opposite direction.

The man's face was unlike all the other faces in the room. His countenance was calm. But his focus was intense. He was headed out of the hotel.

Dunleavy thought he saw the man put something in his right pocket. He then made a very human mistake. He wanted to find Robert Kennedy.

Kennedy was lying on his back. His eyes were glazed. There was no doubt he had been hit.

Dunleavy could not get close enough to touch Kennedy. He just stared for seven seconds.

Dunleavy's analytical brain suddenly kicked in. That man. He might be the shooter. Or one of the shooters. Dunleavy spun around and started running toward the exit. The man had to be found and found quickly.

Dunleavy was pulled short. There was a hand on his forearm. "Where are you going friend?" The man's eyes were dark and menacing.

"Take your hand off me!"

"How do I know you are not involved in this?"

"I'm with the campaign! And if you don't take your hand away, I am going to knock you out!"

The man slowly removed his grip. "Okay, friend. No need to get carried away."

Dunleavy's right hand was balled into a fist. He was a split second from coldcocking the stranger. He resisted the impulse. He took off in a dead run. Where was that man?

Tommy Borsino smiled. He had detained Dunleavy for ten seconds. That was all the time required. The backup got away.

Borsino lit a cigarette. Time for him to leave too. He walked away with disdainful insouciance.

Dunleavy scoured the sidewalk outside the Ambassador Hotel. His target was gone.

Now his priority became Arlene and his son. In a matter of minutes, they would learn about the shooting. Each of them would be frantic.

There would be time enough to visit Bobby in the hospital.

Dunleavy took a second to look at the imposing architecture of the Ambassador Hotel. He knew this building would someday be a tourist attraction. Of the worst kind.

Chapter 60

Curt Holmes could not believe he was sitting in St. Patrick's Cathedral in Manhattan. In a few minutes, he would be listening to a eulogy for another dead Kennedy.

The date was June 8, 1968. Three days earlier Robert Kennedy was gunned down in California.

The entire Kennedy clan was present. So were hundreds of politicians, celebrities, and ordinary Americans.

Holmes brought his wife, Helen, and their two boys, Mark and Thomas. He wanted his boys to experience firsthand the challenges that life had in store for all of God's children.

Tomorrow is promised to no man. Status, wealth, power, nothing was a guarantee.

Holmes was trying to save three spots for Stuart, Arlene, and little Michael.

Then he saw Stuart. He was in the northeast corner of the cathedral. He had managed to pigeonhole Teddy Kennedy.

The two men were having a very animated conversation. Aides to Ted Kennedy kept trying to intervene. They wanted the last remaining Kennedy brother to mingle with the crowd.

Ted Kennedy kept waving them off. Whatever Stuart was saying, it was obvious Teddy wanted to hear it.

Fifteen minutes was a long time to corner Ted Kennedy. He was the most important man in the building, and everyone wanted to shake his hand and offer condolences.

Holmes watched as Kennedy and Dunleavy grabbed each other's forearms and then embraced. Dunleavy then directed his wife and son over to Holmes's pew.

Arlene and Michael sat down. Dunleavy signaled Holmes with his index finger.

Holmes stood up and the two men walked five feet away from the assemblage.

"Arlene and Michael are visiting her mother Monday next. Can you come by the house after work?"

"Sure, I can, Stu. What's up?"

"Not now. Not here. Just come to the house with an open mind."

A strange request. Now Holmes was consumed with curiosity.

The men who spoke before Ted Kennedy were mere window dressing. The whole world was waiting for the senator from Massachusetts.

Kennedy was grim when he ascended to the podium. "My brother need not be idolized or enlarged in death beyond what he was in life. He should be remembered simply as a good and decent man who saw wrong and tried to right it, saw suffering and tried to heal it, saw war and tried to stop it."

Ted Kennedy was at that moment the most important man in America. Everyone knew he was going to be the Democratic nominee for president in 1972 should Richard Nixon ascend to the White House.

It was even conceivable he could be the nominee this year. But the convention was too close in time. And Kennedy was too distraught to make a strong run for the job.

Robert Kennedy, like his brother John, was a navy man. He would be buried next to his brother at Arlington Cemetery.

Holmes noticed that Dunleavy was stone-faced and quiet. He seemed deep into his own thoughts.

The next day was a Sunday. Holmes picked up the telephone. He was dying to talk to Dunleavy. But he put the receiver down. Arlene and Michael would be in the house. It was clear Dunleavy wanted to speak to him without anyone else present.

All day Monday Holmes kept staring at the clock. Then it was time to go.

Twenty minutes later, he was knocking on Dunleavy's front door. He had not even finished knocking when the door swung open.

"Come on in, Curt. Let's go out to the veranda."

On the veranda were two chairs, a table, a bottle of Jim Beam, and two glasses, each one holding one ice cube.

Dunleavy poured exactly one ounce into each glass. The two men did not touch glasses. A toast seemed inappropriate.

"Thanks for coming, Curt. Sorry I was so uncommunicative Saturday."

"Don't give it a second thought, old buddy. How are you doing now?"

"I am mad, Curt. Madder than hell."

Holmes took a small sip, swallowed, and put his glass down. "You were right there, Stu. I can't imagine seeing something so awful."

"Curt, what do you want to bet the LA police conduct an investigation and reach a conclusion that states Sirhan acted alone?"

"It is a little early for such an accusation."

"What do you want to bet J. Edgar Hoover picks up the telephone, calls the LA chief of police, and tells him the death of Robert Kennedy has national security implications?"

"Where are you going with this, Stu?"

"I was twenty feet away when Bobby was shot. The gun kept going off again and again. It was chaos. But I saw something for just a split second. I saw a man bend down just inches from Bobby's head. Then I heard a report. The man immediately stood up and put something in his right pocket."

Dunleavy stopped to take his first sip. Then he continued. "He did not run, but he walked away with a very deliberative purpose. I should have followed him. But I wanted to see Bobby. I wasted valuable seconds looking at my friend lying on the ground. Then I realized I might have allowed a second shooter to get away."

"What did you do?"

"I went after him. But some guy grabbed me. He wanted to know who I was. He wanted to know if I was involved in the shooting."

"Did you know this guy?"

"No, he delayed me. I threatened to flatten him, and he let go. But I could not locate the suspect."

"Did you see this guy shoot Bobby?"

"No. But he did not act like everybody else was acting. It looked as if he had a purpose for being there."

"Stu, do you think our Mob friends were involved in this?"

"That is exactly what I think. Here is a question I would like you to answer for me, Curt. The decision to leave the embassy room and walk into the kitchen was a spontaneous decision. We had planned to take Bobby back to his room via a different route. But somebody said the press wanted to interview Bobby. And the quickest route to the press room was through the kitchen."

"Tell me, Curt. How did Sirhan Sirhan know we would be going through the kitchen?"

Holmes rubbed his chin. "I don't know."

"Logic dictates Sirhan would have been in the embassy room. He would have stormed the podium, his gun blazing. But no, he was waiting like a spider in the kitchen, waiting for Bobby to walk toward him."

"Are you implying someone on Bobby's staff turned traitor?"

"I don't know! But I will be watching to see if the LA police grill a dozen people about why Bobby's exit protocol was changed. If they don't chase down this line of inquiry, we will know something isn't right."

Holmes downed his remaining bourbon. "Pour me another one will you, Stu? One ice cube please."

Dunleavy stood up to fulfill his social obligation. "Sirhan had a revolver that held eight bullets. I am told he emptied his chamber. Five people besides Bobby were hit. Without question this proves that Sirhan was an untrained, uncoordinated first-time killer. The Mob would never put all their eggs in this one inept basket. They'd have a backup plan."

Holmes asked an obvious question. "Sirhan was a Palestinian with a grudge. Isn't it possible he killed Bobby because of his support for Israel?"

Dunleavy dismissed this with a wave of his hand. "Curt, give me the name of just one politician who has national aspirations who doesn't support Israel."

"You got me there, pal."

"Sirhan was selected precisely because Palestinians and La Cosa Nostra have no mutual connections. Sirhan is the shiny object designed to draw everyone's attention away from the truth!"

"What's to stop Sirhan from spilling his guts now that he is facing the death penalty?" Holmes thought the question was reasonable.

"How about 'you open your mouth and your entire family dies'? The Mob certainly has used that tactic in the past."

Holmes rattled his glass so the ice would melt and smooth out the bourbon. "Okay, Stu. Let's say the Mob killed another Kennedy. What do you want to do about it?"

Dunleavy rested his elbows on his legs and bore his eyes into Holmes. "I am not going to put up with it, Curt. I am going to become proactive."

Holmes was not certain what that meant. "Proactive how?"

"I want to find out who actually put a bullet into my president's head. And when I am done learning the truth in that case, I want to find out who ordered Bobby Kennedy's death."

"What are you going to do? Become an FBI agent?"

"With J. Edgar Hoover at the helm! That would be a sure path to failure."

"Stu, you are not thinking of becoming a vigilante, are you?"

"I am going to become a crusader for the truth. And I might have to employ some rough tactics."

Holmes took a deep swallow and killed his second ounce of bourbon. He did not order another one.

He stood up. "Stu, you have a wife and a son. The people you are going after are heartless killers. Are you willing to take that chance?"

Dunleavy got to his feet. "I am not going to go on some cross-country killing spree. You have to trust me. This is not a suicide mission. But for reasons I cannot comprehend, my government seems incapable of conducting honest investigations into any case involving the name Kennedy. Maybe I can do better."

"Maybe you can join John and Bobby in Valhalla."

"It would be an honor. But I don't plan on seeing them for many decades."

"Stu, you don't have a job. How are you going to support your family?"

"I may not have a job, but I do have one hundred thousand dollars."

"Did you rob a bank?"

"Didn't have to. Let me explain. On June 3, I marched into Robert Kennedy's room. I told him I was going to quit following the California primary if he didn't upgrade his security. He smiled and walked over to his desk. He pulled out his checkbook and wrote the sum of one hundred thousand dollars. He handed it to me and said, 'Use this money as you see fit. Hire your own men.' Curt, he made out the check to me personally. How is that for trust?"

"Stu, now that Bobby's dead, the family is going to want that money back."

"No, you are wrong. I spoke to Teddy Saturday. You saw me. I told him about the money. I explained what I intended to do with it. Teddy signed on right then and there. He wants to find out who killed his brothers as much as I do."

"Okay, now let me ask you this. Are you going to bring Arlene into your confidence? Do you think she'll sign off on having her husband risk his life?"

"No, I can't tell Arlene. She won't understand. This is where I need your help."

"What can I do?"

"I want you to write a letter on NSA letterhead. The letter will state that Stuart Dunleavy has been hired as an independent consultant for the agency. The term of the contract is one year. I promise you she'll buy it."

"And what if Arlene brags to her friends her husband has a fancy new job at the NSA? That kind of information would get around town pretty fast."

"I will tell Arlene the job entails clandestine activities, and she cannot discuss it with anyone. She'll keep quiet."

"Is this the only favor you are going to ask of me, Stu?"

"No. I need someone who has access to information and intelligence. I need the resources the NSA can provide. I need someone I can trust who can double-check facts. I am going to be on the road quite a bit. The information I garner has to be crosschecked for accuracy."

Holmes just stared at his friend. He didn't want to say no. But using NSA resources for an unauthorized investigation could be a job-killing enterprise. Holmes had his own family to support.

"I don't know, Stu. Are you sure you have thought this through? How are you going to get these Mob guys to talk? Instead of giving you information, they might give you a pair of cement shoes!"

"I intend to use technology instead of brawn. I am going to need some miniature recorders and listening devices. And, Curt, keep an open mind when I tell you this."

"What?"

"I am going to need a hypodermic needle and a sleep agent."

"Oh my god." Holmes slapped his forehead with his right palm.

"Certain you don't want another drink?" Dunleavy was trying to lighten the mood.

"Getting me drunk won't get you the answer you want."

Dunleavy put his right hand on Holmes's left shoulder. "Curt, I know, I am asking you to take a big risk. But there is something wrong with this country. You and I both know who killed the Kennedy brothers. But the government doesn't want the truth to come out. For the life of me, I don't know why. I don't want to end my life sitting in a rocking chair and thinking if only I had done something. Curt, I need to know right now. Are you in or out?"

Holmes looked at Dunleavy's countenance searching for any sign of insincerity. There was none. If he helped Dunleavy, he might be contributing to his friend's death.

Stuart Dunleavy was willing to risk his life. Holmes told himself he would only be jeopardizing his job.

Holmes knew that without backup, Stuart Dunleavy's chances were slim to none.

Holmes extended his right hand. Dunleavy grabbed it. "I'm in."

Chapter 61

The year 1968 was turning into a disaster of epic proportions.

First the Tet Offensive in Vietnam. Then Martin Luther King Jr. was gunned down. Six weeks later a similar fate befell Robert Kennedy.

People were in the streets denouncing their political overlords. Lyndon Johnson was now just a spectator. He stayed inside the White House just waiting for the calendar to free him from his prison.

The Democratic Convention met in Chicago on August 26, and from day 1, it was chaotic.

Johnson did not plan on attending. His mere presence might have inflamed passions and led to violence.

Two years earlier, Mayor Dick Daley had lobbied Johnson for the right to hold the convention in Chicago. Daley had enough clout to get his way.

Daley could not have known then that volcanic political events would turn his planned happy convention into a raging donnybrook.

Radicals of all stripes were descending on the Windy City to make a statement. If that statement involved violence, then so be it.

Daley was no pushover. He blanketed the city with police and national guardsmen. He told his lieutenants they did not have to be polite when dealing with troublemakers.

Daley's antagonists just loved to poke the bear.

Abbie Hoffman and Jerry Rubin were leaders of the Youth International Party, better known as Yippies. Hoffman and Rubin sent out press releases stating their intentions. The water supply in the city was going to be contaminated with LSD. Young people would roam naked and defecate in the streets. The police would be bombarded with all manner of homemade missiles.

Daley believed all of it. He had no intention of losing a fight with a bunch of snot-nosed spoiled brats. Television viewers all over the world watched as police used billy clubs to subdue the crowds of protestors.

When Hubert Humphrey ascended the stage to accept his party's nomination for president, he could smell the tear gas from outside the building.

Stuart Dunleavy was not in Chicago in August of 1968.

He was in New Orleans.

A month earlier, Dunleavy had spoken to Holmes. He asked Holmes to find out if Marcello was in Dallas or Louisiana. Marcello was top dog in both locations.

The two men had concocted a communication system that would not leave a trail. It was only used when Dunleavy was out of town.

Five days a week after work, Holmes would drive to a coffee shop exactly halfway between his house and the NSA building. From 5:30 p.m. until 5:45 p.m., he would sit on a bench next to a phone booth. If Dunleavy needed anything, he would dial the number inside the phone booth and speak with Holmes.

Dunleavy was stalking Carlos Marcello. Holmes was feeding him information.

Holmes had a close friend in the New Orleans office of the FBI. The agent sent Holmes documents and photos of Marcello and his confederates. Holmes then transmitted this information to Dunleavy.

At great risk, Holmes manufactured a phony driver's license for Dunleavy to use on his travels. For no particular reason, Dunleavy chose the name Max Fesenbender.

Dunleavy was staying at a nondescript motel ten miles from Bourbon Street.

Each night Dunleavy called home and spoke with Arlene and Michael. Dunleavy told his wife he was in New Orleans on a clandestine assignment for the NSA. He told her he was staying at the Jackson Motel under the name of Max Fesenbender.

His wife bought all of it. Dunleavy asked her if any of their friends were questioning her about his whereabouts and job prospects. She said they were.

"I'm deflecting them, honey."

"Good girl. I can't wait to get home and see you."

"I miss you so much!"

"When my contract with the NSA is over, I'm taking you and Michael to Hawaii."

"Boy, am I going to hold you to that promise!"

Each time Dunleavy hung up the phone after speaking with his wife, he doubted his sanity. "What am I doing? Why am I taking this risk?"

An hour later, his determination would return. He was not going to abandon his goal.

Before leaving for New Orleans, Dunleavy gave Holmes an assignment. "These goombahs always have a favorite restaurant. Can your FBI buddy tell us where Marcello hangs out?"

"I'm sure he can." Holmes picked up the phone and made a call.

Holmes's contact came through.

Twice a week Marcello dined at Monticello's Italian Restaurant in the very heart of the city. Each Monday and Friday Marcello and his entourage would march through the doors of Monticello's like an invading army.

Two tables were always set aside for Marcello. One table backed up against a wall so no one could approach from the rear.

The other table was for five bodyguards. They were permitted to eat, but they were not allowed to drink alcohol. Marcello wanted them sharp as a tack at all times.

The very first time Dunleavy entered Monticello's, it was on a Monday. Holmes's FBI contact said Marcello always arrived exactly at 6:00 p.m.

He sat far away from his target. He brought along a newspaper to hide his features. At exactly 6:00 p.m., Marcello walked in and sat down.

Dunleavy noticed that Marcello seemed to be very friendly with one young male waiter.

He decided his first visit would be nothing but reconnaissance. He was coming back on Friday.

Dunleavy was two miles from his motel when he noticed a sign that read "Available for Rent." It was a free-standing garage. It was not in good shape. The price would be reasonable.

An idea formed in his head. There was no way he could kidnap Marcello. The man was too well guarded. But Dunleavy correctly assumed his second in command might not have the same level of security. It was worth a shot.

Dunleavy wrote down the telephone number on the sign. He called the owner an hour later.

The next day, Dunleavy had secured a garage for one month. The nearest building was one hundred yards away. It was perfect.

Friday afternoon, at 5:30 p.m., Dunleavy was inside his motel room. He picked up the garage keys and put them in his pocket.

He put on his shoulder holster. He checked his .45. He put on a blue leisure suit and headed out the door.

He was headed back to Monticello's. Dunleavy looked up from his newspaper and watched Marcello lead his army into the restaurant.

There were four men at his table. His bodyguards took up their posts.

Dunleavy noticed the same waiter again handled Marcello's table. He decided to take a risk.

Twenty minutes went by. The waiter approached Dunleavy's table.

"Excuse me, young man. Can I ask you a question?"

"Sure."

"I'm a tourist. Is that Carlos Marcello?"

"The one and only. But please don't go over there and ask for an autograph. He hates that."

"Oh, I would never have the courage to do anything like that. Are there any other celebrities at that table? Who is the guy on Marcello's right?"

"That's Marcello's number two. His name is Pete Donatelli. A very powerful man. But he does not get any press attention. The government knows who the hell he is, but the public doesn't have a clue."

"Thanks. I promise you I won't bother Mr. Marcello."

"That is a very wise decision, mister. Can I get you anything?"

"Just my check. Thanks."

Dunleavy wanted to pay his bill so he could leave the restaurant instantly if necessary. He sipped coffee and pretended to scan the newspaper. Marcello was like a robot. He was programmed to stay two hours at Monticello's and not a minute longer.

At 8:00 p.m., Marcello stood up. Each bodyguard rose with him. Two men walked just ahead of the boss. Three men walked behind him. The last man in the train turned his head and walked out, looking behind him all the way to the door.

Marcello stood in the door while his bodyguards scanned the parking lot. Only then did he exit the establishment.

The four men who had been sitting at Marcello's table lingered in the restaurant. One by one they got up and exited.

The last man sitting was Pete Donatelli. Dunleavy watched as he nodded his head in the direction of a very pretty waitress. The young woman went over and sat next to him. The body language was as clear as a bell. These two were having an affair.

Dunleavy had to make an instant assessment. He knew Donatelli would be leaving by himself. The girl would have to finish her shift before the two of them could reunite.

He very slowly got up and headed for the door. Once outside Dunleavy did a terrain assessment. The parking lot was empty. It was dark.

This was an opportunity. *Can I do it?* Dunleavy decided this was the moment of truth. Either he had the stones or he didn't.

He looked through a window. Donatelli was rising. He kissed the girl on her cheek. He put on his coat.

Donatelli was fifty-five years old and more than a little overweight. But he looked like he could put up some pretty stiff resistance. This was not going to be a cakewalk.

Donatelli stormed out of the restaurant and displayed absolutely no situational awareness. He did not scan the parking lot. He marched to his car knowing he was Pete Donatelli, and no one would mess with him.

He was completely unaware that twenty feet behind him a man was walking on cat's feet.

Donatellli opened a car door. He slid in and belched in contentment. A second later he felt cold steel against his temple. "Don't move and don't speak." The voice was strong and clear.

Donatelli panicked as he felt a hypodermic needle entering his neck. He jerked involuntarily, but the voice said, "Move and I'll kill you!"

In twenty seconds Donatelli was unconscious. Forty-five minutes later, Donatelli's brain began to awaken. His eyes fought to refocus. He tried to move. He could not budge. He was duct-taped to a chair.

"Welcome back, Mr. Donatelli."

He knew that voice. "Where the hell am I?"

"Where you are is not important. Why you are here is the only thing that matters."

Donatelli jerked his head to the left. He saw nothing but a wall. He turned his head to the right. He saw a man sitting in a chair. The man was wearing a non-descript Halloween mask. He was casually holding a large handgun. His hands were covered by white latex gloves.

"Who the fuck are you?"

"I am the man who, at this moment, decides if you live or die."

"Do you know who I am? Do you have any idea what kind of a shit storm your life is about to become?"

"You are not holding any cards, Mr. Donatelli. This is not a traditional kidnapping. There won't be any ransom demands. No one knows you are missing. In one hour, you will either be alive or dead. And it all depends on one thing."

"What's that?"

"Information. Either you tell me what I want to know or you don't."

"Who do you work for? The government?"

"I am an independent operator, Mr. Donatelli. The government has no role in this little drama."

"If you are not doing this for money, then what the hell do you get out of it?"

"Truth."

Donatelli started shaking his head. "This is all bullshit. If you let me go right now, I might be able to save your life."

"Mr. Donatelli, I want you to look straight ahead and tell me what you see."

Donatelli squinted. The lighting was poor. There was a table. And on the table, there was an electric drill.

"I bought it this morning at Sears. A very reliable item. You can see it has a nine-inch drill bit."

"You wouldn't dare!"

"I'm going to start with your ankles. Then we will move on to your kneecaps. But all this unpleasantness can be avoided if you just tell me what I want to know."

"All right, goddammit. What do you want to know?"

"I want to know the name of the man who actually murdered John Kennedy."

Donatelli in a thousand years would not have guessed this was coming. "Are you insane? This is why you brought me here?"

"The clock is running, Mr. Donatelli. Will you or will you not cooperate?"

"You want to know who killed Kennedy? Read the damn newspapers! Lee Harvey Oswald killed him."

"We both know that isn't true. We both know Oswald was a patsy who had to die so he couldn't spill his guts in court." Dunleavy continued, "We both know Jack Ruby worked for Carlos Marcello. Please do not waste my time."

"Why are you doing this? What do you get out of it?"

"My motives are not the issue here. The issue here is your cooperation or the lack thereof."

"I don't have the information you are seeking, pal! So just cut me loose."

Dunleavy slowly got up from his chair. He put his .45 in his shoulder holster. He walked over to the table. He picked up the drill and plugged in the cord.

"Time to begin, Mr. Donatelli." The drill roared to life.

Donatelli held his ground but only briefly. Dunleavy bent over and rolled up his left pant leg. He pressed the twirling drill bit against his flesh.

"Hold on! Wait just one damn minute! You can't be serious!"

"I am as serious as a heart attack. Shall we continue?"

"Put that damn thing away! You want a conversation, let's have a conversation."

"I will put this back on the table, Mr. Donatelli. But if you stonewall me again, I will bring it back, and this time there will be no stopping."

Dunleavy put the drill down. He casually walked over to his chair and folded his arms in front of his chest.

"Please continue, Mr. Donatelli."

"All right, I want to help you, whoever the hell you are. But I have a big problem. If Carlos Marcello finds out I spoke to anyone about John Kennedy, I will be killed and so will my entire family. I have four children and fourteen grandchildren."

"Mr. Donatelli, we have a window of opportunity here. No one on earth needs to know what is transpiring here. I certainly don't intend to tell anyone, and I seriously doubt you will. That girl you spoke with tonight. Are you supposed to see here later?"

"Yes."

"What time?"

"Eleven p.m."

"And your wife, what about her?"

"She knows the line of work I am in. If I don't come home for days, she understands."

"Well, Mr. Donatelli. We have at least two hours to conduct our business. More than enough time for me to cut you loose so you can keep your appointment with that tantalizing young lady."

Donatelli saw a ray of hope. If he was let go in a timely fashion, no one would know he had been kidnapped.

"How do I know you will keep your word?"

"You don't, but what choice do you have? If you show up in a hospital with drill bit wounds all over your body, Carlos Marcello is going to want to know how that happened."

Donatelli took four seconds to explore his options. "Okay, mister. Ask your questions."

"Was Lee Harvey Oswald a patsy?"

"Yes."

"Who shot John Kennedy."

"Well, I don't actually know his name."

"Oh, Mr. Donatelli, just when I thought you understood the rules."

Dunleavy walked back to the table and picked up the drill.

"Wait a minute! Just wait one minute! I can explain!"

"Mr. Donatelli, your expressed ignorance of the killer's name strikes me as noncompliance. I warned you about this."

"Just give me a minute to explain, will you!"

"I'll give you ten seconds."

"I don't know his name, but I know his...what do you call it, nom de guerre."

Dunleavy laughed. "His nom de guerre! Please, Mr. Donatelli."

"What if I told you even Marcello doesn't know his real name."

"I would say that is impossible."

"Hear me out! There is only one man on the planet who knows his real name. That man is Santo Trafficante."

"Okay. You have bought yourself a few more seconds. Keep talking."

"Marcello and Trafficante are tight. When the decision to kill Kennedy was finalized, the actual shooter had to be selected. Trafficante said he had a man in his organization who never missed."

"Marcello expressed no interest in the man's identity?"

"He did. So did I. Trafficante said we would just have to trust that he could get this man but that no one besides himself would know who he was."

"This is a very interesting story, Mr. Donatelli. But I am afraid I am going to need some kind of corroboration."

"I guess you are just going to have to kidnap Trafficante. Good luck with that!"

"Mr. Donatelli, I am afraid this does not rise to the level of full cooperation. You are going to have to give me something more."

Donatelli's mind was racing. If his captor picked up that drill one more time, it would be over.

"All right, wait a minute! Can I offer a suggestion?" Dunleavy nodded.

"Go to Tampa. Find some library. Dig up old newspaper articles about the Trafficante/Charlie Wall war back in the early fifties."

"Keep going."

"I heard Santo Trafficante Sr. had a guy on his payroll who was deadly from a thousand yards. According to the newspaper writers, Wall's men kept getting killed, and no one ever saw the shooter."

Dunelavy pondered Donatelli's story. It seemed too good to be a concoction. No one could manufacture such a tale in the stress of a few seconds.

"Okay, Mr. Donatelli. You have provided me just enough to save your life. Here is what is going to happen. You are going to experience another sleepy time episode. When you wake up you will be in the passenger seat of your own car. You will never hear from me again. I suppose that is music to your ears." Dunleavy stood up. "And I assume you don't intend to discuss this with anyone?"

"Brother, you can count on that."

"One more thing, Mr. Donatelli. What is the shooter's nom de guerre?"

"The Cobra."

Chapter 62

Stuart Dunleavy was ecstatic when the airplane wheels hit the pavement at Dulles International Airport in Virginia.

He was minutes away from kissing his wife and tossing his son in the air. He spent the entire flight from New Orleans thinking about his actions.

Dunleavy knew he had sunk to the level of the Mob in order to garner information.

He had kidnapped a man. Threatened him with torture and death. Do the ends justify the means?

Dunleavy thought, *If the government would do its job, none of this would have been necessary.*

In any event, Dunleavy decided he would not engage in this type of activity again. His pursuit of truth would stay academic and not descend to the barbaric. If, at all possible.

Arlene looked like a million dollars. His son could not stop hugging him.

"Let's go find a steakhouse, honey. I don't eat airline food."

At the baggage claim, Dunleavy told his wife he wanted to call Curt Holmes. "I'll be back in five minutes."

Holmes picked up the phone at his house. "Damn, Stu, it's good to hear your voice."

"Can we do lunch tomorrow, Curt? I'll pick you up at work."

"It's a date."

Dinner with the family took two hours. Dunleavy wanted to just sit and talk with his wife and son. He told Michael, "You can have all the ice cream you want."

Arlene protested, "Stu, I don't want to raise a little butterball."

Dunleavy laughed and grabbed his son. "Don't you worry. This kid is going to play sports seven days a week. He'll be thin as a reed."

Four hours later, when Michael was fast asleep, Dunleavy surprised his wife while she was in the shower. She did not complain.

She thought his lovemaking had extra zest. She sometimes wondered what healthy males did when the wife was hundreds of miles away.

Dunleavy said "I love you" so many times she was convinced he behaved like a Trappist monk on his journeys.

Arlene decided that this was the night to tell her husband she had come to a major decision. "Stu, I want another child."

Dunleavy bolted up in bed. "Honey, that's fantastic!"

Four years had passed since Michael's birth.

Arlene was stunned by the transformation of her body, thanks to biology. Pregnancies cause women to gain weight and become frumpy. Looking in a mirror she said, "I can't live like this."

Following Michael's birth, she immediately went on the pill. A pharmaceutical methodology for preventing birth was brand-new.

Arlene worked hard to get her figure back. She succeeded beyond her expectations. Her husband was not displeased.

Arlene's friends were jealous of her success. She looked like a high school prom queen. "It's not fair!" She heard that a lot at lunches.

Now it was 1968, and her biological clock was ticking.

One day it hit her like a bolt of lightning. She wanted a daughter.

Dunleavy always wanted more children, but he was not going to force his wife to accept his wishes. If they did have a daughter, Michael could play the role of a protective brother, and the age difference would make it possible.

Dunleavy kissed Arlene. "We had a good start tonight. Let's try again tomorrow."

"What's wrong with right now?" Arlene tossed off the sheet to expose her perfect figure.

Dunleavy moved with the speed of a trapdoor spider.

At 11:55 a.m., Dunleavy picked up Holmes in front of the NSA building in Fort George C. Meade in Maryland.

"You seem to be in an awfully good mood, Stuart."

"Arlene wants another child."

"So that's it. Well, it's about goddamn time."

"I'm buying today. Curt. How about Nelson's Diner?"

"How about the 21 Club in New York?"

Dunleavy laughed. "That's not lunch! That's an expedition."

The two men did not discuss business until their hamburgers and French fries were gone. Dunleavy noticed Holmes had brought a large manila envelope into the diner.

"What's that, Curt?"

"Remember when you asked for documents and photos of Marcello's henchmen? I thought you might like to see the faces of the men who work for our friend, Mr. Sam Giancana. These two families work together quite a bit."

Dunleavy took the envelope from Holmes and slowly opened it. Inside were twenty photographs. It was photograph number two that caused Dunleavy's eyes to widen to the size of saucers.

"Curt, who is this?"

Holmes took the photo and examined it. "That's Tommy Borsino. Giancana's underboss."

"Holy shit on a shingle!" Dunleavy leaped to his feet and grabbed the photo back from Holmes.

"What the hell is going on, Stu?"

"This guy was at the Ambassador Hotel when Bobby was shot! He's the guy who grabbed my arm and kept me from following the second shooter!"

Now it was Holmes who was on his feet. "Are you sure? There's no chance you are mistaken?"

"I will swear to it in a court of law! I was six inches from his face!" Dunleavy got in Holmes's face for dramatic effect.

"Let's sit down, Stu. People are starting to stare."

Each man eased back to their respective chairs. Dunleavy downed a glass of water in one gulp. Had it been bourbon, it would have suffered the same fate.

"Curt, this is the final proof. Do you have any doubts whatsoever that the Mob killed John and Robert Kennedy?"

Holmes took five seconds to answer. He wanted to weigh any possible explanations that were contrary to Dunleavy's assessment.

He could not think of one. "Stu, there is only one reason why Tommy Borsino would be in the same room with Bobby. To make certain the deed was done properly and definitively."

"You are righter than rain, my friend."

Dunleavy then grabbed Holmes's forearm with great force. "So why is the government so determined to find alternative theories? Why don't they look at the most obvious theory? The Mob had motive. The Mob had the means. And the Mob had the will!"

"Are you going to tell me what you found out in New Orleans?"

"Yes, I am. And if you needed any more reinforcement, I've found it."

"Just answer me one question. You didn't kill anybody to get this information, did you, Stu?"

"I give you my word I did not put anybody in the ground. But it is better you don't know the details surrounding exactly how I got this information."

"Oh, boy. Knowing you is going to cost me a lot of sleepless nights."

Dunleavy told Holmes he had an impeccable source who confirmed the hit on John Kennedy was ordered by Marcello, Giancana, Trafficante, and Roselli.

"I am also convinced Jimmy Hoffa knew what was going to happen, but he was not part of the operational planning."

"Did your source confirm that?"

"No, but Hoffa was in bed with all four of these hoodlums, and it is reasonable to conclude he would know." Dunleavy saved the best for last. "I also have a lead on the actual triggerman in John Kennedy's death. Curt, I am going to spend some quality time with my family. Then I am going to Tampa. I will need some NSA excuse, and I will need you to keep supplying information."

"That's Trafficante's territory. Watch out!"

"Hey, my wife just told me she wants another kid! I am going to be as cautious as I can be!"

Chapter 63

In the first week of November 1968, Republican Richard Nixon's eight-year quest for the White House reached fruition.

He and running mate Spiro Agnew defeated two candidates. The most formidable opponent was the Happy Warrior, Democrat Hubert Humphrey. He and running mate Edmund Muskie came within a whisker of winning.

The election would have been a blowout for Nixon, except for one thing: Alabama Governor George Wallace wanted the job.

Wallace formed a third party and picked WWII hero Gen. Curtis LeMay as his running mate. LeMay was in charge of the bombing campaign over Japan.

A more right-wing confederation could not have been imagined.

Wallace and LeMay garnered just under ten million votes. Had these gentlemen sat out the election, about 95 percent of these votes would have landed in Nixon's column.

Nixon received 31,783,783 votes. Humphrey received 31,291,839. Nixon was sworn in exactly one year after the Tet Offensive.

The country was wracked by street violence and the creation of an incipient terrorist organization called the Weather Underground.

There was also a growing number of Americans who doubted the government's version of what happened in Dallas in 1963.

The first crack in the dam occurred in 1966. American lawyer Mark Lane wrote *Rush to Judgment*, a scathing indictment of the Warren Commission.

Holmes and Dunleavy devoured the book. They enjoyed having company in their quest for a reassessment of the assassination.

Lane's book triggered an avalanche of critical news stories and editorials about Earl Warren and his conclusions.

As long as Lyndon Johnson sat in the Oval Office, there would be no reevaluation of the report. Richard Nixon never spoke publicly against the Warren Report. Privately he believed it was a piece of junk.

Nixon did not want to reopen the Kennedy assassination. He wanted to push his own agenda, and that meant getting out of Vietnam before the United States imploded.

Asking Congress to form a commission to reexamine Kennedy's death would have been hugely divisive.

The country was divided enough.

Holmes and Dunleavy decided they had three months to finish their clandestine activities. Once Nixon was sworn in, there would be a housecleaning. Nixon would put his own people in charge of every agency.

Curt Holmes was the number three man at the NSA. He might survive. Then again, he might not.

Holmes's removal would cripple the cause of finding John Kennedy's true killer.

Dunleavy had another problem. His mother's health was declining. Death was not imminent, but one never knows.

The entire family was going to congregate in West Palm Beach for Thanksgiving. That included Dunleavy's two older siblings, Matthew Francis and Kristin.

Matthew had four children. Kristin, who was married to a lawyer named John Tunsten, had five.

Patricia Dunleavy's spacious house was going to be alive with the laughter of children.

Stuart was outnumbered. He could not wait to tell his mother and siblings he and Arlene were going to have another child.

In early November, Arlene visited her doctor. She learned she was two weeks pregnant.

One day on the telephone, Patricia told Stuart she was going to stay alive to see the birth of that child "come hell or high water!"

One week before Thanksgiving, Dunleavy asked Holmes to meet him after work for a cup of coffee. "I will be leaving Mom's house three days after Thanksgiving. Here is what I want to do. I will drive Arlene and Michael to Tampa Airport. I am going to stay behind. I will tell Arlene the NSA, meaning you, wants me to investigate something and there is no reason to fly to Washington, turn around, and fly back. I just need you to know this in case Arlene brings it up."

"I have your back. Stu, are you going to confront anyone in Tampa? Do I have to worry?"

Dunleavy laughed. "Old buddy, this will be strictly academic."

"You aren't just saying that?"

"Curt, I am going to spend one whole day just reading old newspaper articles. Unless the librarian is on Trafficante's payroll, I should be perfectly safe."

"Okay, buddy. I will tell Arlene an alien spaceship was sighted in central Florida, and you are the only one qualified to handle it."

"Curt, if anyone can sell that story, it's you!"

Thanksgiving weekend in West Palm Beach was an elixir. Patricia's spirits soared with the inundation of family members.

Arlene was subjected to goodhearted humor about being "slow on the job" when it came to producing children. Matthew ribbed Stuart. "Are you taking enough vitamins?"

Dunleavy felt uncomfortable discussing his employment. All Americans are consumed with curiosity when a family member has a job that is described as clandestine.

"Are you a spy?" Dunleavy heard that question a dozen times.

He would parry with "Come on, guys, there's a football game on."

From Thursday through Sunday, this Irish clan bonded over alcohol and the consumption of heavily caloric food. The only thing missing was Mike Dunleavy Sr. His photo was prominently visible in the living room.

Stuart watched his mother cry several times over that extended weekend.

On Sunday morning Dunleavy packed his wife and son into a rental car and headed toward Tampa. He hugged Arlene and Michael for a long time at the departure gate at Tampa International Airport.

"I wish you were coming with us." Arlene did not want this separation.

"I'll be home in two days."

Dunleavy did not leave the airport until the jet carrying his precious cargo was out of sight. That Sunday night, he and Arlene talked for two hours.

Monday morning found Dunleavy at the Tampa Public Library. He spent three hours perusing old articles about the Trafficante/Charlie Wall Mob war in the 1950s.

Dunleavy concluded that Pete Donatelli might be telling the truth. But he was not satisfied. Dunleavy wanted to talk to the man who wrote those articles.

The byline on most of the articles was written by a man with two first names: Scott Dennis. Dunleavy found a pay telephone and dialed the number for the *Tampa Tribune*.

Founded in 1895, the Tampa Tribune was thriving. This was the halcyon years of newspapers, when classified ads raked in millions of dollars.

"City desk, Johnson. How can I help you?"

"Hello. I was wondering if Scott Dennis was still employed at your paper?"

"Scotty! Nope, he's retired. But he still lives in Tampa."

"How can I find him?"

"Simple. Every night at seven p.m., he has dinner at Brodie's Bar and Grille."

At exactly 7:00 p.m., Dunleavy walked through the doors at Brodie's. It was a high-class eatery with a well-dressed customer base.

A waiter pointed to Scott Dennis sitting at the bar. There was an empty stool just to the right of Dennis. Dunleavy eased his frame into the spot.

Dunleavy debated using small talk to break the ice, but he abandoned that idea. Dennis might be the cantankerous type who rejected strangers.

"Just jump right in" seemed a better strategy.

Dunleavy shoveled his right hand into Dennis's view. "Scott Dennis?"

Startled, Dennis shook his hand. "Yeah, who are you?"

"Max Fesenbender. I used to read your stuff in the *Tribune* all the time. You are quite an accomplished writer."

"Thanks, pal. Were you ever in the newspaper business?"

"No. But if you let me pick your brain, I will be more than happy to relieve you of your bar tab."

Dennis chuckled. "Mister, you can't afford to make that promise. Newspapermen can outdrink any other class of people on the planet."

Dunleavy produced a wad of cash. Most of the bills had the numeric number of one hundred.

"Permit me to make an effort."

Dennis was mightily impressed. "Okay, pal. I'm all ears."

"I've led a boring, law-abiding life. But I have always been fascinated by gangsters. Your articles on Santo Trafficante and Charlie Wall were extremely interesting. Tell me, what were those men like?"

Dennis snapped his fingers. "Harvey! Another scotch. Easy on the ice."

While Harvey did his ministrations behind the bar, Dennis resumed his conversation with Dunleavy. "What were they like? They were gangsters. They made their money selling vice. People like to gamble. People like sex. Whenever the government outlaws something, people want to have it."

"Why couldn't Wall and Trafficante work out their differences? Why didn't they divide Tampa into two territories, you know, like Capone and Moran did in Chicago?"

Dennis snorted in derision. "And how did that work out? Capone and Moran got along for maybe a year and then they went to war. When mobsters make deals, they can't go to civil court to resolve their issues. They go to the mattresses."

Dunleavy waited for Harvey to place a drink in front of Dennis. Then he continued his interrogation. "Did you ever meet Wall or Trafficante in person?"

"I met Wall once. Didn't like the guy. He was a prick. But I knew Trafficante pretty well. I wouldn't say we were friends, but I could talk to him about anything."

"Really! A gangster opening up to a newspaperman! Isn't that counterintuitive?"

"Hey, there were rules, you know. Just about everything he told me was off the record. But I used that information to get facts I would not have access to without his cooperation. Believe me, I wasn't stupid enough to stab Santo Trafficante in the back."

"What caused the two men to go to war?"

Dennis took a heavy swallow and belched in contentment. "I started at the *Tribune* in 1946, right after I got out of the Marine Corps. I missed all the gang fighting that took place in Tampa in the 1930s. Charlie Wall and a hood named Ignacio Antinori spent that whole decade shooting bullets at each other. The bodies really piled up. The war ended in 1940 when Wall cornered Antinori and one of his men opened up with a sawed-off shotgun. Goodbye, Ignacio! Guess who picked up the pieces of the Antinori gang? None other than Santo Trafficante. Wall was weak from ten years of gang fighting. Trafficante had the stronger organization. Wall was forced to bide his time."

Dunleavy did not interrupt Dennis's soliloquy. The man was on a roll.

"Trafficante kept Wall caged for a whole decade. Then in 1950, the Kefauver Commission came calling. The commission hit Wall with a subpoena and forced him to testify. Trafficante wanted no part of the government asking him questions. He and his son moved to Cuba and started buying into casinos. While both Trafficantes were out of the country, Wall started feeling his oats. He hired more torpedoes and took over portions of Trafficante's empire. As soon as the Kefauver Commission completed its work, Trafficante and his son came back to Tampa. This is when I became close to the man. He wanted to know what Wall was up to, and he believed a seasoned crime reporter would be a good source."

"Excuse me, Mr. Dennis, allow me to ask a delicate question. Were you ever on Trafficante's payroll?"

Dennis smiled. "Nope. But when I was with him, I never picked up a drink or dinner tab." Scott Dennis winked at Dunleavy.

"Please continue, Mr. Dennis."

"So now Wall thinks he is the rooster in the barnyard. He tells Trafficante it is time to retire. He actually told Santo he would 'allow him to live' if the entire Trafficante organization moved out of the city."

"I'm guessing Mr. Trafficante rejected Mr. Wall's kind offer."

"You are a funny guy, Fesenbender. Hey, what kind of a name is that, anyway?"

"German. But I'm half Irish."

"A kraut and a mic! Hell, I've got the same two bloodlines myself!"

Dennis raised his glass. Dunleavy responded in kind. "It seems like you killed that glass of scotch. Care for another?"

"Do you really have to ask?" Dennis chortled at his rejoinder.

Dunleavy wanted to get back on track. "I'm guessing this was when the war started. Why did Trafficante prevail?"

"You know, right at the beginning of the conflict, I told Santo, 'You better be careful. Wall has thirty men, all of them trained killers.' Santo just smiled. Then he said, 'Wall has bazookas and hand grenades. I have a human nuclear weapon.' I asked what the hell that meant. He said, 'Just keep monitoring your police radio. You'll understand.'"

"Did you ever find out?" Dunleavy was genuinely curious.

"Yeah, I did. Wall's people started dropping like flies. It was always the same. One of Wall's guys would be sitting at a traffic light, and then his head would disappear in a cloud of blood. It was a high-caliber bullet each time. Except no one ever saw the shooter or heard the rifle."

Dunleavy was now paying attention with clenched fists. "You are telling me Trafficante's secret nuclear weapon was a trained sniper?"

"Not just trained. This guy was the best. Nine guys were killed the same way. Always a head shot, never the torso. After one year, Wall's men were afraid to leave the house. You can't run a crime organization from your basement."

"Did Trafficante lose any men?"

"He nearly lost his son in 1953. Santo Jr. survived an attempted assassination. Then the old man died of natural causes in 1954. A year later, Santo Jr.'s men found Wall and shot him dead. Trafficante the younger has run Tampa without hindrance since Wall departed this earth."

"What can you tell me about the sniper?"

"What do you want to know?"

"Is he still around? Did old man Trafficante ever tell you his name?"

"His name! No, do you think I would be stupid enough to ask his name? Santo's tolerance of newspapermen did have its limits, you know."

"That's a shame. It would be one hell of a scoop for any reporter to find out who he is."

Dennis killed his scotch. One more time Harvey was summoned.

"Oh, I heard scuttlebutt. I heard he was an Englishman. Served with Montgomery in North Africa. Killed Germans by the boatload. The Nazis even gave him a nickname."

"What name was that?"

"They called him the Cobra."

Chapter 64

The clock was ticking. It was now December of 1968.

Richard Nixon would be sworn in on January 20, 1969. Would he clean house? How many Democrat holdovers would be shown the door?

Curt Holmes was high enough in the NSA bureaucracy to qualify as a potential target for removal. Plenty of Republicans would like to have his job.

Dunleavy and Holmes were having lunch together at least three times a week. Dunleavy told Holmes he was absolutely convinced that Pete Donatelli's observations were factual.

Donatelli's story was backed up by Scott Dennis.

"That newspaper guy never met Donatelli, yet they both used the same nom de guerre to identify the sniper. This guy is real, Curt. But how do we find him?"

"Are you sure you want to find him? From what you have told me, this guy is death on a stick."

"If we can just get his name, maybe we can turn it over to the FBI. Who knows if Nixon is going to keep J. Edgar Hoover?"

Holmes chuckled. "You don't think Hoover has enough information on Nixon to blackmail him? I think old J. Edgar is going to die sitting in a leather chair inside his federal office."

"You are probably right."

After having six lunches, neither man had developed a strategy for finding the Cobra.

The situation became critical a week before Christmas. Laurence Frost was long gone. The head of the NSA in 1968 was Marshall Carter.

Carter called Holmes and four other top supervisors into his office. He got right to the point. "I just found out Nixon is going to appoint Admiral Noel Gayler as NSA director. Gayler told Nixon he would accept the job only if he could appoint his top people. You know what this means. You gentlemen are out. I promise I am going to give each one of you a glowing recommendation for whatever private-sector job comes your way."

Holmes exited Carter's office and immediately called Dunleavy.

In exactly five weeks, all the resources of the NSA would be out of reach. Holmes's job would be gone, and Dunleavy's make-believe job would also disappear, as it only existed under Holmes's protection.

"What do you want to do, Stu? Call it quits?"

Dunleavy's right hand gripped the telephone so hard it hurt his fingers. "Can you meet me immediately after work?"

"I can meet you right now. It's two p.m. What are they going to do? Fire me for leaving work early?"

"Great! You know the place! I'll be there in half an hour!"

Dunleavy watched as Holmes entered the coffee shop. He waved him over. Dunleavy had two cups of black coffee on the table. He picked a location as far away from other people as possible.

"Well, Curt, how does it feel to be unemployed in your mid-forties?"

Holmes smiled. "Kind of liberating. I always dreamed of playing tennis seven days a week."

"Keep your racquet in your closet. I have a plan. It's a real long shot. Do you know anyone in England who holds a security clearance?"

Holmes rubbed his chin. "Well, two years ago I made a phone call to the number two guy at MI6. We talked for a long time. I think I established some level of rapport."

Dunleavy smiled. He could not think of a better conduit. "Tomorrow, I want you to find out if this guy is still with MI6. If he is, get him on the phone. Tell him to expect a visit from a man named Stuart Dunleavy, who is under contract from the NSA."

"Stu, where are you going with this?"

"Do you think this guy has enough clout to forage through British military records and find a name?"

"The number two at MI6! He would absolutely have the clout."

"Good. Then I am going to start making plane reservations."

"Stu, he is going to want to see a piece of paper attesting to your bona fides. It means I am going to have to use NSA letterhead and sign my name at the bottom."

"That's right, Curt. And if you get caught, you might get fired!"

Each man laughed.

"It's still a risk, Stu. It is one thing to walk away from a job because of a change in administrations. It is another to get fired for unethical behavior."

"I know it's a risk. But if we stop now, we may never know who killed John Kennedy. Will you do it?"

Holmes stared at Dunleavy for a long time. The pros and cons of this conspiracy bounced around his brainpan. He could be black-balled by private employers because of the manner in which he exited government.

He might end up running his own lawn service. He could also end up in a rocking chair at age ninety, cursing his cowardice back when he was still a young man.

"Dammit, Stu. Let's give it a shot!"

Dunleavy beamed. "I owe you big time, pal."

The next day Holmes wasted no time in calling London. The Brits were four hours ahead of America. His 8:00 a.m. call meant it was lunchtime at MI6 headquarters.

The British were renowned for their intelligence service. Both Kaiser Wilhelm in 1914 and Adolph Hitler in 1939 found out the hard way.

The Secret Intelligence Service is commonly referred to as MI6, or military intelligence, section six. It is housed in the SIS build-ing in London. Its counterpart in the United States is the Central Intelligence Agency.

The Brits outfoxed Hitler for six years. Not so Joseph Stalin.

British intelligence was plagued with treason. This was an out-growth of a fascination with Marxism that gripped British elites in the 1930s. Five traitors kept Stalin informed of everything Britain was doing during the war and long after the conflict ended.

These traitors were Donald MacLean, Guy Burgess, Kim Philby, Anthony Blunt, and George Blake.

The number of human assets murdered by the Soviets because of these men was in the high hundreds.

It was not until the 1980s that the CIA learned MI6 was riddled with communist sympathizers.

In 1968, the duplicity of these men was still unknown. In 1966, Holmes called MI6 and spoke with Sir Thomas Higgins. Holmes was instructed to find out if the British had surpassed America with a new telemetry invention.

Higgins was surprisingly forthcoming. Holmes thanked him for his cooperation.

This was the door Holmes and Dunleavy hoped was still open.

On a snowy mid-December day in 1968, Holmes learned that Higgins was still at MI6 and he still held the number two position.

Higgins also remembered Holmes. The two men bantered for over half an hour before Holmes got around to the purpose of the call.

Holmes asked if Higgins could find time somewhere in his busy schedule to see a man named Stuart Dunleavy.

Holmes told Higgins Dunleavy was an NSA employee. Holmes hoped Higgins would accept this declaration and not follow up on it.

"May I inquire what this is all about?" Higgins had a rich accent that clearly labeled him upper crust.

"I would prefer the nature of Mr. Dunleavy's visit not be discussed over a telephone line. Is that acceptable?"

"Of course! Let's see, with the holidays coming up, I can see your man on the second Monday in January. Can he accommodate that date?"

"He can indeed, Mr. Higgins. And thank you very much. Oh, permit me to give you my private number at the NSA in case you have any follow-up questions."

Holmes was being clever. He wanted Higgins to speak only to one person at the NSA.

Holmes told Dunleavy he had to be in England on the exact date mandated by Higgins. They would have just one shot at getting the information they desperately sought to acquire.

Dunleavy spent the next three weeks attending to his wife's every wish. He wanted her to be happy as a lark before telling her he was going to England without her.

He knew she would accept it. She would not like it. But she would accept it.

After all, everything her husband did was hush-hush.

New Year's Eve was a blended party with Holmes, his wife, and his children and the Dunleavy family getting together.

Holmes handed Dunleavy an envelope. Inside was a letter of introduction. It respectfully requested that MI6 provide the holder of the letter with "any and all information pertaining to a national security matter important to the United States."

Dunleavy said, "Thanks, Curt. I know the chance you are taking."

Holmes downed his cocktail. "See you on the unemployment lines, Stu."

Both men appreciated the perverse humor.

Dunleavy landed in London on January 12, 1969. He could have come earlier and spent some time sightseeing. Arlene put the kibosh on that plan.

"You are not going to see London without me, Stu. We are going back together. With Michael!"

Dunleavy did not complain. He happily acquiesced.

Dunleavy's appointment with Sir Thomas Higgins was scheduled for 10:00 a.m. the next day. His hotel was five blocks from the SIS building. He walked there in the bitter winter weather.

Dunleavy showed security credentials that labeled him an active member of the NSA. This was another gift from Holmes.

Two men escorted him to Higgins's spacious office. Following introductions and handshakes, Higgins retired behind his desk. Dunleavy sunk into a large leather chair directly facing his counterpart.

"Tea?"

"Thank you, Mr. Higgins. With lemon, please."

Dunleavy briefly stood to hand Higgins his bogus letter. Higgins put on his reading glasses and took his time reading the contents. Dunleavy hoped he might hand back the letter. He did not.

"Well, Mr. Dunleavy. How can Her Majesty's secret service help our American cousins?"

"I want to thank you very much for seeing me, Mr. Higgins. I can imagine how busy your schedule must be."

"Please, Mr. Dunleavy. Do not give it a second thought. Without the United States, I might be digging ditches and speaking German!"

Both men appreciated the veracity of that remark.

"In the interests of not wasting anyone's time, may I ask if you have the authority to examine all British military personnel records?"

"I most certainly do have the authority."

"Wonderful. We are interested in locating a British national who may have committed a heinous crime in the United States."

"Mr. Dunleavy, normally we would receive such a request from your state department. And they would be acting on behalf of your FBI."

Dunleavy had to think fast. He was up to the task. "Quite true. In 1961, former President John Kennedy signed an executive order allowing the NSA to cooperate in a limited capacity with the FBI. That order is still in effect."

"I see. Well, whom are you seeking to apprehend?"

"We don't have a name. We do have some details about his life."

"Please continue."

"The man we are looking for served in the British Eighth Army in North Africa. He was a sniper."

Higgins sniggered. "The British Army had many snipers, Mr. Dunleavy."

"I know. But this man was exceptionally efficacious. He was so deadly he terrified the Nazis. They even gave him a nickname. They called him the Cobra."

Dunleavy was stunned by the change in Higgins's demeanor. The man's eyes doubled in size. His body became rigid. He seemed at a loss for words.

"Mr. Higgins, have you heard of this individual?"

Higgins cleared his throat and tried to recover. "Mr. Dunleavy, what crime is this man suspected of committing?"

Dunleavy had hoped he could secure Higgins's cooperation without getting too specific. That boat just sailed.

Now Dunleavy was slow to find his words. "We have credible information this man may have been involved in the assassination of John Kennedy."

"Mr. Dunleavy, you represent the United States government. Do you not?"

"I do."

"Is it not the official position of your government that John Kennedy was killed by Lee Harvey Oswald and that Mr. Oswald did not have any confederates?"

"Mr. Higgins, half the country does not believe the Warren Commission. The commission's findings are not sacrosanct. We have an obligation to explore all possibilities."

Higgins knew American politics. He knew Lyndon Johnson would never countenance this revival of his predecessor's death.

But in one week Johnson would be out of office, and Richard Nixon would be president. Did Nixon greenlight this investigation? Higgins pondered that possibility.

What Higgins was not prepared to do was make a determination here and now. "Mr. Dunleavy, I will take your request to my superiors. Can you come back tomorrow?"

"I can and will. Thank you, Mr. Higgins. Good day." Dunleavy noticed that Higgins's parting handshake was a lot less robust than the first one.

Dunleavy did not leave his hotel. He honored his promise to Arlene not to see the sights. He did talk to his wife and son for a full hour. Damn the cost.

He made one short call to Holmes. "Halfway there" was all he said.

Under no circumstances was Dunleavy going to expound on an open telephone line about his investigation.

At 10:00 a.m., Tuesday, Dunleavy was again at the SIS office. This time Higgins had company.

Three men sat on chairs against the southeast wall of Higgins' office.

"Mr. Dunleavy, these gentlemen are from MI5."

Dunleavy knew that MI5 stood for military intelligence, section 5.

Much like the CIA and the FBI, these two agencies had different jurisdictions. MI6 was responsible for international intelligence. MI5 handled domestic intelligence operations.

The three men extended their hands, but they did not speak.

"Mr. Dunleavy, after conferring with my superiors, a determination was made that Her Majesty's government cannot help with your investigation."

Dunleavy was not prepared for this dramatic declaration. "Do you have information that this man actually exists?"

"I can neither confirm nor deny." He continued, "Any information concerning the death of John Kennedy is classified at the highest level. To declassify this information, a formal request would have to be made by your president directly to our prime minister."

"I see. But is there a man formerly connected to the British Army who has the moniker the Cobra?"

Higgins smiled. "Mr. Dunleavy, I am afraid your quest must now return to America. Can you get an appointment to see Mr. Nixon?"

The statement was mocking and disrespectful. But it was clear there would be no cooperation.

Dunleavy rose slowly. "Thank you, Mr. Higgins." He did not extend his hand.

Nor did he even glance at the three MI5 men sitting close by.

Dunleavy would now be returning to America empty-handed.

Higgins waited until Dunleavy had left his office. He glanced at his three compatriots. "You know what to do."

The three men nodded and left. They would stalk Stuart Dunleavy until the very moment he got on his flight home.

Sir Thomas Higgins never did confer with his superiors. Higgins had his own skeletons to protect.

Higgins knew the identity of the Cobra. He was a veteran of WWII. He served in the British Eighth Army.

In 1943, Higgins was in Tunisia. He was wounded and lying on a dusty road. He could barely move.

A German scout car was heading right toward him. It was clear the three occupants were going to run him down. The Germans were laughing.

Higgins knew death was seconds away.

Suddenly, the left front tire of the scout car blew up. The Germans attempted to exit the open-air vehicle, but their efforts were for naught.

Higgins watched in amazement as the heads of the Germans disappeared in a sea of blood. There was silence for sixty seconds. He rolled over and saw a tall muscular soldier cradling a rifle.

"Need a hand there, mate?"

It was the Cobra.

The soldier picked up Higgins and carried him to a field hospital. Higgins and the Cobra became friends. It was a battlefield bond, the kind of bond that lasts for life.

Since 1945, the two men had spoken to one another at least once a year.

Now it was Higgins's turn to save his friend.

Higgins buzzed his secretary. "Judith, I need to make an overseas call."

Chapter 65

In March of 1969, Richard Nixon was constructing a foreign policy initiative that would extricate America from Vietnam. Nixon decided it was time for the South Vietnamese to take over the bulk of the fighting.

America would supply the armaments. The young men of South Vietnam would supply the blood.

There were half a million American soldiers in South Vietnam. Their presence was radicalizing an entire generation of Americans. Nixon's election did not stop the street protests. They became more violent.

The troops had to come back, or Nixon would face the wrath of the voters in 1972.

Nixon's other great fear was a man sitting in the United States Senate named Edward Moore Kennedy.

There were a hundred senators, but only one strode the earth like a colossus.

All the smart people knew Ted Kennedy would be the Democrat nominee for president in 1972. He would be but forty years old. That fact would be subsumed by the emotional attachment millions of Americans had for the last surviving brother.

Richard Nixon was convinced Ted Kennedy would be the nominee.

He told his two top advisors, John Ehrlichman and Harry Robbins Haldeman, that Kennedy probably would not face a single challenger in his own party.

"They are going to give it to him by acclamation," Nixon said.

Nixon ordered Ehrlichman and Haldeman to begin researching Ted Kennedy's life from his birth in 1932 to the present moment.

"Spare no expense!" Nixon lost one presidential race to a Kennedy, and he could not stand the possibility of losing again.

In the early part of 1969, Ted Kennedy had almost as much clout as the sitting president. Reporters followed him everywhere. Most of these news people were fawning sycophants who existed not to challenge Ted Kennedy but to help him expel the hated current occupant of the White House.

Nixon knew that beating Kennedy would be a Herculean task. He could not know that in just five months, Ted Kennedy would commit political suicide in a little town called Chappaquiddick.

The death of campaign aide Mary Jo Kopechne would doom Kennedy's presidential aspirations for all time.

Nixon did not know this. No one knew it. It had not happened.

There was one man in the winter of 1969 who could prove invaluable in keeping Ted Kennedy out of the White House. That man was J. Edgar Hoover.

Hoover was now seventy-four years old. He was long past the mandatory retirement age for federal workers.

Hoover did not want to retire. Power was Hoover's heroin. He could not give it up.

Nixon called Hoover into his office. Nixon knew Hoover's weaknesses and desires. "J. Edgar, you should be sitting in a rocking chair enjoying your sunset years."

"Thank you, Mr. President. But I am in excellent health, and I would like to serve you and the nation for a few more years."

"Well, J. Edgar, I think we can keep you on for at least awhile. But we both know there is a mortal threat to my reelection, and your job. Do you really think Ted Kennedy is going to let you stay on and run the FBI?"

Hoover did not have to respond. Both men knew the answer.

Nixon moved in for the kill. "J. Edgar, I am your boss. And I have the legal authority to declassify any document created by the executive branch. Do you agree?"

"You absolutely have that authority, Mr. President."

"If I call you and ask you to bring over a document you keep squirreled away in that secret room, you won't have a problem producing that document, will you?"

"Mr. President, I give you my word that anything you want will be expeditiously processed."

"Thank you, J. Edgar. You may resume your duties."

Nixon intended to scour FBI documents he knew existed on the entire Kennedy clan.

Ted Kennedy was conflicted about his future. He knew he was the titular head of the Democratic Party.

He also knew that his two older brothers had fallen victim to bullets fired by assassins who had not been caught.

At least the men who organized the killings had not been brought to justice.

Running for president in 1972 could be very hazardous. Kennedy believed he would not be able to resist the millions of Americans who would insist he run for the good of the country.

Democrats hated Nixon like the devil hated virtue.

Kennedy had received a visit from Stuart Dunleavy in late January. Dunleavy told him about his unsuccessful encounter with MI6.

"Senator, if we are going to get that file, we will need you sitting in the Oval Office talking person to person with the prime minister."

"I understand."

"You won't be sworn in until January of 1973. I do not want to wait that long. I have an alternative plan."

"What is it?"

"Since money is not a factor, you should send me back to London. I will hire the best private investigators. These men will find and interview soldiers who served in North Africa. There are probably a hundred men who know the identity of the Cobra."

Ted Kennedy liked that idea. "How about you, Stu? Are you and Curt still job hunting?"

"Curt and I will be just fine, Senator."

"I want both of you men to find jobs here in Washington. I want to have you close by so we can have face-to-face conversations. Let me see what I can do."

Ted Kennedy had fame and power.

The titans of industry did not want to disappoint a man who would certainly become president someday. When Ted Kennedy called, the heads of corporations snapped to attention and picked up the phone immediately.

In one week, both Holmes and Dunleavy had high-paying jobs that demanded their presence in the nation's capital.

Holmes and Dunleavy were grateful. They loved their houses, their children's schools, and the excitement of life in Washington, DC.

They also knew that mutual proximity meant their grand quest to find the killers of John and Robert Kennedy would be enhanced.

Dunleavy wondered why Ted Kennedy did not demand a reassessment of the Warren Commission report. He had wondered the same thing about Bobby Kennedy.

Dunleavy did not know that Ted Kennedy was constrained for the same reasons his older brother held back. Immediately after Bobby Kennedy was schooled by J. Edgar Hoover, Ted was summoned to his brother's office.

Robert Kennedy told his younger brother that Hoover had the family by the throat. "Teddy, we have to go along with it. But I promise you, our day will come!"

Ted Kennedy could not tell Dunleavy or Holmes about the blackmail. He simply changed the subject.

But he never lost sight of the truth. The Kennedy family had tens of millions of dollars. Money that could be used to uncover facts that were being hidden deliberately by the Mob.

Ted Kennedy told Dunleavy and Holmes he was willing to spend the money.

Dunleavy's return trip to England was on hold. His wife was now very pregnant. He could not tell her he was making a second trip to London so close to the first one.

Nor could he take a week off from his new job. Holmes faced the same dilemma.

Dunleavy's second child was due in July. Arlene's parents would have no problem looking after the infant while he, Arlene, and Michael spent a week in England.

August or September in London. It sounded fantastic.

Dunleavy believed his life was better than the lives of 99 percent of humanity.

It was all sunshine and roses as March and April came and then disappeared into the history books.

The month of May brought warm weather and outdoor activities. May 17 was a Friday.

The very next day three astronauts were scheduled to lift off for the moon. The mission was called Apollo 10.

Thomas Stafford, John Young, and Gene Cernan were going to come within eight miles of the lunar surface. But they would not touch down.

This was the final dress rehearsal for a man landing on the moon. The world would have to wait until July to see if Neil Armstrong and Buzz Aldrin could perform a controlled descent to the lunar surface and survive.

And leave it alive.

Young Michael Dunleavy had fallen in love with the space program and everything connected to it.

He asked his dad if they could have a cookout on Saturday, May 18, 1969. The entire day was going to revolve around the television screen.

Stuart Dunleavy said yes to everything his son wanted. At 5:00 p.m. on Friday, Dunleavy left work. He drove to a supermarket five miles from his house.

He thought about getting hamburgers but decided the magnitude of the next day and his son's anticipation of it demanded steak. Rib eyes.

Dunleavy loaded up a cart full of root beer, baked potatoes, steak sauce, ice cream, and of course, hand-carved meat.

He exited the store whistling a Beatles' song. It was "Yellow Submarine."

He unlocked his rear car door and deposited the edibles. He slid into his front seat and adjusted the mirror.

At that very second, his right front passenger door swung open.

In the blink of an eye, a man sat down. A man with a gun. In a microsecond, the gun was pressed against his ribs.

"Don't move. Just listen. This is not a robbery. But if you behave in a foolish manner, it will be your last day on earth!"

Dunleavy stared at his intruder with saucer-sized eyes. The man was wearing a mask. And he had on white surgical gloves.

Dunleavy could not see the handgun. He did not know it was a Walther PPK .32 ACP. An additional accoutrement was a silencer.

"If this is not a robbery, I assume it is a kidnapping."

"Wrong again."

"My instincts tell me I should make a play for that gun. If we leave this parking lot, my chances of surviving are probably very low."

"Your chances of surviving this encounter are very good, but only if you do not do anything stupid."

"Do you mind telling me what you want?"

"I want to have a friendly conversation with you. Nothing more. Nothing less."

"Then why the mask, the gloves, and the gun? You could have walked up to me, shaken hands, and asked for a moment of my time."

"But you might have said no. And my feelings would have been hurt."

Dunleavy thought that statement was flippant. But it also demonstrated confidence on the part of the intruder.

"What is it you want?"

The gunman produced a pair of handcuffs. "Attach one end to your steering wheel. Place the other end on your right wrist. And let me hear the snap of the locking mechanism."

Dunleavy slowly complied. Once his right wrist was firmly attached, the intruder pulled the gun out of his ribs. "Thank you, Mr. Dunleavy. Your cooperation has earned you points."

"How the hell do you know my name?"

"I know a great deal about you, Mr. Dunleavy. I know you have a wife named Arlene. A son named Michael. And a little fellow on the way."

He continued. "And I know you want to see them again, more than anything on earth. But first, we have to move to a less congested spot. This is a large parking lot. I want you to start your engine and very slowly move all the way to the very end of this property."

Dunleavy started his car. He contorted his left hand to reach the ignition.

"Mr. Dunleavy, if you gun your engine, there will be a bullet in your brain in less than a second."

Dunleavy did not exceed ten miles an hour. "Is that a Bela Lugosi mask?"

"Yes, it is! I saw Bela Lugosi in the very first Dracula picture ever made. I was a kid. It scared the pants off me."

"What should I call you?"

"Well, since we are never going to be friends, I will call you Mr. Dunleavy. You can call me Mr. Lugosi. Or Bela!"

"If it is all right with you, I will call you Bela."

"Excellent. Now do you see that tree? Park the car directly under it. And shut off the engine."

Dunleavy did as instructed. His fear was subsiding. But with his right hand attached to his steering wheel, no heroic actions would be forthcoming.

Dunleavy's car was far away from any third-person rescue. Now he would have to use his wits. "All right…Bela. If this is not a robbery or a kidnapping, do you mind telling me what it is?"

"Mr. Dunleavy, we are going to discuss your immediate future. You are facing two scenarios. In one, you and your family will live long and happy lives. In the other scenario, you will first be a witness to, and then a victim of, a holocaust."

Dunleavy wished he could see the gunman's eyes. He wanted desperately to get a read on him. But it was impossible.

"Who are you?" Dunleavy spoke loudly and with determination.

"I'm the man you have been looking for, Mr. Dunleavy. I am the Cobra."

Stuart Dunleavy's jaw dropped two inches. He was speaking to the man who he believed killed John Fitzgerald Kennedy.

"Mr. Dunleavy, I presume there are some questions you want to ask me. I possess a mountain of information. I am here to clear the air. But we cannot sit here all day. Please move with alacrity."

Dunleavy suddenly realized the man was speaking in a high-brow English accent. Everything he had learned about the Cobra indicated he was an Englishman. "Did you shoot President John F. Kennedy?"

"I did."

The man behind the mask did not hesitate in his answer.

Dunleavy gulped. "He was a good man. Why did you kill him?"

"I did it for two reasons. First, for the money. Second, to win the war."

"What war?"

"The war between the Kennedy administration and La Cosa Nostra. I thought the motives for the killing were obvious. To my great surprise, your government never even considered the obvious."

"Who were the men behind the assassination?"

"Oh, I think you know the answer to that question. But if you want absolute verification, I can provide it. The man who organized the entire operation was Carlos Marcello. His co-conspirators were Sam Giancana, John Roselli, and my boss, Santo Trafficante."

"Why are you telling me this? I could use that last statement in a court of law!"

"A statement! What statement? Made by whom? You do not know who I am. And if you told anyone about today's encounter, no one will believe it. What are you going to say? That you were kidnapped by Bela Lugosi?"

"Ted Kennedy would believe it."

"Ah, yes, Senator Ted Kennedy. The last Mohican."

The Cobra adjusted his frame. The handgun was now lying on the dashboard. He did not fear a potential aggressive move by his prisoner.

"You might want to have a long talk with Mr. Ted Kennedy. He should think long and hard about seeking the White House. The people I used to work for cannot afford to have anyone named Kennedy sitting in the Oval Office."

"Are you telling me you no longer work for La Cosa Nostra?"

"My dear Mr. Dunleavy. When one has killed a US president, one has reached the apex of one's career. I have been retired for five years."

Dunleavy was losing his fear of the Cobra. "Explain to me why you should be allowed to live out your life in freedom? Explain why you should not be covered in chains and hauled before a judge and jury?"

The Cobra was smiling under his mask. Dunleavy would have been enraged had he the capacity to see it.

"You really are a true believer, are you not, Mr. Dunleavy? You idolize the Kennedys. Millions of Americans feel the same way. But by wearing rose-colored glasses, you don't see the dark side." The Cobra leaned into Dunleavy's personal space. "Can you stand to hear some inconvenient truths? Let's see."

The Cobra took a second to look out the rear window to see if anyone was approaching their position. "Okay, Mr. Dunleavy, I will invest the time. Let's start with the fact that Joe Kennedy made his money in the same way my employers did. By breaking the law. He used his money for personal aggrandizement. He used it to buy the White House. Along the way, he asked my employers for help. He made promises. He had the power to control his second son and keep him in check. He did not do that. John Kennedy came after us with all the resources of the federal government. We, who had done so much to put him in power. But that is not even the most galling part. Following the Bay of Pigs, John Kennedy came back to us and asked for our help."

"First, he wanted the president of the Dominican Republic dead. He also asked for our help in killing Fidel Castro. We kept our end of the bargain. But the Kennedy boys, after asking for our resources, still did not abate their legal campaign to put every member of La Cosa Nostra behind bars. Do you see the problem here? He held out his right hand in friendship. In his left hand he held a dagger to plunge in our backs. This kind of duplicity could not go unchallenged."

Dunleavy did not want to surrender the moral high ground. "Sometimes good men have to bend the rules in order to prevail over evil men."

"Do good men betray and abandon other good men? Those fifteen hundred patriots who invaded Cuba were told the United

States Marine Corps would be right behind them. Who got cold feet and left them to be slaughtered? The very man you worship as a demigod."

For the first time the Cobra's voice rose in anger.

"And I have personal reasons for despising John Kennedy. I was sent to the Dominican Republic to help bring Rafael Trujillo's reign of terror to an end. I and my fellow conspirators were told we would be protected. Not so. Only I escaped. My friends were left in the country to be massacred. You want more proof that John Kennedy was no better that Carlos Marcello? Three weeks before he was assassinated, Kennedy greenlighted the murder of President Ngo Dinh Diem of South Vietnam. That is two heads of state killed in three years. One could almost say that a powerful Mob boss was taking care of business."

Dunleavy did not like the direction the Cobra was taking him. He had never even thought about these matters until this very moment.

"You are obviously a very educated and intelligent man…Bela. Why become a hired assassin? There are ten thousand other ways to make a living."

"I was born with a special talent. There are maybe a hundred men on the planet who can hit a moving target at one thousand yards. God gave me the eyes of an eagle and the soul of a barbarian. This is who I am."

"If you truly are a barbarian, then my chances of surviving this encounter are quite small."

"Mr. Dunleavy, do you believe a man, even a very brutal one, can experience an epiphany?"

"I suppose anything is possible."

For a second time, the Cobra looked out the rear window. He saw nothing.

"We have time for one more informational digression. I suppose you are wondering how I found you."

"I was curious how all this came to pass."

"You went to England and spoke to a man named Higgins. Mr. Higgins and I served together in North Africa. I saved his life. He informed me about your efforts to find the name of a British soldier."

Dunleavy thought, *Oh my god, what are the chances of that?* "I was betrayed by the number two man in MI6?"

"A soldier's bond is greater than the bond between a man and his wife. Higgins had to know that by contacting you he was condemning me to death. Do not judge Mr. Higgins too harshly. He mentioned two possible scenarios. One involved your demise. The other involved your cooperation. I originally chose the easiest solution. I was in your neighborhood yesterday. At exactly 5:36 p.m., you exited your house and went to your mailbox. Do you recall?"

Dunleavy thought for a moment. He did get his mail at about that time.

"I was in a white panel truck exactly four hundred feet away. I was pointing a Weatherby elephant gun at your head. The trigger was halfway compressed."

"Do you know what saved your life, Mr. Dunleavy? At that exact moment, your son came running out of the house. He jumped into your arms. You tossed him high in the air. You caught him, hugged, and kissed him."

Dunleavy now knew the story was completely true. Every detail of the Cobra's recitation was accurate.

"Had I pulled that trigger, your son would be covered in your blood. He would be traumatized for life. He would never know a normal or happy day again. I lowered my rifle and decided I was going to follow scenario number two. I decided I was going to meet with you, Mr. Dunleavy. I decided you might be receptive to certain immutable facts."

"I'm listening."

"I worship my freedom, Mr. Dunleavy. I am not a man who can be caged. You represent a threat to all I hold dear."

Dunleavy brashly countered: "A wise man once said, 'Let justice prevail, though the heavens may fall.'"

"The good guys do not always win, Mr. Dunleavy. In this case, it is manifestly important to your family that I not be pursued."

"I would appreciate it if you would not threaten my wife and son."

"You have two options. You can walk away from your crusade. If you choose that path, you and your family can sail through life on gossamer wings. Option two is dramatically different. If you continue to try to bring me to justice, you need to know what is at risk."

The Cobra picked up the Walther PPK and pointed it at Dunleavy's head. "I have never once shown a target mercy. You are the very first one. That is the very definition of the word 'unique.' Do not squander this opportunity."

Dunleavy felt the tip of the PPK enter his ear canal. "If I learn you are still looking for me, this is exactly what is going to happen. Someday your wife will be in a parking lot very much like this one. Michael Dunleavy will be with her. The first to die will be Michael. His head will explode. Your wife will be covered in your son's blood. For a few horrible seconds, she will scream in absolute agony. Then another bullet will end her misery. I will allow you to live for one year. Each night you will come home alone, pour a drink, sit in a chair, and dwell on the holocaust you could have prevented. I will then end your sad and miserable life. Maybe I will do it while you are getting the mail. Oh, and your friend Mr. Holmes! Dead. His wife. Dead. His children. Dead."

Dunleavy no longer saw the suave and erudite assassin who entered his car half an hour earlier. He was now hearing the voice of a man who possessed all the moral trappings of a reptile. A Cobra.

"Are we finished here?"

"Yes, I believe we are."

The Cobra reached into his pocket and pulled out a ten-inch file.

"It should take you about half an hour to file through those handcuffs. I will be miles away. Give me your car keys."

The Cobra exited the car. He turned and stuck his masked face back in the window.

"I truly hope this is our last meeting. If I am forced to come back, the results will be too awful to contemplate. Goodbye, Mr. Dunleavy."

The Cobra walked away with a calm demeanor. Dunleavy watched as he removed his mask. But all he could see was the back of his tormentor's head.

He strained to see what type of car or truck the Cobra brought to the parking lot. He failed.

It took forty-five minutes for Dunleavy to free his right hand.

He slowly opened the door. He walked to the front of his car. He leaned against the hood and folded his hands across his chest.

"I am alive. I should not be, but I am."

Dunleavy did not doubt the sincerity of the Cobra. "What gives me the right to put my family at risk?" Dunleavy did not think it was odd he was talking to himself.

He started walking back to the supermarket. He would have to call Arlene for a ride. He would invent some story about losing his keys.

"How do I tell Ted Kennedy I am out? How do I tell Curt Holmes I have feet of clay?"

Dunleavy stopped walking. He let his mind go back in time. Back to those terrible days in the South Pacific. He thought of John Kennedy risking his life over and over to save his crew.

John Kennedy was not a perfect man. No man carries the crown of perfection.

But Kennedy was the living embodiment of a young and vibrant nation. He was murdered in the very prime of his life. His own government lacked the courage to run down the facts.

A man who made a living murdering human beings had just thrown down a gauntlet. Back off. Crawl into a hole and hide. *Do not even think of intruding into my life.*

Dunleavy raised his eyes to a cloudless blue sky.

"I will see you in hell, Cobra!"

About the Author

Jon Dietz has had a lifetime passion for three intellectual outlets: history, politics, and current events. After graduating from Miami University in Oxford, Ohio, Dietz landed a job as a reporter for the Sarasota Herald-Tribune. He had multiple responsibilities, including crime reporting, featuring writing, military historian, and weekend metro editor. He interviewed Presidents Jimmy Carter and Ronald Reagan. During his days as a newspaperman, Dietz went to Honduras with a bounty hunter. They successfully returned to the United States with a drug dealer who had fled the country to escape prosecution. Dietz also covered the Ted Bundy murder trial for a foreign publication. His writing attracted the attention of the top people in the European Union Parliament. He was offered a one-month travel grant to visit Germany, France, and England. After fourteen years as a newspaperman, Dietz changed careers. He was hired as an investigator for the Office of Public Defender, Twelfth Judicial Circuit. He was promoted to the homicide division. He and Public Defender Elliott C. Metcalfe Jr. handled several high-profile murder cases. Dietz's first novel, The Jerusalem Train, can be purchased on Amazon.

CPSIA information can be obtained
at www.ICGtesting.com
Printed in the USA
JSHW021559210622
27206JS00001B/2

9 781662 455636